THE NOMAD AND THE LION

A novel by

Ronnie H. Hall

The Nomad and the Lion

This novel is a work of fiction. Names, characters, places and incidents are either the product of the author's imagination or are used fictitiously. Any resemblance to actual events or locales or persons, living or dead, is entirely coincidental.

ISBN: 979-8-218-06241-5

PROLOGUE

Twelfth Century Scandinavia

The small log house was his grandfather's and he never bothered to knock unless the door was latched. It wasn't so he stomped the loose snow from his boots and slipped in.

As usual these days his grandfather was slouched in his big chair gazing into his fireplace far off in his mind to some other place and time. A deer hide ravaged by years of hungry mice lay across his lap. A soiled, moth-eaten wool shawl was draped around his drooping shoulders. The boy loved his grandfather dearly and every day since the old man had woken with one side of his body numb and useless, he'd checked on him to make sure he had something to eat and firewood close by. The boy crept beside the old man, and as he stood looking down on him he thought back to when not that long ago the old man was still strong and agile and able to hunt with him in the snow up in the mountains. But the curse had changed that and had made him old and feeble overnight. The sight of him now shuffling about on his walking stick so unsteady and weak and fragile disturbed the boy and made him feel sad. It'd become a hard chore lately just for the old man to fetch a few sticks of firewood from right outside the door. After a long while the boy grew restless and put his hand out to touch the old man's shoulder to bring him out of his dreams, but then he drew it back. He waited on for a time longer and finally lost patience and was about to slip away and leave the old man when he slowly raised his head and then blinked the boy into focus. "I didn't hear you come in," the old man said. "Have you been here long?"

"No. Just a short while."

The boy realized he'd been caught in the lie when the old man's teeth appeared through his silvery whiskers and his sparkling cobalt eyes fell to the puddles of melted snow and ice pooled around his boots. "So, I see," the old man said with a wink. "If I were one of those hares you hunt, I wouldn't be much sport as addled as I am now."

The boy smiled, and said, "I killed a fat buck this morning. Ma said you should eat with us tonight."

"Well, thank you. I believe I will. She's as fine a cook as you are a hunter. There's no better meat than rabbit if it's cooked right, except for maybe grouse." He smelled the sharpness of the spruce and hemlock and the cold on the boy and remembered how it'd been. He loved the boy more than anything and held out his arms and the boy bent and hugged him. Then he went on. "The howling wind woke me at daylight this morning. By the looks of your cheeks it must have been brutal up there. Was it a long stalk?"

"Almost to the big mountains, but the fresh snow made tracking him easy."

"That's a long way. You must have really wanted to kill the poor thing."

A sinister smile appeared, and the boy pretended to draw a bow. "As always," he said. "More than anything. It's what I live for."

The old man tilted his head and raised a finger as if testing the direction of the wind. "Now what do you suppose makes you want to kill an innocent rabbit so bad that you'd freeze and exhaust yourself wading through miles of snow against such a wicked wind?"

The boy thought and then shrugged. "I don't know. It started when the spell came over me that night after the great blizzard. I slipped out after it passed and walked for hours trying to find one and when I did, I wanted to kill it more than anything. But I didn't have a bow then, so I chased it with a stick till my legs gave out. Since that night all I want to do is to hunt and kill hares. But I've told you that. Don't you remember?"

"Oh, I remember. I just want to be sure you do. A great storm awakens things inside a man just as it does the animals. Mostly their will to survive."

"Sometimes I think I'm crazy I want to kill them so bad."

"You're not crazy. I was the same way. We're just different from others. We'll talk about that later."

"Let's talk about it now."

"We will, but first I want to talk about making you a new bow. Soon you'll be old enough to hunt deer and you'll need a heavier one. You need to start practicing with it to build your strength so you can draw and hold it properly when the time comes."

The boy gazed about the room and admired the collection of heavy antlered deer skulls the old man had taken in his younger days. Their sight sent his thoughts to the broken timber in the high mountains and to killing the wise old harts that hid there. He couldn't think of anything grander than killing one. When he was alone in the mountains, the sight of one bounding away through the clouds of stirred white powder with the sun reflecting off its massive-polished antlers made him shake and shiver and his heart pound for a long time from the rush it caused.

After a while the old man touched the boy's shoulder and stirred him from his imaginings. Then he leaned and spoke softly as if he were shielding a secret. "Do you ever dream about a man from long ago that hunts with a spear?"

The boy was so taken aback his lips moved, but nothing would come out. "How did you know? I've never told anyone about those dreams," he finally managed. "They'd think I'm crazy."

"There's nothing wrong with you. I've been having the dreams since I was your age, too, but the man doesn't hunt animals in my dreams anymore. Now he hunts peoples' souls with a lion." The boy

thought as he studied the old man's face. "Now why that dreadful look?" the old man said.

"I'm afraid they'll come for you."

The smile came again. "Oh, they'll come alright, and soon, I think. Look we all must go away. Some sooner than later. Like your pa." His eyes became sad and he paused and swallowed hard before going on. "And your grandmother. She left me after your father was born. She was too young to go, but sadly she did. She was a small woman and not so strong and never could recover from your father's birth and died soon after. I loved her from the time I first saw her, and I've missed her every day since she went away. I still have dreams we're together and happy again. And as you know, I raised your father by myself. It was hard, too."

"Then why didn't you get another wife to help you raise Pa?"

"You're young and don't understand. I suppose I don't either. You don't love a woman because you want or need to. I can't explain why you can love one woman and you can't another. I think because I loved your grandmother so much, I couldn't love another woman. I tried but never could. I don't know why." He turned and smiled and looked hard into the boy's eyes. "All I do know is that she and I'll be together again – and soon."

"I don't like you talking about going away, but how do you know that?"

"Look, when those two come for you, the Lion takes your soul, but then the Nomad does a wonderful thing. He lets your spirit live again in any animal you want, like a wolf or a lynx. I believe he'll let her come back, too, to be with me again. I don't know why I know – I just do."

Now the old man's eyes were dripping tears. The boy thought at first it was because of the sadness of thinking of his wife, then he realized by the old man's smile they were instead tears of joy.

Then the boy thought about coming back from the dead in the form of an animal and doubted such a thing was possible, but he didn't want to be disrespectable and dispute his grandfather. He finally decided the old man was just so lonely and wanted to be with his wife so much that his imagination had taken him over. So, to appease the old man, he said, "Then what animal will you come back as?"

The old man was quick and emphatic. "A gyr."

"But why a bird?"

"A gyr can travel and hunt wherever he wants, and he gets to eat hares and grouse whenever he likes. What could be a better life than that, especially if you're with the one you love?" The boy's countenance revealed his dilemma as he considered what animal he'd want to be if he could somehow come back. After a time, the old man said, "Don't worry with that now. You have years to decide. Now, would you like to hear the story of the Nomad and why you're so possessed to kill those harmless rabbits?"

"Yes, but why haven't you told me all this before?"

"I've been waiting for the right time and I think that time is now. If you'll bring in some wood, I'll tell you." The old man knew the time was now because he was sure the Nomad and the Lion were coming for him soon. He'd had too many dreams of them lately and could feel their presence stronger every night as he struggled in his loneliness in the dark trying to sleep.

The room was close and sweltering after the boy had been out in the cold all day, but for the old man's sake he brought in an armload of logs and stoked up the fire. Then he took a seat on a footstool beside the old man and began rubbing his knees in anticipation of the coming tale while the old man packed and lit his pipe. The exhaled blue smoke at first crept towards the fire and then went gushing away up the chimney like a fleeing ghost.

"Understand this story didn't come all at once," the old man began, pointing his pipe stem at the boy. "It's like a puzzle with all the parts and pieces of dreams I've had. It's taken most of my lifetime to sort them out."

The old man settled back in his chair, fixed his gaze on the livening fire, and began his story. "My dreams of the Nomad take place in a time when herds of strange and giant animals roamed this land. Winters lasted a good part of the year then and were so brutal that every living thing would freeze and die if it didn't go south. Then in the spring, to escape the unbearable summer heat, the herds would turn and drift back north as the deep snows melted. They'd fatten up on the lush grasses that sprang up on the plains along the way to survive the next coming winter. So, you see the animals were always moving back and forth up and down the plains with the seasons. Men called nomads lived and fed their families by following and hunting the herds. The man we dream about was a nomad and you and I are kin of his. What you mostly need to know about this nomad is that when he was about your age he lost his family to some disease or something and didn't have anyone to teach him how to survive; how to hunt or make spearheads or shelters or fires. He had to learn those things on his own, and he survived to learn them because he had such a strong will to live and an undeniable passion for hunting and killing. His passion to hunt and kill was so great in fact that it's still as strong in his kin as it was in him. But not all his kin. Your father wasn't afflicted, nor are your brothers. They hunt for enjoyment, not for the relentless desire and passion of the stalk and the kill that you and I do. They're not inflicted and driven like you are to hunt those hares. You have that great passion because the Nomad's bloodlust is in you and it can't be denied.

The fire was crackling and popping wildly now and almost a roar. The old man slid the reindeer hide off his legs and onto the floor and flipped the shawl off his shoulders. He looked over at the boy. His eyes were wide with attentiveness staring into the fire and sweat was running down his face. A bead was dangling from the tip of his nose. The old man smiled and went on. "Back in those times if a man didn't hunt, he'd starve. And not only would he starve, his family and clan likely would too. But it's not a necessity for men to hunt these days because we now raise animals to slaughter when we need to. Or meat can be bartered or bought from a market hunter or a herder down in the village. And since we aren't required to hunt anymore, sadly

I believe the compassion to hunt is being bred out of us." The old man let the boy contemplate what he'd told him, then said, "Do you understand what I've told you so far?"

"Now I understand why I'm so different from my brothers, the way I want to hunt and kill all the time. It's all I think about when I'm not up in the mountains chasing hares. It's all I want to do."

"I was the same way, but for some reason your father wasn't like us. Like your brothers he had no real passion for hunting. Now do you understand why I believe the bloodlust compulsion is being bred out of us."

"I think I do. Now go on with the story."

"But as the Nomad grew older, he was overcome by an even greater passion than for bloodlust, and that was the passion for raising his son." He turned his gaze from the fire to the boy. "Since your pa died, I've felt a great responsibility and duty towards teaching you about life and to be an upright man. I don't feel that way about my other grandsons. Maybe it's because you're the youngest and need it most. Or maybe it's because you're so much like me that I'm drawn to you to do it. Anyway, I just hope I've done enough, and you've learned all you need to know."

"But, Papa, we still have a lot of time to spend together. You can teach me more."

The old man's eyes became empty. "I'm not so sure." A long moment passed as he pulled a glowing ember from the fire and relit his pipe. Then he began to tell how the Nomad came to have his son by a strange girl he came on one day swimming in a river after he'd wandered way far to the south.

"The sight of her naked stirred him so that he went and dragged her out of the river and then forced himself on her. She fought him at first, but he finally had his way and then they coupled over and over till they were too tired to couple anymore and then they fell asleep. It wasn't long though till the Nomad was stirred awake by some unknown fear that caused him to grab his spear and to start running blindly for the river. When he did, a cave lion broke out of the brush after him.

The Nomad was barely a stride ahead of the cat when he dove off the riverbank and planted his spear against a rock. Then he pointed the chipped obsidian point so it would ruin the lion's heart as it came down on him. His aim was true, and as the cat recoiled from the pain, the Nomad dove and swam out into the river as far as he could. He was expecting the cat to be on him when he came up, but instead it was dead on the bank laying in a great pool of pink-frothy blood.

"He stroked the cat's rich fur and ran his fingers up and down its long ivory fangs admiring the beast for some time. Eventually his mind settled, and he remembered the girl and as he started to go look for her, a band of dark-skinned men came out of the brush and stopped him. They were big boned and heavy and towered over him. Some had clubs and others spears and they were about to kill him when the girl came running up grunting and moaning and got between them. She jabbered as she motioned and some of the dark men followed her, and on seeing the lion with the spear through its back, they became wild and started jumping and shouting, rejoicing the fair man's kill. But as they went about skinning and quartering the creature, they took more notice of the stranger's looks and started to wonder how such a small and frail man could have killed such a terrible beast. They began to jabber to one another as they pointed back and forth from the little man to the sky. Eventually they all agreed he must have been sent by their gods and they should welcome him into their clan. And when the dark men started for their cave with the meat and tawny hide and head of the lion, they motioned for the Nomad to follow.

"The Nomad spent that winter with the girl and her people, and they treated him with great respect and kindness, and he was content. But when spring came, he'd become bored with the girl and the clan's dull way of life, and as always, his lust for blood rose and forced him to leave to go chase after the herds.

"That summer he was content being on the move along the river and across the plains killing again, but by fall he'd become lonely for the girl and headed back south to her and the clan. On his return,

though, he wasn't welcomed and respected like before but was instead ignored and treated with scorn. And the girl was gone, and it took him days to find her hiding in a cave with his newborn son. She'd been forced to hide from him because the clan thought their fair baby was deformed and cursed and they'd threatened to kill her and her child if she mated with the Nomad again.

"So now the girl was so afraid for herself and her child, she wouldn't have anything more to do with the Nomad. And though the girl and the clan now rejected him, the Nomad wouldn't leave because of the strong attraction of his son and he stayed with the dark people again that winter. But the yearning for killing and migration was stronger than even the love for his son and it drove him to follow the herds every spring, but he always returned in the fall to spend the winters teaching his boy how to hunt and survive.

"Fifteen years or so passed, and when the Nomad came back that fall, he found the clan had cast his son out after his mother had died. The boy had survived on his own only because of what his father had taught him through the years. And now with the girl dead, and the scorn of the clan greater than ever, the Nomad and his son left the dark people for good the following spring and struck out across the plains for their true home in the North.

"One afternoon along the way they found a cave in some foothills overlooking a river to stay the night. The stench of lion piss and scattered bones made the boy anxious, but the gusting wind smelled of rain and he didn't want to sleep outside in the storm. Anyway, the Nomad knew how animals feared fire, so they gathered a store of wood and slept in the cave that night knowing the fire would keep them safe.

"The next morning the boy was restless to be on the move and woke early. The storm had passed, and he stoked and fed the fire and went to watch from the hills as the great herds moved over the rolling plain bellowing and bawling and raising great clouds of dust ambling along. In the glare of the rising sun he could see waves of ochre-colored insects in their mating dances shimmering over the river. Fish were

rolling and splashing feeding on the ones falling spent and dying on the surface. He became so captivated in the sights that he never gave thought to the dying fire or to the lion till he heard it roar.

"The cat was so busy mauling his father it didn't notice the boy running into the cave. But it felt the searing pain of the spear passing through its heart. The lion growled and turned on the boy for a moment, glaring menacingly before it started heaving and coughing up great spouts of lumpy blood. Then it collapsed and died where it stood. And though the boy had killed the lion, he was too late to save his father.

"He grieved all that day carrying wood to the cave, and that night he cremated the Nomad and the Lion together. That was how those two came to be eternal partners, when their spirits left the cave together under the veil of smoke and darkness to begin a journey through time hunting the restless souls that would be spawned from the Nomad's lineage.

"The next day the boy was terrified of being lost and alone, but the need to move forced him to go on. He began to travel north again and crossed a mountain range some days later, and as the hills fell to the plain, there were great sheets of ice groaning and moaning creeping down the slopes. There were forests of fragrant evergreens, and when he saw a band of fair hunters like himself, he knew he was home.

"The Nomad's son lived a long time among his half relatives and raised his sons to be great hunters and good fathers just as his father had done for him. And it's gone ever on for centuries since. You and I and the dreams are proof of it. Whether you've been blessed or cursed, I'm not sure."

The boy had listened intently to the story and as the old man refilled and smoked his pipe, he sat in silence considering what he'd been told. Because he'd had dreams of the Nomad like his grandfather had just described, he believed all that the old man had said. He agreed that he and his grandfather were decedents of the Nomad, but the fact that the Nomad's son had been so careless as to have let the fire die so the Lion could kill him was inconceivable. He'd never be so thoughtless with his grandfather as much as he loved him.

After a while the old man interrupted the boy's thoughts. "Do you remember enough from making your first bow that you can make the next one on your own?"

The boy studied the old man curiously. "I'm sure I could, but why wouldn't you help me?"

"Because I might not be here." At that, grief overwhelmed the boy and the old man saw it in his tortured face. "Don't look at me like that. The time we'll be apart will be short. A lifetime passes quickly. You'll see. Don't mourn my death. Celebrate my life instead. I've had a long and good one." He paused and grinned in hope of softening the boy's sorrowful mood. "Anyway, I miss your grandmother and I'll be happy to see her again dressed all in her beautiful white feathers. I might have seen her fly by the other day while I was out getting some wood."

But what the old man said did little to comfort the boy and tears welled and streamed down his wind-ravaged face. Then the old man's voice became stern. "I hear your stomach growling like a pack of angry wolves. I'm sure that hare is ready. Your mother won't be happy if supper gets cold. Now dry your tears and don't be afraid. You'll be fine when I'm gone."

The hare was seasoned to the old man's liking and cooked to perfection. When dinner was over the boy sledded the old man back to his house. On his way back home, thoughts of the Nomad's son letting the fire die made him stop to consider. He couldn't remember if there'd been any wood stacked beside his grandfather's hearth and he turned to go back to make sure, but the bite of the wind was harsh, and he changed his mind. A bad storm was brewing, so he hurried on home.

All that night he dreamed of the Nomad and the Lion. In the most vivid one, he saw them passing in the blizzard going down the road towards his grandfather's house in the cold dark. He wanted to run to warn the old man, but he was too weak. His legs felt like iron when he tried.

The next morning, he woke tired and groggy from the restless night's sleep. The storm had passed, and it was bitter cold, and he knew the hares would be out feeding and it would be easy tracking them in the fresh snow. He dressed hurriedly and grabbed his bow and quiver and on his way to the hills to hunt he decided to stop by his grandfather's house to tell him about the dream of the Nomad and the Lion passing in the night.

When the old man's house came into view, he noticed there was no smoke coming from the chimney and he scorned himself for his laziness and neglect. And though he pounded on the door for a long time, his grandfather never came to unlatch it. Then he noticed the three sets of wind-blown tracks leading into the dark forest. And as he stared in awe at the cat's great strides, two white falcons cruised by so near he could feel the rush of wind off their wings. He watched them twist and turn rising ever higher into the brilliant blue sky. Then they came together as they rolled and stooped as if making love in midair and went out of his sight forever.

BOOK 1

CHAPTER 1

Oldale, Ga. 28 July 1950

"It's your own damn fault you're having to leave. Only reason you joined was for that dumb promise you made to Jacob. If you hadn't made it, you wouldn't be in this fix. And you ain't doing me, so keep your cold paws off."

"It'll only take a minute. I promise."

"I feel the morning sickness coming on and it's been kicking all night and I ain't slept a wink. Just leave me alone. I ain't in the mood for none of your foolishness right now."

She rolled out of bed and her footsteps made scratchy noises sticking to the tacky linoleum floor. The bathroom door slammed and then I heard her retching and coughing, and then tinkling before the toilet flushed. When she began brushing her teeth, I felt the faint vibrations start. The trembling grew. Flickers against the aged, opaque drawn shades began. Then the bed started to shake as the rumbling built. The windows rattled, then the dishes in the cupboard. The flickers grew into brilliant strobing lights that danced across the walls like lightning flashes from a hot evening storm. Then a deafening horn exploded above it all. As the engine's roar faded, the metronomic clacking of the wheels against the track joints began. Finally, the maelstrom eased as the early freight faded out of town. The morning became quiet and still again, but the lingering, noxious scent of burnt diesel remained. I despised the trains that passed by only feet from our front door, but what I hated most were the sympathetic looks of the folk in the plush coaches as they sped by. The shanties where we existed were in advanced states of ruin – loose shutters, carboarded windows, peeling paint, and all of it covered with a deep layer of poverty and despair and topped off with an unctuous coating of diesel exhaust and coal grit from the switch yard locomotives. But more than anything, what I hated most was the way the passersby looked down on us like they did as they sped past.

"Get me warm, Henry." She was trembling from the chill of the early damp as she slid back into bed and snuggled against me. I hugged her tight. "Not so hard. You might hurt the baby."

Feeling her shiver and the sound of her meek voice caused my dread to swell for having to leave her. My chest felt heavy and a sick feeling formed in my gut. I didn't talk at first for fear my words would come out as sobs. "Look, I'm sorry I'm having to leave you like this," I finally managed. "I just wish you didn't feel this way. It's not what I wanted. They gave me orders and I've got to go or go to jail."

"But what if one of them Japs kills you like they did Jacob? Where will that leave me? A widow alone with a baby with no money and nobody to help me."

"I'll be back soon, Ginny. And it's Koreans this time and not Japs." I hugged her tight against me again. She didn't complain this time. "Remember when I get back, I'll be able to get a GI loan and buy you a nice house. I'll be able to get you out of this miserable shack away from these godforsaken tracks and lowlife people. You'll be alright with the allotments I send you. Mama's going to see you're looked after. Everything's going to be fine."

"You'd better hurry and get back if you know what's good for you, Henry Ball. I ain't waiting on you forever."

It was starting to light outside. A few birds were chirping. A car from an early mill worker clattered across the tracks down the way.

"What do you mean by that? You know you'll be here when I get back."

"I might and I might not. You shouldn't be leaving me like this. They shouldn't be making you leave me like this. If I'm not here even if you do get back, it's your fault. I can't raise and support a baby on my own. It's just not fair you doing this to me and I hate you for it."

"You don't mean that if you love me like I do you. You're everything to me and you know it. You shouldn't be saying things like that when I'm about to leave. I'll be worrying enough about you without thinking about you leaving me while I'm gone. It's always been you and me."

"What about that Martin girl you went off with that time? You forget about her?"

My heart picked up and it suddenly felt hot under the covers. "Why can't you forget about her? She didn't mean anything to me, and you know it. It was just a fling. Nothing happened. And what about you and Donald? Did anything happen between you two? I've always wondered."

"And what if it did? It was you that left me for that hussy. Donald at least made something out of his self. You don't hardly make anything working at that stupid newspaper for old man Hughes. If you don't get back soon, I just might look Donald up. I bet he'd take care of me and my baby."

"It's our baby, Ginny. And please don't say things you don't really mean."

"You sound like you might cry, Henry. Now you know how it feels to be scared like I am. You'd better get up now and get your uniform on before you miss your train."

She got up and went back to the toilet. Having to go to war was bad enough, but the thought of her leaving me while I was gone was too much to bear. I did almost cry. If she did leave, it would kill me. She always meant what she said and that's what scared me most.

Chapter 2

The Chosin Reservoir, North Korea
1 December 1950

As the sky began to lighten, the Chinamen started slipping back into the spruce-covered hills to hide from the Corsairs for the day. That was when I first saw the wavering black line stretched across the pale winter sky. I thought at first it was some ominous creation God was sending to kill the scourge of us all for what we'd done to each other during the night, but it turned out to only be a bunch of starving birds that wheeled over us and then scattered out over the valley. They kept their distance from the dead men for a while, but then inch by inch they crept closer while twisting and turning and slanting their heads, looking and listening. When they seemed satisfied there was no danger, they began their gory feasting. They hissed and screeched as they fought over the eyeballs and pieces of nostrils and ears or any other chunks of flesh they could tear loose from the blank, ashen faces. I've always wondered how they knew about the bodies and where they'd be that morning after our first battle beside that godforsaken-frozen lake.

Three days had passed now since that first assault and the mob of carrion crows had come faithfully to feast every morning since and they'd grown in number as the number of dead Chinamen had.

I'd been studying their gory feeding for over an hour while glassing the hills for prowling gooks when I first noticed the little puffs of steam coming out of the snow. I didn't understand why the birds kept their distance from them at first, but then I reckoned it had to be something alive they were afraid of. Pit Jenkins was on watch in the fighting hole beside me and I wasn't about to let the chance to mess with him slip by. "Hey braindead, you noticed those little clouds coming out of the snow over there by that blown up spruce?" I said while pointing. "You got to look hard before the wind blows them away."

Pit jettisoned a stream of cigarette tobacco juice that turned into sparkling ice crystals before hitting the ground. "Yeah, I done seen 'em. It's just some phosphorous from a mortar round still smolderin'."

"That's what I thought it was at first, but it's not. Phosphorous wouldn't disappear that fast."

"You ain't makin' no sense. What is it then?" he said in his squeaky, nasally voice.

"A yellow man that ain't dead yet."

His face contorted and his eyes narrowed as he adjusted the focusing wheel on the big field glasses he jerked from my hands. "Bullshit, that ain't no gook. He'd be froze by now covered with all that snow."

"That's what it is, redneck, and the birds know. That's why they won't get near him."

I took the binoculars, refocused them and looked over the valley again. The little vapor clouds were easier to spot when you knew what to look for. They were always where there were no birds. "And there's another one, and another one there," I said, pointing out the faint steam clouds.

He took the glasses again and turned the adjustment knob back and forth as if he were trying to focus the truth away. "Oh, shit, there's a bunch of 'em ain't dead. Spose they're just playin' and get up and come after us again?"

I almost laughed but stopped when the cracks in my lips started to split. "They're not playing. They're just human and have a strong will to live and don't want to give up the ghost just yet. You shouldn't be surprised there's some still alive with all the ones we've shot. We couldn't have killed them all."

"How many you think there is? Dead and alive ones I mean."

"I counted over four hundred this morning, but it's hard to tell with all the new snow. All I know is there'll be more and if the cold don't get us the shambos surely will." As I searched for more vapor plumes Ginny came to mind. I lowered the glasses and turned to Pit. "Damn I wish I'd got that letter off to my wife while I had the chance."

"How many times you goin' to say that? It don't make no difference. She's thousands of miles from here and can't help you none. She's probably bangin' one of your asshole buddies right now and don't give a damn about you or no letter no how."

I grabbed his collar and pulled him close. "I got a good mind to kick your dumb, country ass for saying that."

He wrenched my hand loose. "I didn't mean nothin' by it. Why you always a wantin' to fight somebody when they joke you about your old lady?"

I leaned back against the wall of the fighting hole regretting I'd lost my temper. Pit was one of the few friends I had in the company. "Look, my wife's everything to me and I won't have any of you lowlifes talking like that about her. She's not like that, so don't even joke about it."

He stared back with expressionless eyes. Tobacco spittle had frozen drooling out the corners of his drooping lips. He could never understand the feelings I had for my wife, so I dropped it. "It's time for Robinson and Rogowski to take over. Give them the glasses," I said. "I want to sleep a few minutes while I've got the chance." He took the glasses and crawled out of the fighting hole. I rolled out my sleeping bag and crawled in and was asleep before my head touched the ground.

Corsairs dropping napalm and artillery bombardments out of Hagaru kept the Chinamen away during the day, but they came out in droves at night when the planes couldn't fly. For the past four days we'd watched them form on the surrounding hills at sunset. It was hard to tell in the dull light in their pale uniforms, but they seemed to stage in groups of forty or so. Occasionally we'd send bursts of fire towards them, but they were always too far away and quick to hide to do any damage to. The skipper finally told us to stop wasting our ammo after a while, that we were just as well shooting at ghosts. After dark when they'd formed and were ready to assault, they'd start blowing horns and whistles and banging drums and clanging cymbals. There wasn't any music to it, only scary racket performed by an orchestra of lunatics. I figured they did it to un-nerve us even more than we already were, and to let their comrades know they were in place and ready to charge up the hill to kill us.

I hadn't been asleep long before somebody kicked me awake. I peeked out of the sleeping bag hoping it wasn't a Chinaman with a bayonet at my throat. Thankfully it was only Pit. I stood up and looked around. To my great relief there were no gooks about to as-sault the hill either, only stretcher bearers carrying casualties from the night before off the hill. "What is it, hillbilly?" I said.

Pit was amused like everybody else in hearing. Everyone in the area was looking at me wearing big grins. "You was screamin' like a little girl down in that hole. I heared ya all the way over there by Robinson's gun. You must of been havin' another dream about that lion. Damn, you're shakin' like a dog shittin' peach seeds, you scared motherfucker."

I was a kid when the dreams of the little man began. Before I'd wound up here in this death trap, he'd hunted Ice Age animals with a spear alone on an endless plain along a great river. Those child-hood dreams weren't so bad, but the man has a huge saber-toothed cat with him now, and they aren't hunting giant sloths and wooly mammoths anymore. It seems all they want is my soul, and even worse than the dinks do. The dreams aren't like normal dreams.

They're far more real and intense. I can even smell the piss-stench of the lion a long time after I wake.

"Yeah, he and the little man get closer to killing me every time I try to sleep now. That big furry bastard had his paw on my chest, and I couldn't breathe."

"You are one more fucked-up asshole, Ball. When we get back to Pendleton you can get out of this shit on a mental discharge if you try. And I'll be your best witness." Then he waded off through the powdery drift spouting clouds of laughter. When he got to Jim Robinson, he pulled him around by his sleeve and pointed back at me. He said something, and Robinson started laughing, too. Then they lit cigarettes and turned their backs on me. I needed sleep but didn't want to deal with another nightmare featuring the smelly lion, so I pulled the charging handle on my weapon to be sure the bolt hadn't frozen and as always started thinking about Ginny.

"Ball, you look like you're going to a minstrel show with all that gun smoke caked on your face. You ought to go take a hot shower." It was Captain Johansson our company commander making his rounds. Thoughts of Ginny flew out of my head. "You got everything squared away for tonight?" he said, standing over me with his hands on his hips. He was still chuckling about his idiotic hot shower joke.

"I need another ammo bearer and some new gun barrels, Sir. These are all shot out."

"Take a little initiative and get somebody then. And I can't shit miracles. You're not getting any new gun barrels. You'll have to make do with the ones you have." He stared down on me a few more moments, then said, "You look like a starved scarecrow, Ball. You been to mess today?"

I couldn't remember the last time I'd eaten. Chow was always half frozen and gave all of us dysentery. It was agony having to pull your pants down in the brutal cold and bare your ass, so nobody wanted to eat so they wouldn't have to, but the Skipper made us anyway. "No, Sir."

"Then bring your lame ass with me. You know better. You got to eat. I hear lobster bisque and lambchops with asparagus is the main entrée today. With a bottle of Chateau Gilette okay with you?" He chuckled again and walked away motioning me to follow.

We slid, slipped and fell down the several hundred meters of ice incrusted hill from our perimeter to the battalion center. Other than cussing when he took a spill Johansson kept quiet until we got to the mess tent. It felt steamy and hot inside, but the mess men were serving out chow in heavy overcoats and gloves like the rest of us wore. When Johansson spoke, thick fog plumed out his mouth. "Spoon us up some of that nasty shit and give this skinny body some extra," he told the head messman.

Blue flames were glowing under the blackened pots, but when I took a bite of the c-ration beans and franks, it was slushy and crunched. Johansson watched with amusement as I choked down what was on my plate as he ate his. Then he checked his watch and a startled look came on his face. "Oh, shit," he said, and turned to the mess sergeant. "As always, excellent cuisine. Compliments to the chef." The mess sergeant just shook his head and he nor anyone else in the serving line seemed amused.

After we left the mess tent, I followed Johannsson at a trot to the command post. I figured he'd want me to wait outside, but he motioned me on in.

It was noisy inside the tent with the wind flapping the canvas and whistling through the bullet and shrapnel holes in the walls. A half dozen pogues were listening to staticky PRC radios crackling out barely intelligible messages. The other company commanders were gathered around Colonel Hayes, our battalion commander. Hayes crossed his arms and narrowed his eyes when me and Johansson came in. "Johansson, you finally decide to come down off your mountain for my briefing," he said.

"Sorry, Sir. It's busy up there and time slipped me by."

Hayes pointed at me. "What's with the Lance Corporal? You have a staff now I guess."

"No, Sir, we had chow together. Didn't want to leave him out in the cold."

"So, you held up my briefing so you could enjoy a nice hot breakfast."

"Sorry, Sir. I didn't realize the time."

"Excuses are like assholes, Johansson. Everybody's got one. Now let's get down to it."

Johansson and the other company commanders gave their reports on troop strength and equipment readiness. Casualties from the weather and battle had us down to less than half strength. After the reports, Hayes crossed his arms, dropped his head and started pacing. Then one of the pogues listening to a radio jumped out of his seat, and said, "Sir, it's Hagaru," and everyone craned their heads toward the radio. "Be advised," the metal box spouted out. "Intelligence reports confirm you're surrounded by sixty to a hundred and twenty thousand Chinese. Be prepared for intense nightly assaults. Standby for organized withdrawal update. Command clear, over, out."

We already suspicioned what the report had said, but no one imagined we were up against those kinds of odds. If the human wave assaults we'd survived the last three nights weren't intense assaults, then I wondered what was about to come. The only good news in the report was the withdrawal plans. I thought it'd better happen soon, as in hours, or no one would be left to withdraw. After a while the radiomen put their heads down and went to taking notes again, and the company commanders slipped out one by one. Johansson gave Hayes a disparaging look and shook his head and I followed him back to the foot of the hill and we started back up the icy slope to our perimeter.

Gunny Gains, the senior enlisted man in the company now, was waiting at the top of the hill to hear the latest from command. After Johansson told him about the Chinese and their suspected number,

Gains kicked up a cloud of snow. "Damn, Skipper, I been in some bad shit before, but nothing like this. That's more than six to one in their favor. With odds like that it's going to take a fucking miracle to get us out of here."

"Brilliant deduction, Gunny. You're practically another Einstein. If I thought you knew how, I'd order you to say a little prayer for us, but coming from you, I'm sure it'd only make things worse." Johansson walked off a few steps, then stopped and turned back. "Ball needs an ammo bearer, Gunny. Make sure he gets one and that those automatic weapons are ready. So far they've been our salvation."

Gains put his hands on his hips and started ranting. "I call bullshit on that, Captain. Why can't that scum bag do it? He's a lame ass Reservist. Why's he in charge of the automatic weapons section in the first place. He don't know shit about leading Marines." After a long moment under Johansson's glare, the fire left Gains' eyes and he dropped his head.

"He's got rank, that's why he's in charge, Gunny. Haven't you noticed he's a lance corporal and those other shit birds in his section are all privates or PFC's. Maybe you should take over if you don't approve of the way I'm commanding this company?"

"I wasn't aiming that at you, Sir. I'm just pissed at the situation. It just don't seem right for a Reservist to be over regular Marines, rank or not, especially the way things are now."

Johansson held his stare long enough so that Gains knew not to ever question his authority again. "I agree, but I don't make regulation – and neither do you. I'll be back before dark and you'd all better get your heads and asses wired together if you want to make it through this night. It's going to be the worst fucking nightmare yet. And I guarantee it."

I'd been activated to regular duty because of a shortage of automatic weapons personnel. Gunny Gains, like most of the regulars, didn't like me because I was a Reservist. They didn't think I was a real Marine and called me a weekend warrior, among other things.

And the fact that casualties to the NCO's in the automatic weapons section had made it necessary to put me in charge of the company's three machinegun crews made them despise me even more. I didn't want to be in charge, and it wasn't my fault I had rank over the few machinegun crewmen that were left.

I went back to my section and told the handful of men about the report of the numbers of Chinese flooding over the border, then I sent several to the mess tent. I was so tired I could hardly stand and needed sleep, but instead because of the inevitable horrid dreams of the lion, I made sure my weapon and the others in my section were operable and of course I started thinking of Ginny back home all alone and how I needed to get back to her.

It'd been well over a month since I'd heard from her, but that was no surprise. The Division had moved so fast past the Thirty-Eighth Parallel that mail hadn't been able to keep up and now we couldn't send mail and mail couldn't reach us. In her last letter, she said the baby was past due and they might have to induce labor. I'd just like to know if it was a boy or girl and that everything had gone well. Thinking of her with my child in the pitiful shack among the trashy folk filled me with despair. I felt if I didn't get back to her soon, I'd lose my mind. Then Gains' irritating voice brought me back to the Chosin.

"You ready for the gooks' visit tonight, shit for brains? The last planes are gone for the day and the yellow bastards are already forming up. The Skipper's calling in artillery, but as usual it won't do us no good."

I'd been so absorbed thinking of Ginny that I hadn't noticed the Chinamen. I watched as a bunch appeared momentarily on a distant hill. Others even closer moved through the trees our way and then were gone. Their sight caused a jolt of fear to surge through me. Gains saw the dread wash over my face and came and stood over me. "Ball, you're a worthless douchebag. Have you even bothered checking your section yet?"

I knew he'd call me a liar if I told him I had. "I was just fixing to, Gunny."

"You scumbag." He pulled me out of the fighting hole by my hood and threw me on the ground. "Get your shit together, Ball, before I rip your balls off and stuff em up your ass. It should have already been done."

As I was getting to my feet, he drew back to hit me, but a voice caused him to pause. "I wouldn't do that, asshole." Gains dropped his fist and shoved me away. I fell hard back into the fighting hole with the wind knocked out of me. I got back on my feet and looked over the rim of the fighting hole. Jim Robinson was squaring off with Gains. He kept poking Gains' chest as he talked. "Why don't you fuck with somebody more your size, you hoggy piece-of-shit?"

"This ain't none of your concern, convict. Stay out of it or I'm going to write your ass up."

"Write me up, but I'm going to stomp your ass first." As Robinson drew back, Gains turned and broke into a trot. He passed into the failing light and blowing snow like a ghost dissolving into fog. I crawled out of the hole still trying to get my breath as the others were bent and laughing at Gains' fast exit.

"Damn, slim, I think Gains' got a hard on for you cause you're a weekend warrior," Pit said.

"He better keep away from here or there's going to be an unfortunate accident," Robinson said. "Like my bayonet stuck up his fat ass."

"You redheaded ape, you're in enough trouble for punchin' that duty officer back at Pendleton," Pit said. "It don't matter if you was drunk, you're still goin' to do time over it. You don't need to make it worse gettin' into it with Gains."

"Don't none of it matter no how cause none of us is getting out of here alive anyway."

Pit's eyes grew wide. "Yes, we are. Gains told me second and third battalions are on the way here and we're goin' to linkup with 'em. Then we're goin' to fight our way back to Hagaru."

"Bullshit, hillbilly. Ain't going to happen. Gains is fuller of shit than a Christmas goose."

"But it's true. He told me this mornin'."

"It don't matter if the whole damn division comes. We ain't getting out of here with all them damn gooks surrounding us, and there's more coming every day. You're either going to be dead or a bitch to one of them chinks any day now, you dumbass. Time you understood that."

"Don't talk like that," Pit said.

"How could God have made such a moron, you Mississippi redneck? Do you think they're going to disappear if we don't talk about them and pretend they're not here? Shit. I'm going to get me some ham and limas. You ready for supper, ass wipe? You coming, Ball?"

"I'm not over the shits I got from the beans and franks I ate for breakfast," I said. "And what Pit said about the linkup is true."

He gave me the finger. "Fuck you. I still don't believe it. Let's go, idiot."

After Pit and Robinson disappeared down the hill, I went back to my weapon and to thinking about Ginny.

The early winter darkness came fast. The last bombing run of the day had long since passed. Johansson had called in an artillery barrage, but as usual it'd had little effect. Just after it'd ended the Chinese came out fearlessly in the open and formed on the hills in the last few minutes of light. Now I could hear their unintelligible jabber and crunching footsteps on the crusty snow in the dark below.

When the weird symphony of their whistles, drums, horns and cymbals struck up, thumps from our mortars launching illumination flares started. The first pops of brilliant light revealed the staged masses in the valley below, and then the deafening roar of our gunfire erupted. Muzzles flashed, tracers flared, and bullets whined ricocheting off bone. From our assigned fields of fire, the hillside became a slippery red obstacle course of screaming Chinamen tripping, sliding and clambering over each other and their dead as they ascended the hill to our perimeter. The ochre-clad masses firing and moving towards us looked surreal under the slowly descending, swaying and spewing parachute flares. Red, green, and blue tracers streaked through the sky and white phosphorous mortar rounds exploded in the background like great fireworks displays.

There were so many of them moving up the hill we couldn't kill them all for having to reload and from our weapons malfunctioning. Eventually they got into hand grenade range, and then they were inside the perimeter and hand to hand fighting broke out.

I fired as fast as my crewman could load and went through belt after belt of ammunition until my weapon over-heated and a case burst in the chamber from the intense heat from all the firing. The action jammed and wouldn't clear, so I took up a rifle and began firing and reloading again and again.

When I was down to my last few rounds, I crawled out of my fighting hole to get more ammo, and through the choking miasma of spent cordite shrouding the perimeter, I could see men everywhere struggling with each other against death.

I started towards a Marine grappling with a Chinaman, but before I could get to him, another one stabbed him from behind. I used my last few rounds splattering their brains when they started rummaging his pockets.

I chased after some other Chinamen dragging a screaming Marine away, but they vanished with him down the hill before I could catch up.

Then I came on Johansson. He was dancing and twirling and dodging like an unhinged ballerina jabbing and swinging a bayonetted rifle at three Chinamen trying to keep them away. I drove my bayonet into the first one's spine, and when I tried pulling it out, it wouldn't come. Then I was bashed from behind and on the snow in a daze with my head pounding as millions of swifts screamed in my ears. I raised on my elbows and watched as the other two Chinamen dragged Johansson towards the edge of the hill. He was limp, and a red line was being drawn on the snow from a wound to his head. I forced myself onto my feet and grabbed Johansson's rifle. The Chinamen kept losing their grip on Johansson's boots and I kept tripping and falling but managed to catch up just before they disappeared down the hill. I buried the bayonet into the first one's back and for a moment he lay still, then exploded flipping and flopping and bleeding like a lanced tuna on the deck of a boat. Then the other one blindsided and tackled me and I lost my grip on the M-1 and we started struggling, screaming, punching and kicking like two crazed animals. I was weak and still dazed from having my head bashed and he soon had my arms pinned against the snow with his knees. Then there was a glint from the flares as he drew out a knife and raised it over his head. His eyes widened and glimmered with hate as he started the blade down, but his face exploded as he did, and I was blinded by the gore. The taste was hot and pungently bitter, the stench putrid like a gut-shot deer. I spit and gagged and wiped my eyes and tried to stand, but the Chinaman's spasming body held me down. Then the twitching man lifted, and Robinson was straddled over me grinning and wide-eyed like an excited child. "Get off your worthless ass, Ball. We got gooks to kill." Then he kicked the faceless Chinaman and went off laughing insanely. As I lay on the snow with my head in agony, my adrenaline receded, and I slipped into a comforting sleep.

When I came to somebody was shaking and slapping me. I forced my eyes open and the blows stopped. Johansson was kneeling over me with a blood-stained field bandage wrapped around his head. His lips were moving, but I couldn't make out what he was saying. Then in stages his voice grew into comprehension. "Wake up. Can you hear me, Ball? If you don't get up, you're going to freeze." He helped me to my feet and then put a handful of snow in my hand. "Here, wipe that shit off your face before I puke." I scrubbed the frozen brains off as good as I could and then he gave me a shove. "Now get to your section and see to your men."

Flares were still spewing overhead, and an occasional gunshot still rang out, but the assault had been stopped. As I ambled through the bent and twisted bodies now frozen in their contorted positions of death, I tried avoiding their gazes, but I was spell bound by the illuminations of the flares reflecting off their empty-glazed eyes. It was impossible to turn from their waxen faces shrouded with countenances of varied fears and anguish. The smell of burnt cordite, gore and death-induced shit added hideous effect to the nightmare.

When I got to my fighting hole my head had cleared somewhat, but the throbbing pain was still there. Quiet had come over the perimeter, but there was some unusual desultory artillery night fire far off in the distance. I watched the bloom of pink on the horizon as the rounds detonated long before the crump of the explosions came. To be chancing night artillery I figured someone was going through a worse assault that we'd just gone through. And then I realized how lucky I was and felt an exhilaration that made me feel more alive than I'd ever been.

Pit was the only one in my section I could find. He was wrapped in a sleeping bag down in his fighting hole sobbing uncontrollably. I got down in the hole and was leaning over trying to console him when Robinson came up and kicked me between my shoulder blades. I thought my head would come off.

"You cowards can come out," he said and laughed. "The gooks are all gone now."

A fantastic rage replaced the searing pain in my head, and I crawled out of the hole and grabbed Robinson by his collar. "You'd better leave while you can, motherfucker."

"Try me, you little piece of shit."

He lost his grip on his pistol when I hit him. He was goggle-eyed and dazed when he got up, but not so that he didn't realize I had his 1911 pointed at his face. "Nobody's going to know or really care who put a bullet in your head. Now leave or die." He ambled off and didn't look back.

When we'd left San Diego in August there were 98 Marines in I Company. When daylight came only eighteen of us were left fit for duty. Frostbite was responsible for almost half our casualties. With the odds so against us I was amazed we hadn't been overrun and decimated already. And with the number of Chinese growing and our ranks so depleted, another night of their assaults and we undoubtably would be.

While we moved our dead and wounded from the hill down to the command center, Johansson went to report to Hayes. He was back in an hour, and every time I looked his way, I caught him glaring at me. I'd seen him talking to Robinson earlier and figured Robinson had told him about me putting the pistol to his head and my threat to kill him. My court martial was likely already in progress, I supposed. Johansson called what was left of the Company together when the hill was clear of casualties.

"Orders just came down, men, and we're pulling out of here in a few hours," he started. "Second and third battalions are rendezvousing just to our south and we're going to attempt linking up with them. Then we're going to fight our way back to Hagaru. I Company's part in the withdrawal is to guard the rear of the convoy from here to the linkup area. Except for the machine gun crews, all of you collect your gear and load it on the last transport truck." Then he turned to me. "Ball, you and your section hang loose."

The men leaving the hill went about joyfully collecting their equipment like a mob of death row inmates just given stays of execution. It didn't take long before the hill was deserted, except for the four of us. When the last man disappeared down the hill, Johansson spoke up again. "I don't like this, men. I did everything but get court martialed refusing to give these orders, but that's the way it is in the Corps. There's nothing fair about it. Now listen up, you three are going to stay here and keep the gooks off the road so the column can get a head start out of here. I know it sucks, but it's the best and only chance of saving what's left of the battalion.

I have complete confidence knowing you three will persevere. Any questions?"

Johansson waited as we stared back and forth at one another in dismay. I was too overwhelmed by the feeling of betrayal to say anything. "Why the dreadful looks?" Johansson said. "Did you think you were signing up for a weenie roast when you joined the Corps?" No one answered. "Since you seem to be okay with the orders, you've got time to get some chow or to go see Chaplain Kelly. You two are dismissed, but I want you back here by 1400. Ball, I want a minute with you."

As soon as Pit and Robinson went out of sight down the hill, Johansson turned to me with his hand out. "I appreciate what you did last night saving my life. I didn't know till this morning when Robinson told me. I was out when it all happened."

His hint of compassion was so out of character it threw my thoughts out of kilter. I shook his hand, then said, "It wasn't no big deal, Sir."

"It was to me, and it's a miracle you didn't get killed. If that lamebrain hadn't happened up when he did and given that gook a face lift, you wouldn't be here. He made a special point of telling me all about that as well."

"I'm sure he did."

"Look, in my position I'm not supposed to be saying this, but I'm sorry you're in this mess. I'm giving you my word that I'll do everything I can to get you out of here. I wanted to stay with you, but the Colonel won't let me. Now you'd better go do what you need to do. Time's getting short, so you'd better hurry it up."

Nothing was left to do on the hill. The automatic weapons, what was left of them, were as ready as could be. There was plenty of ammo stacked nearby. I'd felt starved before Johansson had come back from the command tent, but now those pangs of hunger had been replaced by ones of fear. Then I thought of Ginny and the letter I'd written weeks before but had never had the chance to mail and decided I'd go see Chaplain Kelly. And then the thought came that if by some miracle we weren't killed, what was I to do to get the three of us back with the battalion. Johansson had just turned to leave when I stopped him. "So, Skipper, what do we do after the battalion gets away?"

He turned back to me with a ridiculous look of confusion and started stammering and stuttering and I knew he hadn't considered we'd have any chance of getting off the hill alive and hadn't made any prior plans. Though he was befuddled at first, his eyes started dancing as his brain worked, and he quickly invented a half-assed bullshit story. "Damn, Ball, think I haven't worked that out? I've got a 105-howitzer battery at Hagaru registered on this hill. When it starts, you'll know we're at the linkup, and when the first-round falls, you'd better haul ass out of here because I'm going to walk hell over every inch of this hill. Hide out in the timber until dark and then head south and you'll find us. Just don't take the easy route on the road. Stay out of sight in the timber on the hills."

When Chaplain Kelly opened the flap to his tent, I thought I was at the wrong place. He was a big, mean looking bastard with a severe scar running from his white, lifeless left eye down to his chin. He didn't look very religiously devout to me. "Come in, son," he said, motioning with his hand. I followed him to his field desk that had nothing on it but a Bible. After sitting behind the desk, he joined his hands. "What's your name, Corporal?"

"Henry Ball, Sir."

"Where you from?"

"Georgia."

"Well what do you think about that? My wife is from the South. She says it's hot as Hell down there." He smiled trying to raise my mood, I guess. I didn't see the humor. "News travels fast in the Corps, Ball. I heard about your upcoming mission. It's a bad predicament, but I understand the Colonel's reasoning. Did you come here to pray?"

"No, Sir, I didn't come to pray. Seeing all the squandered dead over the last four nights has caused me to lose faith. The reason I came was to see if you'd get this letter to my wife," I said, and handed him the envelope. "I want her to know that my love for her is what's kept me alive through all this and I'm doing everything I can to get home to her as soon as I can."

The intense stare from his good eye was hard to stay locked onto for the several long moments that passed in silence. I figured he'd become perturbed because I'd disavowed my faith and didn't want to pray. "I'll do my best," he said, and stood and placed the letter in his bible. Then he pointed towards the door. On my way out I reckoned the odds and figured Ginny would never get my letter.

The command center had been disassembled by the time I'd finished my visit with the Chaplain. The dead and wounded had all been loaded in or tied onto the vehicles, and the convoy was ready to move out. With a rackety, smoke belching bulldozer plowing the way, the battalion started for the linkup.

As expected, the Chinamen knew what was up, and as soon as the trucks started moving they came running and screaming out of the hills like crazed banshees, and we began cutting them down in droves with the automatic weapons from our perimeter on the hilltop. They were an uncontrollable mob chasing the convoy and in their great excitement seemed oblivious we were annihilating them at first, but then we started taking small arms fire. Though it was inaccurate, there was enough of it to worry about a lucky round finding a mark. Then a few mortar rounds started coming in, but they were exploding randomly at a harmless distance.

With our machinegun support, the convoy disappeared in minutes into the hills seemingly unscathed. If there was only light resistance along the road and no mechanical problems, the trucks should make the staging area in less than an hour. Our only chance of getting off the hill was to slip away during the artillery barrage Johansson had promised, and the sooner the convoy got to the linkup so he could get the bombardment started the better for us. But now that the trucks were well away, and they couldn't follow because of our fire, the Chinamen turned their full attention on us, and now I had to concentrate on saving my own ass.

When I first noticed the tiny spotter plane buzzing overhead, I figured close to an hour had passed since the convoy had left. We'd killed a lot of the Chinese during that time. Most of which were trying to get past us down the road with intentions of overrunning the departing battalion. We'd done our job, but Pit had paid the ultimate price by taking a round to the head in doing so. And the last man I'd figure to break would be Robinson, but he was curled sobbing convulsively beside Pit like a frightened child. I'd taken some shrapnel in my side from a mortar round that burned like hell but didn't seem to be that bad. I was running so high on fear and adrenaline, though, my whole side could have been shot out and I wouldn't have felt it.

I was screaming like a frightened girl as I went about springing from weapon to weapon jumping in and out of fighting holes, emptying ammunition belts as fast as I could shoot and load. I was out of my mind with fear and time flew by and I don't remember much until I heard the first whistling roar of incoming 105 rounds. That's when I felt some hope that I might have a chance to survive even with the mortar rounds raining in and the waves of green tracers whizzing by like mad hornets. Then a noise of crunching metal came, and when I looked up a chunk of the spotter plane's tail was spiraling down. It hadn't left the area in time and had gotten in the way of one of the howitzer rounds. I was watching it heading out over the reservoir losing altitude fast when the first incoming round exploded on an adjacent hill. The blast so near was incredible and shook me to the core. A giant column of black smoke rose from where it'd impacted. The gooks were well acquainted with our artillery and started running away when they heard the distinct sound of the first incoming rounds, and I was inclined to do the same.

I kicked Robinson to get him up, but it had no effect. At first the 105 rounds started impacting at a safe distance but now were walking closer towards the perimeter by the second. I slung an M1 over my shoulder and kicked Robinson again. "You'd better come on, asshole, or they'll be sending you home in a cigarette pack." He was apparently so traumatized he couldn't feel or hear me. I couldn't leave him, though, and helped him up and we started sliding down the hill as artillery rounds began impacting in the perimeter.

A waning moon rose out of the hills while we hid in a spruce grove waiting for dark. Then I herded Robinson towards the direction I'd last seen the O-1. After reaching the road, I could see the glow from a fire out on the open reservoir and figured it had to be from the burning plane. I thought hard about turning around and leaving since most likely no one could have survived the fiery crash. And if anyone had they'd surely have been captured by the Chinese by now. But whoever had been in the plane had directed the artillery barrage precisely and had made it possible for me and Robinson to escape and I was going to be sure of their fate before I left.

I went out on the reservoir far enough to be sure the heavy smoke and fire was from the plane. Robinson was such a liability I left him there and went on alone. I hadn't gone far when I heard faint shouting off to the north. I deviated from my path and went towards the direction of the loud voices. As I got closer somebody in either a great deal of pain or anger, or both was screaming profanities in English. The screams were punctuated with bouts of laughter. I slipped on till I made out two Chinamen kicking a screaming man on the ground. They were so intent in their amusement I slipped in and butt stroked one from behind and bayonetted the other in the chest when he turned with an astonished look. Then I finished the first one for good with a slash to his throat.

For a moment I was amazed on finding their victim to be Johansson, but then I reckoned he was the one most likely to have come back to help us as he'd promised. The two Chinamen had given him a hard time. His face was a bruised and a bloody mess all beaten and battered. The gash from the headwound he'd gotten the night before was bleeding again.

"Damn you got a loud mouth. You better be glad none of the other gooks heard you or your ass would be on the way to a prison camp. What about the pilot?" I said.

Johansson cleared his throat and spit a wad of blood onto the snow. "I don't think he made it. He told me to jump out just after we touched down, then the plane flipped and burst into flames. The gooks must not have seen me jump. They went straight for the plane."

"So, what're you doing here anyway?"

"After we got to the linkup, Hayes ordered the pilot to fly me back to see if you were still alive before I called in the barrage. Are you the only one that made it?"

"I left Robinson back near the road. He's out of his mind in shock. Poor Jenkins didn't make it, though. Look, I don't think it wise we hang around here. Can you walk?"

"Hell no. My knee's ruined. I twisted it when I jumped out of the plane. You damn fool, don't you know you committed suicide coming here?"

"That's the thanks I get. Now put your arm over my shoulder and get off your fat ass and let's get moving."

I'd intended using the cover of night to reach the linkup area, but Robinson was of no help with Johansson. I did the best I could, but we made little progress. With the adrenaline of the battle gone, the pain of the shrapnel wounds had become overwhelming and then exhaustion overtook me. We were all done in when we got back to the road, so we crawled under an outcropping of rock in the lee of a ridge out of the wind to rest and soon we were asleep.

When I woke it was just at sunrise and I was all but frozen. My wounds had stiffened, and the pain was unbearable when I tried to move. I had no idea if Johansson or Robinson were alive. Neither would respond to my feeble shaking or strained voice.

Then I heard the unmistakable whooping of chopper blades coming our way and wanted to run out and wave it down when it came into view, but all I could manage was a foolish wave of my hand as it hovered over the area of the command post and our old perimeter. I supposed they were looking for any of us that might have survived the last assault on the perimeter, or most likely they were seeking the fate of the crashed O-1 and its crew. Then the chopper banked and headed toward the smoldering plane. Now that there was enough daylight, I could make out dozens of Chinamen crowded around the charred rubble trying to get the last of its warmth. They looked like a covey of quail exploding in all directions when they realized the chopper closing in. I watched the door gunner have his way while the pilot chased them across the open reservoir. First there were spouting clouds of snow as the bullets chased and then gushers of red as the fifty caliber rounds caught up. It was lucky for us this happened, because as the chopper was leaving, the pilot spotted the muzzle flashes in the shadows of the lee from the M1 I began firing in his direction in desperation. Thankfully he came to check it out.

The last thing I remember of the Chosin was being loaded onto the chopper and then a medic at the link up area saying he couldn't get glucose thawed enough to get into me. "Wrap him in a sleeping bag and tie him to a truck fender and tag him 'Unlikely'," he said. But he took some morphine ampules from his mouth and shot them into my leg anyway and I was soon asleep.

Before they had me lashed to the truck fender I was dreaming of the Nomad and the Lion. The filthy little half naked blond man with dazzling cobalt eyes and the giant brown cat that always stayed faithfully at his side began trailing me across a seemingly endless plain along a great river. They stayed on my trail for days, and every time I looked back, they were closer. It was his way to test my will I guess since they could catch me anytime they wanted. Only the thought of Ginny gave me the fortitude to keep ahead. Then one night I couldn't go on, not even for her, and they closed in that moment I gave up. I thought the cunning little man with his spear would be the one to do me in, but instead he sent the cat to do his bidding. But when the Lion stood on my chest forcing the life out of me, my resolve to live surged and the Nomad called him off. Since time was of no consequence for those two revenants anyway, they could come for me anytime, and I knew they would someday. Then dreams of the Nomad and the Lion ended for a time.

I woke with a start in a pool of cold sweat to the feel of motion and the throb of powerful engines. It was pitch dark in the bay of the ship. The medicinal and antiseptic stench was atrocious.

CHAPTER 3

"You are one lucky son of a bitch, boy. If you hadn't been half frozen, you'd have bled to death getting to Hungnam tied to that truck. And we did lose you one time, but the corpsman here beat on your chest till he got you going again. Now that was a real miracle. And I came close to cutting some of your toes off a few days ago, but I think now they're going to stay on. I want the truth now. How do you feel?"

"Fine, Sir."

"You're so full of shit, Ball."

I'd been bedridden in the foul-smelling sickbay for over two weeks. The infirmary reeked of the usual chemical smells that all hospitals do, and the constant odor kept me nauseous. I thought if I didn't get some relief from the stench, I'd die anyway. "Okay, I hurt like hell, but can I go up on deck for a while? I've got to get out of this stinking hold before I choke."

"I doubt you can make it, but you're welcome to try. Just don't mess around and open any of those wounds or I'll have your ass in a sling. I got most of that shrapnel out, but the rest is going to have to work its way out over time. Some of it may never come out."

Layers of black skin were peeling off my feet and my toenails were gone. Putting weight on them was excruciating. I was a rack of bones encased in saggy, pale skin. The doctor wisely sent a corpsman to help me get around.

I held the corpsman's shoulder and gripped the metal railing of my cot to keep my balance. It'd been close to three weeks since I'd stood, and the vertical position made my head swim. The pain from the wounds caused dots to dance in my eyes. I hobbled around for only a short time before I was exhausted. The corpsman got me back in bed and was almost out the door when he stopped. "Say, Ball, now that you're mobile again, how about giving us a break and take a shower?"

It'd been months since I'd felt hot, running water. A shower sounded wonderful. "In an hour, Doc?"

"I'll be here. You'll make a lot of us happy."

Johansson came to check on me later that afternoon, like he'd done every day since we'd boarded ship. We'd become very close over that time. "Damn, Ball, least you don't smell like a dead gook anymore," he said, after seeing I'd shaved, and my hair had been washed.

"Yes, sir, and it'd be nice to have a smoke and some coffee and to get away from this stench for a while."

Johansson wandered around the infirmary and found a wheelchair. He could barely walk and had to use a cane as he pushed me along. I didn't want to put him through the effort to get me up on deck, so he rolled me to the mess hall instead and a galley man brought us wonderful mugs of steaming, strong coffee. Then as we talked and smoked, it became apparent Johansson was preoccupied with something and his lack of attention started to annoy me. My curiosity eventually got to me. "You act like you got something on you mind, Sir."

He shifted his gaze and stared long and hard at me. I began to feel uncomfortable by the time he started. "You know if it wasn't for you, I'd be in a Chinese prison camp, or most likely I'd be dead now. You saved my life during that last assault. And the convoy would have likely been decimated if you hadn't kept the gooks off the road like you did. Nobody would have stood up under that kind of fire. And you saved Robinson and came after me after the plane crash knowing in all probability you'd be killed. There is something on my mind, Ball. I'm recommending you for a Medal of Honor for what you did. I've talked it over with Colonel Hayes and he agrees. You deserve it and I'm going to see that you get it."

I figured it was one of his lame jokes he was so bad at. I waited for the punch line, but by his unyielding, stolid expression I realized he was serious. "I don't deserve or want any medal. I'm getting out of the Corps as soon as I can, and it won't mean anything. All I care about is getting home to my wife and kid. Ginny needs me and I've got to get back to her."

"I'm an officer. Don't argue."

"Aye, aye, Captain," I said, and smiled.

"By the way, it's Major Johansson to you now." I glanced at his captain's bars. "I'll get the oak leaves when we get back to the states."

I shook his hand and congratulated him. He got the cigarettes out again as a group of boisterous Marines came filing in. One re-filled our cups and Johansson nodded his thanks. "Heard anything out of your old lady yet, or did she wise up and leave your sorry ass?"

Though he was only joking, what he said unsettled me and I didn't answer at first. "Only letters I've received in weeks are from my mother. She wrote that the baby had come, and everyone was doing well. It was a girl and Ginny named her Sara."

"I hope she favors her mother and not your ugly ass. Your old man ever write? I've never heard you mention him. Is he dead or something?"

"No, he's not dead and I'm glad he doesn't write. If he was dead and I never saw him again it'd be fine with me."

"You and your old man didn't get along, huh? Same way with mine. He was enlisted in the Army and loved kicking my ass when he drank, which was all the time he was off duty, and a lot of times when he was on. First thing I did when I got home on leave from

Parris Island was kick the shit out of him when he started in on me. I cut my leave short and reported to my duty station early just to get away from him. Never saw him again after that. Didn't even go to his funeral."

"Sounds as bad as my old man. But if you went through P.I. you had to have started out as an enlisted man."

"I was a corporal when my platoon commander thought I might have some potential to be an officer and got me into O.C.S. I've been on both sides of the fence, Ball. Your doctor told me the frost bite injuries to your feet are bad enough to get you medically discharged if you want to get out. It's up to you if you stay in or not. If you do decide to stay in and want me to, I'll help you get a commission. With your record, you'd have a hell of a career. If the only thing holding you back is your marriage, don't worry, you can get a nice house and live with your wife on base at the government's expense."

"Thanks, but I'm getting out. I've had enough of the Corps. I think I've done my share. And I've put my wife through enough already."

"I guess you have. So, what made you want to join the Corps in the first place?"

"I had an uncle that pretty much raised me. My Uncle Jacob was the opposite of my old man even though they were brothers. He was religious and never drank that I knew of. And he was gentle and patient, not mean and intemperate like my old man. By the time I could walk he had me out hunting and fishing. When I was old enough, he took me to the mountains to trout fish and he always kept good birddogs and we quail hunted all the time. I wish he'd been my father. He got killed on Bougainville. You see he was a Marine and I joined because he wanted me to be a Marine. But I didn't want to serve a two-year enlistment so I joined the Reserves so I wouldn't be gone but for six months because of Ginny. I swore to her I'd never leave her again after I got back from active duty, but here I am. Been gone for months."

"That don't make sense, Ball. Maybe you shouldn't have joined at all if you need to cling to your old lady like that."

"You're probably right. Having her back is all I want and ever will want. I made it through that hell we just went through just for her. I won't ever let her out of my reach again no matter what. And that includes a career as an officer in the Marine Corps. So, after hearing all that does it mean you'll forget about that medal?"

"Not a chance."

CHAPTER 4

Regulation required I remain on active duty until I'd recovered sufficiently from my wounds and frost bite before being re- leased from active duty and returned to my reserve unit. I was sent to Bethesda Naval Hospital as soon as I arrived back in the States to recover.

Because of his injured knee Johansson was also sent to Bethesda to rehab and recuperate before being cleared for further combat duty. He wanted another tour in Korea to pay back some unsettled debts for nearly a company of deceased Marines. He checked into the hospital a week after I did and then found my room. I slid out of bed to greet him when he came in. "Damn, Major, it's good to see you. Those oak leaves look good on you. Where you been?"

"Trying to get your worthless ass a medal, but some Colonel Army doggie on the board don't like Marines getting decorated. We just got to be patient, Ball. I'm still working on it. It would have gone through without any hitches if Robinson hadn't died and could have been a witness."

"I wish you'd let it drop. It's not a big deal to me."

"Damn it, it is to me, and I'm going to see it through! By the way, the lady at the front desk asked me to give you this."

In the left upper corner of the large brown envelope 'Ginny Ball' was included in the law firm return address. This was what I'd been dreading but knew all along was to be. As I read the decree, I strained to hold back my emotions, but Johansson could see I was overwhelmed by the way I was trembling and the pain on my face. After I finished reading it, I handed it to him.

He picked through the legal stuff and reread parts like the papers had been served on him. He shook his head as he handed them back. "Sorry, Henry. I know she and your daughter are everything to you. It says there's thirty days before its final after it's filed. Hopefully she'll come to her senses and reconsider during that time. Do you know her reason for it?"

"I believe she left me for another man for his money. According to her last letter Mama thinks so, too. She said Ginny got scared I wasn't coming back when she found out we'd been surrounded and so outnumbered. According to Mama from what the news was saying nobody thought any of us were getting out of there alive. Mama thinks she latched on to him for her and Sara's sake. The day I left for Korea Ginny threatened she would do just that if I didn't come back soon. That she'd leave me for an old high school boyfriend. Looks like she came through on her threat."

"All you can do is hold out for hope she reconsiders. I'm sure with you being in the position you were in and with a newborn baby she was under a heavy strain. Give it a little time and I bet she changes her mind and forgets all this."

I thought I'd learned what the feeling of hopelessness was at the Chosin, but that was nothing compared to how I felt after the divorce decree. I knew the war would end one way or the other. Either we'd win or lose, and I'd go home, or I'd be killed. But the agony of losing Ginny would be forever or for as long as it took to get her back.

That night I started what was to be a nightly routine until I was released from the hospital. I slipped out of the infirmary and hobbled to a nearby liquor store in a set of corpsman whites I stole from the hospital laundry and a coat I heisted from a waiting room rack. I sat in the snow in the alleyway behind the store and drank a pint of cheap whiskey with a group of homeless drunks who'd begged money for food on the street during the day then took what they'd panhandled to buy whiskey to get drunk on that night. I staggered back to my ward half frozen and made sure I woke everyone on the floor. From then on, I'd try to instigate fights with anybody that seemed willing. Anyone and everyone that had to deal with me came to detest me and my defiance. I had no conscience for consequence anymore. I was a moment away from going to the brig when my release from Bethesda came. Then they shipped me home on a bus so someone else could deal with me and my problems.

I'd only been home a few days when orders came for me to report to the reserve armory in Rome to discuss my future with the Marine Corps. My Commanding Officer now was the Reserve I&I Officer Captain Glenn Rogers. We shook hands and I sat down across from him at his desk.

"Corporal Ball, it's a wonder you're not getting kicked out of the Corps with a bad discharge," Rogers began. "For a man recommended for such a high decoration, you've gone to flat out shit. It's inconceivable to me that the short time you were in Bethesda you were written up for drinking, fighting, unauthorized leave, and insubordination so many times. You must have set a record. Seems you would have gotten your fill of fighting in Korea."

I said nothing and stared back without concern, which undoubtably incensed Rogers.

"Nothing to say about that, huh?" I shook my head. "Okay then. Though it's against my better judgement it's my duty to ask you to stay in the Corps. A Major Johansson called and told me about your experiences in Korea and about your recommendation for the Medal. He said if you stay in, he's also recommending you for O.C.S." He paused for a long moment as if to let what he'd said sink in, then he went on. "He also informed me about your divorce, and

I have empathy for that. I'll get all this cleared from your record if you think you can square yourself away, but if this is the way you're going to conduct yourself in the future, I'd suggest you get out. You could have a hell of a career in the Corps with your combat record. And just for your information you've been meritoriously promoted to corporal. Now, do you want to sign these medical discharge papers, or do you want to discuss staying in?"

"Fuck yes, I want to sign those papers. I want out of this shit as fast as I can get out."

Rogers seemed dumbfounded. "You don't even want to discuss it? You've got such an opportunity here."

"Fuck no. The Marine Corps has ruined my life. I'm handicapped from wounds and frostbite from fighting a bunch of crazy Chinese soldiers that our great commander General MacArthur wouldn't even recognize we were fighting until it was almost too late in thirty below weather with winds that you couldn't stand up in. But most of all I've lost my wife because of the Marine Corps. I know I'm not mentally the same person that left here last summer. If not for General Smith I wouldn't even be here. I doubt any of the First Marine Division would have gotten out if not for him and some other great leaders, like Major Johansson. You see, Captain, they're men that have balls. They're real Marines not pogues like you that fill their time skating behind a desk. If you were a real Marine, you'd leave this petty job and volunteer for combat. No, I'm not staying in. I've sacrificed all I'm going to. I think it's your turn to go fight the Chinese."

Rogers had a look of shock – or maybe it was devastation – when I'd finished my little sermon. "You can't talk to me like that, Ball. I'm an officer. I'll write you up for insubordination again. I'll bust you back down to private if you don't shut the fuck up."

"Then what else, Sir? Make me get a haircut and send me back to Korea?"

I didn't know or really care that the I&I First Sergeant from his office across the hall was listening to our conversation. I guess my attitude pissed him off because he stormed into Rogers' office without permission and began ranting. "Who do you think you're talking to, Ball? I'm going to drag your sorry ass out of here and stomp the shit out of you." My insolent stare enraged him more and he shook his clinched fist in my face. "You're treading on thin ice, boy."

Rogers spoke up. "First Sergeant Makilhaney, I think it best you wait outside."

The big throbbing vein in Makilhaney's neck had turned crimson and looked on the verge of exploding as he stormed out.

"Okay, Ball, sign here and you're discharged. I want you out my sight forever. Don't ever come back here, understand?"

"You don't have worry about that."

"If you've checked your gear, get off this base. I'll have your ass arrested if you ever step foot back on it again. Your discharge will be mailed to you. Any questions?"

I flicked a sarcastic salute, did an about face, then started marching out of his office. Just before I went out the door, I turned and said, "See you assholes in the funny papers, Sir."

A brass Iwo Jima Flag Raising paperweight came flying by my head and knocked a big chunk of plaster out of the wall. "Ball, you are one more despicable piece of shit!"

I didn't stop laughing till I passed through the gym going to the rear parking lot to my old truck. There, I became somber as memories came flooding back of the weekends I'd spent at the Armory in classes, the days in the field training for combat and of the rigor and harassment of Parris Island. I thought about the friends I'd made during my duty, especially the ones whose lives had ended in Korea. I should have been happy being out of the Corps, but happiness for me had become a thing of the past. I wanted to go someplace far away to escape the despair and bitterness of the divorce. But maybe Johansson was right. Now that I was back, maybe Ginny would have a change of heart and take me back. I'd hang around a while and see.

When I went out the back door, I wasn't surprised to see Makilhaney standing shirtless beside my truck still red faced and livid. "Get over here, Ball," he bellowed. "I'm about to stomp your sorry ass."

He started towards me in a boxer's stance way overconfident, and I surprised him with a hard right that sent him stumbling backwards. Then I stayed low under his punches and he kept backing with each one I threw. When he tripped over the curbing and tried to stand, I used my boot heel on his nose. It crackled like an eggshell and he went down for good. I'd probably been charged with manslaughter if the shock of a gunshot beside my head hadn't stopped me pounding his face. When I turned, a .45 was pointed at my head. Rogers was peering down the barrel with a look of agitated wonder. "Get your ass in your truck and leave, Ball. I've had all your shit I'm going to take."

I looked down at Makilhaney, then back to Rogers. "Tell him if he ever fucks with me again, I'll kill him. And next time you point that pistol at me you'd better use it, or I'll stuff it up your sorry pouge ass."

As I walked to my truck, I couldn't constrain my laughter and sounded like an amused imbecile sliding behind the wheel. I turned the key and hit the floor starter and the motor caught. After the engine redlined, I popped the clutch, then watched in the rearview as Rogers disappeared in a black cloud of burnt rubber.

I was finally free of the Marine Corps, but now that I had my freedom, I had no idea of where to go or what to do. I decided to stop at a tavern I passed on the way home and wound up getting drunk trying to figure it all out. Later, my temper exploded when some redneck pushed me aside at the bar so he could order a beer and I started a fight with him and ended up spending my first night as a civilian in jail.

CHAPTER 5

Montana, the Judge, the Compulsion
3 April 1951- Oldale, Georgia

Having to deal with the divorce and the aftermath of the war was bad enough, but then Mama got a call from Mr. Newcomb, my bank president, saying I needed to drop by his office. I always thought I'd like to be a banker because they all seemed to make a lot of money doing nothing other than bullshitting and blowing smoke up customers' asses. They all wore flashy clothes and drove fancy new cars and I was excited thinking that maybe he had a job offer for me. I couldn't come up with any other reason he'd want to see me. The next day I dressed up in my Sunday suit for my visit with Mr. Newcomb all excited and pumped up expecting the good news of a plushy, high-paying job offer.

When I informed the receptionist, who I'd gone all through school with, that Mr. Newcomb wanted to see me she acted as though she didn't know me. "Mr. Newcomb said he wanted to talk to me, Jennifer. How are you – "

"Wait here, Henry. I'll see if he's busy." She hurried off with an irritated sigh and came back seconds later and plopped down behind her typewriter. "You can go in now," she said, without bothering to look up.

Remembering her as a sweet person, I was surprised by her rudeness. "How're things going, Jennifer?"

She opened a drawer and stuck her head in it. "I'm really busy. He's waiting on you."

Mr. Newcomb wrapped his hands behind his head, leaned back in his padded leather swivel chair and propped his polished wingtips on his desk when I went in. He didn't offer his hand and wore an unusual smirk and held an intense stare. "How goes it, Henry? Glad to be home?"

"Yes sir, I am. And I'm ready to get back to work. I'm looking for a job."

"Thanks for coming in. It's good to see you but I've got some bad news." He shoved a piece of paper across his desk toward me. It was a check I'd written a few days before for my light bill. I picked it up thinking I'd forgotten to sign it. But 'Insufficient funds' was stamped on the face of it in red ink. I was dumbfounded. "This just can't be right, Mr. Newcomb."

"Oh, but it is right, Henry. Ginny came in and emptied that account just before she left town."

"Well then I'll transfer some out of my savings account to cover it. I sent home plenty in allotments while I was gone. I only kept enough out of my pay to live on. I was going to use the rest towards a down payment on a new house for her."

"Sorry, but she took that too. And there's more. I've been waiting till you got back so I could send somebody out to pick up that furniture and those appliances you financed when you first married. She didn't make a single payment after you left and they've got to go back. You've really put me in a bad spot, Henry."

"There's no need for that. You know I'll pay you what I owe. You act like I'm a criminal. None of this is my fault."

"No, but it is your responsibility. It's your signature on the note. And you should have checked on your accounts before you started writing checks. Now get it taken care of before I get lawyers involved. I'll have someone out to your house to pick up those appliances and furniture this afternoon. And by the way, good luck on finding that job you're looking for."

I was waiting in the front porch swing for the repossession people to come when Rosco Lipscomb, my landlord, drove up. I'd known Mr. Rosco all my life. He was a close friend of my Uncle Jacob and we'd hunted and fished together a lot over the years. I stood and waved as he pulled to a stop. He simply raised a finger off the steering wheel in greeting before unfolding his long, gaunt frame out of his truck. I jumped down off the porch looking forward to his visit. "Mr. Rosco, it's good to see you. Still got those fine bird dogs?"

"I do, Henry. Glad you made it home alright. How's your mama?"

"She's doing well. Church and playing at weddings keep her busy."

"Sorry Ginny run off on you like she done. She was a cutie. Didn't get to see the baby. Who'd she take after?"

"Me, I guess. She's got blond hair anyway."

All the pleasantness left his face. "Ain't going to sugar coat this, Henry. You're going to have to get out before the weekend. Got new tenants moving in Saturday."

"What do you mean, Mr. Rosco?"

"Ginny didn't keep up the rent while you was gone and I couldn't wait no more. Hell, I didn't know if you was ever even coming back."

Just then a moving truck pulled up. Two stout men got out. "One of you be Henry Ball?" one said.

I raised my hand. "Guess you've come for my furniture?"

"We have."

"Door's open. Go on in and get it then."

"They come for your stuff huh, Henry?" Mr. Rosco said, bent over glaring down at me, hands buried in his back overall pockets.

"They did. I'll have what's left out in a day or two. Ain't much."

"Where you going to go to, Henry?"

"Back in with my folks I guess, at least till I get back on my feet and can afford another place."

"She really put it on you didn't she, boy? I think you're as fine a man as Jacob was. Hate seeing you go through this, but sometimes things work out for the best. Keep your head up and don't let it get you down too bad. Maybe we can bird hunt some this fall. Be seeing you, Henry."

I'd been home for over a week and hadn't had any communication with Ginny. I didn't know where she and Sara were, only rumors they were living in Atlanta somewhere. I was going crazy with her silence and one day I broke down and called the law firm she was using and asked for her home address or a phone number where I could reach her. I was put on hold for a long time until an unpleasant voice came on and informed me that he was Ginny's attorney and that if I had anything to say to her, my attorney could talk to him about it. I was speechless. After a long pause the unkind and rude voice, said, "If that's all you have to say I'll see you in court," and hung up.

The court hearing date we had to appear in front of Judge Elway Harper came a week later. I didn't have the money to hire a lawyer but an attorney that had been friends with Jacob assured me I didn't need legal representation because Judge Harper was the most impartial and ethical judge there was and would treat me fairly.

When I entered the courtroom Judge Harper was sitting behind his bench talking to an old man kneeling beside his chair. It took a minute, but I realized the man was Judge Rupert Armstrong who Jacob had told me stories about that had retired from the bench years before. In his younger days Armstrong was a bootlegger that had been caught and convicted several times. He'd started his law education while serving time in Reidsville State Prison. Jacob told me he was the biggest poacher in the county hunting out of season and shooting over his limit in everything including ducks and doves and that he liked to get drunk and jack light rabbits at night. Jacob said Armstrong always considered himself above the law. When I walked into the courtroom Judge Harper looked my way and said something to Judge Armstrong. Judge Armstrong then looked up at me and nodded. After Harper nodded back, Armstrong left through the back door of the judge's chamber.

I hadn't seen or talked to Ginny since the day I'd left for Korea. An awful feeling of grief and loneliness came over me on seeing her. And knowing the reason she was there was to shut me out of her life forever was agonizing. Judge Harper stared hard at me the entire time the lawyers and clients from the preceding case were leaving the room and I became more uneasy by the minute.

After the people from the prior case were gone the clerk stepped up and read from a document. "The divorce hearing of Ginny Ball versus Henry Ball is next on the docket, your Honor."

About then I heard the courtroom door open and close. Then someone came and sat down behind me. I didn't think much about it till I glanced over my shoulder and saw First Sargent Makilhaney in his dress uniform gawking back at me. That's when the truth hit, and I remembered that Judge Armstrong was Donald's uncle and Makilhaney was there to testify against me. I felt as defenseless as when the Chinese were forming in the dark below our perimeter.

"Will the attorney for the plaintiff step forward," Judge Harper said.

Ginny's attorney got up from beside her and went to the bench. "Your Honor, I represent Ginny Ball who is seeking divorce from Henry Ball on grounds their marriage has been irretrievably broken."

"Why has the marriage been irreconcilably broken?"

"Henry Ball has abandoned her and their daughter Sara. He's left them living in a state of destitution. And for mental abuse and he suffers from alcoholism and becomes violent when he drinks."

"I see. Come forward please, Mrs. Ball," Harper said soothingly.

Ginny was dressed in a plain, rumpled flowery-faded dress that showed a lot of wear. She wore no jewelry and her hair was disheveled and looked as if it hadn't been washed in some time. She looked poverty stricken. The sight of her made me feel sorry for her. She sat down in the witness chair beside Judge Harper.

"Mrs. Ball, when did your husband abandon you and Sara?" her lawyer began.

She looked down at her folded hands on her lap like a frightened child and I had to strain to hear her meek voice. "Last July when I was seven months pregnant, he left to go to Korea. He wanted to go even though I was pregnant and begged him not to. He's been back several weeks now and today's the first time I've seen him. He's never seen his daughter that came while he was gone."

"I see. And that has caused you mental anguish I suppose?"

"Yes, your honor. It's been hard for us to scrape by. I've used what little we had saved up and don't know what I'll do when the rest of it's gone. They tell me he's drinking up what money he brought home from the war. They even took our furniture because he wouldn't make the payments."

"So, you think you and your baby would be better off with Henry out of your life?"

"From what I hear about him he stays drunk and fights all the time. I'd be afraid to live with him again the way he is now."

"So, he wasn't like that before the war?"

"No. I think it was the war that changed him. He was a good man before he left."

"You may step down." Harper turned to Ginny's attorney. "Anyone else you want to call, counselor?"

"Yes, your Honor. Will First Sargent Edmond Makilhaney please come forward."

Makilhaney went to the witness chair. There were still faint black splotches under his eyes where I broke his nose and some brown from fading bruises on his cheeks. Unlike Ginny, he glared at me the entire time he was on the stand.

Ginny's lawyer started the questioning. "First Sargent Makilhaney, are you acquainted with Henry Ball sitting there?" He stretched out his arm and pointed without looking my way.

"I am." His voice boomed and echoed around the cavernous, almost empty chamber.

"How, sir?"

"I was and am the senior NCO Inspector-Instructor at the reserve armory in Rome where Corporal Ball served in the Marine Corps Reserves."

"Were you there last summer when he decided to leave his pregnant wife and go off to war?"

"Yes, I counselled him on the pros and cons of volunteering."

"What was his attitude about going?"

"He seemed very motivated to go."

"Even though he would have to leave a pregnant wife for no telling how long?"

"Yes, sir."

"What kind of attitude did he have when he came back?"

"He was full of hate and defiance. When his commanding officer Captain Rogers interviewed him on staying in the Marine Corps, he started a verbal altercation in his office that got so heated I had to intervene. Then when I escorted him to his truck, he hit me from behind and knocked me down. Then he kicked me unconscious. That's where these bruises on my face came from. If Captain Rogers hadn't pulled a pistol on him, I'm convinced he would've killed me."

"Are you familiar with his service record?"

"Yes sir. Corporal Ball was written up numerous times for drinking and fighting while he was on active duty. I can't understand why he wasn't kicked out of the Marine Corps with a bad discharge considering all the times he was in trouble."

"So, in your opinion do you consider Henry Ball a violent alcoholic that could be a danger to his wife and daughter?"

"I would, sir."

"You may step down. Oh, by the way Sergeant Makilhaney, I requested that Captain Rogers come testify. Why'd you come instead?"

"Captain Rogers volunteered to go to Korea. He's taking over a grunt Company as soon as he gets there. He's on a boat heading there now."

"He didn't mention he was leaving to me when we spoke on the phone a few weeks ago."

"It was kind of a sudden thing. He just got it in his mind he needed to go. I didn't ask him why."

"Heroic he'd volunteer for combat when he had it made sitting behind a desk. Thank you, Sergeant. Your Honor, I'd like to call Henry Ball to the stand."

I was so shocked from the lies and deceit it was all I could do to get on my feet and walk to the witness chair.

"Mr. Ball, why haven't you tried to contact your wife or sent money to her since you returned from Korea?"

I was confused and found it hard to collect my thoughts and to respond. "I didn't know where Ginny was to send her money. Nobody I know knew where she was. And when she left, she took all the money we'd saved, and I'd sent home while I was away. I was going to buy her a new home with it, but she took it all. I didn't have any money to send her."

"If what Sargent Makilhaney told us is true, I can't blame her for hiding from you. I would too. But you've had money to buy whiskey, right?"

"Not really. Look, I wasn't like that till she served the divorce papers on me. Her divorcing me drove me to drinking. You can ask anybody that knows me that I never drank before. And I called you and asked for her phone number, but you hung up on me."

"Yeah, I'm sure you didn't drink before, and I'm sure the divorce decree was the reason you started. You could have sent money to my law firm and we would have seen to it she got it. When you called me, you didn't seem to have any concern with her wellbeing. Or at least you didn't ask if she and your daughter were okay. You should have been smart and hired an attorney. A good attorney would have made sure you sent her money."

"She has a boyfriend taking care of her and my daughter. Everybody knows that and so do you. As soon as our divorce is final it's common knowledge they're going to marry. You know that. I'm sure he's paying Ginny's legal fees and furnishing her with a place to live and anything she or Sara needs. He's a doctor. And I didn't volunteer to go to Korea, I was ordered to go."

"I have no more questions, your honor. Mr. Ball isn't making any sense."

It was quiet for a long spell before Judge Harper spoke again. "I think the divorce is justified in this case considering all I've heard. Henry Ball, I'm going to give you visitation rights to see your daughter but if I hear of you drinking while she's in your care I'll put you in jail for as long as the law will allow and see to it you never get to see her again. If you ever harm her in any way, I'll see to it you're a very old man before you get out of jail. And the same goes if you threaten or harm Ginny Ball. I have no patience with men like you leaving a family to fend for themselves while they go off on some dreamworld vainglorious jaunt when they should be home working and taking care of them." Then he pointed his finger at me. "If you know what's good for you, you will start taking care of them. And one thing for sure, you never want to come before me again regarding drinking or violence unless you like living in a prison cell."

As I was leaving Ginny came up to me with tears streaming down her face. "I'm so sorry I had to do this, Henry. I still love you, but I had to do what's best for me and Sara. I was so scared. I didn't get any letters from you for weeks letting me know how you were. Please believe me that I really thought you were dead and were never coming back." She opened her arms like she wanted to hug and kiss me but stopped. I think because she was afraid someone would see.

"I still love you and feel dead inside from grief that you're doing this. I'll always be waiting if you ever change your mind and want me back."

"You'll find another woman to take my place and then you'll be happy again. From what I've been told, even by your mother, you're not the same man that left here last summer. They say the war made you crazy and you're dangerous now. I couldn't trust you, especially around the baby. It's best for me and Sara that I go through with this. But I'll always love you, Henry."

"I'll never be happy again without you, Ginny. Please think this through and take me back."

Things went as well as could be expected between me and my father the first few days after I'd moved back home, though he made it clear he resented me being back by the annoyed and disgusted way he looked at and spoke to me. Then one night at dinner after he'd had a few drinks the old truculent Hank that I knew all too well reappeared. I'd been drinking too and was talking to Mama about Mr. Rosco's setters and how good they were and how much I liked setters because of their disposition and natural beauty when the devil reappeared.

"You're full of shit and don't know nothing about bird dogs," Hank broke in. "Pointers are the only dogs for the South. Setters is what them damn Yankees use to hunt timberdoodles with up north. They're like you, not worth a shit for nothing."

"Jacob used setters. He knew a lot more about dogs than you ever did. Or about anything else far as that goes."

"I know enough to stomp your smart little ass if you don't stop talking back at me. You're an uppity little shit since you come back, and I don't like it."

I'd lost any fear I had of him or pretty much of anything else at the Chosin. I felt one of the unusual anger episodes that had developed since the war coming on. "Let's go outside and see if you can back that up, old man. You're nothing but a bunch of hot air when you get some of that rot-gut hooch in you."

Mama worked herself between us after we jumped up and turned over our chairs and knocked some dishes off the table. Somehow in the turmoil of cussing and pushing and shoving she was able to keep us from throwing any serious punches – though I did draw a little blood out of Hank's nose. It was the first time I'd ever stood up to him and I think it took him off guard. In the past I'd always sat trembling in fear expecting a backhand and taken his scorn. I left with mama crying and screaming in hysterics and Hank calling me every son of a bitch and bastard he could come up with. Then I went off in my old pickup to ride and drink the backroads till I couldn't keep it out of the ditches anymore. Sometimes during the night, I stopped to piss and passed out behind the wheel when I got back in. I was in the middle of nowhere on a rutted, red clay road and didn't come to until sunrise. I made a point of missing dinner at home from then on and went to my bootleggers instead to buy Stillbrook whiskey and Blatz beer to chase the whiskey down with. I started spending evenings cruising the backroads on lonesome highs thinking of Ginny till a couldn't keep out of the ditches anymore. Then I'd stop in the middle of nowhere on some dirt backroad and pass out. Sleeping in my truck in the cool North Georgia nights wasn't bad after the Chosin, especially after being numbed by the booze.

The fact that I was able to reclaim my prewar job selling retail newspaper ad space at the Oldale Herald for owner and Editor Chuck Hughes was the only good fortune that came my way after I returned home. Though Hughes' frugality was legendary, and he paid his employees as little as he could get by with – and I was no exception – the job was still a godsend. I was soon reacquainted with my accounts and easily fell back into the routine of making ad layouts for customers to proof. Everything was going smooth in my opinion as far as my job was concerned anyway. Work was a simple matter of showing up on time and being cordial to my clients, which can both become very boring in a short matter of time after you've become accustomed to a hellish life of death and war.

A few months after my return, the circulation manager Floyd Burch and I slipped off to the poolhall for a few games of Snooker after having several pulls off a pint of cheap bourbon I kept in my briefcase to help me through difficult days. Unfortunately for us Hughes was on his way back to the newspaper from the post office while we were in the billiard parlor, and as he drove past, he saw my truck parked out front and made a screeching halt and a fast turnaround. Everyone in the billiard parlor watched through the front windows as he came into the parking lot sideways, his high finned powder blue Cadillac kicking up gravel and dust as it slid to a stop.

When he sauntered into the poolhall he acted as though he'd caught two spies in an act of treason. I was leaning on a cue in the hazy blue wafting cigarette smoke waiting to hear what he had to say. The crack of pool balls and foul language silenced when he pointed his finger at us. "I want to see you two in my office – immediately!"

As he strutted out, the riffraff clientele laughed and shook their fingers at me and Floyd. I didn't feel much emotion though. For some reason Hughes' angry demeaner didn't ignite the fear the Chinese human wave assaults had.

We mulled our situation over in the circulation department while we waited for Hughes to call us to his office. I sipped on what was left of the pint of whiskey and decided I was going to tell Hughes where to shove his newspaper. I don't know why I had such an attitude. Hughes was just doing what any sensible boss would have done, but after the war my reasoning wasn't rational. I was always looking for conflict and my hostility was compounded when I was drinking. I wasn't like that before the war, and I never drank before going to Korea either.

Hughes called Floyd in first, and a few minutes later he came moping back like a paddled schoolboy. "He's madder'n hell, Henry. I thought he was going to fire me, and I've got a wife and a kid you know. Let him chew on your ass a little and maybe he'll keep you on. He knows it's all your fault."

"You've got to be shitting me. You put the blame on me?"

"It was your idea, Henry, and you had the whiskey, too."

"I ought to kick your ass, you miserable little turd."

I killed the last of the pint and broke the bottle flinging it into a metal trash can. Then I left to go see Hughes.

I bounced off doorways and stumbled into furniture staggering to Hughes' office. After I fell into a chair in front of his desk, he sat for a spell staring at me livid and determined. But after studying my countenance for a while his eyes started to dart around the room and he dropped his gaze and round doughy head. Then he began doodling on a notepad and had a hard time getting his words out. "Henry, your attitude's been deplorable since you've come back. I know you're drinking on the job. You reek of it now. Your work is terrible and you're taking Floyd to the poolhall and getting him drunk, as well. You leave me no choice but to let you go."

It took a moment for what he'd said to soak into my inebriated brain. As it did my anger escalated. "Round man, you don't have to fire me. You can stick your paper up your fat ass. You're like those self-righteous merchants downtown that get drunk at the country club on Saturday night and then show up at church smelling like a liquor keg on Sunday morning pretending to be devout Christians that never had a drink in their lives." I stood and put my fist in his face and slurred on. "Pay me and I'll leave, but if you ever cross me again, I swear I'll kick your ass all the way down main street and back again."

His hands came up with the palms out. "Okay, if that's the way you want it, Henry."

After he left wide eyed and trembling heading to the bookkeeper to figure my pay, I went to the doorway. Halfway to the bookkeeper's desk Hughes stopped as two Oldale cops came in the front door. A big lumbering sergeant did the talking. "Floyd called and said you might be a needin' us, Mr. Hughes. Said Henry Ball was in one of his crazy moods."

"Thank goodness you're here. Yes, he's drunk in my office. I just fired him, and I want him out of here. He's causing a scene and making threats towards me."

When I heard his comment, I charged out of Hughes' office and couldn't stop in time and wound up stumbling into the sergeant so hard he fell backward onto a small table near the front door. After I eyed him and the other cop up and down, I turned to Hughes. "You sawed-off lying runt, you didn't fire me, I quit." Then I turned back to the cops. "Say, Robert, you and Craig come to arrest me?"

Robert, the sergeant who I'd known all my life was glowering down on me. "Look here, Henry, nobody wants no trouble with you, so just get on out of here."

"Soon as I get my check I will." I jabbed his belly with my finger. "Looks like you been eating good, Robert."

He bent and put his face close to mine. "You ain't a damn bit funny, boy. Your boozin' and attitude's a goin' to get you in a lot of trouble if you don't straighten up. You done lost your job. What you goin' to do now, be a drunk vagrant?"

"It's none of your damn business what I do, but I'm going to leave this shit-hole town to get away from you country bumpkins. I'm going somewhere out West far away from here where there aren't any people to bother me. Someplace where I'll be left alone and in peace."

He chortled. "May as well get as far away from here as you can. Nobody in Oldale's going to hire a street drunk like you after all the trouble you've caused around here. I'm sure there's someplace out there that needs somebody like you to shovel horse shit for 'em."

I started poking him again. "Least I won't be sitting in a car all day eating doughnuts and helping old ladies cross the street."

He pushed my hand away. "If I catch you drunk again, Mr. Ball, I'll show you what else I can do."

I slapped his finger out of my face. "Better hope you got plenty of help."

He gripped his night stick and pulled it part way out of his pistol belt. "Get your pay and get out, Henry. I'm about to run you in, and if you cause any more trouble I will. People have put up with you round here cause of what happened to you in the war and your wife a runnin' off on you and all, but those days are bout over."

I eyed his night stick and realized the other cop had slipped behind me. As bad as I wanted to fight, I figured it best I back down.

"You don't have to worry about me, lard ass. I can take care of my own self."

The bookkeeper had finished writing my check and she handed it to Hughes. Hughes turned and offered it to me. "Here, Henry. Now please go. We don't want any real trouble out of you."

I snatched the check from his hand. There were a dozen or so framed photos of Hughes receiving awards hanging around the front door. I heard several fall and glass breaking when I slammed it going out.

I met Ginny at a restaurant parking lot in Atlanta one Saturday morning in May to get Sara for a weekend visitation. We'd met there several times before. None of mine and Sara's visits had gone well either no matter how hard I'd tried to be a father. It was terribly frustrating to drive fifty miles to get a daughter that seemed to despise me. She cried anytime I held or tried to feed her. Only when Mama took her up did she seem to feel comfortable and stopped screaming. I'm sure she repulsed me because she could feel and sense my anxiety of her responsibility. Donald was Ginny's husband now, and as always, he was in the background watching from his Mercedes with murder written on his face. Ginny was dressed in a white dress and matching hat. She was well tanned, and her long black hair contrasted sharply with the outfit. She looked incredibly beautiful that spring morning glowing in the bright-morning sunlight. As usual, Sara was screaming and kicking in her arms as though she was protesting having to leave with me. Ginny had her bag of diapers and bottles and baby things strapped over her shoulder, and along with her appearance and Sara's wild protest, something inside of me snapped and the next thing I knew I was on my knees at her feet blubbering like a fool. "I can't live without you, Ginny. Please take me back. I didn't know I'd be gone so long. I couldn't help it. But now I'm back and things can be the same again."

"Henry, for heaven's sake you're talking like a crazy person. Get up and take Sara. I'll see you back here tomorrow night at six."

I got up and composed myself best I could. I glanced over at Donald. He was standing outside his car bent and shaking with laughter. I'm sure he'd gotten out thinking there was going to be trouble when I first went out of my head. I took Sara and the bag, moped to my truck and strapped her in the baby seat. She screamed all the way back to Oldale till mama took her. Next evening when I met Ginny, I was so humiliated from our last meeting that I couldn't look her in the eye. Neither of us spoke. I got drunk driving home that night and decided it was time that I got out of Oldale for a while. I was doing nothing other than making myself and everyone around me miserable. Several times since I'd come back from the war, I'd put the muzzle of a Government .45 in my mouth that I'd bought from a Marine aboard ship and managed to smuggle home. I came close to doing it too, but the thought of leaving Ginny forever kept me from it. I'd never known the hell of depression, but I was learning it now. I'd never felt so weak and helpless. I thought if I could get away from my troubles for a while my life and attitude might change back to the way it'd been before the Chosin and the divorce, then I could make everything right again.

So, I decided it'd be best for everyone if I left Oldale and went someplace else. I felt that no matter where I wound up, it couldn't be worse than what I was living with now. I scrounged up what money I could over the next week selling off some old guns, a Schwinn bike and some other things I didn't need. In the end my cash worth tallied just over $150.00.

It was a beautiful early June morning when I loaded my belongings and told Mama I was leaving. She walked off crying and told me to wait. She came back a few minutes later and slipped me another hundred she'd saved and kept hidden from Hank. I left Oldale without saying goodbye to anyone else, and made special effort avoiding Hank.

CHAPTER 6

I started out driving north to Chattanooga and then rambled on to Nashville. From there I drifted west and then north through steep rolling hardwood forests and row crop farms of corn and cotton. It was mid-morning the next day when I crossed the Mississippi and got to the outskirts of St. Louis and realized I hadn't had a drink in several days and stopped at a rundown tavern. The beer can and whiskey bottle littered parking lot was already filled with dilapidated cars and banged up trucks much like mine. I started out drinking a few beers at the bar, then switched to whiskey later in the afternoon. After several more drinks and a few games of nine ball with some local rednecks, I spotted a woman sitting alone in the gloominess in the back of the bar at a small table and went over and started a conversation with her. From a distance sitting in the dark she looked quite attractive, but up close the truth shown out. She was acne scarred and had terrible teeth and was overly painted with rouge and lipstick. She was gauche and our conversation was boring and short. Her vulgarity put me off so that I soon lost interest in her. It turned out though that one of the bouncers was her boyfriend and when I went to pee, he and three of his buddies followed me into the restroom.

"I ain't never seen you around here before. Where you from, slick?" the boyfriend asked.

"Georgia," I said, while shaking off. "I'm headed west."

"You fucked up stopping here. That's my lady you been flirting with. What you got to say about that?"

If I'd simply apologized it might have saved me, but instead, I said, "Damn, she's uglier than my dog's ass and when I kissed her it tasted about the same."

I don't remember much else until I woke in the bed of my truck sometime during the night. My eyes were black and almost swollen shut. My nose was broken, and I thought a shoulder might be. Several ribs were bruised, and I could hardly breathe.

Next day I ate headache powders and chugged beer as I drove on west to Kansas City and then north into Iowa then west again through Lincoln and on till I hit the North Platte at Ogallala. The rich Nebraska landscape was rolling and immense. I passed occasional rundown farmhouses with dilapidated barns and rusted-out farm vehicles and implements strewn about seemingly where they'd died. There were some cattle, and chickens roamed the yards. Billowing clothes were drying in the incessant wind. Tall corn fields stretched forever.

In eastern Wyoming cultivation all but ended. Little traffic traveled the open roads across the open prairie and there didn't appear to be much life other than sparse sage brush and scattered bovine dotting the cracked, broken and wind scoured grey and brown landscape. But during the night under the beams of my headlamps scores of luminous-eyed deer and antelope appeared along the highway. It was as if they'd come out to see what dregs of society might pass through in the night.

As I approached Shoshoni the landscape began to change as I entered the mountains and wound up the pacing Wind River to Thermopolis. I drove on through Cody and entered Yellowstone Park at the East Entrance. Grizzly and black bear were staged along the roads begging for handouts like corpulent, furry mendicants. The ambling herds of elk and bison grazing in the open lush meadows and the pungent-thermal clouds from the pots of bubbling sulfurous mud caused me to feel I'd been there or someplace like it before. I waited for over an hour with a bunch of babbling tourists to see the gusher at the Old Faithful Inn. They oohed and awed and clapped and cheered when the hot-smelly stream of water spewed out of the ground. It was a great overrated disappointment to me. The superstructure support beams of the Inn were much more impressive.

It didn't take long for the pokey traffic to get to me and I exited the Park through the West Entrance and wound up in West Yellowstone, Montana. Though West was small, the roads were running rampant with tourists. I eased down the pocked gravel streets with the heavy traffic in a haze of dust studying the souvenir shops and cafes. The atmosphere was like a carnival with the smells of cheap food, the boisterous sightseers and flashing neon lights in the windows of the endless gift shops.

I stayed in a campground just out of town a few nights and poked around in the Park during the day. I managed to catch a few trout out of a creek called the Gibbon and roasted them on a stick over a fire and ate them mushy and half raw for supper that night. Then I got drunk and into a fight with a cattle truck driver from Ennis in a bar the third night and wound up in jail. I didn't start the fight, but when the chief of police released me the next morning, he was emphatic. "You'd better leave in a hurry and never bring your worthless ass back here again or you'll sorely regret it."

I headed north and rolled into Helena a few days later. There were painted placards and overhead banners everywhere advertising a Fourth of July Rodeo. The sidewalks were crowded with upstanding people milling about dressed in colorful western attire. I went strolling, too, but as out of place as a hobo at a debutante ball in my tattered service dungarees and food and blood-stained t-shirt. The soles had separated on my boondockers and I made flopping sounds plodding along. I hadn't shaved or bathed in days and could smell the putrid sourness of myself.

I liked Helena so much I thought it might be the place I'd settle, so I decided I wouldn't drink that night so as to avoid a fight and chance getting thrown out of town, but everyone was celebrating in high spirit and I couldn't help myself. After roaming the streets for a while, I got thirsty and spotted a tavern down the way and went in.

I'd been at the bar an hour or so minding my own business having a few beers when I noticed a big cowboy across the way drinking with a homely, lanky girl. He'd take a swig of beer and then wipe the foam off his mustache with his sleeve and then point in my direction. Then he'd say something, and they'd laugh. When I looked behind me to see who was so amusing, no one was there, only a deplorable reflection of myself gazing back in the mirror. Though I couldn't make out what he was saying, I decided it wasn't nice, and my anger started to rise and I went over and ground the toe of one of his fancy-reptile-skin boots with my dilapidated brogan. At first, he seemed surprised, then he got mad. "Why you little bastard," he said, and punched me hard in the face.

I got in close and started pounding him solidly. When blood began spouting from his nose, the girl screamed and busted her beer bottle on my head. I went down face first in the spilled beer, snuff spittle and squashed cigarette butts. I tried to stand but his boot heel smashed me back down. I tried getting up again, and he kicked me down again.

I lay there till the pain had eased and I'd regained my wits somewhat before I got up. I guess he thought I was finished because he was back at his place at the bar drinking again. Just as I got to him, he picked up his beer to take a drink, and when he turned, I hit him, and he went down like he'd been lightning struck.

I'd just started jumping up and down on his face when someone grabbed me from behind and slammed my face down on a tabletop. My hands were cuffed behind me, and I was dragged out by my collar and thrown into the back of a car with a sluggish revolving red light on top. A door inscribed "Helena Police" slammed behind me, and that's the last I remember of that night.

I woke the next morning in a dim jailcell sprawled in a pool of piss. I tried to sit, but an overwhelming pain came in my head that forced me back down. Then I heard a chuckle and realized there were men sitting on the floor leaning against the steel bars all around staring at me with amusement. Their gawping made me mad, but I felt too bad to say or do anything about it. In slow degrees, I raised myself and crawled to a vacant spot and sat with my back against the bars like the others. Eventually a grinning elf spoke up. "Hot damn, boy, you shore had a good time last night, didn't ya?"

He broke into a hacking laughter that turned into a coughing fit. It sounded as though his lungs were coming out, but it was just a glob of green slime that he spat onto the floor.

A portly, somber Indian with long, greasy grey streaked braids spoke up. "You look like hell, man. Did you win?"

I stared long and hard into his cold, black eyes. "Think I broke the bastard's jaw. I felt something go when I hit him. And when he went down, he didn't get back up."

"Sounds like you broke something. Where'd it happen?"

"Hell, I don't know. Some honkytonk downtown."

The Indian smiled and seemed to be enjoying taunting me. "Which honkytonk?"

"I don't fucking know, I told you."

"Describe it to me. Bet I been there."

"Hell, man, it looked just like every dive I've been in since I got to Montana. An elk head hanging over the bar, or maybe it was a moose or a buffalo. Hell, I don't remember. There was a bunch of redneck drunks and ugly women standing around yakking at each other. Some of them were making fools of themselves trying to dance to the jukebox that was playing way too damn loud."

The Indian smiled again, and the other men chuckled. Only the Indian had a full set of teeth, and the few the others had were bright yellow or black. One had a gold one.

"You're right. They do all look the same. Know who it was you had the run-in with?"

"Hell no, I ain't from around here. He was a big guy dressed up fancy. Had on a flashy yellow shirt, a loud vest, and fancy lizard or snakeskin boots. Ain't sure which. All I know is he likes using them to fight with," I said, rubbing my swollen, bruised cheek.

They laughed harder this time, and the Indian called to the jailer. "Say, Mr. Jimmy, know who the kid here beat up last night?"

A portly-uniformed man with a jaw bulging with tobacco eased around to the cell door. His hands were on his hips. He didn't wear a gun, but had a big, shiny wooden baton slid through his belt. He spit a brown stream onto the floor, and said, "Messed up, Laurence. Put the Judge's ranch hand in the hospital."

The Indian stared at me in disbelief. "Hell, you mean this scrawny punk kicked Donnas Donavan's ass?"

"Sure did. Judge Mason ain't going to like it neither. Broke Donnas' jaw and he won't be able to work again for a spell. I doubt that kid'll get out of here before fall."

After the laughter stopped, the Indian spoke up again. "I'd hate to be in your shoes, boy. You can bet Donnas will be waiting when you get out. He's a damned good boxer. Semi-pro at one time. You must have got in a mighty lucky punch or he was mighty drunk one."

Except for desultory coughing and farting, the cell was quiet for some time. I noticed the Indian still giving me the eye. "So, tell me, chief, how do I get out of this stinking shithole anyhow?"

There was momentary silence, and then the jail block erupted into an uproar. Most of them were pointing at me as they laughed. I glared back, but it only caused them to howl louder. I could hear the jailer's laughter over the inmates. After the room quieted, and another bout of hacking and coughing, the elf spoke up again. "Boy, you ain't getting out of here till you work your debt off. You'll be slinging grass on a road crew for months before they let you out of here."

I sat there all day hurting all over, especially where the girl had split my head with the bottle. I thought they'd have at least shown enough sympathy to have let me wash the blood and piss off.

Instead I was treated like a caged-wild animal. Once, though, they did offer a piece of white bread and a spoonful of scrambled eggs, but I couldn't eat.

During the night, somebody kicked me off my cot and took it over. I lay on the wet concrete feverish and shivering and couldn't sleep. Next morning bright and early Mr. Jimmy roused me out and handcuffed me and then escorted me to the visitor's area.

The room was empty except for a man that could have passed for a cowboy movie star. He was leaning back against the wall in a straight-back chair reading a newspaper. His white shirt and jeans were starched and sharply creased. He was deeply tanned with thick, heavily pomaded and combed-back-black hair. A pack of Home Run cigarettes, a Zippo lighter, and a steaming coffee cup was sitting on the table beside him. A white Stetson hung on a nearby chair. He seemed astonished when he shot a glance at me over the newspaper.

Mr. Jimmy introduced us. "Here the little fucker is, Judge."

The man didn't look up. "Thanks, Jimmy. Uncuff him and go on. I'll be okay."

The man read on for some time unmindful of me. When he did look up, though, his stare came sudden and intense, like he'd forgotten and then realized where he was. "You lowlife, stinking piece of shit. I can't believe a miserable, disgusting wretch like you caused all that trouble the other night at that redneck shithole dive."

"Go fuck yourself. Who're you anyway?"

"Don't worry about who I am. Just answer me, you filthy miscreant. Whether you realize it or not, you're in an ass of trouble."

"For what? I didn't do anything."

"That's not what I understand. It's not polite to stomp on a cowboy's dress boots and then hit him when he's not looking."

The man smiled, and his immaculate set of teeth seemed unusual after my most recent company. I wasn't in the mood for his humor, though. My head was pounding, I was starving, and most of all I was shaking from need of a drink. "He shouldn't have fucked with me. I wouldn't have started anything if he'd minded his own business."

"Well, they say you started it, and now it's done, and you've been charged with assault, public drunk, destroying private property, and disturbing the peace. There're other charges, but I can't remember them all. You figured out how you're going to get out of this mess?" He started pacing the room and had to stoop to keep from bumping his head on the hanging light globes. I didn't answer and he went on. "The man whose jaw you broke happens to be my ranch foreman. Without him I'm going to have to do his work. I don't like that. I've got other things to take care of, and I don't have the time." He stopped and glared at me. "What do you think I should do about it?"

"I don't give a big shit. Hire somebody else if you're too damn lazy to work."

"Good help's hard to come by around here with the war on. But I doubt the likes of you even know there is a war on."

"I know about the war. I've been there."

"I'm not talking about a beer parlor brawl, like the one you were in the other night. The one Louisa Bassett won with her beer bottle."

"I know where you're talking about. I've been there I told you."

"Bullshit. Where?"

"The Chosin Reservoir with the First Marine Division."

"Awe, bullshit!" He leaned over me with his hands on the table. "You expect me to believe that? A reprobate like you? I guess you were a Colonel. Hell no, a squared away individual like you would have to be a General."

"No, asshole, I was a lance corporal and the only one in my section that got out alive."

He was still glowering down on me, but now seemed more curious than mad. "I'm going to find out the truth about you, smart ass."

As he was leaving, I noticed his stature again and decided I wouldn't want to fight him. Anyway, for some reason I felt trust in the man, something I hadn't felt in anyone in a long time. He was hard but seemed genuine. Mr. Jimmy came back after he left.

"The Judge is mad as hell about you banging up his ranch hand, boy. It wasn't good you gettin' on the bad side of him. He's got a lot of high stepping friends around here. He even drinks with the Governor sometimes. You're going to have hell to pay for this. And then you're going to have to deal with Donnas before it's over with."

I took the opportunity to swipe one of the stranger's Home Runs and smoked another one before he came back thirty minutes later and sent Jimmy away again.

"Okay, Henry Ball, you told the truth. The Oldale Chief of Police said you were a good man before you went off to Korea. Said you were up for a decoration for something you did over there. And he told me about your divorce." A puzzled look came on his face. "Why'd you fall into this mess? You crazy from the war, or is it the whiskey?"

"I just want to be left alone, but people won't let me. They're always doing things to piss me off, like that asshole the other night. He egged it on, so I gave him what he was asking for. I don't start fights, but I don't back down either. And so I drink a little, but what's it to you?"

"Do you drink to escape the war or the divorce?"

I began thinking of Ginny and started staring into space as my mind wandered off. "I liked the war compared to what was waiting on me when I got home. Sometimes I wish I'd gone back. I'd probably been better off." Then my presence of mind came back. "But ain't none of this your concern. Mind your own damn business and leave me alone, you prick."

"So, it is the woman. Should have known." He looked at me now as if I were a misguided child, shook his head and went on. "Listen to me now. You need to get off the hooch till your mind clears up and you get over your troubles. You need an environment that's free of people antagonizing you. One that's full of hard work to keep your mind off your troubles and that'll sweat all that booze and hate and bitterness out of you. And I've got just the cure you need – if you'll take it."

We sat in silence for some time while I contemplated, and his patience finally wore thin. "Now listen, if you know what's good for you. I need some help till my ranch hand gets over the ass whipping you gave him. Come work for me and I'll get you out of here. I'll even pay you a little salary to boot. If you don't want to do that, you can work your wormy ass off for the county slinging grass all day in the hot sun with those other reprobates in there."

"I'd run away the first chance I got, and I ain't no damn reprobate."

"You're right about that. You're several rungs down the ladder. I don't think they even have a word befitting somebody like you. And go ahead and run. We'll find you. You leave a trail of drunken brawls wherever you go. How much money you got?"

I checked my pockets. My wallet was gone. The little money I had left was missing along with my knife and keys. "Those sorry bastards robbed me!"

"No they didn't. Don't flatter yourself. You didn't have anything worth stealing, even for that bunch in there. Jimmy's got your stuff."

"Hell, I don't know how much I got left. I've pretty much blown it all, what little I had."

"You've got a grand sum of thirteen dollars and some change, unless you've got some ratholed in your rig. Do you?"

"Why hell no."

"Okay, genius, you make the decision. Stay here and sling grass for the county twelve hours a day for the next six months and live with your new friends back there or come work for me and do as I say. I'd think hard on it if I were you. Some of those boys back there look like they'd enjoy having their way with a tender young thing like you." A sinister smile appeared before he lit a cigarette and went to a barred window on the far side of the room to watch life out in town.

An out of balance ceiling fan bumped gratingly and kept interrupting my thoughts. I for damn sure didn't want to go back to the cell after remembering the way some of the inmates had smiled and winked at me. And I was almost broke for a fact and didn't have any other place to go. I thought back on my ramblings and fights and the days living off nickel beers and greasy meat and vinegary-tainted boiled eggs that I filched from the fly-ridden trays that'd been laid out in the sleezy bars and smelly taverns to attract early afternoon clientele. I hadn't slept in a bed or bathed in weeks, only soakings in stagnant stock ponds or dirty creeks. I'd sobered enough to realize what the man was offering was what I'd gone searching for when I'd left Oldale weeks before. I looked over at the man at the barred window. He really had no use for a squalid tramp like me, yet he was offering me salvation and a chance for redemption for some reason and I seized on that chance. "Hey, hard ass, if I agree to work for you, when can I get out of here?"

The man smiled and flipped his cigarette butt through the bars and turned to me. "Right now, if you'll stop acting like a horse's ass."

"All right then, I'll do it."

He grinned and pointed back towards the jail. "Smart choice, even though it's going to break some hearts back there."

After he left to pay my fines and for the bar damage I'd caused, I went to the prison bath area to clean up. While I was showering Jimmy brought in some well-worn clothes some charity had donated to the jail for people like me. The water felt good even though it was numbingly cold. It hurt like hell dry shaving with the dull community razor, but I looked better even though I cut myself a few times because my hands shook so bad. But I still needed a haircut and my face was bruised and puffy; an eye was shiny black.

I had to squint when Jimmy showed me out the front door of the jail and told me to wait there. It felt wonderful being in the clean, dry morning air and bright sunshine after having to endure the reek of the stinking, dim-lit prison cell the past few days. I despised the stench of the jail even more than the septic smell of the ship's infirmary and vowed to never find myself in either again. I'd sobered up over the past two days and my head had cleared, but I still wanted a drink and had a good case of tremors.

I was leaning against the jail wall with my shabby black charity Stetson pulled down over my eyes and a bundle of worn-out clothes tucked under my arm when a fancy new pickup pulled up. The man that got me out of prison stuck his head out the window. "I hardly recognize you, boy. You clean up pretty good. Let's go get some chuck."

It was Sunday morning and church had just let out. The cafe was filled with seemingly upstanding and well-dressed people of prosperity. Everyone seemed to know the man and spoke pleasantly to him or at least nodded, but they scrutinized me in my goodwill clothes all wrinkled, faded and missized. I guess my battered face caused some curiosity as well. Their meddlesome looks made me uncomfortable, so I headed to the rear of the cafe and took a seat with my back to them. The man sat down across from me grinning. "You shouldn't be embarrassed just for looking so ridiculous in that miss-fitted and raggedy hand-me-down outfit. Looks like it came off a dead panhandler – like it was tailored just for you."

An attractive neat waitress in a blue plaid apron and white dress brought two big white porcelain mugs and a steaming coffee pot. She poured the mugs and waited while we studied the menus. "Eat up. It's on me," the man said. Then he turned to the waitress. "Texas omelet, extra order of bacon, and a large milk, please. Hold the hotcakes. And you, Henry?"

"Same for me, and I'll take his hotcakes." The smell of cooking food had me drooling like a starving dog. I tried but couldn't recall the last time I'd eaten. Probably three days, maybe four. A surge of gratitude swept through me for what the stranger had done, and I intended to let him know. "Mister, I appreciate you getting me out of that shithole, and I want to apologize for all those bad things I said back there. I'll work off what I owe you, and you don't have to worry about me running away, either. But after all you've done, I don't even know your name."

"Well I'll be. You might be coming to your senses. Maybe you're not quite the imbecile I thought you were." He stuck out his hand. "James Mason."

He released his grip and I massaged my fingers till the pain faded away. "They call you Judge. Are you really one?"

"Not anymore. Was for a spell when I lived in Houston. Wish it'd go away. But if I was still a judge, I wouldn't have had to pay out my ass to get you out of jail, then would I?"

I laughed. His sense of humor reminded me of Jacob. "How'd you wind up here?"

"Old man left me a chunk. Made it big in the oil business back in Texas where I grew up. You ever been to Nacogdoches?"

"Never even heard of it."

"Didn't think so. Hell, nobody has. Anyway, I fell in love with Montana the first time I came here. So much so that I bought a ranch so I'd have an excuse to live here. Montana is a paradise for hunting and fishing, and what's so good is that not many people are willing to live here. Winters are too harsh. This country won't ever change. Anyway, unless you ranch, there's not much else to do to make a living. So, nosy, what did you do before you became a drunk drifter and a bar brawler?"

I laughed again. It'd been so long since I had I couldn't remember when. If it'd been anyone other than James Mason who'd said it, I would have been ready to fight, but coming from him was different. It wasn't so much because of what he'd done for me. He had a natural, commanding air that few people I'd met had, but it wasn't condescending. It was much like Johansson. You trusted and respected him to the extent of vesting him with your life. Though I'd only known Mason a few hours I felt that same respect and trust in him. "Worked for a newspaper selling advertising."

"Damn, I'd never figured you for a white collar. Didn't you like it?"

"Good enough to stay on before the war, but after I came home, I hated it and everything and everybody involved. I haven't liked anything since the war and my divorce, except traveling, fighting and drinking. You married?" A pained look came on his face. "I say something wrong?"

As fast as it'd appeared, the hurt faded. "No, it's just that I lost my wife not long ago, too. In an accident," he added. "Tough isn't it, losing your wife?" He said it so I'd realize his empathy. I nodded and swallowed hard.

While I ate, Mason wouldn't stop asking me about the Chosin. "Was it as bad as they said it was?"

I talked between gulping down mouthfuls of food. "Hard to believe it can get that cold. If you slowed down even for a minute, you'd freeze. Some nights it went to thirty below with a wind that would blow you down sometimes. All of us got frostbite. A lot of men died just from the cold. My feet still hurt from the frostbite I got."

"No, I mean was the fighting that bad?"

"I didn't like seeing my friends get killed, if that's what you mean."

"Having seen all that death and violence must bother you?"

I took a big gulp of milk to wash a mouthful full of food down. The milk was cold and tasted good, maybe even better than a drink of whiskey, I thought. "I can't sleep without having bad dreams any-more, and the least little thing sets me off. Yeah, I think it messed me up now that I think about it. The war did things to me I can't explain."

"I can't imagine what the fear of those human wave assaults must have been like."

"Shit my pants a lot. I got so scared so many times that nothing much seems to scare me anymore. Sometimes that's not so good, though. That's why I'm here and your ranch hand's in the hospital with a broken jaw."

He thought as he stared hard and long at me. Finally, he shook his head and then went to pay our tab. After he peeled a small for-tune onto the table for our waitress, we left.

CHAPTER 7

Mason's ranch was an hour's drive north of Helena just out of a hole-in-the-wall town called Wolf Creek. The town center consisted of a combination grocery and mercantile store that was plastered with soft drink, cigarette, paint and petrol signs. A hand operated gas pump was sitting out front of the log-planked, weathered emporium. Three old geezers in straight back chairs sitting on the porch threw up their hands as we sped by. Mason set down on the horn and waved out the window as we blew by in a cloud of dust.

The drive from Helena took us through a lot of beautiful sage brush prairie country teeming with antelope and mule deer. Most of it was set against a backdrop of mountains. Some of the taller ones had splotches of white on their peaks. When Mason wasn't talking about his ranch and its operation, he had me laughing at one of his endless tales. I didn't think about a drink the entire way.

Once we were on Mason's property, brown and white cattle were grazing everywhere in knee deep grass. We stopped numerous times to let them amble off the graveled road leading to his house. He told me the cattle were registered horned Herefords. When we came to a high point he stopped and pointed out the boundaries of a portion of his land. The Missouri River bordered the eastern section and I could see it glistening through the swaying lush green cottonwoods that marked its course several miles away.

Then we came to a wooden fenced corral and a herd of a dozen horses or so came galloping up raising a cloud of dust. They ran alongside us till we passed by a huge weathered grey wood-planked barn, then they turned and went thundering off in the other direction where the fence ended.

Mason had explained what he expected of me during the drive. It was outdoor work that mostly entailed hard physical labor. Though I still felt like hell from the weeks of drinking, fighting and not eating or sleeping, I wanted to start working that day, but Mason said he'd show me around the ranch first. Since it was Sunday, we'd just spend the afternoon in leisure.

His log home was a massive two-story structure with stone chimneys poking up everywhere and bejeweled with big picture windows mirroring the brilliant high-prairie sun. While he was backing under the garage, a pair of Irish setters and a graying black Lab went crazy running and jumping and barking from a kennel in the yard. When Mason stepped out of the truck, he raised his hand and they quieted.

While we were moving my few belongings up to a small apartment over the garage where I was to stay, my ragged gun cases and dented rod tubes caught Mason's attention. "What you got there?" he said, nodding towards the guns and rods.

I proudly uncased the two Parker shotguns and two Winston rods my Uncle Jacob had left me and laid them across the single bed. He broke one of the guns open and looked down the barrels and then shouldered it. "Damn, for a destitute reprobate, you've got some mighty fancy equipment. These Parkers are nice. Where'd you steal them?"

"My uncle left them to me. The twenty gauge is for quail, the twelve was his duck gun."

"I'm truly impressed. Can you shoot?"

"Yeah. Haven't shot birds in a while, though. I'm probably rusty."

"Shooting's like riding a bike, once you've got it, you never lose it. Show me those rods."

Pride engulfed me again as I jointed the two Winston cane rods. "I use the light one for trout and the heavy one for bass."

He flexed the light one and peered down it for a set. "Nice rod, but can you cast it?"

"Fair, I guess. Jacob taught me, but I doubt I'll ever be as good as he was."

"Tell you what, I've got a couple of chores to take care of, but I'm thinking about going to the creek where we cut a hayfield the other day to see if the trout might be looking for a grasshopper. Care anything about going with me?"

"That creek we crossed back down your driveway?"

"Yes. The Little Prickly Pear."

"Hell yeah! I'd love to."

He smiled. "Let's get a bite of lunch then, take care of a few light chores, and we'll go later then."

For lunch, we had beef brisket sandwiches with homemade horseradish sauce. "I smoked the roast and ground the horseradish myself. I like horseradish hot and fresh. I made the bread, too. What do you think?"

I was wolfing down a second sandwich. Tears were flowing, and snot was streaming from the bite of the horseradish. The brisket was deliciously seasoned and tender and melted like butter in my mouth. The breadcrust was crunchy and the bread like a foamy cloud with the hint of yeast. "Best sandwich I've ever ate. I ain't just saying that either."

"Glad you like it. Next to hunting and fishing cooking's my favorite hobby. I'll be back after I change into some work clothes and we'll go to the barn."

When the horses saw us coming through the corral gate, they came galloping up and I thought they were going to trample us. I'd had little dealings with livestock and Mason thought it was hilarious when I cowered behind him. "They're not going to hurt you. Just don't get behind one and spook him and get what little brains you have kicked out. Even though you are practically worthless, I still need you."

I liked the barn. It was dim and cool and smelled syrupy and sour from hay, leather polish, sweet feed and horse manure. A choking dust cloud soon filled the bay from the horses milling around. After Mason chased them out, the wind quickly cleared the air. "If I was trying to get them in here, I'd have to chase them half the day," he said, and pointed to the loft. "Throw down a couple of bales of that hay. Maybe it'll keep the pesky bastards occupied while we get these few chores done."

I climbed the ladder and heaved two bales out the loft door. It was hot in the trapped air. Dislodging the hay stirred a fine chaff that started my eyes burning and snot flowing worse than the horse radish had. I clambered down coughing and sweating and rubbing my eyes. Mason was at the bottom grinning. "Like it up there?" he said.

"How do you get those bales up there? They must weigh sixty pounds at least."

"Don't worry. You'll find out soon enough. Now get a pitchfork from that tool closet," he said, motioning with his chin."

Mason backed a small tractor with a wagon into the barn and I started forking the horse shit and stale hay from the stalls onto the wagon. As Mason disappeared into the tack room, I thought back on what Robert had prophesized at the newspaper the day I was fired.

It took over an hour to get the old straw and dung out of the stalls and loaded on the wagon. When I'd finished, Mason came from the tack room rubbing leather oil off his hands with a dirty rag. "Now pull the tractor around back and empty the manure into the honey spreader," he said.

"What's a honey spreader?"

"It's that contraption there that slings horse shit on the pasture for fertilizer," he said, pointing to a weird looking implement out behind the barn partially hidden by tall grass.

"Oh. But I don't know how to drive a tractor."

"Damn, you really are worthless."

He explained how to operate the tractor and I managed to get the honey wagon hitched to it without breaking anything. Then it took another hour of loading the spreader and slinging the honey over the horse pasture. The sun was well into the west when I'd finished, and I could well feel the toll of the liquor and hard living of the past months. Mason came out of the tack room when I shut the tractor down. "Still want to go fishing?" he said.

"Hell yes. Why?"

"Cause you look on the edge of death, that's why. Get your tackle together and meet me at my truck."

It didn't take five minutes to gather what little equipment I had. Mason hadn't come out yet, so I sat my rod and creel by his truck and went around to the front door. It was unlocked, so I went in.

The room I entered was enormous. The roof beams were gigantic. It was sunlit by two large windows that framed a range of distant ragged mountains. Strange looking game heads lined the overhead walls. A rug made from an angry lion baring his teeth with wide, ferocious red eyes lay in front of the fireplace. There was a painting above the gnarled pine mantle of horse soldiers carrying a calvary flag chasing a band of Indians across a prairie. I squinted and strained to read the name in the lower right corner. Frederic somebody was all I could make out. Hefty sculptures of cowboys on bucking horses and of buffalo and elk and other animals were sitting around the room on the tables, the mantel piece and bookshelves. A polished oak bar lined with different shaped and sized glasses etched with game bird scenes occupied a corner.

I admired a gun cabinet filled with fine double shotguns and rifles inlaid with gold scenes and stocked with finely checkered walnut. Mine were junk in comparison, and I felt my face flush thinking how proudly I'd shown the Parkers.

I wandered into an adjoining room filled with framed photographs of Mason posing with dead animals and big fish. A beautiful woman was always alongside him. When I noticed a bed, I realized I was in Mason's bedroom and hurried out, but he was outside waiting in front of one of the picture windows gushing the blinding sunlight. "Making yourself right at home I see," he said. His face was undiscernible against the glare of the window and made him appear formidable.

"I've never seen anything like your house before, the game heads and all."

"A weak spirited person would likely say my home is morbidly decorated. They'd probably say my trophies are just my ego on display. If they were on public display, I'd agree, but they're not. They're only for me to see for the memories of the safaris and adventures I loved so much."

"I like seeing them, too, and your guns and those iron animals."

"They're brass, dimwit. Now are you ready to go fishing, or do you want to spend the evening discussing décor and snooping around my house?" He took a few steps out of the glare and I could see he was smiling.

"Look, I'm sorry. I was so amazed at everything I didn't realize I'd wandered into your bedroom."

"Forget it. You're probably too stupid to steal anyway. Got everything you need?"

"The water leaked out of my leader tin and my leaders dried out and rotted and I can't find my fly box."

"I've got leaders and flies. Get moving. You've held us up long enough as it is."

We drove to where the Little Prickly Pear bordered an alfalfa field that had recently been mowed. The crystalline water was rumbling and frothing over its rocky course. It was shaded intermittently with willows and huge cottonwoods. Mason started lecturing, something

I soon learned he loved to do, as soon as we pulled under the shade of one of the big cottonwoods to rig up. "This leader is made from nylon," he started. "I doubt you Georgia hillbillies have heard about it yet. You don't have to soak it to make it soft like you do gut."

He searched several pockets for his reading glasses that he discovered attached to a cord hanging around his neck, then after knotting the leader to my line, he handed me a handful of cork bodied grasshopper fly patterns. "When these fish take, they're quick, so set fast. There're some big ones, so don't be surprised. Fish up from here and I'll fish downstream." He turned his back to get better light and began lining his rod but stopped and turned and motioned towards the creek. "Now get going before you shit your pants. And if you get lucky keep a few for supper."

I went up the creek to the first good looking run and tied on one of the hopper patterns and started fishing. My first casts were sloppy I was so out of practice and the hopper was too heavy for the light rod anyway. The large fly plowed furrows across the water as soon as it touched down and sent wakes of spooked fish scattering in every direction. I pushed my next back cast higher, waited longer for the line to straighten, and overpowered the forward cast. The line on the forward cast straightened and snapped back forming slack in the supple leader and the hopper floated properly with the current. I stripped slack fast as the fly raced downstream on the pacing water. It was a joy to cast and mend line again, to feel, smell and hear the rush of the creek. I felt alive inside for once in a long time. I didn't really care if I caught a fish or not.

As I cast into the riffles and runs my casting form soon returned and became second nature again. My mind then wandered to the north Georgia Mountains, and I became absorbed in thought of better times when me and Jacob fished together. And when the hopper disappeared in a silvery flash, in my complacency, I hesitated, struck late and missed hooking the trout. I stomped my foot in disgust like a child would do.

But soon another fish came to my fly, and anticipating it this time, I set the hook properly. Its strength and speed surprised me boring against the fast water, leaping and shaking in brilliant colors in the sunlight. After the initial run, the fish tried regaining its strength by sulking under a boulder, but I forced it back into the current where it soon tired and floated up gasping on its side. I then led it onto a gravel bar and admired its incredible beauty. It appeared to be made of burnished steel. Deep crimson stripes ran along its chrome sides, and black dots spotted its back. In my enthusiasm, I turned, and holding my squirming prize by a finger through its gill, started to run down the creek to show it to Mason, but the dancing gleam from his bowed rod stopped me. I turned back upstream before he noticed, cussing myself for my vain enthusiasm and glad I hadn't shouted.

I fished on and caught five more rainbows all identical in size. But one fish, a big yellow-bellied brown, pulled free after it went deep into an undercut. I could feel its weight undulating through the light rod, which hadn't the backbone to drive the hook point home, and after getting the right angle, the trout had freed itself. I was satisfied with my catch, though, and felt content and happy, which was something I hadn't felt in a long time.

When the sun went below the mountains, a coolness crept into the air, and pale-yellow bugs with sailboat like wings began to hatch from the stream. The trout then turned their attention to the small and delicate flies and gave no more notice to the massive hopper. I was tired anyway and took a seat on the bank to watch in the half-light mesmerized by the trout eating the bugs off the water and the swallows swooping and diving picking them off as they flew towards the safety of the streamside foliage. The fish appeared weightless in their liquid world floating suspended just beneath the surface. They rose with a distinct rhythm daintily picking off the hatching flies as their noses made slight dimples and bulges.

Then as abruptly as it started, that hatch ended, and swarms of what looked like dark candle flies started dipping and diving onto the water as they moved upstream. The fish then began feeding on the migrants and I tried again but couldn't interest a single fish with the hopper even though every run was lined with trout splashing and slashing recklessly feeding.

I sensed something behind me, and when I turned a bachelor group of floppy eared mule deer coming down from the hills to feed and water were milling around in the cut alfalfa field trying to figure out what I was. Their velvety racks were silhouetted in the afterglow of the sunset. They stamped and stomped and craned their necks and flared their nostrils and studied me till they caught my scent and then went bouncing back into the hills. Again, as in the Park, that feeling that I'd been here or someplace like it came over me.

It was getting late and the fish had quit feeding when Mason came up. "How'd you do?" he said.

"I caught five rainbows and lost a nice brown. Then they started eating those damned yellow bugs and I couldn't catch anything. What are those things anyway?"

"Well, I'm surprised you even noticed them. I figured you'd have been digging around trying to find some worms to fish with instead of studying the hatch. The light-colored ones are mayflies called Pale Morning Duns. The dark ones are caddis flies. If you can read and are interested enough, I'll loan you a book on aquatic entomology. Part of the book also explains how to tie flies that imitate the insects." I said nothing, and Mason went on. "All in all, sounds to me like you got a good ass whipping tonight you might not ever get over. Give me your creel."

Mason didn't keep any fish, but he cleaned the ones I'd caught in silence, first slitting their bellies then pulling out their gills and attached intestines. Then he raked out their kidneys with his thumbnail and washed them in the creek. He spoke up after returning them to my creel and rinsing off his hands. "Even though in your childish pouting you didn't have the courtesy to ask how I did, I'll tell you anyway. I caught over a dozen rainbows. All of them were bigger than those dinks you caught. I did land one brown of about three pounds. And I don't appreciate you killing every one of my trout you catch. From now on keep only what you want to eat so they'll be some left to catch when we come back."

I started to remind him that he'd told me to keep some for supper, but before I could speak, he'd started to his truck. After we loaded our gear, he climbed behind the wheel and took a flask from the glove compartment. When he turned it up, drops of the golden-brown liquid trickled down his chin and formed dark spots on his khaki shirt. When I caught the scent of the bourbon, my mouth watered as I imagined the sweet mixture's burn going down, the warm glow it would make spreading through my body, and then the soothing numbness that would follow. But when Mason turned to me smiling and offered the flask, I refused it. "Thanks, but I'm going to try to lay off it for a while. You've given me an opportunity to get my life straightened out and I want to use it the best I can." He offered the flask again. I shook my head. "No thanks."

"Well, maybe you're not as hopeless or quite as dumb as I thought. My old man always said that a whiskey glass and a woman's ass was the ruination of many a man. People of inferior intellect like you should keep that in mind."

"Look, I want to apologize for the way I acted tonight. We don't have hatches like that back home. It was so beautiful and amazing seeing all those fish feeding like that, but so frustrating not being able to catch even one. I came close to breaking my rod over my knee."

"Fly fishing is considered one of the most challenging sports there is. It not only takes hours of practice and execution to achieve flawless casting and presentation, you've got to know and understand aquatic and terrestrial entomology as well. You need to learn to tie your own flies because you can't always buy the right imitations. You've got to learn to read the water so you'll know where the fish are holding. I'm only skimming the surface. There're too many variables to be a hundred percent successful all the time, but if you study and try hard enough you may get to where you can fool them most of the time. You're going to have to put a lot of time and effort into it, though. You're going to find it doesn't come easy. You've got to really want it. You've got to love and appreciate fantastic challenges and learn to accept and use constant failures as learning experiences."

When we were back at the house the breezy hot day had receded to a cool evening. The livestock had quieted and the yapping and howling of prairie wolves readying to hunt started out in the growing dark. The glow of a rising crescent moon outlined the blue and ragged Little Belt Mountains to the east while in the west the lingering radiance from the long past set sun seemed would last forever. Mason had told me on the drive up that though the summer solstice had passed, and the days were growing shorter, there were still several months of haying season left. He emphasized that baling as much alfalfa as possible would be my primary job. He said without the rich, nourishing hay, the cattle couldn't survive the brutal cold and raging winds and blizzards that would come howling out of the north as soon as winter set in.

First thing Mason did when we went inside was mix a drink. Next, he took a slab of bacon from the refrigerator and tossed it on the counter. "Slice some of that pork belly while I get out the corn meal and seasonings. And slice it thin."

He took an iron skillet from a rack over the counter, then lit the stove and adjusted the flame. I watched the edges of the bacon slowly turn translucent as it began to steam. Then grease started spewing and spattering as the bacon shrank and curled.

After Mason salted and peppered the fish, he shook them in a bag of corn meal. "Think two'll do you?"

"I can probably eat three."

"Damn, you sure eat a lot for a scrawny runt." He added another trout to the bag and started shaking again. "Sure you won't have a drink? Mighty good bourbon."

He said it in a way that caused me to feel he was testing me. I almost said yes, but instead, "I think I can make it if I can just get some food in me."

"Suit yourself. Watch that bacon while I go mix me another one."

After he left, I realized an ease had settled inside I hadn't felt since before the war, and my life didn't feel quite as hopeless. Being sober felt strange it'd been so long since I had been, but I believed I could get used to it again if I could stay off the bottle for a few more days.

When Mason came back his drink was several shades darker than the one before. He took the bacon off and put it on a bag to drain. "Eat some of that swine if you want, Henry. It gives me heartburn if I eat it when I'm drinking."

The bacon fat was smoking when Mason slid the first trout in, and the grease erupted. We stared into the pan like medieval alchemists preoccupied with an experiment waiting to see some mystical occurrence transpire, but all that happened was the slit where the fish had been gutted slowly widened as their eyes turned marble white.

When Mason was satisfied the trout were cooked precisely like he wanted, he laid them on the paper sack to let the grease drain. He cooked the other two and they came out slightly charred from the accumulated burned meal. "You can start if you like. I'm having one more drink before I eat," he said.

I ate the trout even though the steaming meat scalded my mouth, and I consumed a mountain of fried potatoes, too. I felt ashamed for being so hoggish, but the trout were the best I'd ever eaten. Mason told me to eat one of his if I wanted, that he really wasn't hungry. I finished it with the same gluttony as the others.

While Mason picked at his dinner, I washed the dishes and then we moved to the big room off the kitchen that was filled with the strange animal heads. After Mason settled in his big leather easy chair in front of the fireplace, I took a seat on the sofa next to him.

I was curious about the game heads, but I was most interested in the lion sprawled on the floor at my feet and asked how he'd come to kill it.

He narrowed his eyes and started moving his hands as if he were smoothing something invisible. "We were in the tall grass when my professional hunter sensed we'd become the prey instead of the predators. We stood back to back with shouldered rifles and waited. I've never had such a time just breathing. My heart was pounding so I thought it was going to come ripping out of my chest as we stood in the waning light waiting for those cats to make their move." He bolted to his feet and began slinging his arms with great animation. His voice rose several octaves. "I saw a blur parting the grass and didn't have time to aim. I just pointed and snapped off a shot. I owe all the years of quail shooting to saving my life because, as you can see," – he stopped and pointed to a hairless dot on the cat's forehead – "I instinctively hit the scoundrel right between his eyes. He came rolling to a stop at my feet stone dead. But by then his harem had surrounded us, and after an eternity of their grunting and growling slinking and slipping around us hidden in the grass, they slunk off in the dark." He sat back down and raised his glass, and in a calm and relaxed voice, said, "It's a damn miracle I'm alive, boy."

The weight of my eyelids had become unbearable towards the end of the story. The last I remembered of the night was Mason explaining the joyous reception from the dancing and chanting Africans at camp that he and his professional hunter received on their return with the cat draped over the hood of a Land Rover, and the great celebration that ensued the rest of the night.

CHAPTER 8

Next morning, I woke to the noise of Mason's boot heels tapping and clogging on the kitchen floor as his out of tune voice tried harmonizing with Hank Williams'. I thought it was way too early for the radio to be cranked so loud playing "Hey Good Lookin". I had to massage a crick out of my neck that had formed from sleeping in a contorted position on the hard sofa. I rubbed as I stared out at the mountains trying to come fully wake. The sky had just begun to lighten and the horses racing around the corral looked like ghosts floating in the mist. Then the sound of Mason's voice got me up and moving. "You going to sleep all day in there? Get off your lazy ass and get in here and eat so we can get some work done."

I followed the smell of cooking food and brewed coffee and found Mason wearing a well stained and raggedy yellow apron, Texas two stepping around the kitchen. I couldn't help but laugh.

"Stop your guffawing and go take a shower. These hot cakes are about ready, so hurry it up. Here, take this coffee with you."

I realized that for the first time in months I didn't have an ax splitting my head from having drank too much whiskey the night before, but I still had the shakes and I'd thought about having one when I first woke and saw the bottle Mason had left out on the bar the night before. Again, I thought he'd done it to test me. I figured he was too neat and tidy not to have put it away the night before.

After I showered and ate, we headed to the barn. Mason used a bucket of feed to entice his horse inside, a big bay named Quanah Parker, and a small black mare for me. "Molly's the gentlest horse in the bunch. She's as meek as a newborn lamb and will be a good one for you to learn to ride on," he assured me.

I watched as he explained how to blanket and saddle a horse as he went through the procedures. Then we led the horses out to the corral, and he swung up on Parker. I felt awkward struggling up onto the mare being the first time I'd ever been on a horse.

As soon as my butt touched the saddle I was launched into space. I felt like a cat clawing at the air trying to land on my feet, but instead I fell on my face in a heap of horse turds. When I'd regained my senses, Mason was looking down on me with a broad grin. "Good ride. Now wipe that shit off your face and get back on and let's go."

I swung back up onto the horse ready this time. Mason laughed and whooped while I somehow hung on as the mare jumped, kicked and twisted until she bucked out. "That's what happens when you don't ride them regularly. But I've never seen her act like that," he said, still chuckling.

As we rode the property, Mason pointed out fences needing mending and alfalfa fields ready for cutting. Pheasant and Hungarian Partridge with their half-grown broods flushed from the fields and mule deer does with their spotted fawns bolted to cover at our approach. We eventually came to the cut field where we'd fished the afternoon before.

"We've got to get this field done and start cutting the others. I want to get at least one more cutting before fall, and I'd like to get two. Hay can get mighty scarce here during a long, hard winter."

After we made a round of the ranch, we swapped the horses for a large tractor and Mason led the way in his truck back to the cut hayfield. Then Mason spent an hour with me on the tractor explaining haying procedures and was very explicit about one. "Of all things you've got to remember it's this, Henry. When uncured hay is baled it can generate enough heat to catch fire. That sorry Donnas put a load too green in the barn one time. If I hadn't seen the smoke coming out of the loft it would have combusted and I'd lost the barn, the little tractor, and maybe even some horses. But we lucked out and only lost a loft full of hay." After feeling confident I could operate the tractor, Mason left for the house.

The sky was cloudless, the sun beat down hot and heavy and a stiff wind soon came up. Grasshoppers rose in waves ahead of the tractor, and when I raked along the creek, trout exploded like small bombs taking advantage of the windfall. I had to fight the urge to go to the house for my rod every time I made a pass near the stream.

When I'd finished raking late that afternoon my shirtless back was burned and I was coated in sweated salt, dust and chaff. Grit crunched in my teeth. Wads of black boogers and grainy snot streamed out when I blew my nose. My eyes burned and I realized what a miserable several months I was in for. I kept thinking of the hefty bales in the barn and remembered Mason's sinister grin when he said I'd find out soon enough how they got into the sultry loft. I stripped and let the numbing currents of the Pear wash the grit and chaff away before I started the long drive back to the house.

I wanted to get back to the creek to fish as soon as possible and the slow tractor ride seemed to take an eternity. Mason had dinner ready, and we ate hurriedly and went back to the same stretch of the Pear we'd fished the day before. He explained it was too late in the day to fish hoppers, but the aquatic insects would soon emerge again, and the trout would rise to them just like the night before.

Everything Mason told me about the hatch was true, but I couldn't get the tiny flies he'd given me to float right, and the fish ignored my pitiful offerings. But every time I looked downstream, his rod was bowed and dancing. At dark, I was more dejected than the evening before and had just started to the truck when Mason came up. "Get your head out of your ass and stop pouting. Read those books I told you about and you might learn how to catch a trout on a fly," he said.

As soon as we were back at the house I asked about the books and Mason went to his bedroom and came back with a copy of <u>Trout</u> by Ray Bergman. He said it was a great source for a beginner to learn the rudimentary concepts of fly fishing, and he was right. I read it cover to cover over the next three nights. It was filled with tales and effective techniques to use fishing the East and West. There was a section with step-by-step photographs on fly-tying instruction at the end. Then he produced a copy of <u>A Book of Trout Flies</u> by Preston Jennings that contained a great deal about aquatic entomology as well as fly-tying instruction and needed materials. After reading the books, fly-tying fascinated me so that I asked Mason where I could buy the needed equipment and materials to tie. "Come in here," he said, motioning me to follow.

We went through his bedroom to a connecting office. On a desk in a corner was a mountain of cured hides and hackle capes and bags of feathers. A Thompson tying vise was clamped to the table holding a pitiful monstrosity of a fly in its jaws. I laughed and pointed at it, and then regretted doing so after I realized how bad I'd hurt his feelings.

"Look at that. It's sad, but not funny, Henry. I've tried to tie, but I'm not dexterous enough. I'm all thumbs. Let's pack all this stuff up and move it to your room. Then you can try your hand at it."

I attempted tying a fly that night. Initially it seemed impossible, but after several tries, my patterns began to take form. After several nights, I started turning out imitations that looked almost as good as the store-bought ones Mason ordered from back East. A few days later I caught a trout on one I'd tied, which gave me a great deal of pride and satisfaction. That night I turned out a dozen of the same pattern, and the next evening we both had good success with my creations. Mason was unusually complimentary and seemed genuinely impressed. "I've got to say your flies look good and work remarkably well for a man that shakes as bad as you do."

Fishing was secondary though. Haying and cattle were the priority. Workdays were long and hard. My main job was haying, but I also mended fences and helped inoculate cattle and with branding calves. My favorite job was halter breaking high-graded yearling bulls to show at sales. I kept the stalls cleaned and alternated riding the horses and gradually developed into a decent rider. Everything on the ranch seemed to be running smoothly. I loved what I was doing and didn't want anything to change it, so I was dreading Donnas' return knowing I'd likely be unemployed when he came back. I had no idea where I'd go, and I didn't have much time to figure something out, either. One recent morning at breakfast after Mason had been to a cattlemen's meeting the night before in Helena, he broke the news. "I heard a lot of rumors last night that Donnas is out on the town again, either in the bars dancing and chasing whores, or training in the gym. Guess it won't be long till he's back here at work pestering hell out of me."

Still devastated from my divorce and because of the long hours of work and the distance to town, I didn't have the time or convenience nor motivation to look for a woman. The few locals I saw at the mercantile in Wolf Creek were either married or too old. But one Saturday night when we went to Helena for dinner a waitress changed all that when she leaned over to write up our orders. I couldn't take my eyes off her magnificent cleavage no matter how I tried. Then after she smiled and left, I locked onto her spectacular swaying ass until she went out of sight, and Mason let me have it. "Cut it out, you imbecile. Everyone's looking at you. Next time why don't you just reach out and give one a good squeeze?"

"I couldn't help it. I've never seen a woman with jugs and an ass like that."

"She knows what she's doing. She's showing you those things hoping you'll ask her out, but you're too dumb to realize it."

"She wouldn't go out with me. She's too classy for a lowlife ranch hand. Besides, I'm sure every available man in Helena is after her."

"How do you know she won't go out if you don't ask? You're just chickenshit is all."

"I might ask her out, but I don't need lame advice from you. And why don't you ask her out?"

"She's too young for me. It would start a scandal. It'd do you good getting away from the ranch some at night, especially with someone like her. Ask her out and I'll loan you my truck to date in."

"And what's wrong with my truck?"

"It's a rundown piece of shit, that's what's wrong with it. My dogs wouldn't ride in that ratted out wreck. Personally, I'd be afraid to set out to Helena in it, much less expect a classy woman like her to ride in it. You'd been better off to have let the chief of police keep it."

"I'll take her out and she'll be happy riding in my truck. But I wouldn't mind an advance on my pay to buy some new clothes. Mine are pretty much shot now."

"Now? They were rags when Jimmy gave them to you."

Mason was relentless about me asking her out. I got sick of listening to him and finally said I would if he'd shut up about it. Before we left the restaurant that night, I managed to work up enough backbone to ask her if she'd like to go see a movie and to my surprise she said yes.

I'd gotten my truck back from the Helena police chief a few weeks before after Mason had assured him I wouldn't run off during the night. "I doubt I'll ever get rid of him now that he's gotten used to my trout stream and cooking," Mason had told him.

I gave serious thought about taking Mason up on his truck offer but decided I wouldn't give him the satisfaction and cleaned mine up best I could and bought some new jeans and a fancy blue silk shirt. I brushed the mud and manure off my boots and polished the scuffs out, and on her next night off, I took the beautiful waitress to an old Gary Cooper western. About as far as I got that night was holding her hand. I thought about trying to kiss her goodnight, but I couldn't find the courage.

Her name was Laney Pfeiffenberger. She told me she'd come from Pennsylvania a chorine with a traveling show and had wound up stranded in Helena because she'd lost her job there. She claimed the manager had abruptly released her because she was too short and thick legged and didn't fit in with the other chorus line dancers. That didn't make sense to me because he'd hired her the way she was to begin with, and her legs looked plenty long and mighty fine to me. But I didn't really care how she'd gotten to Helena. I was just glad she had.

I didn't say how I'd come to be in Montana or on the ranch and she didn't ask. I was glad she didn't. If she'd learned all the sordid reasons, I doubted she'd had anything else to do with me.

After a few weeks we'd had several dates, and so far, I felt I'd bored her immensely. I was intimidated by her beauty, class and charm and felt anything and everything I did or might say would offend her. A movie or dinner and conversation about little was all, but finally she did kiss me goodnight. I began to sense she was getting bored and tired of me, but I didn't know what else to do to entertain her. On the way to town for our next date I tried to come up with something new and entertaining to do, but I was stumped because I didn't know of anything else to do in Helena we hadn't already done, so I decided to let her make the decision.

"Yes, I'd like to do something else besides going to another stupid movie, Henry," she said. "Let's get some food and have a picnic down by the river."

"Sounds good to me. We could stop at Gus' and pick up some sandwiches."

"It'd be peaceful and cool at sunset by the water. The moon's going to be full tonight. It'd be romantic, don't you think?"

Before I could answer she went to her bedroom and rummaged out several quilts. Her short skirt rode up when she bent over to get a picnic basket from the pantry and her tanned-muscular legs showed up to her panties. When she caught me gawking at her, she responded with an inviting lewd smile. After that my focus was only on one thing.

We ordered sandwiches from Gus' Diner and bought a carton of beer at a honkytonk going out of town. The ride to the river was long and dusty on the rutted and rocky roads, and it wasn't long till sunset when we arrived at an out of the way spot on the Missouri. Laney was right about it being peaceful and cool by the river. I hadn't had a drink in weeks and knew I shouldn't, but I had a notion it was going to be a special night and was so excited I decided to get the best out of it I could and had already had three beers on the drive out.

She didn't seem to care how much her panties showed rolling around on the quilts as she sipped her beer. She indeed knew what she was doing, and after she put the food out, I was so randy I couldn't eat.

As the sun had gone down the glow from the rising moon had backlighted the eastern skyline. At first it rose as a big orange ball, and then shrank to a glowing white dot after struggling above the Belts. Laney was sprawled beside me watching the simultaneous sunset and moonrise. "Beautiful, isn't it?" she said.

"We were lucky to get a sunset and a full moonrise together like that. It doesn't happen very often." I figured that sounded stupid and tried to come up with something intelligent to say, but she intervened.

"It's so romantic isn't it?" Her eyes were filled with amorous intent as she rolled over against me and smiled. The moonlight sparkled in her eyes and glistened off her teeth. When she puckered and closed her eyes, I started kissing her. Then we were gasping and rolling around like crazed animals. I wanted to grab her tits but couldn't mount the courage. She was obviously wanting the same thing because she took my hands and placed them there for me. The more I kissed and groped, the harder she pushed and rubbed. When I couldn't hold back anymore, I pulled her skirt up and tugged on her panties. She wiggled her ass and I slid them off. I fumbled with her bra till she giggled and unsnapped it for me. Her boobs were even more spectacular than I'd imagined. I got out of my jeans as fast as I could and crawled on. In less than a minute what I'd been dreaming about for weeks was over.

"That was fast," she quipped. "You could have at least waited till I had one."

"Give me a few minutes and I'll make it up to you, I promise."

She rolled on top of me and squirmed and hunched and licked and kissed. I thought my heart would explode when she slid down to my waist and had her way with me there. Then we screwed till the quilts were drenched with sweat and we were exhausted. Her warmth felt wonderful snuggled against me afterward. "All I been thinking about since the first time I saw you is getting your panties off," I said.

"You seemed so shy the night we met that I was afraid you weren't even going to ask me out. Then after our second date I knew I'd have to make the first move. I was beginning to think you were funny the way you kept your hands away. Even gentlemen don't hold back as long as you did."

"I was afraid you'd get mad if I tried something, and I didn't want to take the chance."

"It's an insult to ignore a female that way. You don't know much about women, do you?"

"You're only the second woman I've ever been to bed with."

She giggled. "You're almost a virgin then, but okay for a man with so little experience. Maybe a little quick, though."

Asking how she would know almost slipped out. It made me wonder about her being so experienced and uninhibited for a woman just turned twenty-one.

"I don't want to get pregnant, so from now on you've got to use a rubber."

"But I hate those things."

"It's better than having a kid, isn't it?"

"If I get some then can we start coming out here all the time?"

"Don't start thinking I'm your whore. You're still going to treat me like a lady, or you can go whack your own self off."

"I didn't mean it that way. I know you're a lady. I told Mason you were the first night we met. That was the reason I was afraid to ask you out at first or then to put my hands on you. I figured a woman like you wouldn't go out with a ranch hand like me in the first place. I figured you'd want somebody rich like James Mason."

"Oh, Henry, you're so stupid. You know Mason's dating Lula Mae Jordon."

I was too dumbfounded to answer, and Laney knew it by my expression. "Why, Henry, you look like I just cut your willy off."

"Mason's got a woman? He's never mentioned her to me."

"Yes, and she's very pretty, too. Her husband drowned in a stock pond several years back trying to get a calf unstuck from the mud. Some people think he somehow got kicked and knocked out, either by the calf or its mother. Anyway, they met at a church social. They date regularly, but not openly. They're very discreet about their affair, but everybody in Helena knows about it."

"I'll be damned. And I thought he was going to cattlemen's meetings all those nights."

"He's only human, Henry. Don't you think he likes to screw like everybody else?"

I had to think on it and went to the river for a beer. After I fished one out, I decided to cool off and waded out into the flow. I held the beer over my head and went under and Laney waded out to me. Her body was hot pressing against mine in the cold water. "I never thought about Mason having a woman because he seemed so devastated over losing his wife. But I'm sure glad he does. Maybe he's not as lonely as I thought."

"And now you've got a woman, too, and she needs you back on the blankets."

We didn't let up till the moon was near setting and I was so given out it was all I could do to stay awake on the drive back to the ranch after taking Laney home. The dull headache from all the beer I'd drank didn't make it any easier.

When I got to the ranch, daylight was starting to show. I saw a light on in the kitchen while I was still a good distance from the house, so I cut my headlights and parked down the way beside the barn and slipped into my room and took a shower. Since nothing was mentioned of my early morning arrival at breakfast, I figured Mason hadn't seen or heard me pull in.

I was dreading the coming day. I had a fifteen-acre field of haybales to load and stack and knew it was going to be hot. It was scorching by ten and sweat was pouring out of me in buckets. I'd moved about a fourth of the bales and stacked them in a corner of the field and was already all but done in when I went to the house for lunch. I felt so bad I was going to tell Mason I needed the afternoon off, but it was as if he was anticipating what I was about to say. "The hay you're moving today is the best quality of any I grow, and I want it for the horses, so fill the barn loft before you stack anymore in the field," he said.

"Can't the barn wait till tomorrow? The heats already getting to me. I was thinking about taking the afternoon off."

"Yeah, they say it's going to be the hottest day of the year, so be sure to drink plenty of water. Throwing those sixty-pound bales around can milk it out of you, especially in that hundred-degree loft." His cynical little smile came. "Hope you got a good night's sleep. Damn, could you imagine having to do it hungover? Oh, and by the way, it's supposed to rain by morning so we can't put it off. You don't want to put wet hay in the barn and start a fire like that idiot Donnas did, do you?"

It didn't rain again for over three weeks.

CHAPTER 9

I was in the barn graining the horses when Donnas came strolling in ignoring me. It was his first day back at work since I'd put him in the hospital, and I'd been dreading it. Things were going so well for me on the ranch that I didn't want it messed up by another fight with him, and I was afraid Mason might not need me anymore with his return anyway and for the time being I didn't want to leave. I tried sounding friendly and sincere. "Hello, Donnas. Glad you're back."

"Yeah," was all he said and grabbed some fencing tools and left without even looking at me.

I told Mason at dinner that night about our meeting and that Donnas didn't seem to have any animosity towards me, but he scoffed at that notion. "Bullshit, even though I warned him not to make any trouble you can bet he will. And I'm telling you what I told him. If there's another fight both of your asses are gone from here. I won't tolerate it. Do you understand?"

"Yes, sir, you won't have to worry about me starting anything."

"Just be ready. That ill bastard won't be happy till he kicks your ass for what you did to him. Not just for the ass whipping you gave him, but mainly for the shame you put him through."

And as usual Mason was right. A few days later I was raking hay and noticed Donnas galloping towards me on his pinto. After he drew up in a cloud of dust, he motioned for me to get down off the tractor.

"Guess you think I'm going to forget our fight, don't you, you little faggot?" he said.

I hadn't intended on doing anything so stupid as to start a fight, but what he said and how he said it hit me wrong. The anger I'd brought home from the war began to stir. The warning Mason had given flashed through my mind, but the uncontrollable fury took over my reasoning. "No, Donnas, I knew it was still on your feeble mind. Now climb off that nag and let's finish it here and now. I kicked your ass once and I'll do it again for you. Right now."

As I unbuttoned my shirt, the confidence drained from his beady eyes. "I don't want Mason to know, so meet me at the gym tonight at nine and we'll get this settled," he said.

"No, asshole, get on down here and let's get it on here and now."

"Not here. At the gym at nine."

"I wouldn't miss it for the world."

Except for Donnas, the sweat and liniment smelling gym had emptied by nine. He had a key, and I heard the lock rattle and click behind me after I came in. I took off my shirt and boots and pulled on the set of gloves he offered. When I crawled through the ropes, he was in the ring jumping and rolling his shoulders getting loose as if he were Max Baer or some other great boxing champion. Watching him made me want to puke.

After Donnas laid out the basic rules of boxing we squared off and he threw the first punch. Streaks of blood stained my forearm when I tried wiping the burn out of my cheek. Another left cut me again. I came back with a solid right hook, but it didn't seem to faze him. He just grinned, and after several more jabs he got me with a right that turned my legs into rubber. Brilliant flashes went off inside my head as I stumbled against the ropes. I waited till the room stopped spinning, then I hit him with several solid jabs that again didn't seem to have any affect. I couldn't understand why my punches weren't causing any damage knowing Donnas wasn't that tough after I'd taken him out so easily in the bar.

He jabbed, cut and punched me at will, and chuckled each time he did. Just minutes into the fight I could barely hold my gloves up. My legs were trembling and mushy and about to buckle.

Then he went to my ribs. The pain became so intense I could hardly breathe. I was about to go down and he knew it. It was the moment he'd been waiting for. He put the weeks of hate that had festered inside him into that one final punch and it put me down and out cold.

I didn't know how long I'd been out when icy water streaming on my face brought me back around. Donnas was standing over me holding a bucket. His voice sounded distant. "I want you awake for this, you little piece of dog shit." Then the steel bucket echoed banging across the concrete floor. "Now I'm really going to fuck you up." When he kicked me, it incensed me. And when he kicked me in the side of the head again, anger induced adrenalin surged and I caught his foot and twisted until there was a loud pop and he went down screaming and writhing clutching his ankle.

I was overwhelmed with rage and finished with his refined way of fighting. Now that he'd broken them, I was done with the rules he'd laid out. I pulled my gloves off and motioned for him to get up. He struggled getting on his good foot and then I knocked him back down and sat on his chest and pounded his twisted face until it relaxed, and I couldn't raise my fists anymore. After I struggled out of the ring the pain and fatigue started building as the adrenalin began to wane and my anger cooled. My hands hurt the worst, but my ribs were almost as bad. Breathing was excruciating. Donnas was still down and hadn't moved, so I figured I'd better call an ambulance and then I went and unlocked the back door.

A short while later I heard a siren and saw red flashing lights pulling up out back. Then some ambulance guys came running in.

After they'd dragged Donnas out of the ring and loaded him on a gurney, one came over to check on me. "Damn I'd love to have seen that," he said, while giving my face a close examination. "That bastard finally got what he deserved. Maybe he'll think more before bullying people around now. Sure you don't want to go with us? You look bad, man."

"I'm alright."

He was holding the gloves they'd taken off Donnas. A strange look came on his face when he looked over at the ones on the floor I'd been wearing. He went over and picked one up. "Were these the gloves you used?"

"Yeah, at least till he made me mad and I took them off. Why?"

"Why'd you want to give him such an advantage. Or did he just take it?"

"What do you mean?"

"You couldn't have hurt him with these no matter how hard you hit him. They're for sparring. The ones he used are unpadded and for working out on the speed bag. It's a wonder he didn't kill you."

I tried getting to Donnas, but they held me back till they got him loaded inside the ambulance.

Later that night Laney cleaned the cuts on my bruised and swollen face and put cold towels on my ribs. I felt like hell the next morning and looked even worse when I left for the ranch. I was late for breakfast, and when Mason saw me, he knew what'd happened. He angrily threw the dishrag he was holding onto the floor. "Damnit, you two just had to do it. By the looks of your face he gave you one hell of a beating. But what about him? Did you put him in the hospital again?"

"I guess. He was still out when the ambulance took him off. Look, Boss, I'll take half the blame, but the fight was his idea. He wouldn't fight fair and I lost my temper. I didn't mean to hurt him that bad. I just couldn't help it." I explained everything down to the gloves. After I finished, Mason didn't say anything, he just turned and tromped off.

I figured my employment at the ranch was done and I waited in the kitchen to learn my fate dreading whatever it was that was about to come. Mason came back after what seemed like hours. He put his palm on my forehead and moved my head around examining the damage to my face. "Maybe now all this will be over between you two degenerates. Anyway, a good ass whipping never hurt anybody. Maybe it even did Donnas some good," he said. I noticed his slight grin.

He took out a plate that had been warming in the oven and sat it in front of me. "Eat some. Maybe you'll feel better."

I ate a few bites of egg, sipped some coffee and didn't have the appetite for anything else. "I hope that's the end of it, too, Boss. I don't like fighting anymore."

"Yeah, I'm sure you don't, just like you don't like screwing that waitress anymore." When I laughed some scrambled egg shot out of my mouth and onto his shirt. "Damn, you make me sick the way you eat. Guess I'd better ride to town and check on him," he said, while brushing the egg off his shirt. "Why don't you go with me and make amends? I think you need to let a doctor look you over any-way. Your hands are swollen. You might have broken something."

"I got things more important to see to."

"Oh bullshit, what in hell have you got to do? You're too beat up to do any work. Come on, ride into town with me. I'll buy you dinner."

"Only reason you want me to go is so you can get drunk and I can drive you home."

"Awe, go to hell then. I'll go by myself."

He stomped off to his bedroom and then came back a few minutes later with a grip. I stopped him as he was going out the door. "Say, Boss, give the Widow Jordon my best, will you?" I said nonchalantly with a smile. He stood a long moment staring back at me wide-eyed and slack jawed.

"You kiss my ass and mind your own business, you little shit," he uttered, then drove off slinging gravel in a great cloud of dust.

CHAPTER 10

By the end of August haying was pretty much done and I had more time to fish and spend with Laney. She started coming to the ranch on most of her days off. I took her several times trying to get her interested in fishing, but she didn't care for it. She did like horse riding, though. At times though I got the impression that her main intention for coming to the ranch wasn't to be with me but instead was to flirt with James Mason.

I'd been writing Mama about how things were going with me and the ranch, and she kept me up with Ginny and Sara. She'd recently forwarded a letter from Major Johansson saying things in Korea weren't going well, but that it was nothing as bad as the Chosin. He was executive officer of Third Battalion now and was still working to get my Medal of Honor approved. Otherwise he was doing well and looking forward to seeing me when he returned to the States. But that would be difficult now because I had no plans of leaving Montana, unless Ginny wanted me back. I hadn't given up hope that she would someday, and never would. Having her back was all I really wanted, then I'd truly be happy again. I just had to bide my time.

By mid-September the ranch was ready for the coming winter. Feeding the livestock and checking fences was all I had to do. One morning after I finished breakfast and was heading out to grain the horses, Mason stopped me. "Henry, now that we're caught up on the ranch let's go fishing."

His comment sounded odd since we fished the Pear so often anyway. "Sounds good. I'm not doing anything tonight. I saw some fish rising to blue wings yesterday when I was riding fences."

He was reading a newspaper and looked at me over his reading glasses. "I don't mean the Pear. I want to go to Yellowstone. Would you like to go?"

"Hell yeah, more'n anything since I've read so much about it lately. But who's going to watch the ranch while we're gone?"

"That sounds like a lame excuse so you can stay here and screw that girl. Just forget about it. I'll find somebody else." He raised the newspaper back over his face.

"No. I want to go. She can do without me for a few weeks."

He kept me in suspense for a spell longer then dropped the paper. "Donnas said he could get around good enough now to take care of the few things around here. Said he'd be glad to move in for a while to help us out. Hell, truth of the matter is all he really wants is to bring his whores out here to impress them and to drink my whiskey up. He could give a damn about doing anything to help somebody."

"I want to go really bad. Just tell me when you want to leave, and I'll be ready."

"Let's leave right now. How long will it take you to pack?"

I was standing by his truck in twenty minutes with my gear loaded but had to wait on him for over a half hour. Then it took several trips to fetch all his baggage and equipment from the house and load it. After we tied a tarp over the bed of the truck we finally left for Yellowstone.

"Hope you brought warm clothes, Henry. It can get mighty cold up there this time of year. It'll more than likely snow on us."

"I've seen it snow before, Boss, but I don't have a decent coat. I'll buy one when we go through Helena. Mind if I stop and tell Laney we're going?"

"We'll eat lunch at the restaurant then. I'm sick and tired of cooking for your sorry ass every day. Hell, you don't appreciate it anyway."

"You cook better than my mama. I've put on fifteen pounds since I came here."

"Yeah, I feel like your mama sometimes."

It didn't seem to concern Laney that I was leaving for several weeks. Instead she seemed indifferent, maybe even glad and relieved I was going. Later down the road when I had time to think more about it, her unconcerned attitude made me wonder if she were seeing someone else and wanted me out of the way for a while.

I'd been drunk the whole time I'd been in Yellowstone Country before. It was a lot different now that I was sober. It was even more beautiful than I remembered. After we got into the mountains at Big Sky, the coolness of the high altitude felt wonderful after the oppressive heat of the prairie all summer, even though the thin air gave me a headache. Mason said he could feel the difference too, because half the whiskey made him twice as high. We were both in good spirit winding along the curvy highway running along the Gallatin River. I'd been driving and enjoying the ride and in no rush since we'd left Bozeman, but Mason started getting anxious when we got into the mountains and he saw the rushing and sparkling waters of the Gallatin cascading by. "Step on the gas, Henry. We need to get to West Yellowstone so we can find a good place to stay. The tourist will have all the rooms taken."

"If we're going to stay in a hotel then why did you have me pack all that camping gear? I figured we were going to camp most of the time. I was looking forward to it."

"We might sleep out some. There's lots of bears around though, so we'll stay at the Kozey Inn mostly. They've got a good restaurant and a well-stocked bar as well."

"I know. I got drunk in that bar several nights on my way to Helena. Had some trouble there too."

"For some reason I'm not surprised."

"But I'm not like that anymore. My days of hard drinking and bar fighting are over."

"Tell it to your preacher. I'm not buying any of that bullshit. I'll bet before we leave, you'll get falling-down drunk and in a brawl. Let's bet something on it. How about one of those Parkers of yours against any gun I own? You seem to like eyeing that little Boss twenty with the gold grouse scenes. Come on."

"Nope, I'm not going to take advantage of you, but I'll prove it. Wait and see."

Puddles of water were standing in the pocked gravel streets when we pulled into West Yellowstone. The cloud that had brought the shower had dissipated and the late afternoon sun was shining brilliantly. Except for a few lingering retirees and fishermen, it seemed everyone had left town. Some businesses had already closed for the winter, but the tackle shop was still open. I pulled in so we could find out which streams were fishing best, and to buy some needed tackle. An Army surplus raft strapped to a trailer parked outside the shop caught my attention when we pulled up. A wooden rowing frame with brass rowlocks and a set of long oars were lashed to it. "What's that thing for?" I said, pointing to it.

"You fish out of it while a guide rows you down the river. I floated the Madison last summer in one and really enjoyed it. Caught a ton of fish. Want to try it?"

"Yeah, but how much does it cost?"

"Don't ask. You couldn't afford it anyway."

The shop was well stocked, especially with high end split cane rods and expensive English fly reels. Large mounted trout of various species were hanging all around on varnished pine plaques. A chalk board above the checkout counter displayed up-to-date fishing reports of the local rivers.

Mason milled about like a woman in a boutique and soon built a nice tab. He spent a good deal of time flexing rods and examining reels. Then after piling his merchandise on the counter, he booked the raft for a couple of days on the Madison.

I bought a few spools of tippet material and several items for fly tying I needed. I checked the book section and found a recently released copy of a book titled <u>A Modern Dry Fly Code</u> that sounded interesting and decided to buy it. We paid after the cashier totted our bills and then went back to the truck. I got behind the wheel and as I started to drive away, Mason sat a box on the seat next to me. "What do you think of this, Henry?"

I opened the box and took out its contents – a Hardy Perfect fly reel. The agate line guide was beautiful, and I fingered its polished silkiness. Then I turned the handle and felt the fine liquid feel of the pawls clicking inside. My reels were junk in comparison. I handed it back. "It's nice, Boss."

He pushed my hand back. "It's yours. Put it in your fishing bag."

I shoved it back. "I can't take that. You've done way too much for me already."

"Just shut up. Here, I got you a new fly line, too. I don't know how you fish with that archaic-worn-out mess of yours. Take it as a bonus for all the hard work you put in this summer. Now be quiet about it and let's go check in." I tried thanking him but couldn't get the words to come out. "Don't cry on me now. It's just a piece of fancy metal," he said."

We then registered for two rooms at the Kozey Inn. I was so elated about the reel I insisted on unloading our gear as a show of gratitude. Mason gladly accepted and headed to the bar. After I stowed our things in our rooms, I went downstairs and joined him.

"Let me buy you a beer, Henry," he said, after I took a seat at the small table across from him. "You deserve one after all the driv-ing you did today." But when our young waitress came, I ordered a whiskey instead and Mason's face soured. "Sure you want to do that, Henry? You've been sober for a long time now. You hardly even shake anymore."

"I'm just going to have one. One can't hurt can it?" But those few ounces of whiskey brought back the wonderful feeling I so craved, and I had to have another, and then another.

At some point during the night four men had come in and sat down at the table beside ours. I hadn't noticed them in my inebriated stupor, but then their sarcastic voices and vulgar remarks to our young waitress grew so loud and harsh they caught my attention. The initial euphoric high that makes drunks so clownish and fun in the beginning, but eventually and ultimately changes them into mean and brutal tyrants came over me. I started to get up to say something hoping to start a fight, but Mason put his hand on my arm. "Just ignore them. Maybe they'll leave soon," he said.

But they'd riled me, and there was no dialing it back now being that I was loaded beyond reason with alcohol. I couldn't keep my attention from what they were saying. "If that little bastard gets up again, I'm going to stomp his ass," one said.

"He's got a hairdo like them jarheads that's getting their asses kicked over there in gook land," another said.

I turned to them again. "What you looking at, you wormy little prick?" the biggest one said. "I'm going to kick that ass for you if you ain't careful."

I was trembling with rage and started to get up again, but Mason grabbed my arm and held me back. "Let it ride. We don't want trouble. They're just drunk. Let's get out of here and call it a night." I didn't want to leave and broke his grip from my arm and started to get up again. He grabbed me again. "Let's go to the restaurant and have some dinner. Come on now, let's get out of here."

I gave in and we left heading for the dining area. We were almost out of hearing when their last comment came. "Look, Clem, the chicken shits are running out on us. Probably going to change their rags." A roar of laughter erupted.

Nothing was going to allow me to let it pass, not even my respect for James Mason. Then an idea came to me. As we were going by the men's restroom, I stopped. "Got to take a whiz, Boss. I'll be right there."

He gave me a doubtful look. "I'll get a table. Just don't wind up back at the bar, okay?"

"Are you kidding? Those four gorillas would stomp me into a greasy spot. I'll be right there."

I went into the restroom and washed my face with cold water and my rage began to subside and some reason started easing back into my brain. It came to me that facing all four of the hulks at once would indeed be suicide. I reconsidered going back to the bar to face them alone and decided to drop it.

I'd just started peeing when one of the four buffoons walked up to the urinal next to mine. I was going to ignore him and do nothing, until he said, "A sawed off shit like you shouldn't get so far away from your boyfriend. Somebody's liable to wash your ugly face in one of these pissers."

Anger came over me again. I made a half turn and started spraying his boots, and then said, "Were you talking to me?"

He grabbed my throat, then pushed me back against the wall and took a swing. I ducked, and there was a loud bang as his knuckles shattered against the metal divider separating the urinals from the commode. He let out a howl and grabbed his wrist and I knocked him down with a hard right, then punched and kicked his face till he lay still.

I finished peeing and was washing my hands when two of the others came in. When they saw their buddy on the floor, one caught the back of my shirt and slung me around. The other drew back to punch me, but he was too slow, and I hit him before he swung. He slipped backwards on the piss-slick floor and his feet shot up into the air. I knew he wasn't causing any more trouble by the ripe watermelon thump his head made hitting the stone tile. I spun loose from the other and gave him a solid kick to the balls. When he doubled over, I put a knee hard into his face and he went down and tried but couldn't get up. I gave him a good kick behind the ear with my bootheel, and he stopped squirming. I figured I'd better get going while I had the chance.

I was hurrying out when the last one came stumbling in. When he saw two of his buddies out cold and the other floundering on the floor like a beached whale, a look of wonder came over him. Before he could react, I slammed a standing metal ashtray that was sitting near the doorway against the side of his head and he went down with the others.

Mason had already ordered and was flirting with the waitress when I sat down. "Damn, boy, I was beginning to think those four buffoons might have jumped you."

I jerked a menu off the table to cover my grin. "What you having?"

"Ham and eggs. Eat up, it's on me."

"It's always on you. How about letting me get this one for a change?"

He made a big deal out of it by spreading his arms. "By all means do, big money."

We talked fishing and made plans for the next few days as we ate. When we'd finished Mason went to pee, but he was back in minutes. He took my wrists and inspected the damage to my hands. They were swollen and several knuckles were showing white. "Damn you, Henry Ball! I told you not to start trouble with those men."

"What men?"

"You know who I'm talking about. They're still laid out on the floor in there."

"They ganged up on me and I had to protect myself. What else was I supposed to do, beg for mercy and take a beating?"

"With you it's always the other guy that starts it. Nothing is ever your fault. Now let's get the hell out of here before the law comes."

"That's probably a good idea."

I thought it was a bad dream, but the banging kept getting louder as I slowly came to. I staggered over and opened the door. It was Mason with his fist up ready to bang some more, pert as ever, grinning broadly. "Wake your sorry ass up and let's go," he said. "It's getting late."

"Be down in a few minutes."

My brain was a swollen sponge. I puked a few times in a trash can while I was on the toilet shitting water. Mason was laughing and joking with two other fishermen sitting at the table next to him when I finally made it down to the dining area. "There's my old buddy. Hey, Henry, want some scrambled eggs?" he said, with his cynical little smile.

I felt dry heaves coming on and covered my mouth with my hand. "Just coffee."

"Looks like you had a rough one, boy," one of the men said. I managed a nod.

"These gentlemen had great fishing yesterday on the Yellowstone down the Howard Eton Trail, Henry. Let's hike down there and take the grill and cook some trout for lunch. That way we can stay all day."

As bad as my head was pounding, I didn't care what we did and nodded agreement again.

As Mason was finishing his breakfast, I noticed the Chief of Police standing in the entranceway surveying the restaurant. Even though I'd been drunk when he ran me out of town back in July, I remembered his face distinctly. I hoped he hadn't recognized mine as he headed our way.

"James Mason, good to see you again," he said when he got to our table.

Mason stood to shake his hand. "Good to see you, Bill."

The Chief started giving me a hard look, so I dropped my head and pulled my hat down over my face.

"Bill Stanfield, meet my friend –,"

"Where's the fish biting at?" I said, cutting Mason off.

I figured Stanfield was squinting at me so hard because he was trying to recollect where he'd seen me before. "Don't ask me. I don't have time to fish," he said, and turned back to Mason. "Were you in here last night, James?"

"We ate dinner here. Something wrong?"

"Know anything about the fight in the restroom?"

"Oh, lord, a fight?"

"Four men from Minnesota got beat up in the urinal. I'm trying to find out who ruffed them up so bad. For some reason they won't say. Must have been a bunch of rough ones. Probably the usual suspects – them cattle truck drivers out of Ennis. Always drinking too much and starting trouble." He looked back at me again with narrowed eyes. "Don't I know you from somewhere, boy?"

"No, sir, don't think so."

He leaned down to get a better look. "I don't forget faces. You look mighty familiar. What's your name?"

"Pit Robinson."

"Ever been in West Yellowstone before?"

"No, sir."

Mason seemed surprised at how well I could lie and realized why and knew we needed to make a fast exit before Stanfield remembered who I was. "Pit, sure you're not hungry?" he said.

"I'm ready to go if you are, Boss."

"Hope you catch those ruffians, Bill. We've got to get going. We need to have dinner one night soon. I'll stop by the station so we can make plans." Then Mason dropped a wad of bills on the table and we made a fast exit for the truck. Just before going out the door I turned, and Stanfield was still staring hard at me.

"Damn you, Henry Ball," Mason said, when we were outside. "Why'd you lie like that? You're going to get us both in a hell of a lot of trouble. Bill Stanfield is not only the chief of police here, he's also a good friend of mine."

"Because he told me not to ever come back here. He might have remembered me by my real name and put me in jail again. Anyway, don't worry. We won't see him again."

"I hope to hell we don't, at least if you're around."

Mason enjoyed the hike down the Howard Eaton Trail. It was like a death march to me. My head was still pounding, and I was weak from lack of sleep and from having heaved my innards out. Carrying the duffle bag full of cooking utensils made it even more miserable, especially the camp grill.

The Yellowstone River was low and clear and fishing was even better than the old men had predicted, but I was disappointed with the Yellowstone Cutthroat trout. Their beauty paled in comparison to a rainbow or brown, and for their size, their fight was unimpressive, feeling like wet socks wavering in the current on the end of my line. Not once did they test the drag on my new reel. And they ate my fly too eagerly like hogs at a trough on almost every cast, and it didn't take long before I became bored with their stupidity. After a while I stopped fishing and decided to take a nap beside a blowdown that had fallen partly into the river. I hadn't been asleep long before Mason came up and nudged me awake with his boot. "Why aren't you fishing?" he said.

"I still feel like shit from last night."

"Oh hell, you're so damned worthless." He went on downriver shaking his head.

I fell back asleep in minutes, but with the warming sun bearing down on me, I soon woke drenched in alcohol sweat with my heart racing. I couldn't swallow my throat was so parched, so I crawled the few feet to the river and buried my face and drank till my teeth ached. The water and nap revived me somewhat, but I wanted a smoke before I started fishing again.

As I was watching Mason fishing peacefully downriver, a buffalo appeared from around the bend from below. When the bull saw Mason, it stopped and lowered its head and began pawing up clouds of dust. I could see his flanks and shoulders were ripped and bloody from a recent fight, and it appeared he was going to take his frustration out on Mason. I jumped up and started screaming and pointing, and Mason must have heard, but not understood over the rush of the river because he waved and then went back to fishing. I broke into a run as the bison charged.

Mason turned when the bull splashed into the river. The sight of the beast pawing at the water froze him for a moment, but then as he turned to run, his feet flew up and he fell hard on the shallow-water rocks. Just as the buffalo started after him, I bounced a grapefruit sized boulder off its head, and then it turned on me. "Get out of here you ugly bastard! Get, damn you! Get on now."

I ran out into the stream to get closer and connected with an even bigger rock. That was enough for the buffalo and he left shaking his head as he went bellowing and bucking into the trees above the river.

Mason couldn't get his footing and kept slipping and floundering, so I waded out to help him. I had to carry him most of the way back and then had to drag him up on the bank. "Damn, Boss, I think that son of a bitch was going to hook you."

His agonized face revealed his pain. "I think my hip's broken, Henry." His cigarettes were soaked, and he was shaking so bad I had to light one of mine for him. "Weren't you afraid of that thing?" he said, after he'd regained some composure.

After working with cattle and horses all summer and halter breaking yearling bulls, I'd lost all fear of livestock and I foolishly considered the buffalo with the same attitude as the farm animals. "They're nothing but overgrown cows. You just got to show them who's boss."

"Bullshit. They've lost their fear of humans here in the Park and are extremely dangerous, and the rut's got them crazy as well. You don't know how lucky you are he didn't kill you."

"I think you're the one that's lucky, Boss."

I went searching down the river and found his rod. The line had tangled in a deadfall and after I straightened it all out and brought it back to him, he said, "Thanks, Henry. I owe you, and I don't mean for the rod either."

"You don't owe me anything, Boss. You saved me when you pulled me out of that jail and got me sober and helped me get my life back together."

"A lot of times I think I should have left you in there, and you don't know how close I came to doing just that especially after the terrible way you talked to me. But something wouldn't let me. Though you were a disgusting, deplorable and defiant drunken retch, I felt compelled to try to save you for some reason. Just don't ask me why. Now get the grill out and start a fire, and I'll cook us up some lunch." Then as an afterthought, he said, "I should have whipped your ass in that visitor's room that day. Nobody would have given a damn."

He was so intent in watching for buffalo while grilling the trout that he burned them to the point they were inedible. And his hip hurt so bad he couldn't fish, so we decided to call it a day. He struggled and stopped often going the mile back up the trail, and I winced when he showed me the bruise on his hip oozing blood when he changed out of his wet clothes when we were back at the truck. But after several pulls from his flask and some headache powders his pain and apprehension seemed to ease. I took the wheel and we headed back to West Yellowstone.

"Guess you'll have bad dreams of buffalos tonight," I said.

"I'm sure I will. You're a crazy son of a bitch. You know that?"

I laughed. "Course I do. So how did you and Stanfield get to be such asshole buddies?"

He shook his head and took a long pull from his flask. "Several years back while I was in a cafe eating breakfast somebody came along and heisted my favorite Leonard rod from the back of my truck. I knew I should have cased and locked it inside the cab, but I was in such a hurry to eat so I could start fishing I didn't.

"I went to the police station and reported the theft and Stanfield told me to come back the next morning and he might have my rod, and by damn he did. He suspected that some kids he knew had stolen it, and after having a talk with their parents the rod miraculously appeared. I was so happy I took him and his wife out to dinner that night and we've been friends ever since. But now that you're along and have screwed everything up as usual, I guess our annual dinner will be cancelled this year."

"I can make myself scarce. Don't change your plans on my account."

"I wish you'd made that bet with me."

"What bet?"

"That you'd get drunk and start a fight before we left town. It was our first night and you didn't let me down for once. How many more will there be before we leave?"

"None. I'm not like that anymore, and I'm never touching another drop of whiskey again for as long as I live. I swear it. I've learned my lesson this time."

"Bullshit. A leopard never changes his spots and neither does an ignorant redneck."

Later that evening in the Kozey Bar, a handsome, slim young man sat down at the table beside ours. He looked like he might be a fisherman by the way he was dressed and by his sun-ravaged face. Mason must have figured the same and thought he could get some fishing information from him and became very cordial. "Say young man, can I buy you a beer?"

The man produced a big grin. "You bet."

"I'm James Mason. Good to meet you."

"I'm Ethan Macstatts. The way you guys are dressed you must be fishermen."

"We try to be. And you?"

"You betcha. Having any luck?

"Henry and I had a great day at LeHardy's today. How about you?"

"I caught a few on the lower Madison. Kind of slow now that the hatches are over. Where you guys from?"

"Wolf Creek."

"You talk like you're from the South."

"You're right. I was born in Texas but live up on the Missouri now at Wolf Creek."

Macstatts turned to me. "How about you?"

"I work for Judge Mason."

"What did you say your name was?"

There was something familiar about this guy, and he seemed to be searching for more than fishing information and it put me on guard. "Pit Robinson."

"Thought your name was Henry?"

"The Judge's getting old and gets confused sometimes when he's drinking. The other man that works with me is named Henry. Ain't that right, Judge?"

Mason glared at me for making him lie, but he realized why. "Yeah."

"By the looks of that close haircut you must have been in the military."

"I was."

"Bet you're glad to be out now with the way the war's going."

"Sure am. Where you from, Ethan?"

He hesitated. "Spokane. Me and my wife are here on vacation."

"What do you do back in Spokane?"

"Ugh, college professor."

"And what do you teach?"

"Physics."

I was about to choke holding back my laughter. "Ever fished out here before?"

"Been coming out several years now."

Where did you say you were staying?"

"Ah, the Pioneer Inn."

"Nice place?"

"Okay, I guess. Look, I'd better be getting back to my old lady. Maybe see you guys fishing somewhere tomorrow?"

"We're going to the lower Madison. I'm sure we'll be seeing you again," I said.

Next morning, I fell in love with the Madison River. It was like a giant Little Prickly Pear the way it paced and in its make-up. The rainbows and browns were selective, and presentation had to be perfect to fool them into taking my fly. They were wild and beautiful and incredibly strong and the light, smooth drag of my new reel proved its worth.

After I'd fished for several hours, my back felt like a sword had been driven between my shoulder blades from standing crouched over for so long, and my feet felt like blocks of ice from standing in the frigid water. The burning pain from the Chosin frost bite made it worse. I waded to the bank and took a seat on a log to rest and thaw out. I'd just started gnawing on a piece of jerky when I spotted a fisherman heading my way. As I expected it was Ethan Macstatts. Even though I suspicioned he was trying to connect me with the fight, I was still glad to see him. I really liked the guy for some reason even though I'd known him only briefly. I wondered how long he'd been looking for me along the many miles of the Madison River.

"I'll be damned, Pit. What a coincidence I ran into you." His big snowy smile appeared. "Catching any?"

"A few. Have some jerky." I offered the bag.

He put up his hands. "Too hard for me to chew."

Then questions began flying again as he tried connecting me to the fight. It was so obvious what he was up to. When he started asking about my past I left and went back to the river before I broke down laughing and embarrassed him. I didn't fish long, though. The sun was getting high and the fish had stopped feeding. My back started cramping again so I waded back to shore. When I sat down,

I noticed the flies on Ethan's fleece hatband. "Where did those come from, Ethan?" I said, pointing to his hat.

His grin melted. "I tied them. Why?"

"They're beautiful."

The smile returned. "Why, thank you. Do you tie?"

"Started a few months ago. Mine catch fish, but they don't look as good as yours do."

He gave the flies on my fleece-drying pad a look. "They're not so bad. A lot better than most people turn out. You cast well, too, except your back cast is a little low."

"I appreciate the advice. I'll keep it in mind."

"How do you like Yellowstone Country, Pit?"

"I've decided to move here if I can find a job. I'm going to ask around while we're here."

"My wife Emma and I are opening a fly shop in West next spring and we'll need some help. Would you be interested in working for us?"

My heart rushed for a moment with excitement, but then I figured it was part of his scheme to somehow link me with the fight and I felt disappointment set in. "Sure, but I don't know anything about working in a fly shop."

"We don't know much either, but we're going to learn. We'll need a guide, too."

What he told me sounded too good to be true. There was nothing more I'd like than to live in Yellowstone Country and be on the water every day and get paid for it, too. But there was still the matter of the fight and my doubt in his word. "I'd at least be willing to try. When will you know if you're going through with it or not?"

"We already know. We're ordering stock now."

He seemed so sincere in what he was saying, and I wanted the job so bad, I decided to gamble and come across with the truth. "Look, Ethan, my name is really Henry Ball. I'd take that job in a heartbeat if you're serious, but there's a problem. Last summer when I was here, I got in a fight and got locked up. Stanfield told me never to come back to West Yellowstone." Ethan looked at me oddly and then started rocking with laughter. "What's so damn funny?" I said.

"I remember you now. Yeah, I remember now," he said, pointing at my face. "Stanfield backed you against the wall at the station and told you never to come back. But you don't resemble that guy at all now or I'd have remembered you last night."

"But that's not the bad part, Ethan. I'm the one that beat up those four buffoons in the Kozey restroom the other night. One of them caught me alone and started it. He threw the first punch."

"I bet he didn't have any reason to."

I had to look away. "Not until I started pissing on his boots."

"About what I figured. But there were four of them. They were big guys too. Mason must have helped you."

"Oh no, he was mad as hell about it. He had absolutely nothing to do with it. He was in the restaurant eating when it happened." I explained it all, that I'd drank too much, how it'd started and how lucky I'd been that all of them hadn't come into the restroom at the same time or I'd most likely be in the hospital. I added that they were so drunk they weren't in any condition to fight anyway. Then, I said, "You looked familiar last night, and I thought you were feeling me out. That's why I gave you the fake name."

"Yeah, Stanfield put me up to it. He knew he'd seen you before and figured you were involved in the fight. I'd never met Mason before either. That's why Stanfield sent me and not one of the other deputies. And now I understand why they won't say who they had the fight with and why they don't want to press charges."

I was at a loss. "How's that?"

"They're too ashamed to admit a scrawny guy like you whipped them so bad, that's why. And they were here on business and I doubt they want it to get back to their bosses they got drunk and in a fight in a bar in a redneck town like West Yellowstone. I wouldn't worry about them anymore. They're leaving town tomorrow and I doubt we'll ever hear from them again. So don't worry, I'll smooth the fight over with Stanfield, too."

"So, what am I supposed to believe now? You've done nothing so far but lie to me."

He laughed again. "You've told quite a few yourself. The truth is that my wife and I are really from Spokane. I was a fireman and she was a schoolteacher. Five years ago, we came out here on vacation. We loved it so much we've come back every year since. Last spring a job opened for a cop in West, so I took it. And they needed a teacher, too, so Emma hired on. And now we see the prospect for another fly shop here and we're going to make a go of it. If you want the job, I'll take care of Stanfield. He's not quite as hard as he makes out to be. You being friends with Mason will go a long way with him. Now if you want it, you've got a job next spring."

"I say definitely count me in. You saved me the trouble of having to look for one."

"Is your drinking going to be a problem?"

"The night of the fight was the first time I've drank whiskey since last July. I've learned my lesson. You won't have any problems with me drinking, I promise. I just want the chance to prove myself."

"As long as you stay sober and out of trouble you have a job." He smiled and we shook hands.

As usual we were having dinner at the Kozey Restaurant. It was our last night in West Yellowstone, and as usual Mason had struck up a conversation with a stranger that this time was from Chicago. He and Mason talked for several hours about their hunting and fishing travels and at one point the man brought up his duck hunting experiences in the river bottoms of Arkansas. The stories fascinated me. From my early childhood hunting with Jacob, waterfowl had captivated my interest the most, and I listened intently to his tales.

"The White River overflows in the fall and floods thousands of acres of timber. Mallards migrate there from the provinces by the millions to feed on acorns in the flooded hardwood bottoms. Those Arkansas boys call them in right on top of you. It's one of the most incredible experiences in the world watching those big green headed drakes twisting and turning floating down through the trees in the bright morning sunlight right on top of you," he said.

"Where is it you go? And who do you go with?" I said.

The man thought a minute, took a pen from his shirt pocket and then scribbled on a napkin and handed it to me. "Contact this man, Howard Stokes in Boones Bluff. He's the best duck guide down there and a real damn character. You'll get a kick out of being around him even if you don't kill any ducks."

After the man left, I was determined to go to Arkansas to hunt mallards in the flooded timber. Nothing I could imagine excited me more and I started in on Mason. I thought he'd be as excited as I was and all in for going. "Boss, let's go down there. It sounds like a kick in the ass to me."

"Down where?"

"You know. Arkansas, to the river bottoms. To kill those big greenheads in the timber."

"Hell no. My old man took me there one time. I almost froze to death. It was miserable."

"You wouldn't want to try it again?"

"Forget it. We can kill ducks on the Missouri back home."

"But it isn't the same."

"To hell it's not. Killing ducks is killing ducks."

"No, it's not. I want to hunt mallards in the timber and I'm going even if I have to go alone."

He gave me a long and determined look. "If you're depending on me, you'll be going it alone."

CHAPTER 11

As Mason expected, Donnas left his house an inexcusable, disgusting mess. The kitchen smelled putrid from overflowing trashcans and unwashed dishes piled in the sink and on the counters. The beds were unmade, and the linen was stained with sweat and love juice and tainted with dime store perfume. But the worst thing of all, Donnas and his whores had drunk the whiskey cabinet dry. I followed Mason around the house as he stomped and ranted. "That worthless son of a bitch. Bastard had some real parties. Ruined my floors dancing around with that damned cast on his foot. Some of that whiskey was rare and expensive and too good for the likes of them. They probably drank it in Royal Crown."

It took two maids a day to mop, wash, polish, and scrub the house back to order, and a substantial load of whiskey I had to fetch from Great Falls to restock the bar.

Mason was still livid that night and halfway through dinner he left the table and started stomping, ranting and slinging his arms again. "I'll fire that sorry bastard if you want his job, Henry. He's the biggest no nothing I ever saw. He's got shit for brains."

I'd been reluctant to break the news about my new venture with the Macstatts, but knew I had to tell him at some point. Now seemed as good a time as ever. "I've already got a job with the Macstatts working in their new fly shop next spring."

He cocked his head, and with a confused look, said, "Oh yeah? Well that's the first I've heard about it. You can tell them you changed your mind."

"I've given my word and I won't go back on it."

He slumped back down in his chair. "Well, hell, I can't fire Donnas then. As bad as he is, it'd be hard finding somebody to replace him. At least you can stay till spring."

"I told you I'm going to Arkansas in a few weeks, but you never listen. And you don't need me now that the ranch is ready for winter and Donnas is back. I feel like a charity case staying here as it is."

"Damnit, why do you want to do something so stupid? Forget about that god forsaken place."

"I've already written Mr. Stokes that I'm coming. Can't you understand that going to Arkansas is something I want to do?"

"Awe hell go on then. When you get down there and see how dirty and featureless it is, you'll come running back – if those crazy people don't rob and kill you first that is."

I couldn't wait to get to town to get Laney in bed the next day. Wednesday was her normal day off, but she didn't answer the door after I banged for five minutes. I peeked through the crack in the front door curtain, and things just didn't look right, so I went to the restaurant and asked one of the waitresses if she knew where Laney might be.

"Nobody's seen her in over a week, Henry. Her landlady said she left what she owed for rent and disappeared that night. I'm so sorry. I know you loved her, and we miss her so much."

I drove back to Laney's place with my innards feeling like they'd been through a steel jawed clothes wringer. The landlady came over from across the street after I pulled in. "Wasn't you one of Laney's boyfriends?" she said, through squinted eyes. "I seen your truck parked here more times than the others."

I was taken aback at first, but then what I'd suspected all along came as clear as the blue sky overhead. "Guess I was dumb enough to think I was her only boyfriend. You don't know where she went, do you?"

"I don't know. She just left one night. I loved that girl so much."

"Yeah I did too, and I thought she loved me." I gave the flowers I'd bought for Laney to the old lady and left.

Mason's expression didn't change as I spieled the news of Laney's mysterious disappearance. He didn't seem one bit surprised that she'd left town in the middle of the night like she had. "I was expecting something like this. So, nobody has any idea where she may have gone?" he said.

"Nope."

"You must have been suspicious about her. Nothing about her made sense – how she came to be here and all. Look, I'm telling you this because I don't want your feelings hurt any more than they already are. But if this is pissing you off, I'll stop."

"Go on."

"I did some checking and got the story from the concierge of the hotel where they stayed when that dance thing she was in came here. She was humping the manager and his old lady caught them. It was either fire her or get divorced. That's how she wound up in Helena. She even propositioned me here on the ranch several times when you weren't around. Don't think you were her only lover. There were plenty of others banging her and paying a lot for the pleasure. I got that from several of her customers I talked to at the cattle association meetings. They were married men but even they couldn't keep from bragging about it after they got their guts full of liquor."

"I knew something like that was up, but I didn't want to believe it."

"I know it hurts, but we all go over fool's hill, especially when emotions and women are involved. Remember what I told you about a whiskey glass and a woman's ass?"

"Worst thing is I can't show my face in town again. I'm the biggest idiot in Montana."

"A lot of men in town will be envious when they find out you were getting it for free, and some women will be curious as to why, so it just might work out to be beneficial to you, especially with the women. And now that you know the truth about her and she's gone, you don't have to deal with her ever again."

"But, Boss, I think I loved her, and she was so good in bed."

He leaned over and slapped my knee. "Well, hell, you got to enjoy it for a while and it only cost you a little beer and gas money. I think in a few days you'll realize that what you felt for her was just lust and not really love and you'll be over her in no time. Anyway, another one will come along soon."

"But why did she pick me out to be her lover and act like she cared so much for me?"

"I guess she wanted a normal relationship just like everybody else. The other was just business to her I suppose."

"I'll never figure women out."

"Nobody will. Now get her off your mind. There're more important things to think about, like getting your hunting gear ready. Did you forget bird season opens tomorrow?"

Next morning, I was so excited about bird season opening that I couldn't sleep and for once beat Mason to the kitchen. When he came in, I had bacon frying, coffee brewing and pancake batter bubbling on the griddle.

"What in hell are you doing? You can't cook," he said, glaring at me with his hands on his hips.

"Don't eat then."

"I'll probably come down with a terminal case of the shits if I do. What gun you going to shoot today?"

"My twenty, of course."

He poured a cup of my crude oil from the percolator and took a seat at the table. "I'm going to have fun killing my limit and yours today," he said. After he tasted the coffee he grimaced.

"That's Marine Corps coffee. It's not for a candy ass like you."

"It does have a kick, but it's good. What horse you riding today?"

"Molly."

"Not a good choice."

"And why not?"

"She's scared of guns. Ride the grulla."

"But he's the wildest son of a bitch in the bunch."

"Maybe, but he ain't scared of guns."

"I hate that cantankerous bastard, but if you say so."

"Now dish me out a plate of that slop so we can go hunting."

I swung up on the grulla, and after he bucked a few times, we struck out under an immense azure sky with the two red setters casting back and forth well ahead. Mason occasionally spoke soft encouragement to them. Ben, the old graying black Lab, stayed in close to the horses. Mason reigned up and motioned me over when we came to the first alfalfa field. "The birds will be spooky in this sparse cover. Dismount as quickly and quietly as you can and get loaded as you approach the dogs. Getting into position to shoot before the birds flush is going to be testy."

As Mason had expected, the first covey of Huns didn't hold for a point. They flushed wild and beautiful flying bunched and chirping rolling and twisting with the terrain like a rollercoaster ride, their wings flashing in the early bright sun across the creek and down a shallow sage covered coulee. "Keep 'em marked. They'll eventually tire and hold if we can flush them a few more times," Mason said.

The next covey did hold for a point, but as I stepped off the grulla, the birds flushed and went down the same coulee as the first covey had. I started cussing, but Mason cut me off. "They're not tame like those bobwhites you're used to hunting back home. You're not in Kansas anymore, Dorothy."

Soon the dog's tails were beating like wipers in a deluge as they darted back and forth inhaling bird scent. Then they spontaneously turned into burgundy statues with raised heads and high tails. Mason dismounted, and as he approached the dogs, a group of five pheasant came cackling out of the alfalfa. He killed two roosters out of the bunch at the apex of their rises with as many shots. It was a beautiful thing to see. Even though I was impressed by his skillful shooting, I had to say, "A milking boot's harder to hit than them slow-flying gaudy things are."

He turned with a grin knowing he'd put on a grand exhibition and opened the breech of the double. The empty cases spurted out with a loud click and spirals of blue smoke followed. "We'll see how you do, smart ass. We'll see how you do."

My turn came at the end of the field when another cackling rooster exploded under the dog's noses. I missed the first shot but managed to break a wing on the second. The old rooster tumbled down running, but Ben caught it just before it reached a briar thicket.

"No wonder we're losing the war if all you jarheads shoot like that," Mason said.

We hunted on into the morning and killed our limits of Huns and pheasant in less than two hours but managed to kill only two sharptail grouse. Mason was a fabulous wing shot and I don't remember him missing a bird. I had little trouble with pheasant but shot poorly on Huns. We headed in as the morning warmed and the dogs tired.

After lunch Mason seasoned, floured and browned some of the birds and started them simmering in gravy. That night he opened a bottle of fancy red wine, and we ate the birds along with wild rice and asparagus. He was in a good mood because of the fabulous day, or he was until I unwisely brought up the sore subject of the White River bottoms. "You thought anymore about going to Arkansas with me?" The cheerfulness left his face and I cussed myself under my breath for bringing it up.

"How many times do I have to say no? Leave me alone about it." I kept quiet and after a while his temper cooled. What he said next surprised me. "You've done a lot around here that I feel I haven't paid you for, Henry. I'll help you out if you want to go that bad. Maybe if you get down there and see how miserable it is, you'll come back and forget about it. Get the gazetteer out and we'll figure out the best route to get you there. We'll take your truck into town and get it tuned up and serviced. I'm sure you need new tires. You're such a damn fool sometimes, Henry Ball."

As the days shortened and temperatures fell, the chatter and honking and flashing of wings and wavering formations of migrating waterfowl overhead increased. By mid-October the Missouri was covered with ducks and geese. Watching the great exodus of nature caused inexplicable things inside me to stir and encouraged my trip to Arkansas even more.

Mason had inherited several dozen wooden decoys from his father that had seen a lot of years of hard service, so I repainted and re-rigged them with new anchor lines. I set them out in the shallows off a sandbar in the Missouri and built a blind nearby out of driftwood and willow branches. Mason made noises on a call his father had also left him, and though the sounds didn't imitate a duck all that much, I guess the birds were so tired and hungry they came piling into the decoys anyway.

Several times during the first weeks of October, cold fronts brought light dustings of snow. The nights grew colder until the water in the dog bowls had to be broken out every morning. The fields turned brown, the cottonwood and birch trees turned a brilliant yellow and then became stark and bare. One afternoon the wind started gusting out of the northwest. Low swirling-black clouds formed and shrouded the mountain tops as the first real snow of the season bore down on the Little Prickly Pear Ranch.

I was in my room writing Mama, but the howling wind stirring the trees made it hard to concentrate. Then Mason started pounding on my door. "Henry, wake up and bring your bird gun. I'll be in the barn."

I jumped into some warm clothes, grabbed my shotgun and headed downstairs. I went into the barn slapping snow off my hat. Mason had Parker saddled and was tightening the girth on the grulla, who was even more white eyed and fidgety than usual. "Hold this son of a bitch still a minute so I can get this cinch tight," Mason barked. "Now go turn the dogs out."

The windblown snow stung like bird shot as we made for the alfalfa fields bent and watery eyed. The dogs were exuberant bounding ahead of us. We went from field to field and feeding birds were everywhere. In short order we killed our limits of pheasant and Huns. Then we tied the horses and stood on a flight-line pass shooting sharptail grouse flying down to an alfalfa field from a high bench. We were back in the barn in two hours wet and chilled to the core. "Damn, those birds were feeding like crazy," I said, stomping snow off my boots.

"They were feeding up before the storm hits. They know several days of lean times are coming. It's their instinct to anticipate bad weather. That's how they survive."

Late that night, after the storm had passed, I woke in a fit of anxiety after having dreams of the Nomad. For over an hour I tossed and turned until an undeniable urge forced me out of bed to the frigid outside. The dogs set up to barking when they heard me come out. I hushed them and waded on through the snow down the drive.

I didn't understand the compulsion that had forced me out into the cold, and I rambled about the yard for a time in confusion. Then I heard chattering and looked up. Skein after skein of waterfowl frozen out of the provinces were passing in the moonlit sky and I became engrossed in the magnificent sight. Then Mason's voice sounding strange and faraway like in a dream startled me out of the trance. "Inspiring, isn't it? All that wildlife on the move. Kind of rouses your blood, doesn't it?"

"Very much so." I became engrossed again at the sight and sound of the masses of transient life flowing by overhead and became spellbound once more. A long time passed until the searing burn in my feet from the Chosin frostbite shook me out of the trance. "Sure you don't want to go to Arkansas with me?" There was no answer. I had no idea how long he'd been gone.

CHAPTER 12

The White River bottoms of Arkansas

Several days later after the snow had melted off the roads, I was in the driveway loading the last of my things for the trip to Arkansas. Mason had a somber look on his face when he came out to see me off. "So, looks like you're really going. I thought you'd wise up and change your mind about this foolishness."

"No, I haven't changed my mind, but you could change yours and go with me."

"I've got a ranch to run here and I'm not going on some fantasy chase with you to a place I don't want any part of. Look, I need you here and I don't want to be stuck here alone with that idiot Donnas. There's plenty of hunting around here to keep you occupied. Now unpack all that junk and forget this nonsense."

"My minds made up. I've got to hunt those mallards in the timber."

At first, he seemed disgusted and then hurt. He dropped his head, turned and started to walk away, but stopped. "Be careful. There's a lot of meanness down there."

"I'm only going to be gone for a few weeks at most. Stop making such a big deal of it."

"If I believed you were only going for a few weeks I wouldn't care, but I know better. I'll see you when I see you."

He disappeared moping into the house, and I drove away feeling like I was abandoning him after all he'd done for me. If not for him I'd most likely be dead from drinking or being beaten to death or shot in some despicable roadhouse. But even more so, he'd help heal the mental devastations of the war and my divorce. A great dread of leaving Mason and the ranch that I loved so much to go someplace I knew nothing about came over me as I passed through Helena. I almost changed my mind and turned back, but the urge to go south with the migration drove me on.

I traveled through Wyoming into Nebraska and down along the Platte just as I'd come up in July. The Platte was abounding with waterfowl that had stopped to stage and rest until the next cold north wind pushed them on south. Pheasant and prairie chickens were plentiful along the roads and in the barren grain fields along the river, but the upland birds no longer concerned me. Ducks were my interest now, and my goal was to beat them to Arkansas and the White River bottoms.

I crossed Nebraska to North Platte, and then turned south down through Kansas, then I went east at Oklahoma City. Following the directions Mason had laid out, I traveled southeast through Fort Smith till I eventually came to Boones Bluff, Arkansas. Boones Bluff was much like Wolf Creek. It consisted of nothing more than a Post Office and a general store with a gas and kerosene pump. I went into the Post Office and interrupted the postmaster sorting mail.

"I'm looking for Howard Stokes. Could you tell me where he lives?"

The old man stopped and shot me an unfriendly glare. "What you a wantin' 'em fer?"

"I was told he's the best duck guide in Arkansas. I want to hunt with him."

"Oh, thought you might be the law. He's a good'n alright, but the season don't open fer two, three weeks or so yet. Hired hunts out of season his self, but he ain't gonna take no stranger like you."

He turned his back and began sorting mail again, so I left and went to the general store down the street where another aged, but much friendlier man told me where I could find Howard's house not too far away down a curvy dirt road that dropped and ended at the river.

Howard lived in a rundown clapboard house that had been built on stilts to protect it from the White River's winter floodwaters. The shack was covered with a rusty tin roof that creaked with every breeze. Inky smoke wafted from a stovepipe chimney. Junked car parts and sooty tin cans from an overturned fifty-five-gallon barrel of partly burned trash were strewn over the yard. A large assortment of thread bare clothes was drying on a clothesline.

Small wooden boats of various descriptions were scattered all over. Some were upturned and on the ground. Others were on saw-horses in different stages of construction. And there was a tinned-roofed dock with a planked walkway holding even more. If boats were a sign of prosperity on the river, I reasoned the Stokes were wealthy indeed – at least by river standards.

A dilapidated Model A Ford truck parked under a great red oak had its hood removed. A stripped engine block was hanging by a chain from a limb above it.

A redolence of burnt rubber and the rich-sour odor of the river tainted the air. After I'd surveyed Howard's estate, I noticed a boy on the porch staring blankly down on me. I held up my hand to him. "Is Mr. Stokes here?" I called. He immediately slunk back into the house.

In moments a worn and gaunt lady appeared at the door and began glaring down on me. The red-haired urchin was clinging to her worn and faded calico dress. Shreds of graying hair had slipped from under her frayed and faded blue flowery bonnet. Her face was wrinkled, her eyes sad and tired. "Is Mr. Stokes here?" I said.

She dropped her stare as if her courage had failed. "Who's a wantin' to know?"

"I'm Henry Ball. I want to duck hunt with him. I wrote and told him I was coming. A man from Chicago gave me his name."

"He ain't here. Who was that man from Chicargo?"

I gave her the man's name. She must have remembered him because she seemed satisfied. "You can wait here on him if'n you want to, Mr. Henry. He's gone down the river a checkin' his nets. Be back near dark I reckon."

She went back inside and slammed the door. I took a seat on an overturned wash tub under the red oak. I'd been sitting there several minutes thinking I'd made a mistake coming to Arkansas when I realized the boy was standing next to me. It was as if he'd been placed there transcendentally. "What's your name?" I said.

Like his mother, he dropped his gaze and then half spun back and forth with his hands balled and buried in his pockets and wouldn't answer. "My name's Henry. You a duck hunter?"

With that life came to his face. His eyes became dancing emeralds. "Why hell, yeah, I kill 'em with my flip." He jerked his hand out of his pocket and pointed across the river. "There's some of them sumbitches. I hate 'em."

I had to look for some time before seeing the dots over the distant timber that eventually turned into a formation of ducks. "Why do you hate them?"

"Cause I just do, that's why. I'd like to kill every one of 'em thar is. And when I get big enough, I'm a goin' to. Come on and I'll show ya."

He started off at a fast gait and I followed him through the woods down along the river. His stamina amazed me. He was barefooted but moved so fast over the rough ground I felt I was following some undiscovered simian. I had to run at times to keep up.

We traveled for twenty minutes or so before the boy slowed and went into a stealthy creep. Not far ahead, beavers had dammed a creek and it'd backed out into the woods. I could hear a great deal of splashing and squealing not far ahead. The boy pulled out a slingshot from his overall pocket made from a forked ash limb and strips of inner tube. He put a steel bearing in the leather pouch, and we slipped on.

Ducks were all in the backwater and grazing on the banks. There were rows of piled leaves where they'd scratched for acorns. We crept close before the birds realized us and took wing in a great roar. The boy stretched the rubber as far as he could and let the bearing fly into the thickest part of the mass. I heard a whack and a brilliantly colored drake woodduck came tumbling and flapping down broken winged and landed with a big splash and a loud wallop. The boy ran into the backwater and caught the duck by the neck and held it up proudly. "I got me this bastard," he said. There was a crack as he bit down on the duck's skull and then it began flapping madly in its throes of death.

"That's really something. You always kill one?"

"Most of the time. Come on."

On the way back along the river, he'd stop and listen whenever he heard an outboard motor. After several had passed, one came by that caused him to turn. "That'd be Pappy. Guess we'll have catfish or buffalo ribs tonight if he had good luck," he said, and then broke into a run.

When we got to the house, a slender man dressed in blue coveralls was moving methodically about on the dock unloading and stacking wash tubs from a wooden jon boat. The boy ran onto the dock, and after looking in the tubs he started jumping up and down and waving his arms. "Goddamn, Pappy, you tore their asses out of frame!"

"Reckon I did. Who's that yonder?" he said, nodding my way.

"Some man a wantin' to duck hunt. I done took him, though."

"Awe hell. Kill any?"

"One old drake squealer."

"You're a goin' to get your little ass in trouble killin' duck out of season."

"Hell no I ain't."

"Now go dress it and give it to the old lady. Then come on back and help me with these fish when you get done."

After the man finished unloading the tubs, he came from the dock and offered his hand. "Hired Stokes. Ain't time to hunt ducks just yet."

His snuff and whiskey breath was like a buzzard's and brought me near to retching. I watched in mild shock as he disappeared inside the shack, and like his wife, he slammed the door as if to let me know I wasn't welcomed.

I waited outside thinking that maybe the smart thing would be to get in my truck and start driving back to Montana. I was hungry and road weary, though, and decided to wait. After ten minutes Howard came out carrying several knives.

"So, you was the man sent them letters. Got my sister to read em to me. I can't read nor write, so I couldn't answer you. She was a goin' to but guess never got around to it. You come a little early."

"Duck season was open in Montana, so I figured it was here."

"Well it ain't, and I got about a hundert and fifty pound of fish to clean that won't wait. You can help if you want to, or you can head on out. Take your pick."

He waited for my reply staring back hard, head tilted and squinty eyed, snuff drooling down to his chin. "I'll be glad to help."

Like we were about to start a great celebration, he said, "Come on, then," and we went on to the dock.

He threw a catfish on a heavily, blade-scared wood table and made knife strokes under its gills, then caught the severed skin with a set of pliers and gave a pull. The skin peeled off like a silk stocking. After he severed its head with a cleaver, he gutted and then tossed it into an empty tub.

I felt I'd witnessed a fantastic trick by a magician and stood in awe with my jaw dropped. "It didn't take you a minute to clean that fish."

"Clean enough of the stinkin' bastards and you'll be able to. Now separate them cats from them buffalo. Throw them cats up here first and keep 'em a comin'."

I was so preoccupied cleaning the fish I didn't notice the sun had gone down until a damp chill rose from the river and my wet hands became numb and almost useless. The cold didn't seem to bother Howard, though. The boy had long since come back to help with the fish. He was just as deft as the old man with a knife. His name was Seeb and he cussed every other word, and Howard didn't seem to care. His bare feet had turned blue, but he didn't seem to notice.

We butchered fish till well after dark under lantern light. I was in my truck ready to leave when Howard came up and tapped on my window. "Old lady's fryin' up fish, hush puppies, and taters. You're welcome to supper. Town's a long drive and ain't nothin' goin' to be open this late."

"I don't want to impose on you."

He gave me a curious stare. "Now what in hell does that mean?"

"I don't want to be a bother to you or be in your way."

"If you was a goin' to be in the way I wouldn't of asked ya. Now get your ass out and come on. I'm hawngry."

Howard's wife Myrtle didn't speak the entire time she cooked, or during dinner. As night had come on the children had wandered in and waited at the table for her to serve their food. The girls had been visiting neighbors, the boys trapping and hunting. There were eleven children, and all were sullen and quiet except for Seeb, who chattered incessantly when he wasn't gobbling down food. Howard was full of questions, though. It was hard with Seeb's blabbering, but I told him about parts of the war, some about my divorce, and how I'd come to be in Boones Bluff.

"Damn boy you had a rough time here lately. So, you come all the way down here from Montany alone just to kill a duck in the woods?"

"A man that hunts with you told me about it. It sounded like something I had to do."

"Like likker, if it gets in your blood, the want for it never leaves. You know, there's got to be somethin' wrong with a feller that will go to all the trouble and misery he will to kill a duck. It's a sickness. I'm a thinkin' you're one of them kind of fellers. Kinda like me, ain't cha?"

"I guess I am."

He stared at me as he pondered, as if he were sizing me up. "I got a lot of work to do between now and duck season. If you don't mind sleepin' in the shed with my boys, you're welcome to stay and help. I'll learn you all I can about killin' ducks when time comes. It'll be several more weeks 'fore the season opens yet."

"I don't mind work. I'll give it a try if you can put up with me."

He grinned his toothless grin. "Come on then." He put his arm around my shoulder and gave me a slight hug as we went out, as if I might be salvation for him.

He led me to a one room shack that was out of sight behind the house. It was on stilts and contained six cots, a small table and a few chairs made of unfinished boards. The mattresses were homemade and constructed of mainly cloth flour and sugar sacks, but also of various other pieces of quilted material stuffed with duck down and feathers. I moved my things into the shack that night.

The following weeks I helped Howard with his fishing and moonshine business. Most days we gathered catfish and drum from hoop nets we set in various backwaters along the river and others were spent running off whiskey. At night we cleaned the fish to sell to a commercial vendor in DeWitt. Some nights late Howard would leave alone with quart jars of moonshine in wooden crates hidden under a canvas tarp in the back of his truck. Next day he made sure I saw the green bills he flashed in and out of his shirt pockets. But as the days slipped by, we spent less time fishing and liquor making and more clearing shooting holes in the timber and brushing duck blinds on the oxbow lakes. The shooting holes weren't cut because of convenience like I at first thought, but because of topography and the surrounding plants and trees that produced mast that mallards liked, as Howard explained. Among all the other things Howard taught me was how to trap beaver, muskrat, coon and otter. As we constantly rambled through the bottoms, I came to know intimately all the land thereabouts he considered his domain.

That Howard had taken me in like I was family and spent so much of his patience and time in educating me in the ways of the bottoms was mystifying to me, much like James Mason had done with me on the ranch. Howard seemed as perplexed as I was when I asked him why he had, and he pondered for some time before giving an answer.

"There's something about you makes me feel you're some kind of kin. Don't know exactly what it is. I couldn't turn you away. Makes me satisfied learnin' you all this. Hope it comes in handy for you someday."

One morning Seeb went to the bottoms with us to hunt squirrels with his flip while Howard and I brushed a blind. I kept thinking of Seeb and why he wasn't in school as a child his age should be. Curiosity finally got the best of me and I asked Howard why. He stopped working and looked at me as if a great pain had come over him.

"Why, we sent the little fucker a few year ago when he turned six, but they couldn't do nothin' with him. Hell, he can't keep his yap shut and cussed the teacher anytime she told him to do or not to do somethin'. The principal whupped the shit out of him, but it didn't do no good. Made him worse, I think. That boy ain't like regular people. He's got too much throwback in him. Hell, just look at him. He don't favor none of my other kids. He looks like them idjits on Myrtle's side of the family. They're more animal than man. God knows what we'll do with that boy. But ain't nobody goin' to learn him nothin', so we don't try to send him to school no more, and the school folk shore as hell don't care."

"Would you mind if I tried to school him some? He minds me pretty well. Maybe I could get him interested in reading and writing."

He raised his hands into the air. "Have at it, and good luck, by goodness."

The only book I could find in Howard's house was a soiled and ragged Bible, so I went to the Dewitt library and found a Jack London book of goldrush short stories and a beginner's reading and writing book. The boys listened intently as I read them tales of the frozen North by lanternlight in the shack at night. Accounts of man-killing wolves, of faithful huskies and brutal men, of death in a harsh world. Seeb was so mesmerized that he rarely interrupted. For a while, I tried getting his attention long enough to teach him to write his name, but I soon gave up in frustration and hoped that maybe when he got older, I could help him.

We quit fishing when the catch slowed because of the cold, then we trapped, but mostly we readied for duck season. Except for flour, lard, and a few other staples, the Stokes subsisted mainly from the river and the land along it. Adjusting to a diet of mostly wild game was hard and soon I was boring holes in my belt and the welcomed weight I'd managed to put on from James Mason's cooking soon melted away.

One morning Howard and I were checking his trapline. Along the way he would occasionally stop and tilt his head to listen and then go back to what he was doing. At one point he asked, "Do you hear that hammerin'?"

I concentrated and could make out faint tapping of what sounded like somebody nailing boards together. "I hear it now, but it's a long way off. What is it?"

"I'd say some son of a bitch buildin' a blind in my woods."

Howard seemed to know exactly where the hammering was coming from and thirty minutes later, we came on an opening in the woods where two men were building a duck blind. Howard watched them for a while and then told me to keep my gun ready. "If one of em goes for his'n, you blast his ass."

Howard then went towards them with his shotgun at the ready. "What you two motherfuckers think you're a doin'?" He motioned with his gun barrel. "Now get in front of that blind so I can keep an eye on the two of you."

The men were surprised at first, and then the look of fear came over them. One – big, bearded and heavy – started glancing around. When he spotted his gun propped against a tree well out of reach, he seemed disappointed. "Put that gun down now, Hired. You don't want to kill us," the other said.

"I'm a goin' to blow your ugly faces off if you don't get out of my woods. You bastards know better'n comin' in on me. Now get to movin'."

"What about our tools and guns? Ain't you a goin' to let us take em with us?"

"Next time I go to the mercantile I'll leave em thar. Now get to goin'."

The big man that had located his gun started drifting towards it. Howard shot towards his feet and the man started howling and hopping in the other direction. I put my gun to my shoulder just in case. The man cussed and hobbled around a few minutes and then both started away. The one limping fell several times though the other had his arm around his waist trying to help him.

Howard first broke the stocks off their guns against a tree. Then he started a fire and burned their tools and the remaining lumber inside the partially built blind.

"That'll teach them bastards not to come in on me again. There won't be no talk next time."

"I didn't know you owned this property."

"I don't. Black Kettle Timber Company does, but I got squatter's rights to it."

"What's squatter's rights?"

"I took over these woods before anybody else was around. I been huntin' and fishin' here since before me and Myrtle got hitched. These ain't the first interlopers I've run off from here. And there were a few didn't want to run, and shore damn regretted it. Long as I keep the bastards away, I just as well owns it. Black Kettle don't want no fires, so they don't say nothin'. And the law don't never come snoopin' around down here. Long as I keep trespassers out this as well as belongs to me."

"Aren't you afraid they'll come back and bushwhack you when you're alone?"

He smiled. "Not hardly. I got brothers just as mean as me and the people hereabouts knows if they do anything to me, they'll have to deal with them, and they don't want that. Like these two idiots, they have to come in here and test me from time to time. Don't ever think it's always peaceful down here in the bottoms, boy, because it ain't."

When duck season opened the river hadn't flooded out in the bottoms, so we hunted oxbow lakes. We killed ducks, but it wasn't what I'd come to Arkansas for. I wanted to hunt mallards in the flooded timber. The oxbows weren't that much different than hunting on the Missouri back in Montana and I was disappointed. And the ducks we killed were woodducks, widgeon and gadwall, some teal, an occasional pintail, but mallards were rare. It didn't matter that only 'scrap ducks', as Howard called any duck that wasn't a mallard, were around since his paying customers weren't coming till later in the season anyway. We shot our limits and more of scrap ducks most every day, and for a reason.

During hard times, the Stokes main subsistence was duck and they had long since tired of eating them, so we salted, barreled and sold most of what we killed to an illegal game market. Howard made the deliveries alone late in the night and I never knew to who or where and I never asked.

Early in that Thanksgiving week the wind started to build out of the south. We'd been in a blind on an oxbow since before daylight and had nothing to show for the four hours of boredom. What few ducks we'd seen flared at the pleadings of our calls. Despite our glum luck, I noticed Howard seemed peculiarly happy. "Think they're going to fly late in the morning?" I said.

"Why hell no. They ain't a goin' to fly at all. It's too damn hot."

"Then what are you smiling so about?"

"Damn boy, big rains a comin' and the bottoms going to flood. First cold of the fall will be right behind it. What you been a waitin' fer will happen. Timber'll flood and mallards'll pour in."

"How do you know all that?"

"From years of livin' it. Feel that hard, wet south wind? A bi-gun's a comin' from the Gulf. Longer it blows the more it'll rain."

Howard was right about the storm. It blew hard out of the south for three more days and then it poured for almost three. We had to let the dock lines out every six or eight hours because the river rose so fast. Now I appreciated how Howard had set the dock in the shelter of the cove it was anchored in. There was little current there and the endless drift coming down stayed out in the main flow of the river and washed by without wrecking it.

The morning came clear and cool after the rain stopped. The river was choked with drift that'd been collecting on the banks with the falling water since early spring. Huge trees that had eroded and lost their footings were racing downriver in the roiling current, as well as the countless dead logs that had accumulated from years gone by.

But in the timber, it was a different world that seemed enchanted. Unlike the roil and turbulence of the river on the outside, except for faint concentric flow rings coming from the bases of the trees, there was no other perception of current. The rain and wind had cleared the canopy and the sun streamed through the bare branches in brilliant shafts causing wavering reflections of trees on the surface. The water wasn't stained red like the river with mud, but instead had a character of weak chocolate milk, a pleasing color of water I'd never seen. Being in the enclosed wall of timber and water created a sense of security and serenity I'd never felt. The rest of the world with all its misery and injustices was shut out and ceased to exist. It was a peacefulness I realized I needed and never wanted to lose.

As we motored slowly along through the great forest of oaks, pecan, Cyprus, ash, gum, dogwood and poplar, bunches of mallards flushed ahead quacking in pandemonium. Howard was like a kid pointing and laughing at the steady high V formations flowing south. What he lived for had arrived during the night on a wave of cold Jetstream air, and I soon came to appreciate why. Like Howard had said, to some, hunting ducks was a sickness, and shooting mallards in the timber came to possess me more than whiskey ever had.

The first paying hunters showed up a few days after the flood and the arrival of the mallards. My job was to call, retrieve the dead birds and run down the cripples using a small, narrow boat we paddled that Howard had designed to navigate quickly through the timber. We stayed in the bottoms from daylight till the hunters were so tired and hungry they wanted to quit, or they ran out of shells. Some days we killed so many ducks we couldn't carry them all out, so we cut their heads off to take back so the hunters could prove how well they'd done. The next day the piled-decapitated carcasses would be gone. I never asked Howard who would have taken them, and he never said. I figured he most likely tipped-off the illegal game market for a nice commission.

Just after Christmas the man Mason and I had met in the Kozey Restaurant the past September showed up with a group of hunters. After a few days, I recognized and approached him. "Do you remember me?" I said, after taking my hat off.

He studied me and shook his head. "I do not."

"We met in a restaurant in West Yellowstone late last summer. You told me about the duck hunting down here and gave me Howard's name."

After he thought, his eyes lit up. "Well I'll be damned. I do remember you now. How in the hell did you wind up here?"

"I came down in October and helped Howard get set up for the hunting season, and I'm still here. He gets more hunters every year and with his boys in school he only has their help on the weekends and holidays, and he needed me, and so I stayed."

"You fit right in here. Except for your accent, we thought you were part of the family."

"The Stokes are family to me. They treat me like a son and a brother. I'd be happy staying here forever, but I'm obligated to start a job back in West Yellowstone this summer guiding for a new fly shop."

"You going to be able to make a living at it? Doesn't sound very lucrative."

"All I know is I wouldn't be satisfied doing anything else otherwise. The money isn't important anyway."

"Well good luck to you. If I had the courage and wasn't tied down with a family and a job I've invested my life in, I might do the same thing."

Courage for what? For doing what you're driven to do? But I didn't say it.

Seeb ran away and didn't tell me goodbye the day I left Arkansas even after assuring him I'd be back in the fall before the mallards came back. All the Stokes, especially Howard, tried to get me to stay, but I felt an urgency to leave even as much as I loved the Stokes and the river bottoms. Anyway, the mallards had been gone for weeks on their migration north and I was impelled to go, too. I left Arkansas and the Stokes in early March and headed back to the Little Prickly Pear Ranch.

CHAPTER 13

James Mason came out of the barn as I was driving up his drive-way. There was a lively spring in his gait as he hurried towards my truck. "Well, you made it back without getting your throat cut after all, but you look half starved. Didn't they feed you down there?" he said, while shaking my hand.

"A steady diet of fish or squirrel or possum or whatever else we got for the pot. Looks like you've been eating good, though."

"I have and intend always to. I cooked a beef roast for dinner tonight. That okay with you?"

"If only you knew how good that sounds, Boss."

"So, how'd it go? Was it what you thought it was going to be?"

"Everything and more, especially the timber hunting. There's a freedom, serenity and security I feel there like no other place I've been. If it wasn't for my promise to the Macstatts, I might never have come back."

"I guess that means me and the ranch don't matter anymore."

"You know that's not true. I didn't mean it literally. I was just trying to say I loved it and I'm going back next fall."

"I was hoping you'd changed your mind and had decided to work here full time. Donnas has made a total change since you've been gone. He found a woman he's going to marry that's converted him to religion. He claims he got the calling to preach and has taken it up part time. Soon he'll have his own church and won't need his job here." His sinister little smirk came. "You know I've thought about it a lot and decided that that last ass whipping you gave him was what really showed him the light."

"I can stay and work till late May or early June, then I've got to go to West Yellowstone. You're making me feel guilty, like I'm deserting you after all you've done for me."

"I didn't help you get over your problems just so I could bribe you now. I did it because I knew there was some good in you. I won't bother you again about it, but if you ever change your mind there's always a place to live and a job for you here."

"And if you ever really need me, I'll be here. It's just that I've got a calling, too, as strong to me as Donnas' is to him."

The letter from Emma Macstatts came in late May saying it was time for me to start my employment as a fly shop clerk and trout fishing guide. I broke the news to Mason the next day. "That letter I got from the Macstatts says they need me, so I'll be pulling out at first light in the morning."

Though the Little Prickly Pear Ranch was only a matter of hours away from West Yellowstone, I felt bad about leaving James Mason. He'd as much as saved my life, and because of him I'd found peace and purpose again. The only thing that could make me happier would be Ginny taking me back, but now I understood I had no control over that, but I did my life and that's what I had to concentrate on now. I'd never give up hope of having her back again someday though.

Ethan and Emma Macstatts had leased a building on the main drag of West Yellowstone and had placed a large carved and painted wooden sign out front that read 'Yellowstone Fly Shop'. Underneath in smaller letters, 'Hand Tied Flies and Fine Fly Tackle'. Emma was inside with a brush in her hand and a face speckled with paint.

"Henry! Thank goodness you're here." She discarded the brush and came and hugged me like I was her kidnapped child just returned.

"I came as soon as I got your letter."

"Ethan still has a few days left on his work notice for Chief Stanfield and I've had to do all the stocking and pricing and most everything else by myself."

"Well, I'm here now. What do you want me to do?"

"First go out back and see the guide boat Ethan got for you. It just came in."

I was expecting a raft like the one James Mason and I had fished out of the summer before, but under a shed on a trailer instead was a ridiculous looking high sided wooden boat that was pointed on both ends and bent upward from the middle. It had big brass row locks and a long set of heavy oars lashed down its center. There were seats on each end and one in the middle where the rowlocks were. It looked so comical I thought Emma was playing a joke. I went back and asked her what the hell the outlandish looking thing was.

"It's a Mackenzie drift boat, Henry. They use them on the big west coast rivers. It isn't as hard to row or maneuver as a raft and there's more room, and everything inside doesn't get wet going through whitewater. You need to take it out and get used to rowing it before the fishermen start showing up."

I drove to Ennis and had a trailer hitch welded on my truck and started taking the boat to Hebgen Lake to get the feel of the oars. The long sweeps felt strange and I was clumsy at first, but over time I got coordinated with the nine-foot oars and began to feel comfortable rowing the ungainly craft. Eventually I became confident enough to put the driftboat in the Madison.

The first trips down the pacing river were demolition derbies between me and the boulders that resulted in bone rattling collisions that knocked chunks out of the chines, but eventually I got to the point where I felt I could get clients down the river without killing them. Just after July Fourth fisherman started showing up and a few, out of curiosity I'm sure, booked me to guide them. The numbers and size of the fish they caught over the miles of productive water we covered in a day in the dory was amazing. The stories of the new fly shop and its unique guide service quickly got out and circulated in the fishing community and soon we were turning down guide trips because the demand was so great.

I wanted to be – had to be – on the water every day, but there were times that rowing for hours for days on end put me into bad temperament and made me irascible and I became so tired I struggled getting in and out of the boat. Often the high-altitude winds were terrible and frustrating and made it impossible to control the dory and for the anglers to cast. But no matter what hardships and calamities the clientele or weather presented I loved being on the water. The many days I spent on the streams in that paradisiacal and seemingly enchanted setting were all wonderful, just as the White River bottoms were. I became driven and content with life moving back and forth with the seasons being part of nature's scheme. Summering in Yellowstone and then migrating South with the waterfowl in the fall. And even though Ginny's distance in our reuniting again grew ever further over time, I never lost hope we'd someday be together again. My resolve, like my love for her, that we would was total and eternal.

BOOK II

Chapter 14

Sugar Loaf Key, Florida, 8 June 1990

Doc Holmes and I had left my dock on Sugar Loaf Key at 6:00 a.m. With only a slight southerly breeze, it'd been smooth running through the pale light of the coming dawn out to the edge of the Gulf. Just some minor chop and the occasional wake from a cruiser going out to the deep blue to bounce and rattle the Maverick. As always when Doc and I fished, I'd been on the push pole all morning. Doc had fished hard and had a couple of shots at bonefish, but his casts had either been too short and ignored or had landed too close and created explosions of silver wakes that zigzagged in pandemonium to the deeper water off the flats. At low tide at noon, we'd quit fishing and lunched on cold, grilled mangrove snapper and cantaloupe in the shade of a mangrove island. Afterward, we'd napped till the late afternoon tide change. Doc had long lost interest in fishing, but not his determination to persuade me to have a physical. He'd started haranguing me as soon as we left the dock and hadn't let up, and as I poled across the flat in the afternoon sun, I almost regretted taking him along on this rare day I was off from guiding. But at times he could provide interesting conversation to break the monotony when the fishing was slow. The greatest benefit of having to deal with him, though, was that his wife always made a wonderful lunch for us, like the one today. I believe it was her way of paying me for befriending her husband, who was a great physician, but near helpless at anything else.

I drove the push pole into the marl and staked the boat near the edge of a channel where permit would likely be coming onto the flat to feed with the oncoming tide. As soon as I stepped off the poling platform he started again, like a scratched phonograph record playing over and over. "You're getting older, Henry, even though you won't admit it. And stop pretending you don't hear me."

I'd moved from the stern up to the casting deck and was mending a leader. "For the hundredth time I hear you. And for the hundredth time, why should I get a physical? So you can tell me I'm going to die."

"That's a ludicrous answer. It may save your life."

"You're never going to cut on me and I'm sure as hell not ever going through chemo. I'd rather die than suffer through that nightmare."

"You say that now, but if you were faced with it, you'd change your mind. I've seen it too many times."

I tried a hateful glare to rile him even more, but his eyes were already wide as dinner plates and magnified even more by the heavy refracting lenses of his black rimmed glasses. He was such a comical sight I couldn't help but laugh, which angered him even more. "Want to bet?"

"Damn it no, not with a jackass like you. You have everything anyone could want, but you're too dumb to realize it. I'll say it again, you don't deserve what you have, and that's especially true of Hope. How she tolerates you, I'll never understand. Just forget it. Catch one of those god-forsaken fish and satisfy your insatiable ego so we can go home. It just seems that getting a physical isn't asking that much. The only reason I care is for Hope's peace of mind. You could at least do that for her."

I stood and turned to face him. "Why didn't you tell me to begin with it was Hope's idea? It would have saved hours of me having to listen to your bitching and whining. Just set up an appointment and I'll be there. Now shut the fuck up and leave me alone so I can fish in peace for a while."

The brown and green seaweed swayed and undulated like ripe grain stalks in a gentle breeze with the rush of the tide filling the channel. Small sharks and colorful fish began to spill onto the swelling flat. Then I spotted a huge barracuda coming up the cut with four large shadows gliding behind it. This was the opportunity I'd been hoping for. "Here they come, Doc. Be ready now."

I stripped line off the reel, and as the school of permit came out of the channel onto the flat into casting range, I made two false casts and then double hauled. The first two fish cruised by the fake crab as it sank and ignored it, but the third one dashed to it for a look, but then it went on as well. The fly was buried in the grass as the last one came by, so I picked up and cast again. The timorous fish didn't like the impact of the lead-heavy fly so close, and my blood started to boil as I watched the spooked pod of trophies streak away.

"Damn it to hell. A perfect shot and I messed it up."

Though I was livid for ruining the perfect chance, the scene amused Doc. He giggled and spoke as if he were talking to a child. "Now, now, calm down, sport, another one will be by soon."

I shot him an angry look, but then I smiled at his rare stab at humor. "If we don't run out of light first."

Doc was right. Thirty minutes later a shadow I thought at first to be a stingray because of its size started up the channel, but it was moving too fast for a ray. Then my adrenalin rushed as its huge black eye and sickle tail came into focus. As it came out of the cut and onto the flat it slowed and started to feed. Its splayed black tail glistened in the low hanging sun as it nosed through the turtle grass. "Good god, Doc, look at the size of that one!"

I got the line going and managed to drop the fly on its head. At first the fish acted spooked and swam in tight, blinding circles around the sinking fly, but then it turned and took. The rod bowed and the reel shrieked as line and then backing began pouring off the spool. I looked back at Doc. He was apparently paralyzed with emotion at the spectacle. "Get after him, Doc! Stop messing around."

In seconds, the permit shot off the flat back into the channel and headed for deep water. First, Doc struggled with the mooring line, and then after some banging and cussing, got the push pole in the holder. After he fumbled with the controls, the Yamaha roared to life and he ultimately managed to get the boat into deep water just before the reel spool emptied.

A half-hour later the fish hadn't shown any sign of tiring. It'd held deep and gained line at will. My forearms burned and my hands cramped from fatigue even though I was switching hands with the rod every so often for relief. Doc had been quiet for some time now and when I looked back, he was gauging the position of the sun. He hadn't spoken since I'd hooked the fish and I knew landing it meant nothing to him now but getting on the way home before dark was everything.

Then, as the huge golden globe neared the horizon, I heard, "Think we'll have time to get back to the mainland before dark, Henry?"

"Who cares? Stay after the fish."

"I don't want to get killed out here over a damn fish."

"You're whining again. Where else would be a better place to die. Your stinking hospital?"

I'd been after a permit like this one for years. It would easily go over forty pounds. To hook one of any size on a fly is a hard, next to an impossible feat. To catch one this big would be a catch of a lifetime, and I wasn't about to give up on landing it for any reason.

After another twenty minutes of relentless strain, the fish surfaced and rolled up on its side, but after resting a moment it righted itself and churned on. Ten minutes later it rolled up again, and this time except for its gills pumping, it lay still on the surface awaiting its fate. I eased it close enough to the boat to grip its tail, then pulled it alongside and removed the hook. After Doc snapped some photos, I revived it and we watched it swim away.

Now that it was over, instead of the exhilarating sensation of satisfaction I'd expected, I realized a tiredness I'd never felt before. My body began to tremble after I sat down behind the wheel. Turning the key and moving the shifter forward to start us toward home was an exertion.

There was nothing left of the day but a gold afterglow in the west broken by a bank of black storm clouds. The seabirds had already started their way inland, and then a pair of dolphins began running alongside us. I pointed them out. "Look, Doc, good luck."

I'd read in a novel that crewmen on whaling voyages thought dolphin brought good luck, and now I believed it since I'd just caught the permit of a lifetime, an accomplishment I'd pursued hard for a long time. Then I realized the deep tiredness again and figured it was just the aftermath of the adrenalin rush and the physical strain of catching the permit. Or possibly I had a virus coming on, or maybe Doc was right and I did need a visit to his office.

The phone started ringing again for the third time in the past five minutes, but when the answering machine came on the caller hung up again. I'd just finished a miserable day on the flats and wasn't in the mood for conversation. A fifteen-knot wind had risen at sunrise and I'd polled till my back ached looking for bonefish. Then when I'd found them, my client couldn't make the cast. Each time the old man attempted a shot, his line whipped back and coiled around him like an anemic boa constrictor. I hadn't been able to perform any miracles that day, and we'd gone fishless.

The ringing started again a few minutes later. Even though such insistence couldn't be bearing good news, I decided I'd better answer. I didn't mean to but shouted into the receiver. "What is it?"

There was a pause and then a welcomed voice. "How's it going, Dad?"

I hadn't heard from my daughter in months, maybe even a year. We had little to talk about when we did converse. It was a struggle for me to come up with enough small talk to keep the conversation going. How she, her boy and husband and Ginny were doing was about it. Her stepdad Donald had passed several years back. I'm sure it was an ordeal for her to think of anything to say as well, we not having anything else in common to talk about.

"Sara, it's always good to hear from you. I'm doing well. And you?"

"I'm fine but struggling with Mom right now. She's not doing well and I'm having to spend a lot of time with her."

"Oh lord, what's wrong?"

"You remember the colon cancer surgery a few years ago? Well, after the surgery and brutal treatments they thought she was going to be fine, but now it's back with a vengeance. She's helpless and I'm all she's got now. It's hard watching her waste away in all the suffering and misery."

"I'm terribly sorry to hear that. If I can do anything, please let me know." I tried hiding my emotion. My heart was racing, and I realized the receiver was rattling against my ear. A knot of dread had formed in my chest.

"There is something you can do. It's why I called. Matt's missing. He's in Montana and I need you to go look for him. I can't leave because of Mom, and Cal can't go because of his work. Besides, he doesn't know his way around out there. It would take him weeks to find him, if ever."

"But this is my busiest season. I have clients that have scheduled their vacations to fish with me. They've paid deposits and bought airfares. They're clientele I've spent years acquiring and are close friends. I can't just turn my back on them. It's just impossible for me to leave right now. I hope you understand."

"I've never asked anything of you. If there was any other way, I'd do it. I really need you now. Please help me."

I paused to consider what she'd said, and then she started again. "Can I depend on you for once in my life or not?"

"Where was he last time you heard from him?"

"Working at the Old Faithful Inn. You ought to know where that is."

"How long since you heard from him?"

"Over two weeks. He got fired from his summer job for some reason and left. Nobody out there I've talked to knows where he is, or they won't say if they do. Please go find him and bring him home. I can't handle the stress of not knowing where he is and Mom dying at the same time. I swear I'll never bother you again if you'll just do this one thing for me."

"Why hasn't he contacted you then if he doesn't have a job? Why doesn't he come home?"

There was silence again for several long moments. "Because he doesn't want to come home. He made that clear the last time I talked to him over two weeks ago. He loves it out there."

Dread mounted as I thought of Ginny possibly dying plus having to leave during my busiest season to go look for a kid I'd never even seen before. Sara had sent photos of him now and then over the years, but it'd been a long time since I'd gotten one. All I could remember was a scrawny kid with bushy, blond hair. And there was Hope. She wasn't going to like me being gone for weeks looking for a kid I didn't even know. I tried to hide my reluctance. "Get all the information you can on where he might be and send a recent photo of him so I at least know what he looks like."

"Why, he looks just like you. Didn't you know that?"

"I guess not. So, what does he think about me?"

There was another pause. "He's never asked about you, and I've never had any discussion of you with him. He doesn't know or care that you exist as far as I know. I doubt he's ever even heard your name mentioned. So, if you do find him, it might be best if he doesn't know who you are, or he'll know why you came, and he'll likely run away. I don't know how, but you've got to figure out some way to convince him to come home with you."

I felt a pang of remorse that I didn't have any idea what my grandson looked like. I hadn't cared before now, but suddenly I was filled with regret for not knowing. Self-loathing washed through me. "Guess I can't blame you. I was ashamed of my father, too. Sometimes I wish I'd had a Donald like you did to raise me. I doubt I'd acknowledged my real father, either."

"I'm sorry things turned out like they did, but I had no control over any of it. All I have to go on is what Mom told me. Not much of it's good either. All I know is you deserted me when I was a baby for reasons I still don't understand. I've spent most of my life trying to forgive you, but it isn't easy. Maybe someday we'll get to spend time together and you can tell me why you left, and then possibly we can work it out. In the meantime, I want my son back. Please go find him for me."

I let what she said soak in. It hurt, and it wasn't her fault. I should have tried harder to spend time with her over the years, but I was always gone chasing the saber-toothed cats and woolly mammoths of my selfish life halfway across the country. Maybe bringing her son home would make up for a little of the damage I'd done to our relationship. At least it would make me feel better about myself by easing some of the guilt.

"When I get him home and things are back to normal, maybe you could visit me. I'm not quite the self-centered, selfish derelict I was in my younger days. I'm settled here in the Keys now and that's where I plan to stay the rest of my life. I'd love for you and Cal to come down and visit with me and Hope. There's plenty of room."

"I don't know, Dad. I'll think about it while you're gone."

There was a click and I stared at the buzzing receiver. As the shock eased, I wondered how I'd been talked into it so easily. His father should be going after him, but as Sara had kindly said, her husband was near helpless outside his office. Worse than my life and Hope's being disrupted, my clients would have to cancel their trips to the Keys to fish with me. There would be financial losses of cancelled plane tickets unless they could reschedule with other guides. I'd call Timmy Carter that guided and ran the Sugar Loaf Marina and explain I had to leave for a while because of an emergency and get him to take all my clients he could. And I'd call some of the other guides as well. All that could wait, though. First, I had to figure how to break the news to Hope, and then how to accept the fact that I had to leave, and leave soon, to go find my grandson who was hiding someplace in Montana and hopefully was still alive.

When Hope came home from the clinic later that evening, as I expected, she wasn't happy when I told her I was leaving to go look for a boy I'd never seen before and that was almost three thousand miles away. It was hard to argue with her being that I knew she was right that he wasn't my responsibility. But I felt I did owe my daughter the favor. And there was no one else to go find him and bring him home.

"Hope, I don't feel I have a choice. I don't want to go, but I feel like I have to."

"You do have a choice. Call back and say no. What about me. Am I not important?"

"Of course you are. You're everything to me and you know that, but you have to understand I've got to do this."

"I understand you're being selfish as always. You never listen to my side."

"I always listen to your side, but your side isn't always right. It's useless to argue. I'll run him down and come right back."

"I have a bad feeling about this, Henry. Only heartache and no good is going to come of it." She headed off towards our bedroom but stopped short of the door. "Don't forget your appointment in the morning with Doc Holmes to go over the test results from your physical."

"How could I? You've reminded me of it every day for almost a week."

"Won't you feel better knowing you're in good health?"

It wasn't for my peace of mind she'd forced me into the physical. She felt she was cursed and only wanted to protect me. Her first fiancée had been killed in Viet Nam his first day in country while on his way to check into his battalion. A lucky AK-47 round had gone through the copter's floor and out the top of his head. And after a short marriage three years later, her husband had been stabbed to death during a convenience store robbery trying to talk the crazed drug addict robbing the store down. Her father had died recently, and her mindless mother was residing in a nursing home. If anything happened to me, she'd be alone.

"Doc could tell me what he needs to over the phone. I've already wasted a day having the physical. He just wants to put me through a lot of aggravation. I hate that stinking office of his. After tomorrow I'm never going back there again."

"You sound like a little boy. It's just part of growing old, Henry."

"Yeah, and I'm not liking growing old a damned bit."

When I woke the next morning, the curtains were dancing and billowing from the early breeze. The cool air felt nice stirring through the bedroom. Hope was still sleeping. After we'd gone to bed the night before I'd promised and assured her that I'd be gone for only a few weeks and she'd apologized for being so heartless. She had tears in her eyes when she said I should go find Matt for everyone's sake. Good luck had followed me over the years, especially with friends and people who'd cared for me and taken me in and had made my nomadic life possible. But I didn't know how empty and hollow my life had been until I'd met her. She filled a void in my soul I hadn't realized was missing for a lot of years and had made my existence worthwhile and complete again, especially now that the compulsion had let me settle into a more normal life. My existence would be miserable without her.

Hope didn't have to work. Her father had been a successful developer and had left her a substantial trust. She worked because of her ethics and generosity, and she enjoyed her volunteer job of helping children cope with their physical birth defects as well. It's wonderful there are such special people that have the fortitude and magnitude to deal with such tragedy. I often wondered how she summoned the will to do it. For the children's sake her name fit well.

We'd met in a dive shop in Key West when she was on a snorkeling trip with some friends from her hometown in Massachusetts. I noticed her rummaging through masks and fins while I was looking for channel markers. Either her good looks or some blessed intervention coerced me into asking her if she needed help. Then after she smiled, and said, "Yes, please," I started a spectacular line of bullshit pretending to be an expert on diving, snorkeling and all the equipment involved, which was partially true because I often snorkeled for lobster and scallops. And then I invited her to go with me out in the Contents the next day. She was reluctant at first, but eventually acquiesced after some assurance from her friends that I most likely wasn't some pervert trying to get her alone out on the ocean. The trip went well and now we'd been together for over two years. I've never been able to understand what a beautiful and intelligent woman, fifteen years younger than me, could see in a less than prosperous, old and often grumpy bastard like myself. I'd always done everything in my power to see that she was happy, but now that I had a chance to at least partially vindicate myself for all my failures and shortcomings as a father to Sara, I was going to have to make her unhappy and leave her for a while. I rolled out of bed, slipped on my running gear and started my daily jog around Sugar Loaf Key.

By the time I'd finished my run, the trip to Montana and a runaway brat was least on my mind. My thought was focused on Doc Holmes' stinking office and what he had in store for me about the results of the tests he'd run. He'd called personally to tell me he wanted the meeting. I thought it strange he hadn't had his office lady call. I hoped it was courtesy because of our friendship and not because of something serious.

I sat in Holmes' waiting room for thirty minutes before my name was called. Then I had to wait another fifteen in an examination room staring at walls filled with medical posters of human anatomies. The bad side of me came gushing out when he showed up almost an hour late. "How come you made me wait, you inconsiderate asshole? Think your time is more valuable than mine? I lost two days' work fucking around with this nonsense."

"Come on, Henry. I had an emergency and it put me behind schedule."

"Oh dear, did your pharmaceutical stocks hit a skid? Lose a few bucks on the market? Don't worry, you'll make it up on all these old and unfortunate sick people you'll con here today."

"Henry, this meeting is really serious."

"You act like it's the end of the world, Doc. Am I going to die?"

"Cut the bull, this is bad I tell you."

Then he took some papers from his clipboard and handed them to me. I couldn't understand all the complicated medical jargon, so he explained it. Simply put I had a rare blood cancer and was on limited time unless a series of experimental chemo treatments performed a miracle.

The camper had belonged to Hope's father. We'd hauled it back from Massachusetts after his funeral. It was a slide on model Hope thought we might use to explore the Keys in, but it'd sat in the backyard unmoved now for over a year.

I checked the waterlines and had to do some minor plumbing repairs to the head. The inside smelled sour and stale from mildew and mold, but otherwise it was worthy of my upcoming trip. By taking it, I could save money on motels and move about where and when I needed to after I got to Montana. Also, I had a storage compartment full of books, fishing gear, fly tying equipment and materials and a few old and needless shotguns I wanted to get rid of. I was going to leave it all with Ethan Macstatts to sell or give away. I had no use for any of it anymore and should have left it with the Macstatts with my drift boat two years before when I'd left Montana for what I thought at that time was for good. The only things I didn't take that I never used anymore were the guns and rods Jacob had left me.

While I was loading all the junk I was taking to Ethan, I noticed Hope watching intently. "What are you giving me the evil eye like that for?" I said.

"Are you planning to start over out there with all that stuff you're taking with you?"

"It's not stuff. It's my lifetime collection of fishing equipment that's mostly outdated and practically useless now. It may have some value to a collector, especially the books, and I'm giving it to Ethan to sell. He can give the money to a conservation fund or something. Why're you making such a big deal of it?"

"Suppose you get out there and your silly compulsion takes you over and you fall in love with Montana all over again?"

"For the hundredth time I'm coming right back. If only you could understand how much I love you and despise having to leave you to do this. Again, please try to understand it's a small way I can do something for my daughter after ignoring her all my life. Now stop crying and kiss me goodbye and let's get this over with as soon as we can."

CHAPTER 15

I spent a chunk of money I shouldn't have on a case of 18-year-old scotch. James Mason always said it was the best, so I figured it had to be good. Only thing, he could afford it and I couldn't, but I bought it anyway. I also purchased several boxes of high-end cigars at the Marathon liquor store. It'd been years since I'd smoked or drank, but now it didn't seem to matter after Doc's revelation. I often missed having a drink and a smoke and decided I'd enjoy my old vises again while on this trip. Enjoy living a little again before I died. I hadn't told Hope about my condition and made Doc swear he wouldn't either. That could wait until I got back. After I explained the call from Sara and the errand I had to make, Doc raised hell and demanded that I cancel going to Montana and start treatments immediately, but I declined. I didn't think a few weeks would make much difference. I wasn't sure whether I was going to go through the hell of the chemo anyway. Seemed every case I'd heard of when experimental treatment was used it never worked. Just a lot of torture and suffering for a few months of prolonging the inevitable while your loved ones went through an unnecessary hell as well. It didn't seem like a good swap off to me. But I'd have a lot of time behind the wheel to think about all that over the next few weeks.

I drove straight through to Montana, stopping only for gas and short naps in rest areas along the way. I didn't bathe or shave the entire trip and brushed my teeth with bottled water and ate out of drive through windows. My reasoning for constant driving is that for every minute you're stopped, two are wasted. Over the next three days the sordid memories returned of the miles I'd traveled on the two lanes, four lanes, dirt backroads and Interstates over all the many years of my past. The torturous and monotonous hours behind the wheel of constantly dodging and being delayed by the eighteen wheelers along the way with their noise and pollution and their unqualified and bullying drivers made me despise them even more.

I listened to the Eagles, Dan Fogelberg and Jackson Browne on the tape deck. Once during the night when adrenaline was keeping me going and had my imagination running wild, Fogelberg's "Last Nail" made me think of Ginny and a pain coursed through my chest. Then I began to wonder how I could have any feeling, except for hate and resentment, for a woman that had deserted me in my worst times like she did forty years before and had brought me so such misery that I'd come a trigger squeeze away from ending my life. How could I, especially now that Hope had come into my life? But I still loved her and would always want her to take me back. The way our relationship had ended, compounded with the mental devastation of the war must have created a psychosis was the only thing I could reason. A form of insanity I'd never recovered from.

I made the Old Faithful Inn in less than sixty hours, worn, dirty and unshaven – eyes bloodshot and swollen from sleep deprivation. The desk attendant studied me as if I'd come to beg for food, but instead I inquired if she knew Matthew Whitaker. She seemed to know him well. "You mean trout boy? Oh yeah, they fired him a few weeks ago. Never stopped fishing long enough to show up for work on time. Some days he didn't show up at all."

"Any idea where he might have gone?"

"No, but his girlfriend works in the restaurant. She might know."

"Think it'd be alright if I talked to her?"

"We just finished serving lunch and not too busy now. I'll see if she can come up."

The hostess soon returned with a raven-haired beauty with mesmerizing glowing obsidian eyes. Her dangling gold earrings glittered against her dark brown skin. She was obviously of Native American decent and proved to be as bold and short with her words as she was stunning. She turned her aquiline nose up slightly when she looked me over. I wasn't sure if it was because of disdain or my body odor. "I'm Sandy, Matt's friend. What do you want?" she demanded.

"I'm Henry. Forgive my looks. I've just driven straight through from south Florida. I'm looking for him. Know where he might be?"

"Why should I tell you?"

"His family's worried about him. They just want to know where he is and that he's okay."

"Are you a detective or something?"

I laughed. "Do I look like a cop? Of course not. I'm a friend of the family and since I was heading out here anyway, they asked if I'd look him up and make sure he's alright."

She studied me a long moment, then said, "Please don't let him know I told you. I promised him I wouldn't tell anybody where he was. He's a good guy and I like him a lot. But I'm afraid something bad is going to happen to him if he keeps going like he is. It seems that all he cares about is fishing and I'm afraid it's going to be his demise."

"Thanks, Sandy. I won't let him know you told me. I promise."

She was still reluctant to tell me where I could find Matt and stared into my eyes for a spell longer. I think she decided she'd rather put her faith in my word than finding later that something bad had happened to Matt that she could have prevented if she'd told me where he was.

"You'd better not be lying. He called from the Cabin Creek Restaurant a few days ago. Said he was camped there. He's got a little green tent and a sleeping bag. I know he's broke. He must be living off fish and berries down there."

"He likes fishing that much?"

"I wish he cared that much about me."

"He's a damn fool if he doesn't." I thanked her and headed on to West Yellowstone.

As I drove the slow, traffic-filled narrow winding road through the Park to the West entrance, memories of when I first came through the area flooded my mind, especially my insatiable passion for it and I figured that unfortunately the boy felt the same way. After what Sandy had said about his love for fly fishing, I knew there wasn't much doubt.

The main drag of West Yellowstone hadn't changed much in the few years I'd been away. It was the same old crowded streets and lagging traffic, neon signs in every window, smells of cheap food, and the myriad of gift shops selling mostly t shirts, and of course teddy bears. To me it'd always been nothing more than one big carnival.

I passed the Yellowstone Fly Shop as I came into town but didn't stop. I knew so late in the day Ethan and Emma most likely wouldn't be there because they always worked the morning shift. Anyway, I was too concerned about finding Matt than I was to pay a visit that could wait.

Before I went to buy food and supplies, I wanted to shower and shave so as not to look like a homeless transient and lit the water heater in the camper. Then I realized it would take some time for the water to warm, so I paid to shower in a wash-o-mat. When I'd finished, I felt much better with the three days of grit and grime scrubbed away and the beard stubble shaved off. A cold rain had started, and being acclimated to the South Florida heat, the chill persuaded me to rummage out a fleece jacket I hadn't donned since I'd left Montana. Then I went to buy groceries.

My knowledge about young people was vague to say the least, so I bought various foods I imagined a kid might like. All I knew about young people was that their dress was often bizarre and hairdos usually strange, but my recent association with teens had been in the Keys and maybe kids from other places were different. I hoped his hair wasn't pink and he didn't wear tight pants with sequins on the back pockets.

I headed north up Highway 287 towards Ennis down the Madison River towards Cabin Creek Campground. The pressing wind had Hebgen Lake frothing. At an Earthquake marker, I stopped and poured a drink. I tried recalling how long it'd been since I'd had one and couldn't remember, but the taste and feeling it brought were wonderful. I turned up the heat and started on.

At the Cabin Creek Cafe I asked a waitress if she'd seen a kid fitting Matt's description. She lit up and told me what I wanted to hear. "There's a boy like that uses the pay phone outside sometimes. Looks like one of those homeless people back home. Is that what he is?"

"Not really. His folks just asked me to check on him and make sure he's okay."

"Looks starved to me. Started to give him some food once, but I was afraid I'd get in trouble with my boss."

I was so elated over my good fortune in locating Matt so easily and quickly that I thanked her with a five-dollar bill and started driving around the campground looking for a small green tent. I stopped and asked various campers if they'd seen a young man fitting Matt's description camping there. An elderly gentleman from North Dakota in a small motor home helped me. The old man seemed reluctant to open the camper door to let the cold in, so he cracked it just enough to peek out while I stood in the rain holding my hat on. Once he did squeeze his hand through the door to point. "See that caved in tent over yonder? The wind got it a while ago. He's stayin' in that thing. Old lady give him some leftovers the other day. Ate it like a starving coyote. Seen him heading out with his fishing pole a few hours ago. Didn't even have on a slicker or galoshes."

I thanked him and went over and studied the collapsed tent. I spread the door open and looked inside. The tent poles looked bent beyond repair and everything inside was soaked – a sleeping bag, a backpack, some soiled clothes, and an empty sack of jerky and not much else. Other than eating out of trash cans and begging, I couldn't think of how else he would be getting food.

I was drenched and chilled when I climbed back in the truck. I poured another drink and lit a cigar, and then went on searching for the boy. I felt confident I was close on the kid's tail and hoped it wouldn't be long before we were traveling south towards home again.

Fishing the Madison at this stage of the runoff would be ludicrous, but that's where he had to be. I drove slowly the short distance to Quake Lake looking for a fool fishing in the storm. The stream was in full view the entire way except for a short stretch behind a rise just before it emptied into the lake. I didn't see any loonies waving fly rods and decided the kid must be fishing someplace else, but after I turned around and started back, I spotted a form untangling his line from a sage bush on the knoll. I stopped and got out my binoculars.

It had to be him. He looked just like me, except his blond hair was in a tangled ponytail. His tattered quilted jacket and blue jeans were soaked and drooping. When he started back towards the river, I noticed his earring.

His efforts at casting were pitiful. He'd obviously never had instruction and every few casts he'd hang the fly in the sagebrush behind him because his back cast was so low. The river was near out its banks, but he was fishing with what appeared to be a dry fly. Enduring the storm and tolerating the frustration and this misery had to be more than just passion. I realized then that he undoubtably had the compulsion and I likely wasn't going to be leaving Montana anytime soon, not with the boy anyway. The rain increased, and he fished on.

I sipped on the scotch and puffed on the cigar as the wind slammed and shook the truck. The chill made me shiver when I opened a window to let the wind draw the smoke out.

The shards of gale driven mist rushing down the river vanished in a wall of fog that banked and swirled over the austere lake like steam from a great cauldron. The decaying timber circumventing the lake hosted a mob of mantling water turkeys that resembled a macabre rookery of sated vultures. After an hour and nearly dark, the boy finally reeled in and headed to the road. As he passed the truck, I touched the window button and stuck my head out. "Have any luck?"

He stopped a moment, gave me a casual glance and started on again.

I was taken aback by his state of destitution. I figured he'd be dirty and unkempt, but he was abysmal. Strands of snot ran from his nose and coated his sleazy mustache. His appalling pirate sized, gold-plated earring was tarnished green. He wasn't wearing a belt and his jeans hung from the jut of his buttocks. His knees were showing through ragged holes, and his toes were poking out of his Velcro sneakers. Strands of insulation were stringing from his jacket. This is the squalid wretch Sandy cares so much about? I thought. I stopped him again. "Where you headed?"

He stopped and turned and seemed confused. He paused in thought, and then pointed. "The campground across the highway," he mumbled.

I thought he might be suffering from hypothermia because of the way his thought process seemed impaired, but never having conversed with him I couldn't be sure. Maybe he was a dimwit. "If you want a ride, jump in the camper. I'm headed there myself."

He seemed reluctant, but after shuddering from a blast of wind, he nodded. His hands wouldn't function breaking his rod down, so I got out and did it for him. His legs were so numb and stiff from the cold I had to help him into the camper. Then I drove back to the campground.

Before I could back into a camping spot, he was out of the camper trying to set up his tent. After he realized the wind had bent and ruined the poles, he stood staring dumbfounded at the useless heap. I got out and went over to him. "Better get back in the camper till the rain lets up. You're going to freeze if you don't. You can barely function now you're so cold. I've got plenty of supper if you're hungry."

He didn't look up and I could barely understand his reply. "I'd better not."

"I'm cooking steak and fries. Come on in before you freeze."

He accepted my offer by nodding and then rolled up his ruined belongings and dragged the heap beside the camper. I swung the door open and let him in. I wanted to get him warm, and if we were going to share the close quarters of the overloaded camper, I didn't want to smell him. "Better take a hot shower and get the chill out of your bones so you don't get sick. I've got some clothes you can wear till yours dry. There's soap and shampoo under the sink." He nodded and went into the shower stall and threw his nasty clothes out the door. After I heard the shower start, I stuffed them in a trash bag because of the odor.

As I was reorganizing the rod cases and boxes of books to make more room, he ran the hot water out, but that was fine. He didn't look nearly as bad with his shoulder length hair washed and combed, and he didn't smell. Though my old jeans and sweater swallowed him, they were a big improvement. "Warm now?"

"Yeah. Thanks."

I offered him coffee. He took a swallow and started gagging and coughing. "Careful. It's hot," I said. "I enjoyed watching you fish after your beautiful casting form caught my attention. You must have been at it a long time."

"Not really."

"You sure impressed me. Hungry?"

"Yeah, I'm pretty hungry."

The kid salivated like a starving hyena as I seared the sirloin in a cast iron skillet and fried a mound of potatoes. To put himself through this much hell to catch a fish convinced me he was afflicted with the cursed gene just as I was. No normal kid would be over two thousand miles from home, starving, freezing, broke and alone just for the sake of fishing.

I figured I had to play this smart and be careful not to let him know who I was. Sara was most likely right in that he wouldn't have any idea. And in the state of confusion he seemed to be in, I felt confident he wouldn't figure me out. But if he did, I believed like Sara that he'd head out for parts unknown during the night and I didn't want to spend the time trying to find him again. I'd been very lucky locating him so fast, but luck only lasts for so long. Next time it might be much harder to find him.

I only ate a few bites. I was enjoying the high from the scotch and didn't want to lose it, but the boy ate like a famished refugee. When he was stuffed and gnawing on the last piece of steak, I decided I'd better try to persuade him to stay in the camper for the night. I wanted to keep him as close as I could. "With your tent trashed and the weather like it is, you should stay in here tonight. I snore, but it'll be better than sleeping out in the cold rain."

He stared hard at me contemplating for a time. "Why are you doing this for me?"

I thought fast and came up with the best answer I could. "One time when I was about your age, I was in a fix like you're in now and a man helped me get my life straightened out again. I figure it's time I returned the favor. That's all there is to it."

"You're not some kind of whacko that's going to try something with me, are you?"

I hadn't thought about that and couldn't blame him for considering it. I laughed and turned it back on him. "Don't worry about me. You're not funny, are you?"

He smiled. "No."

"By the way, what's your name?"

"Matthew Whitaker. Everybody calls me Matt."

"I'm Henry. Where you from?"

"Georgia."

"So, how'd you wind up in this miserable predicament so far from home?"

He was slow to answer. Maybe because he was reluctant to, or possibly he was fabricating a lie. "Me and some friends signed up for summer jobs in the Park and I got hired at the Old Faithful Inn washing dishes. After a few weeks, I was late for work one day and they fired me. I hitchhiked down here so I could fish the Madison, but it's been so high I can't catch anything."

Thinking back on what the girl at the Old Faithful Inn had told me, I surmised his version of the story wasn't true. "Do your parents know where you are?"

"I don't know – or care."

"Don't you think you should let them know so they won't worry? I'm sure they'd like to have you back home."

"I don't think they're worrying as long as I'm not around bothering them. I'm not going back home anyway. I'm staying out here so I can fish all the time."

"You don't seem to be prospering. You're close to freezing and starving. How long do you think you can hold out like this?"

"When it stops raining and my stuff dries out, I'll be okay. I can eat fish when the river goes down."

"Your tent is trashed, and the river won't be fishable for a long time yet. What do you intend to do in the meantime?"

My inquisitiveness seemed to have riled him, or maybe it was the fact that he realized the reality of his predicament and it made him mad because he couldn't do anything about it. "It's none of your business. Why do you care anyway?"

"I don't care. Just curious. Don't be so feisty."

I figured I'd better ease up for the time being. He'd obviously inherited my temper along with some of my other many negative attributes. He seemed on the verge of walking out and sleeping in the storm just to spite me, but then he opened-up again while I was pouring him more coffee.

"I'll go to West Yellowstone or Ennis and get a job guiding out of one of the fly shops, then I'll never have to go home."

"You have to be experienced at fly fishing to be a guide. You've got to have your own truck and boat, and people's lives are in your hands and you've got to be capable of taking care of them. Do you have any of those qualifications?"

His eyes fired up again and his lower lip started to quiver. I expected him to come across the table swinging. He eerily reminded me of myself when I was his age, so full of anger, defiance and resentment for authority, and emotions arose inside that caused deep feelings of passion for him to rise. I felt I'd known him forever, most likely because he was so much like me. I wanted to reach inside him and let him know everything was okay as long as I was around, and that he need not worry or be afraid. "Is it making you mad that I'm telling you the truth? It's not my fault because things are like they are. I just want you to know what you're up against is all."

"I'm tired of people telling me what to do. And how do you know so much about it anyway?"

"I guided some out here in my younger days and know what I'm talking about. What you need to do is get a job in one of the fly shops. It's the next best thing to guiding. You can start building your knowledge from there. You can learn a lot from talking to customers and guides in a shop. On your days off you can fish and learn more. You can save your money and buy a truck and a drift boat over time. Guiding isn't something you just jump into. You've got to really want it and be willing to work hard for it. First, you've got to do something about your appearance. Nobody's going to hire you to work in their shop looking like you do. You need to get a haircut and shave that growth off your face and get rid of that ugly earring."

"You go to hell. I'm not changing my looks for anything."

"If you're going to get mad whenever I try giving you advice, then I won't give you anymore. I'm just trying to help you."

I needed to get his mind away from the moment to let him settle down. I started feeling uncomfortable thinking he might walk out. "Are you planning on going back to school this fall?"

"I finished high school this spring, and I'm not going to college."

"Why? Don't you have the grades to get in?"

"I was an honor student. I just don't want to go. I want to stay out here and fish."

"Did you play football?"

"I lettered in soccer two years and boxed some."

He didn't look like a boxer. The soccer I could believe. He was small but lean and well developed. The fact that all he cared about now was fishing made me anxious. My primary thought was how to convince him to go home and it didn't seem that was going to be easy. I was beginning to have a bad feeling about this ordeal just as Hope had said. He fell asleep sitting up in the middle of a sentence. I threw a blanket over him and left him snoring and prayed he'd still be there in the morning.

My most immediate and greatest fear occurred while I was sleeping comatosely from the scotch I'd drank too much of the night before and from the exhaustion of the long drive from the Keys. The cold front had moved out during the night, and so had the kid. At first, I figured he couldn't be too far away because he was on foot, but when I checked, his ruined tent was still piled by the camper, but his rod and backpack were gone and it occurred to me that he could have hitched a ride during the night and be miles away by now. But before I left to go looking for him, I unloaded the camper in case he came back while I was gone.

As the sun came up over the mountains everything sparkled, the air was cool, dry and smelled of Christmas trees. The fine morning caused me to lose some of the regret I'd felt for coming on this rescue mission, but it didn't ease the dread of knowing how hard it might be to find Matt again. I wondered if his leaving was because he'd figured out who I was, or maybe it was simply he didn't trust a stranger asking so many questions. The only thing I knew for sure was that he wasn't ready to go home.

I drove down the dirt road along the Madison to Quake Lake where I'd found him the day before, but there was no sign of him. On passing the Cabin Creek restaurant I spotted a pay phone and decided to call Hope while I had the chance. She didn't answer, so I left a message telling her I'd arrived safely and had located Matt. I didn't tell her I'd already lost him but did assure her I'd be headed home soon.

I didn't know where else to look for Matt in the area, so I headed back to the campground fearing he'd hitched a ride after all and was long gone and miles away by now. But when I got back, to my great relief, his rod was leaning against the camper and he was inside sleeping. I put a pot of coffee on and started breakfast. The noise woke him, and he sat up staring at me in a stupor.

"Good morning, Matt. How about some breakfast?"

He seemed to struggle collecting his thoughts. "You don't mind?"

"No. Here's some coffee. I'll need what little hot water we have to wash dishes so go wash up in the campground bathroom while I cook."

He left with his backpack, and when he came back, I caught a strange odor. At first, I figured he'd slipped a cigarette, but it didn't smell like any cigarette I'd ever smelled. Then I realized it was pot. I'd smelled it often in the open-air restaurants in Key West. For a moment I was dumbstruck considering my grandson was a drug user, but I quickly shook it off and started up a conversation as we ate. "Where'd you go so early this morning?"

"Fishing up Beaver Creek."

"That's a long way from here."

"I couldn't sleep for you snoring, so I got up early. It's not that far a walk on the road. I fished a while, but it's still high and muddy and I didn't catch anything."

"I'm not surprised. Beaver Creek takes longer to clear and run off than any stream around here because it carries so much drainage. It'll be at least a week before any of the streams around here are fishable. You'll have to be patient."

"Maybe I'll go back to the Park and fish the Firehole then. It's wasn't high when I left."

"Then why did you leave and come down here?"

He seemed reluctant to admit it at first, but after considering, he confessed. "A Park Ranger made me leave because I didn't have the money to pay for a camping spot."

"Do you have any money now?"

Like the night before, the *I want to kill you* look appeared. Again, I didn't know if his anger was because he resented my prying or that it was at himself for his situation of utter helplessness. He gave me the threating look for another long moment and then went back to gobbling scrambled eggs. I let it drop and we didn't talk again till we'd finished eating and I was washing dishes. "Spread your tent and gear out to dry and go to town with me. I need to see some people and pick up some supplies."

He nodded and left to go collect his worthless belongings.

Ethan Macstatts, as always, was perched on his swiveling barstool chair behind his fly-tying desk hard at work turning out his immaculate imitations when we went into The Yellowstone Fly Shop later that day. He was so glad to see me he almost broke my wrist shaking my hand. "You look good, Henry," he said, after looking me up and down. "You might have even lost some weight. What brings you back to Montana?"

"Just needed to get out of the heat of the Keys for a spell. And I've really missed you and Emma and wanted to see you again."

"Well, whatever the reason, I'm glad you're here. It's damn good to see you. Emma will be so happy."

"Is she here?" He pointed towards the clothing section and I headed that way.

Emma, in her motherly way, was explaining to a young employee how she wanted a clothing display done. She was momentarily stunned when I walked up, then she threw her arms around me. "Why didn't you let us know you were coming?" she said, after releasing me.

"I wanted to surprise you."

Ethan came up and put his arm on my shoulder. "I knew you'd come back, you worthless old son of a bitch."

"Looks like you've enlarged the store again, Ethan."

"Yep, business just keeps booming."

I winked at Emma. "I'm sure it's because of your brains, fame and charming personality."

Emma left giggling back to instruct the girl. Ethan went to his chair behind his desk, but he didn't start tying flies again. Instead he locked onto Matt as he wandered around the shop fondling different pieces of equipment and checking price tags. I made a quick tour of the place and went back up front.

"Well what do you think of the shop?" Ethan said.

"Very nice, though I see nothing in fly fishing equipment has changed much in the past several years. Just more expensive and more cheaply made is all. I still like my old stuff better."

"Or maybe that's your excuse because you're just too cheap to buy new." Ethan then motioned towards Matt with his chin. "That miserable tramp didn't come in with you, did he?"

"Met him down at Cabin Creek yesterday. The weather trashed his tent and he spent the night in my camper out of the storm. He's not a tramp. It's just that those are my clothes he's wearing and they're a few sizes too big."

"It's not just the way he's dressed. It's that ugly earring, his hair and that growth on his face. He's disgusting and not somebody I'd think you'd be associating with. How long are you planning on being here for, Henry?"

"I'm not sure. Till the mood strikes me to go back home, I guess."

"If you're going to be here a while, why don't you stay in the elk cabin? We went up last week and cleaned it and chased all the mice out. The propane tank's almost full. All you have to do is flip the power breaker and carry your toothbrush in."

My first inclination was to say no, but now it seemed it might take more time than I'd initially thought to convince Matt to go home, so I figured I'd better seize the offer just in case. The cabin would be much nicer and easier to live in than the crowded camper, and closer to town than Cabin Creek as well. "That'd be nice, but I don't want to impose."

"Horseshit. I'll take it as an insult if you turn me down."

"Mind if Matt stays with me?"

Ethan's reluctance was obvious, and he had to force the sarcastic chuckle. "No, I don't mind. I doubt he could hurt anything. I'll get the key."

After Ethan left to go to the basement Emma came back up front. "Where are all your guides?" I said.

"On the Big Hole. Salmon fly hatch is going good over there. They didn't get the runoff we did. It'll be at least a week before anything's fishable around here."

"Know where they're staying?"

"Camping at Melrose behind the tavern."

"Cleatis with them?"

"The whole bunch is over there. Ought to get your boat and go over and fish for a few days."

"You're not serious? You still have my boat? I told Ethan to sell it."

"We kept it for emergencies. It's pretty much like you left it. We've kept in the barn."

"I'll be damned. Think I will. I'd like to see that bunch again. Matt, want to go the Big Hole and fish a few days?" He looked up from the fly bin and nodded. There was elation I hadn't seen in his eyes when he smiled.

I picked out a handful of salmon fly imitations, some leaders and tippet for our trip to the Big Hole and went to check out. Emma was at the register. "Drop by around seven tonight for supper, Henry," she said. "Looks like you and Matt could use a good meal."

Ethan overheard the invitation as he was walking up with the elk cabin key. I sensed his resentment because of Matt and declined the offer using our move into the elk cabin and preparation for the trip to the Big Hole the next day as an excuse. I hugged and thanked them, and we left.

All I had to do was turn on the gas, light the water heater and flip the power breaker and the neat and cozy elk cabin was ready. After unloading the boxes of books and rods and other gear from the camper we drove to the Macstatts' place and rolled my old dory out of the barn. It was dusty, and the tires were low, but otherwise it was in good shape being that it'd been stored out of the sun and weather. After pumping the tires, we headed to Ennis and had the trailer bearings greased. Then we hosed the boat off at a car wash and were ready to fish the Big Hole. Matt was obviously beside himself about the upcoming trip, and not just for the fishing. I reasoned his elation was also for his turn of good fortune for now having food and shelter, and of course me for transportation and expenses.

On the way back to the cabin I called Sara and Hope to let them know I'd found Matt and that we'd be heading home soon. I listened to Sara babble and sob as she praised me for ten minutes. All I got from Hope was a generic answering machine voice. I left a message saying I loved her and would be home soon.

A gusher of noise and a cloud of cigar and cigarette smoke billowed out when I swung the log door of the Melrose Tavern open. Inside, a beer guzzling mob of guides and fishermen were all screaming to be heard over the country music blaring out of a jukebox and the cracking of pool balls. I searched the room and spotted Cleatis Jones at a table full of other sun battered and shabbily dressed men.

I went over and most everyone at the table stood and began staring at me like I was a haint, then they all started talking at once.

"You old bastard, where in hell you been? We figured you'd died."

"You ain't changed none."

"How long you out for?"

"Is that your boy you got there with you?"

They eventually settled down enough so that I had a chance to answer. "It's good to see you boys again. It was nice of you to write, especially since I didn't know any of you could."

"Let me buy you a beer and a burger, Henry," Cleatis said.

"I couldn't turn down the chance to get something off you. You hungry, Matt?"

I figured his elated expression was for being among the guides in the festive atmosphere. "I'm starved," he said.

Cleatis gave a shrill whistle and motioned to a waitress who was busy unloading a tray of beers and food at a nearby table. When she'd finished, she rushed over, scribbled our orders and hurried away. She was back in minutes with the beers and as she passed them out, she studied Matt intently. When she'd finished, she pointed to him. "I need ID from you, young fellow."

Matt didn't know what to say, so Cleatis intervened. "Awe, Beth, he's with us. He ain't going nowhere but out back to camp. Let him have a beer."

"Okay, but it's your fault if he gets in trouble."

"He ain't going to get in no trouble. I'll be responsible for him."

"Bullshit. You can't even take care of your own self."

After the laughter died and Cleatis had regained his composure, he held up his beer in a victory toast. "Drink up, buddy. Where you from?"

"Georgia."

"You're from Georgia, aren't you, Henry?"

"I ran into Matt over at Cabin Creek. A storm trashed his tent and I'm putting him up for a few days. I got my old boat out of Ethan's barn and he came over here to fish with me."

"I can't believe the termites ain't ate that artifact," Vic Vickers said.

"It's still like new. Wooden boats are the only way to go. Nothing rows better," I said.

"There's too much damn maintenance in a wooden boat, and I ain't got the time."

"Why can't you spare a few hours varnishing a boat during the off season?"

Vic grinned and made a spinning motion with his hand. "Got to tie flies, man. Turned out twenty-five hundred dozen last winter."

"Holy shit, no wonder you're so demented," I said.

Beer spewed from Cleatis' nose and the table went into hysterics. Even Vance Vines smiled.

"Say, Henry, how's guiding in the Keys?" Cleatis said.

"It pays the bills."

"Bet it's easy after guiding out here."

"It's different, but not any easier. You've still got the wind to pole against. The clients have the same poor skills and unreasonable demands, and flats fish can be even more difficult than trout to catch."

"What planet do these geeks come from? It'd be nice to get one every once and a while that could fish," Cleatis said.

"If they knew how to fish, they wouldn't need to spend their hard-earned money on us morons to show them how, now would they?" I said.

"Damn, Henry, you didn't need to say that."

"All you got to do is be patient and nice to them. How easy do you want it?"

"Fuck, it ain't easy and you know it. A lot of guys try to guide out here, but after a season or two, they find it's too hard and go back to the real world."

"We would too, if we could fit in the real world. How many of you can do bypass surgery or litigate a court case?" They all either looked away or dropped their heads. "That's what I thought. Unlike you, most of your clients provide services that are important and necessary. When your heart is about to explode, they cut you open and repair it. When a tooth hurts so bad you can't bear it, they fix it. When you're about to be put in jail, they defend you. What do you have to offer? A day in a boat with a miserable son of a bitch. Better be glad they can't fish and choose to hire you, or you'd all be driving a forklift in a mill back home."

They all fell quiet. I wished I hadn't said it, but it irked me to hear guides complaining about their work when they get paid so lavishly for nothing more than rowing a boat in paradise a few hours a day. We ate in silent thought until I spoke up again. "Okay, boys, where's the main hatch now?"

"Just out of Divide to here," Cleatis said.

"Anybody caught anything worth bragging about?"

"Vance caught a brown longer'n your arm this afternoon. Ugly hook-jawed bastard."

"Anybody want to fish with me and Matt tomorrow?"

"I will, Henry," Cleatis volunteered.

"Good. Where're you staying?"

"In my sleeping bag in the bed of my truck of course."

"You cheap bastard. You'd freeze before you'd spring for a motel room. I brought my camper. Bunk with us."

"Thanks, Henry. I will."

We tightened our hatbands as a frigid wind came up with the sun the next morning while we were launching my boat. Cleatis chose the front seat and Matt the rear. I took the oars.

Not long into the float the gusting wind began to calm, and as the sun warmed the air, we shed our jackets. With the settling conditions, Cleatis took up his rod and began fishing, but he soon became bored without a rise and reeled in. "No bugs on the water yet, Henry. It's still too cold and we need some of that wind back."

"Be patient. It'll come."

Matt was in yet another mess. He'd already hooked himself in the back twice and tangled the leader to the point that it had to be replaced. Now his fly was stuck to the bottom of the boat and he had his arm in the water up to his shoulder trying to get it lose.

"Say, Cleatis, would you mind helping Matt?" I said.

After Matt retrieved the fly, he wrung the water out of his sleeve. When he straightened everything out and started casting again, Cleatis began spouting instruction. "No. No. Stop the rod high. Ten o'clock on the forward cast and two on the back. Higher is better. And give the line time to straighten behind you. Higher back cast. Higher back cast!"

Matt listened and practiced Cleatis' instructions and his casting began to improve after several tries. "I can feel it in the rod when I do it right," Matt said, after he made a decent cast. "If only there were some fish in this river."

Just after he'd said it a windblown stonefly fluttering back to shore disappeared into a set of gaping jaws, and then the fish ate Matt's fly as well. But Matt panicked and couldn't get his hands to work and didn't raise the rod fast enough and had too much slack in his line to set the hook. The fish was off in seconds. I saw the disappointment in his eyes and tried to console him. "Forget that one. They'll be plenty more. You did the main thing getting him to take your fly."

Moments later Cleatis raised his rod and was into a heavy rainbow. After a few runs and showy jumps, he hauled it to the boat, and I netted and released it. "Good one, Cleatis," I said.

He offered me his rod. "Here, you fish and let me row this apple crate a while to see if it handles as good as you say it does."

"It's about time," I said with a smile, and took the rod and we changed places.

Several more fish took Matt's fly, but he always had so much slack in his line he couldn't set the hook. After I explained while demonstrating how to strip and mend to keep the slack out, a few casts later he managed to hook a twin to Cleatis' rainbow and with the two of us shouting instructions, he got the fish under control and eventually led it to the net.

"That's the first trout I ever caught," Matt said, wonderstruck as he watched the fish swim away after Cleatis released it.

It hadn't occurred to me he'd never caught a trout after all he'd been through and done to catch one. I was flabbergasted for a moment as to the how and why he'd keep at the misery of it failing over and over like he had, but then I understood full well. "That was a good first one and you did a great job with it. Now, let's get to shore. I'm starving," I said.

Cleatis rowed to the bank and began fetching our sack lunches from the cooler. Matt devoured his sandwich in minutes and then went off down the river with his rod. Cleatis watched him disappear around the bend. "Ever hear anything from your daughter, Henry?"

For a minute I thought he might be connecting me with Matt. "Not much."

"Ever miss guiding out here?"

"Not a bit. It wore off after all those years, but I do miss the people I know here, and the mountains and climate. But yes, I finally got tired of chasing around the country like a nomad. I needed a change. Living like that is for the young. But I still need to make a living and guiding is all I know, so that's why I still do it. And it's different guiding in the Keys because it's still somewhat new to me, so I'm not burned out on it yet. And I have a place to call home and don't have to leave it. But most importantly I have a woman there that I care a lot about that's also my best friend. As long as I have her and she's happy, then I'm happy, something else I never quite had out here."

"You sound like you might regret what you did. Suppose you'd spent your life working in a factory, or even worse, in an office?"

"I think about it. I remember how miserable my old man was spending his life working in a tire factory and I'm glad I wasn't like him. I think that's one reason he drank so much. Guess everybody questions what they did in life and whether it was right or wrong. But at least a mill worker has retirement. I don't have anything to show for all those years I put into it. But I realized early on that I wasn't like everybody else and guiding was the only way I'd be satisfied. So, are you planning on doing this the rest of your life?"

The bite of sandwich he was chewing seemed to turn rancid and he flung what was left of it in the river. "You said it last night in your little degrading speech and just said it again now. What else are people like us going to do? It's not by choice I do this, and neither did you. We've got to be doing this because something inside is forcing us to. We're miserable otherwise. I'd have it made now if I'd finished law school and started a practice like my parents wanted, but I'd hated every minute of it. Hell no, I don't have any regrets. Most people have changed with the times, but we haven't. We can't. We're atavisms. We can't adjust and don't fit into these modern, regimented times. We're different and that's all there is to it."

I watched the sandwich disintegrate into a milky cloud as it floated down the river. "I know all that, but what are you going to do when the day comes when you can't physically do this kind of work anymore?"

"I don't think about it. Despite what you say, seems you did okay."

"Bullshit, if not for old man Simington I wouldn't even have a place to live."

"Old man Simington?"

"Horace Simington. You remember him. His only family was the Marine Corps. Why he left his house to me, I don't know. But when I die the house will go to the Key's Conservancy. You see, even my home isn't really mine. It's in a life estate."

"Oh yeah, I remember him. You know damn well why he left it to you. You took care of him. You were patient with him after he got old and nobody else would. What else was he going to do with that house? Leave it to charity."

"Hell, that's exactly what he did. You know I truly liked that old guy. He was a company commander in my division when I was in Korea. Guess that had something to do with it too. I'd still be out here with you boys if he hadn't left me that house. Still living wherever I could find a hole to crawl in to."

Matt came back bleary-eyed and reeking of pot and our conversation of why our lives had gone as they had ended at that point and we loaded up and started fishing again. Several miles downstream we had to make a portage around a small dam. Matt disappeared into a willow grove as soon as Cleatis and I started unloading the boat. We then hauled the cooler, drybags and fishing equipment downriver and lowered the boat over the dam parapet wall by the anchor rope and then reloaded it.

"That burger and beer last night must have given him the shits. That's the third time he's had to go into the bushes today," I said.

Cleatis gave me a dumbfounded look. "Bullshit. Come on, Henry, you know what he's doing."

"I don't."

"He's smoking dope and you damn well know it or you're an idiot."

I looked down and kicked the ground. "Yeah, I'm not that stupid. And I don't like it, but what can I do about it?"

"For one thing he isn't your problem. Get rid of him. Let his folks worry about it."

"Look, he's just like us – just like in the sermon you preached an hour ago at lunch. This is all he cares about and wants to do. He'll be miserable if it's taken away from him. He'd be okay if somebody would take some time with him and show him the way and help him get his life on track."

"I guess you mean like Mason did with you?"

"Yeah, just like Mason did with me. And Howard Stokes and Ethan and Emma."

"If you want to help the kid, talk to him. If he won't listen, get away from him before he gets you in trouble. If he doesn't have money to buy drugs, he might turn to thievery and get you involved."

Matt came strolling back from the willow grove just after we slid the boat back into the river. I could tell Cleatis' dislike for him was growing, not only because of the pot, but anytime there had been work to be done Matt had promptly disappeared. Cleatis rowed and didn't fish again that day and we finished the trip pretty much in silence.

Cleatis was undoubtedly reluctant, but that night I talked him into fishing with me and Matt again the next day. And at the end of the trip I thought he was happy with the way the float had gone, but as soon as we were back at the campground and he and I started cleaning the boat and putting the tackle away, Matt headed to the tavern and I could see Cleatis' face cloud in anger. Since Matt had no money to buy food or play the poker machines, I figured he'd left just to get out of helping us clean the boat. Cleatis thought so too and muttered his sentiment under his breath. It wasn't anything you'd dare say in a church. I pretended not to hear and gave Cleatis some time for his anger to cool before I spoke again.

"He really did well today, don't you think? I've never seen any-one improve so much so fast. Every time he catches a fish it seems to motivate him even more."

Cleatis was sponging the scum line off the side of the boat. "He did okay, but why isn't he helping us do any of this work? We've rowed his doped-up ass for two days and he hasn't done a thing but fish."

"Give him a break. He's no worse than the rest of us were at his age."

"All of us have always done our share of work, and none of us used drugs, either."

"Okay I get it, but I need a big favor, Cleatis. I know you can't stand him, but I want you to stay with him tonight in my camper and let him fish with you tomorrow. I have some business to take care of back in West and he doesn't need to be around."

He stopped scrubbing and rested his elbow on the gunnel in thought. "I don't know, Henry," he said. "I might wind up killing him."

Vance had just walked up. He didn't ever say much, but what he did say was usually worth listening to. "I'll be glad to watch Matt if that asshole won't, Henry. As much as you've done for me, it's the least I can do."

I believe Cleatis would just as soon Vance had broken his jaw than to have given him the look he did. "Alright, I'll do it," Cleatis said, red faced with shame.

"That's good. Now I'm heading to West Yellowstone. Here's some money for his expenses. You can haul the camper and my boat back. I'll be at the cabin. And don't be too hard on him."

It was late and Ethan and Emma had just finished dinner when I got to their house. While Emma washed dishes, Ethan sat at the table across from me as I explained my situation with Matt. I confided in them because they'd raised two boys and I didn't know anyone else to turn to for advice.

"Why do you care anyway? Get away from him. He's nothing but a worthless tramp out to cause trouble," Ethan said, after I'd finished explaining my dilemma with Matt and the drugs.

"Don't you remember putting me in jail? He's no worse than I was when I first came here."

"Bullshit, you were just on a well-deserved drunk because of the war and your divorce."

"Maybe he has problems, too. All he cares about is fishing, just like we did when we were his age. That kid has the same desire I had and if he were cleaned up and given some direction, he'd make a good guide someday."

Ethan's hands shot up and he broke into laughter. "He's got a long way to go. I wouldn't let that puke empty the trash for me, much less guide my clients."

"Come on, Ethan, he's not a bad kid. He just needs a little direction."

"All I can say is good luck, Henry. He's bound for trouble for sure. Don't come crying on my shoulder when he breaks your heart and you find your ass in jail and need someone to bail you out."

Emma sat down beside me. "If he loves it here so much maybe you could bargain with him. Confront him and tell him you're not going to tolerate drugs if you're going to put him up and take him fishing. Where does he get the money to buy it anyway? He's obviously broke."

"He must have bought it before he got fired. I'll try to deal with him your way, Emma. It makes more sense than anything else I've heard here tonight," I said, while giving Ethan a disgusted look.

"So why did you come back here anyway? And why this great interest in that worthless kid? I mean really?" Ethan said.

I sat under their gazes feeling smaller by the second for not having told them the truth they deserved in the first place. I thought that maybe knowing mine and Matt's true relationship would influence Ethan's attitude toward Matt. For better or worse I felt it was worth a try and told them everything, including my cancer diagnosis.

Next morning, I drove to the nearest phone at Slide Inn. Hope answered on the second ring. "Oh, Henry, are you headed home?"

As pleasantly as I could, I said, "How's everything going in the Keys?"

"I'm fine, but are you headed home?"

"Not yet. It'll be a day or two more."

"But you found him four days ago. Why haven't you left?"

"It's not going to be quite as easy as I thought to convince him to leave. If I tell him I was sent to bring him home, I'm convinced he'll run away. He's got problems and needs help. You've got to be patient a little longer."

After the click, I felt the familiar sick and empty feeling form in my chest that only losing someone you care about can bring. Just like after the war, it was happening again. My life was going out of control and I had no bearing over it. I was losing Hope like I'd lost Ginny. While wallowing in my self-pity I decided to call Sara and get that out of the way while I was making women hate me. She answered on the second ring. "Oh, Dad, I'm so glad to hear from you. Are you almost home?"

I stopped reading when I heard Cleatis and Vance pulling in. I folded the newspaper and put it aside as they came in. They'd left Matt sleeping in the camper.

"How'd it go?" I said, after they'd piled in.

"Fishing was great," Cleatis said.

"I know the fishing was good. I meant how did Matt do?"

Cleatis turned and went to a window, then put his hands in his back pockets and began studying the distant mountains. "He's getting the hang of fishing alright, and I believe he has visions of becoming a guide. But we let him row your boat so he'd know that won't ever happen. He knocked some chunks out of your chines and nearly killed us in the process."

"I'll get him out on Hebgen so he can get his coordination down with the oars. It'll be a few days yet before the Madison is fishable. By then I'll have him ready to start rowing the river."

Cleatis turned and pointed at me. "You've lost your damn, feeble mind." Then Matt came stumbling in wearing my filthy and wrinkled clothes. His hair was a greasy mess. Cleatis dropped his stare from me and gave Matt a repulsive look and headed to the door. "We got to go, Henry."

Vance pinched his hat brim and followed Cleatis out without saying a word. I followed them to the porch. "Want me to help you unload the camper?"

"No, just keep Matt out of our way while we do it," Cleatis said.

I went back inside, and Matt had collapsed on the sofa after throwing and scattering the newspaper on the floor. I gathered it up and stuffed it in the kindling bucket. I felt like jerking him up and kicking his ass, but I let it go. "So, how do you feel about guiding now? Rowing that big, heavy, high sided boat in the wind isn't easy, is it?"

"I just know now that's what I want to do the rest of my life."

I cringed. That was exactly what I didn't want to hear. "I don't know if that's a good choice these days. There's lots of competition. It's a tough and often lonely life."

"Wasn't there competition when you started?"

"Not much, but there wasn't much business either except during the summer, which isn't long here. Back then there weren't as many people that could afford to come out here fishing, much less to hire a guide. I had to work in the shop and tie flies to make ends meet the rest of the season, then I worked on a ranch and guided people duck and bird hunting the rest of the year."

"Suppose I got really good at it? Could I make a living at it then?"

"Are you willing to put the effort into it? You've got a lot to learn before you're ready to guide. Anybody can row a boat. That's a small part of it. You've got to know a great deal about fly fishing and entomology and how to relay your knowledge to your clients so they can catch fish."

"I believe I could do it."

"You've got to be positive. You've got to want it more than anything and be willing to work your ass off to get it."

"There's nothing else I want to do."

"There're three kinds of guides, Matt. The worst is the rich boy that just dabbles in it. His daddy keeps him up so he can have something to do after he gets out of college because he's not ready to start a real job. All the rich boy does is screw the real guides out of business they deserve and need just so he can satisfy his vain ego and call himself a guide. Then there's the boy that takes time from school in the summer to row for a dude ranch. All he does is screw the clients because of his ignorance and inability while he goes broke working for nothing so his boss can make a lot of easy money. And there's the real guide that dedicates his life to it because of his passion for it. He can't do anything else because when he's away from the water he's miserable. Which do you want to be?"

"I want to be like you."

"And end up a useless and broke old man?"

"You don't seem old or useless to me."

"Just believe me, you need to go home and get your ass back in school and make something out of yourself."

"I don't want to go to school. I hate it."

"Then join the Marine Corps or something. Don't squander your life away like I did."

"I don't think I'd make it in the Marines. I want to be a guide."

"What are you going to do in the winter when there's nobody to guide?"

"Work in the shop I guess."

"Working in a fly shop in the off season is boring and the pay is terrible. Besides, most of these shops shut down in the winter."

"I could take people deer hunting or something."

"The last thing you want to do is get involved with deer hunters." I started pacing. I had to convince him to go home, and soon mainly because of Hope. She wasn't one to make idle gesture, threats, or dares. When she'd had enough of this folly, she'd leave me, and that was the last thing I wanted. "You need to guide bird hunters. At least they have some class."

"I don't know anything about bird hunting. I've never even been hunting before."

"You don't know anything about fishing either, but you say you're willing to learn. Fly fishing and wing shooting clients are usually professionals that have money and class. Those are the markets to get into."

"Will you help me get started then?"

I suddenly realized I was caught in a trap. My mind was working against itself. Yes, my life was spinning out of control again, but this time it was by my own doing. I had no one to blame but myself this time. I could walk away from this and go home if I wanted to, but I knew deep down what I really wanted was to stay in Montana and save Matt from ruin, even if it meant me losing everything. "If I help you, you're going to have to promise to work hard and do as I say. I can open doors for you that otherwise would be locked, like getting a job guiding for the Macstatts."

The idea of guiding for Ethan Macstatts excited him enough to get him off the sofa and onto his feet. "I promise I'll work hard and do as you say."

"But you've got to agree to something. I will not help you if you don't stop smoking pot and doing drugs. I know you're doing it. I smell it on you. I see it in your eyes. Quit or I'm done with you." A look of astonishment washed over his face. "I'm not as dumb as you think I am, Matt."

"I, I, I'll do my best to quit. I'm almost out anyway."

"If you don't, I'll leave you on the side of the road like I found you. And you better start doing your share of the work around here. I'm not your mama."

We floated sideways and backwards for the first hundred yards and the dory banged off three rocks while Matt flailed and floundered with the oars until we drifted into deep enough water so he could row and get the boat under control. But I still stayed braced expecting another tooth-rattling collision. "You're doing better," I said. "But if you'd waded the boat out to deep water before you got in, you'd been able to row and had the boat under control and have avoided hitting all those rocks. Rock collisions are loud and jarring and unnerving and you need to avoid as many as you can. And remember, always back row. That way you always have the boat under control. And it'll help you stay in proper casting distance of the bank as well. The less you deviate, the less your clients will have to adjust their casts. The more enjoyable the trip, the bigger the tip."

We were floating the Madison from Varney Bridge to Ennis so Matt could get more rowing experience. I'd had him on Hebgen Lake long enough for him to get the feel of the oars. This was the second time he'd rowed the river. I also wanted to do this float to check on the progress of the salmon fly hatch. The much-anticipated giant aquatic insect was overdue because of the excessive runoff and cold water, but I wasn't convinced that in the lower part of the river the insects weren't already crawling onto the banks and up the willows to shed their nymphal shucks. No one else had taken the initiative to see. Several miles downstream into the float I pointed to an island and gave Matt the nod to row in. My instinct was right about the hatch. The willow branches along the island were covered with shed shucks as well as the emerged adults preparing to mate and then lay their eggs.

A stout afternoon breeze sprang up and began dislodging and scattering the flies onto the river as we rigged our rods. Then the sounds of gulps and slurps started as trout began feeding on the wind-blown insects as they fluttered across the surface getting back to land.

"Matt, you fish the outside bank. I'm going down the side channel." An hour later I motioned Matt back to the boat. He'd caught six nice rainbows and I'd caught fish all down the channel. "It's about to bust wide open, Matt. Enjoy today and the next few, because soon the river will be covered with boats and fishermen. It'll be overrun by the weekend."

My prediction proved true. News of the salmon fly hatch attracted a mob of anglers in a matter of days. Guides from all over Montana and Idaho showed up with their drift boats and clients and it was like the Normandy landing all over again, but thankfully there was no gunfire or casualties would have been higher.

Matt worked hard at the oars learning to row over the following weeks. I was impressed at how fast he caught on. His casting improved as well, and more importantly, he had a gift few have which is an intuitive sense of knowing where the fish would most likely be holding, and which fly pattern they would most likely take at a given time of day. It became apparent he was a lot smarter than I'd first thought and more willing to learn than I'd anticipated. If we weren't on the river, he was tying flies. If he wasn't tying flies, he had his nose buried in one of my old books studying aquatic entomology or fishing tactics. My compassion for him grew by the day.

The two weeks I'd promised Hope I'd be gone slipped by, and then it became three, then almost four. I kept lying that I'd be home soon, that I was doing my best to convince Matt to leave. I could sense her growing reluctance to talk to me with each conversation. She knew I was lying and not coming back anytime soon. Then one day when I called there was no answer, nor the next day or the next. Her silence was torturing me, but the overwhelming determination for Matt and his wellbeing was so overpowering I couldn't force myself to quit and go home.

One afternoon near the end of the salmon fly hatch, Matt and I were fishing at Reynolds Pass on the Madison. There were several hours of good fishing left when Matt reeled in and waded to shore headed to my truck. He motioned me to follow. "You sick or something?" I said, when we were back at the truck. "You've never quit fishing till I've made you."

"I need to get back. Some friends are picking me up at eight that I haven't seen since I lost my job at the Inn."

They arrived a half hour late in a pricy German car. I caught a glimpse of the driver, and visions of Charles Manson flashed through my mind. I recognized Sandy as well when Matt opened the backdoor to get in. After the car disappeared down the drive, I did what I'd been wanting to do for a long while.

With Matt gone for the first time since I'd found him, I went searching for his stash of pot. It was easy to find in his backpack inside a metal Band-Aid box. There were some pills, too, which didn't surprise me, but was still upsetting.

I started smoking Prince Albert when I was twelve and knew how to roll a cigarette, but the pot was coarse and seedy and hard to smooth and made bulges in the paper. When I inhaled the first draw, fire shot down my throat and sent me into a hacking fit. Then I smelled something burning and found two smoldering holes in my favorite flannel shirt where some hot seeds had popped out. I doused myself out with the scotch I was drinking. After five minutes with no unusual sensation, I smoked what was left of the joint. Then a few minutes later an odd notion came to go for a walk up the mountain back of the cabin to watch the full moon rise.

An hour later I'd wandered halfway up the mountain watching the smiling orange globe slowly lift above the peaks in the east. Later to the north there was a rare appearance of the Aurora Borealis, and I thought I was hallucinating. When I came down enough to partially regain my thought processes, it seemed hours had passed. I decided to start back down off the mountain then and noticed the lights were on in the cabin and knew Matt had come back.

I stumbled, fell, rolled and cussed most of the way down the switchback trail. Twice I went headfirst into sage bushes and scratched my face all to hell. When I finally managed to get to the cabin Matt was waiting on the porch sullen and cross armed. "You asshole, you stole my pot," he said.

I felt like the thief I was and somewhat embarrassed that I'd been caught, but I went on the offensive anyway. "That stuff makes everything weird. Why do you smoke it? It can't be good for you. It burned my lungs out."

"It relaxes me and doesn't hurt me either."

"Yes, it does. Anything that makes you cough like I did has to be bad for your lungs."

"Whiskey hurts you just as bad. It rots your liver."

"But alcohol is different."

"How?"

He was cunning and I witless in my state. "I don't know. Drinking's not against the law for one thing."

"Drinking and driving is, but you do it."

"Cleatis says it's expensive. How do you afford the stinking stuff?"

"I can't anymore. That was all I had left. You smoked up at least twenty dollars' worth."

I took a twenty from my money clip and tossed it toward him. "Sorry I went through your stuff and stole your pot. I've never tried it and just wanted to know what it's like and why you like smoking it so much."

Matt retrieved the bill and held it out to catch the light coming from inside the cabin. After seeing it was a twenty, he lightened. "Well, what did you think about it?"

"I don't ever want to be like that again. I sat up there on that mountain for what seemed like hours afraid to come down because I thought I might get eaten by a bear or a cat or something."

I'd never heard him laugh so hard. "You just got paranoid, and no wonder, you smoked enough to get ten people stoned. And now I'm out."

"Since you're out, why don't you quit like you promised?"

His humor vanished. "It's none of your business if I smoke, so leave me alone about it."

"That's not what we agreed to. I told you if you didn't quit, I wasn't going to help you. And what are those black pills for?"

He pondered a moment. "Something to help me sleep."

"Bullshit. Get rid of them and don't bring anymore drugs around me. You'd better heed my warning if you know what's good for you."

"I'll move out then."

"Where? Back to Cabin Creek in your ruined tent?"

"I'll get a job guiding and rent a trailer or something."

"Stop talking nonsense and face reality. You don't have a truck or a boat. You don't know how to guide, and nobody's going to hire you to do anything, except wash dishes, and I doubt that."

I was right, and he knew it. He mumbled something under his breath and stomped inside.

When the epic and heralded salmon fly hatch ended, the crowds vanished as fast as they'd come. I was worn out after the days of constant rowing and fishing while following the hatch up the Madison from Ennis to Quake Lake. But by then I'd become confident enough in Matt's rowing ability to let him take the dory down the river alone and the days I didn't want to fish I'd pack his lunch and drop him off at sunrise and pick him up at dark at a takeout downriver.

One morning after he launched, I drove to West to visit with Ethan and Emma. On my way, I stopped at the first pay phone I came to and called Hope, but like the last so many times I'd called, there was no answer – not even the fake obnoxious answering machine voice.

Only one frantic summer employee was on the shop floor when I went in. If the guides and their clients had still been there scheduling shuttles, buying fly selections and tackle, and securing streamside lunches for the day, the shop would have been in chaos. There were always at least two clerks on the floor to help with the morning flurry of anglers preparing for the day, plus Ethan and Emma. As it was, a long line of impatient customers was waiting at the cash register. I started behind the counter to help, but it dawned on me that I didn't know how to operate the charge machine or cash register, so instead I headed for the basement where I found the Macstatts in a dilemma. Before I could say anything, Emma cut me off.

"Henry, I'm so thankful you're here. One of our employees had to go home for a family emergency and now we're shorthanded.

Could you help us out here in the shop for a few hours during the morning rush till we find someone else?"

"I doubt I could learn how to operate those Star Wars machines you got up there, but somebody better get up there and fast. There's a line of impatient people looking more and more like a lynch mob by the minute."

"These damn kids today are just outright undependable and lazy. They come and go as they please, and they don't hardly do shit when they're here anyway," Ethan said, ignoring my concern about the customers upstairs.

"This was unavoidable, and you know it. Don't be so down on him," Emma said.

"Why don't you ask Matt to work for you, Ethan?" I said. "He might step in and give you a hand if you'd stop treating him like dirt."

"Awe bullshit. I told you that tramp's never working in my shop, even if he is your grandson. And I meant it!" He left stomping upstairs.

"Do you think he would?" Emma said, after the footsteps faded.

"I could feel him out and see what he says."

"But how will he get to work? He doesn't have a rig."

"I'll bring him in, or he can hitch a ride with one of the guides staying at Cabin Creek. I'm sure George would give him a ride in if we gave him a little gas money."

"Good idea."

"It'd be good for all of us, Emma. It wouldn't hurt him to make some money for his expenses. My meager savings are going fast."

"Do you think you could convince him to get his hair cut and shave that growth off his face? It would be better if he were more presentable. That's Ethan's biggest problem with him I think."

"For a chance to work alongside Ethan Macstatts, he might just do it."

"If you can get him to work on his appearance, we'll give him a try."

"I'll buy him some clothes and get him cleaned up. I'll have him here at seven, day after tomorrow."

"That'll be great, Henry, and don't worry about Ethan. I'll get him straightened out."

"One more thing, Emma. Just make sure you or Ethan don't slip up and give him any ideas I'm his grandfather."

Matt had fished till dark that night, and dinner was late as usual. I'd grilled a chicken, and after Matt forked half of it onto his plate, I started feeling him out about working for the Macstatts. I felt sure he'd be ecstatic. "I've got some wonderful news for you, boy. The Macstatts want you to work in their shop. What do you think about that?"

I'd expected his face to light up with excitement, but his expression didn't change. He swallowed a mouthful of chicken and took a big gulp of milk instead. "I want to guide, not work in a shop. Anyway, that old man doesn't like me."

"You mean Ethan?"

"Yeah, Ethan. That man hates my guts."

"Ethan doesn't hate you. He's just old and grumpy and full of hot air. Look, they're desperate for some morning help. You could learn a lot working there. Most all guides get their start working in a shop. Think about it, this job could be the doorway for you to guide."

He didn't answer for a long while, but I could tell his brain was hard at work as he gnawed and chewed. "Okay, I'll give it a try, but only for as long as that old guy's nice. If he gives me any grief, I'm out of there."

"Would you be willing to shave and let me trim your hair so you don't look like a castaway?"

He grimaced and looked as though I'd run a knife through his heart. "I don't know about that. What difference does it make what I look like anyway?"

"Most people that come through the shop are professionals and they want to deal with professionals. Appearance is a big part of at least assuming you're a professional whether you are or not. Believe me, you need a shave and a trim. It would make Ethan happy as well."

"Guess I could shave, but I don't have a razor."

"You can use mine. We'll go to town tomorrow and I'll spot you some cash for some new clothes. You can't work with your pants two sizes too big and hanging halfway down your ass. By the way, how was your supper?"

"It wasn't ribeye, but it was alright, I guess."

"Go take a shower and shave and I'll cut your hair so you can go to work and buy your own damn food for a change. Now, how does that sound?"

Matt by no means looked like a choirboy after the shave and trim, but it was a big improvement. I wanted the earring gone, too, but knew just the mention of it would start a fight. We went to West Yellowstone clothes shopping at the Eagle Store the next afternoon and a side of him I wasn't expecting came out.

"You've been looking at yourself in that mirror for ten minutes like a bride modeling a wedding dress. Those jeans look good on you and that canvas shirt fits you well. You've got three sets of work clothes picked out. Now let's get you some new shoes."

"I don't want new shoes. These old boots of yours are fine."

"Those Bird Shooters are dilapidated. I wore them out years ago bird hunting on the prairie. Trust me you need new shoes."

"But I love these boots. They're comfortable and have character."

Suddenly and strangely he'd become picky about how he dressed. If only he'd get that way about his hair, beard and god-awful earring. After we were done clothes shopping, we decided to go to Jean's Restaurant for dinner where I often ate in the old days. The prime rib there was the ultimate. After I told Matt where we were going, he had me stop at a gas station so he could use a pay phone.

We parked in the rear of Jean's down an alleyway, then went through an unmarked door into a small bar and dining room that was known by the locals as 'the rear of Jean's'. The hidden dining area served as sort of a private club with no membership dues where locals could drink and dine unencumbered by the hordes of tourists visiting West Yellowstone. And the food and drink prices were somewhat lower in back than the main restaurant up front. I'd been eating there for years. After Matt and I slipped in, I rummaged what change I had along with a few dollar bills so he could try his luck at the Montana Poker machines that were placed in every available space around the room. As always, the jukebox was playing ancient country music way too loud.

Not long after our arrival three young folks came in. One was a beauty I immediately recognized as Sandy. With a little makeup and out of her work outfit, she was even more gorgeous than I remembered. She was with the same couple that had picked Matt up at the cabin the week before. Sandy rushed over and hugged and kissed Matt the second she spotted him. After speaking to the other couple, Matt gazed around the room and a disappointed look came when he realized the only available booth was the one next to mine. After he and his friends came over and were seated, an aged waitress with thick, ornate glasses waddled up and threw a stack of menus on their table. Then she came over to me. "Ain't seen ya in a spell. Where the hell you been, you old bastard?"

"With all the other old people – in Florida, Alice."

"Hell, you still look like the first time I ever seen ya. Going to be here long?"

"Hadn't planned to at first, but now I'm not sure."

She pointed toward Matt. "That your son you come in with?"

"No. I met him down on the Madison. Storm ruined his camping gear and I'm helping him get back on his feet."

"Never took you for being charitable. Figured he was your boy. Little bastard looks just like ya. What you be drinkin'?"

"Got any good scotch in that selection of rot-gut back there?"

"Hell yeah, but I didn't know you drank whiskey."

"I use it occasionally now to ease my rheumatism." I put my finger to my lips and then pointed towards Matt's booth, and she leaned her head near mine. "Do you know those kids that just came in?"

She spoke softly. "That boy's a local. Little shit's always up to no good. Spent his whole life in some kind of trouble or another. The girl ain't from here, but she's been around for a while. Her daddy's one of them rich computer fucks from California. Bought a ranch down towards Cameron and she stays there most of the time. I don't know that pretty one with your friend."

"I wondered how they knew to find Matt back here."

"Yeah, little bastard comes in a lot. I've always wondered where he gets the money to eat steak and prime rib all the time. Lives mighty fancy for his age. Ain't never had a job I know of. If you get what I mean you might try to keep your friend away from him."

Alice moved her bulk back to the bar and placed my drink order. She took several sips from one she had waiting at her post at the bar and a few drags off a cigarette as the bartender poured my scotch. He took too long, and Alice let him have it. "Goddamn it, Chuck, hurry it up before my friend dies of thirst." He stopped and turned to her with an insolent dare. "You sawed-off wormy son of a bitch, I'll slap that scowl off your ugly four-eyed face if you ever look at me like that again."

She was still huffing and cussing when she came back to my table. "See you haven't lost any of your charm, Alice."

"Awe, that prissy little bastard likes pissing me off. One day I'm going to kick the shit out of him. You ready to order, Henry?"

"Let me drink a while first."

I finished my drink and then stepped over to Matt's booth, which had been in a boisterous state of celebration until my approach silenced them. "Say, Matt, how about introducing me to your friends."

"Sure. This is Sandy." She immediately recognized me, and her mouth fell open. "And this is my friend Henry I told you all about, Sandy."

I smiled and put out my hand. "Good to meet you, Sandy. You must be working for the Park Concession this summer?" After I winked, her mouth closed into a grin and her wonderful eyes became happy again.

"Yes, the Old Faithful Inn."

Matt introduced me to the couple across the table, Cody and Liz. They acted as if I had leprosy, so I gave them a slight nod and turned back to Matt. "What do you want for dinner?"

"Burger and fries."

"Eating with your friends?"

"If you don't mind."

I turned and pointed to Alice. "I was hoping you would. I'm flirting with that waitress there and I want to be alone. I'm trying to get her phone number."

Matt smiled and shook his head as the others eyed Alice strangely and then me curiously. I stepped back to my booth, and either they didn't know I could make out most of what they were saying over the jukebox, or they didn't care.

"Who's that silly old bastard?" Cody said.

"Back off. He's a friend of mine. I'm staying with him for a while."

"No shit?"

"Yeah, no shit. He found me the day my tent got trashed. He used to guide here and he's teaching me how."

Cody laughed. "You, a guide? What a fucking joke."

"That's right, shit head. What about it?"

"Sorry. Didn't mean to piss you off, buddy."

I stuck my menu in front of my face to hide my amusement as Matt went on.

"He got me a job at the Yellowstone Fly Shop, too. I'm starting tomorrow."

"That's another fucking joke. Just like your other job you won't last a week."

Matt got to his feet with clenched fists. "Cody, you're an asshole. Say one more thing and I'm going to flatten your ugly nose."

Cody put his hands up. "Come on, Matt. Don't be so serious. You used to not care."

"Just back off."

"Sure, dude."

Sandy tugged on Matt's arm and he sat down. "Matt, that's great news," she said.

"Henry's done a lot for me and I don't appreciate you running him down, Cody."

"Okay I'm sorry. He ain't funny, is he?"

"No, asshole, I wouldn't be with him if he was, but I wondered at first."

Matt looked my way with a startled expression realizing I might be hearing what they were saying. I had my head down looking at the menu pretending I wasn't paying attention. He turned back around unconvinced. "Hold it down a little. He might hear us."

"I don't care. He's nothing to me," Cody said. But after that they held their voices down.

I was proud of the way Matt handled himself with Cody. And even more so, his excitement about his job at the fly shop made me happy. But it was all dispelled when I was settling at the cash register and Alice motioned for me to turn around as Matt was handing some cash to Cody, obviously the twenty I'd given him for the pot I'd smoked. Cody then passed a small plastic bag from his coat pocket across the table to Matt. "That's why I'd keep your boy away from him. He's the local dope peddler," Alice said.

CHAPTER 16

As I drove Matt in the next morning to his first day of work, I had the same anxious feeling a mother must have taking her child to school the first day. My concern was most about how Matt and Ethan would get along, but I was also worried about how many mistakes Matt might make, and if his blunders would cause the Macstatts financial losses. And the dope transaction the night before was also nagging at my mind. I couldn't let it go and had to bring it up. "I'm disappointed you haven't given marijuana up like you promised. You lied to me again."

I could feel his stare as he pondered. "Oh, so you were spying on me last night, huh?"

"No, I wasn't spying on you and don't try to turn it around on me. Everybody in the restaurant saw you and that little weasel passing money and dope around with no more concern than if it was a basket of bread. Suppose one of the local cops had been in there and seen you?"

"I only bought a little bit. I'm trying to quit. Knowing I have some makes it easier."

"I'm not stupid, Matt. Don't play games with me or you'll regret it."

Matt's uneasiness was apparent as Emma delved out her morning orders. His apprehension wasn't because of Emma, though. It was from the intense looks Ethan kept shooting at him. Though Matt had cut his hair and shaved and was dressed neatly, his improved appearance didn't seem to bear much on Ethan's negative attitude towards him. For Matt's sake I felt I needed to divert Ethan's attention and went to his tying desk.

"Don't you get sick of tying all the time, Ethan?" I said. "You've been sitting there for forty years turning out flies. You can order all you need now from one of those Sri Lanka importers. You don't have to tie anymore. You're going to go blind."

"No, I've got to, Henry. The commercial companies can't keep up with orders, and I have to tie a lot of custom stuff, too."

"You ought to see how nice the flies are that Matt ties. He could help keep your supply up."

Ethan shot me one of his dreadful glares, but I'd put the bug I'd intended in his head and smiled as I headed for the door. "I'm going to Swan Creek. See you this afternoon."

"Keep an eye out for bears. Harold saw a lot of fresh scat in there the other day."

As I strung my rod, I studied Swan Creek from the parking lot trailhead on the hill overlooking the small valley the fertile little stream coursed through. Under the bright sun, Swan Creek was like a glimmering metallic snake slithering through the lush meadow grass. There were numerous bright red signs nailed on the trees warning of bears at the parking lot and along the stream that kept most fishermen away. But there were still a few locals that were either bold or dumb enough to fish there and I reasoned like them. The big brown trout in the small stream made the risk of a confrontation with a Grizzly worth it. It was like having your own high-quality private stream to fish with only the possibility of being mauled and eaten by a Grizzly bear as the fee.

I'd just started up the creek when the foul scent of rotting flesh jolted my senses and caused me to freeze. After the panic passed, my curiosity forced me to follow the stench. The foul odor led to a half-eaten moose calf that had been hidden in a thick stand of willows off the trail. Then as a cloud of flies exploded off a mound of fresh bear scat lying on the carcass, the prickly sensation shot up my neck and fear engulfed me again. I relaxed after nothing big and brown came charging from the grass and I surmised the bear must have left its kill to go into the cool of the timber to sleep until nightfall. I made a mental note to detour the area when I came back through.

I wandered on upstream observing the creek for a feeding fish worthy of casting to, but all I saw were dimples of small fish, so I kept moving. I'd ambled almost a mile through the waist-high meadow grass when I saw the deep concentric rings gliding down the stream's gentle flow I'd been looking for. While I studied the run, beside a deep, log filled undercut a huge hooked kype broke the surface. After making out its pulsing gills and the barely perceptible rhythmic beat of its tail holding just under the placid surface, I discerned its incredible size. I'd caught several large fish from Swan Creek over the years, but none of them compared to this one.

Across the creek and just below the log jam a slight rise offered the perfect vantage to observe and cast to the fish, so I waded across the stream well below the log jam and walked the grass down before taking a seat on the small knoll. Then I started rummaging through my fly boxes for a pattern to try. Knowing that trout this old turn cannibal and only feed during the night on their kin made it hard for me to keep my eyes off the huge fish that appeared surreal in the small environ sipping the tiny duns.

I went through several boxes before choosing a pattern I thought would match the naturals the fish was feeding on and knotted it to my leader. My initial cast floated seemingly perfect over the trout, but it was ignored. After several more casts, the fish made a move toward my offering, and though it didn't take, it was interested enough to drift downstream for several feet with its nose practically touching the fly. Then it turned and went back upstream to its feeding station.

I waited until the fish had begun feeding confidently again before making another cast, and just as it'd done before, the trout floated beneath my imitation for a yard, then turned back upstream. But this time it turned back, rushed the fly and took it.

After I set the hook the fish surged into the logjam. I reeled as I plowed through the thigh-deep water towards the fish. As I neared the jumble of logs, the water humped as the fish raced out and up the creek. The reel screamed before the trout augered into a weed bed in the next bend. I pried and pressured until it fled the weeds and ran up to the next bend in a wake and then held there in a deep run. I pressured the fish as hard as I dared with the light tippet, and after a spell it began to tire against the constant, unyielding pressure of the rod and eventually it floated up spent and gasping onto the surface.

The fish brought memories of when James Mason and I fished for the giant sea run brown trout on Tierra Del Fuego. I couldn't imagine from where this fish had come. The depths of Hebgen Lake most likely, I presumed. Ultimately, though, I felt cheated by how easy it'd been to catch. But as I reached for its tail to drag it to shore, the water exploded, and the hook ripped loose, and the fish swam slowly back towards its shelter of collected dead timbers.

I waited for the sickness to go away, but after an hour the hollow feeling of my unfortunate loss still lingered in the pit of my gut. And then while wading and sloshing back through the muck and mire and thick meadow grass to my truck the compulsion I hadn't felt in years resurfaced and I became obsessed and knew from the many years it'd possessed me that I'd never be content till I caught the misplaced fish.

Daydreaming about the fish as I wandered back to my truck made me forgot about the dead moose calf and the bear. I'd blundered within fifty yards of it again when I heard the noise of a rush that only a big animal makes. Grizzly bear flashed through my mind, but when I turned, through the mayhem of flying mud and churning brown legs I made out a moose. I bolted for the truck feeling like I was in a sack race with my feet sucking loose from the mire and the tangled grass pulling at me like a maze of rough hemp ropes. The hoof beats grew louder, and when I turned to face the mother of the bear's kill, she kicked out a hoof and I dodged and fell back. All I could do was crab backwards and whack her nose with my rod when she came close. Finally, she backed off, shook her head, and before she started at me again, I made a frantic dash up the hill for my truck. For some reason she didn't want to come up the hill and instead went grunting and bucking and slinging her head in rage back into the willows. I cussed myself for not thinking of her. Then I noticed the last foot of my favorite rod was gone.

Thinking about my misfortune while driving back to the shop was tormenting. I figured I'd ruined the only opportunity I'd ever have of catching the huge trout, but I was adamant in my resolve to go back to Swan Creek tomorrow, and the next day and the next, until I caught the thing or died trying. The compulsion would see to that.

The shop was empty of customers when I went in, and as usual Ethan was at his desk enamored in constructing flies. I interrupted his concentration. "How'd Matt do his first day on the job?"

Ethan didn't bother to look up and his answer was lackluster. "Okay I guess."

Emma overheard his comment from the back and came stomping up. "Ethan, you ass! He did great, Henry. I taught him how to issue fishing licenses and run the line machine. The cash register and card machine were easy for him. Thanks to you he already knew his knots and how to fill reels. You're right. He is a bright kid. I've got him in the basement now doing a wader inventory."

"Well, I'll have to say, he can tie a pretty fly," Ethan chimed in. "And he does have a likable personality. He loves to joke and cut up with everybody. I'm surprised at how well he communicates with the customers. If you'd clean him up some more, he might just make it as a store clerk after all."

"Well, a rare compliment from Mr. Macstatts," I said.

"Go to hell, Henry. So, I might have been a little quick to judge him."

"Okay, I'll drop it. Now let's go get some lunch. Isn't it about time Matt was getting off?"

Ethan whip finished the fly he was working on and stepped out from behind his desk. "Anything interesting happen on Swan Creek this morning?" He'd been so absorbed in tying he hadn't noticed I was covered in mud. "Damn, old man, you look like you fell down the shaft of a shit house. What happened?"

"I had a run-in with a moose. She wanted retribution for Harold's bear killing her calf."

"I told you to be careful. Harold wasn't joking about that bear. Maybe you should get somebody to go with you next time."

"I'll take my chances alone. Getting mauled to death by a bear might be an easier way to go than what's in store for me."

"You idiot, why don't you go home and go through with the treatment? Emma and I will keep an eye on Matt now that he's trying to straighten himself out. He can live with us while you're gone."

"He has too much more to learn and I can't chance wasting that much time. Anyway, I swore I wouldn't go through the hell of chemo. It probably wouldn't work anyway, just prolong the suffering.

After a few days of settling into his new job, Matt couldn't wait to get to the shop. It was his fly fisherman's Nirvana. He used what I'd taught him and what he could get out of the guides every morning to help customers select their flies, tackle, and good places to fish. He became Ethan's favorite employee after he started helping to fill the fly bins. Then Emma began insisting he work full shifts, but as much as Matt loved his job, he declined. Afternoons were his and mine to fish together. Learning to guide was his number one concern and main objective, and I was determined to see he achieved that goal.

Though the prime fishing season had just started, the Macstatts were already turning down guide trips because they were short of guides. Soon after Matt went to work, the Macstatts goaded me into running several trips. Those two days on the river reminded me of how I detested dealing with inept clients and rowing high-sided drift boats in the incessant Montana gales. And I'd made that clear to the Macstatts, but several days later Emma started on me again. "Henry, won't you guide for us till we can find more help? We're disappointing customers and losing a lot of money having to turn down trips."

"If it's an emergency I'll do it, but if you need a fulltime guide as bad as you let on, then why don't you hire Matt?"

Ethan cut his angered eyes at me. "He don't know shit about guiding, so drop it."

"I'm better qualified than you are to judge if he's ready to guide or not. I've been working with him every day for weeks now and he can row as good as I can and knows the river and enough about fishing and has the personality. Hell, yes, he can guide. You're just afraid you'll lose your ace fly tier, and worse, have to admit you were wrong about him again."

"I'm not wrong. He doesn't have the physical or mental ability to guide, especially on the Madison. We're not desperate enough to hire him as a guide, and I doubt we ever will be."

I felt my temper starting to rise and knew it was time to leave. "Okay, Ethan, it's your business, but one of the other outfitters are going to hire him if you don't. Matter of fact, Jonas Nowakowski asked me this morning in the cafe if he had intentions of guiding. He's seen him on the river and knows his potential. I bet if Matt went down there and applied, Jonas would hire him on the spot."

"What a joke. Only a fool would hire him to guide."

"Or only a fool wouldn't hire him," I said, and stormed out determined more than ever to prove Ethan wrong about Matt.

Several days later Matt and I were floating the Madison below Ruby Creek. I dropped the oars and the anchor in frustration. "I don't give a damn if you want to fish dry flies or not," I said. "Put the indicator and weight on and fish a nymph like I told you."

"Slinging that gob of junk isn't fly fishing."

"You just started fly fishing and you're already a fucking purist. Just do it, okay? I despise fishing nymphs with indicators, too, but it's an essential technique for a guide to know because it's the easiest and best way for a beginner to catch a trout on a fly." He acted like he was in agony, but he started rigging the nymph and indicator. "You and Ethan getting along?"

"Only when he needs me to tie flies. The rest of the time he's not so nice. I haven't done anything to make him not like me either."

"Ethan's like me, he's old and judges people on first impression, which is mainly by their appearance. That's why I keep telling you to shave and to get your hair cut and lose that disgusting earring."

"All my friends have long hair and wear earrings."

"What have your friends done for you lately? If people don't like you for what you are, they're not really your friends. Are any of them paying your bills?"

Matt tore off several yards of line and made a cast. He put intended emphasis on splashing the nymph rig down as hard and as sloppy as he could just to piss me off. "Of course not," he said.

"To hell with them then. You should be trying to make an impression on Vic and Cleatis and the other guides as well as Ethan. They're your real friends. And wake up. That was a trout that just took your fly."

"Who cares? I'd just as soon not catch a trout as to have to fish this way."

"You're a little shit sometimes, kid. Better get used to doing things you don't like if you intend on being a guide."

Though there were some rough times because of his stubbornness, in weeks I taught Matt guiding techniques that would have otherwise taken him years to learn on his own. He was by no means a finished guide by mid-July, but he'd learned enough to where he could satisfy most clientele, which were novices anyway. All he needed was some confidence and for me to convince Ethan Macstatts to give him the chance to prove himself, and that opportunity arose out of some bad luck a few days later.

I came in on the end of the conversation but got the gist of the story. Then I watched the client mope out of the shop with his head down. "How did that wimp manage to do that to Vic?" I said.

"He thought he was helping him launch his boat. He pushed it too hard off the trailer and Vic grabbed the handrail to slow it down and it dislocated his shoulder," Emma said.

"Clients need to stay out of the way. They don't know what's going on out there."

"He was just trying to help, Henry. Stop being so hard on him. Dan's a good guy," Emma said.

"What are you going to do now? Vic won't be able to row for the rest of the season," I said.

Ethan spoke up. "To be honest, we were hoping you'd take his place."

I felt terrible for what had happened to Vic. Now he'd be subjected to taking clients on wade trips the rest of the season, but his misfortune could be another blessing in disguise for Matt. "I told you, talk to Matt if you want a full-time guide, but count me out."

The Macstatts exchanged desperate glances. I smiled and went to the library section while they pondered. I took out a book and pretended to be reading as I watched Ethan stomp around the shop with Emma chiding close on his tail. I couldn't understand what was being said, but by Ethan's crestfallen and defeated look, I knew it had to be good. I started getting the cozy feeling that Matt was about to be promoted from shop clerk to Madison River guide.

Ethan looked as if he had a case of the vapors when he came storming up fifteen minutes later. "All right damn it! Get him lined up. Old man Grundy's coming to town in a few days. If he can make that cantankerous old bastard happy, he's got a job rowing a boat. Nobody else is going to guide him."

Now that he was going to guide, my next course of action was finding Matt some sort of transportation that would pull my boat and carry two clients and their gear to the river. An old friend who worked for the Forest Service kept an old truck just for hunting and it fit the description. I figured if he still had the wreck, he might be willing to sell it, so I headed to Cam Cook's office to see.

Cam was ecstatic when he saw me standing in the doorway of his office. In our younger days when he was single and had been a smoke jumper, we sometimes hung out together in the Kozey Bar. Cam liked to brawl back in those days and had a knack for starting one and for finishing it as well. It wasn't unusual for his boozing to result in a donnybrook with either the local bikers or the Ennis cattle truck drivers who thought they were tough but because of Cam's skill and passion for fisticuffs found out the hard way they weren't.

After explaining that Matt was guiding for Ethan and had an upcoming trip with Sam Grundy and needed a rig, I asked Cam if he still had the ancient International Harvester pickup and would he be willing to sell it.

"Are you kidding? Think I'd ever part with a machine like that? They don't make them like that anymore. Damn, Henry, anyway that truck's part of my family."

"Bullshit, how much will you take for the pile of junk?"

"Ain't for sale. It may not look like much, but it's still a damn good truck."

"Come on, this is important. If the boy's going to guide, he needs transportation. You never drive that piece of shit anyway. You can't even find parts for it anymore."

"Why are you wasting our time? I bet he don't make it a week guiding anyway."

"He'll make it. Now sell me the truck. I'll give you five hundred for it."

"I want to help you, Henry, and I don't want to knock the kid out of a job, but my sons and I need that truck during hunting season to haul elk and deer out. I just can't sell it."

"Would it make any difference if I told you Matt was my grandson?"

"Your grandson? I'll be damned. I didn't even know you had a kid."

"Guess I never told you I have a daughter. But please don't let him know I'm his grandfather. I'm afraid he might run off if he found out."

"What in hell are you talking about?"

After explaining my situation with Matt, Cam's attitude softened. "I just can't sell that truck, Henry. I need it and it has too much sentimental value. But I'll make a bet with you. If he lasts a week guiding without quitting or getting fired, I'll let him borrow it till hunting season providing he pays for anything he tears up. And if he don't make it you owe me a case of my favorite whiskey."

"It's a deal," I said, and shook his hand before he had time to renege.

"Sipping that free whiskey's going to be mighty fine this winter. He won't even make a day without old man Grundy throwing his ass in the river."

Cam's comment bore truth. Sam Grundy had been fishing the area for years, and his bad temperament was known by everyone in West Yellowstone, especially the guides. His fishing partner, Rutherford Sanders, was even worse. No guide had ever volunteered to guide them, except for me. I liked the old men because they were straight shooters. Maybe they were hard, but they were fair and generous with tips if you did a good job.

The morning of his first guide trip, Matt's usual voracious appetite had vanished. He'd become overwhelmed with apprehension and chewed on his lower lip instead of his usual plate of eggs and bacon.

"Nervous, Matt," I said.

"No, I'm scared to death."

"But isn't this what you've been dreaming of?"

"Yes, but now that it's here and really going to happen, I'm afraid I'll mess it up."

"Look, I've been where you are and know what you're feeling and thinking. You can row and fish, but not sure you can satisfy a client paying $325.00 for a day of your services."

"Suppose they don't catch anything after paying all that money?"

"So, what if they don't?"

"They'd blame me."

"So."

"What would I do?"

"All you can do is the best you can. If they strike out, tell them tough shit and to learn how to fish before they come back to Montana."

"I can't tell them that. Ethan would fire me."

"Then don't guide if you're scared of failing."

The thought of quitting seemed to bolster him. "Okay, I'll do my best. But you say they're mean."

"I guided those two grumpy bastards for years. They're partners in an Atlanta law firm and used to having their way. Just be nice and kiss their asses and give them a long and pleasant day. They're fussy, but they can fish. They tip good, too, if you do a good job."

I helped him hitch my boat to Cam's old truck to be sure in his nervousness that it was done right. He then disappeared in a cloud of dust and blue exhaust down the drive but was back in minutes. I went back out to see what the problem was. "What are you doing back here?"

He walked past me back to the porch and grabbed the boat anchor. "Couldn't make it through a day without this." He placed the anchor in a metal milk crate in the bed of the Harvester so it wouldn't slide around and damage anything and headed back inside the cabin.

"Where you going now? You're already late."

"Got to go again."

I figured his bowels were torn up because of his frayed nerves. I left for town while he was still on the pot.

After catching up on the past with Grundy and Sanders at the shop, I watched with amusement for twenty minutes as Ethan went back and forth from his tying desk to the front window wringing his hands watching for Matt. The old men's patience had long since worn out, and they were letting everyone in the shop hear about it and Ethan wanted their disruption gone.

When Matt finally did pull in across the street the two old geezers were shocked on seeing the window-rattling, smoke-bellowing truck being driven by their ponytailed guide. It had a clutch Matt wasn't used to and it bucked and lurched as he backed the boat and truck into a parking space.

Grundy jumped Matt the second he stepped in the shop. "You think that pile of junk's going to get us to the river? Damn thing sounds like a Sherman tank and smokes as bad as one, too."

"We've been waiting on you for almost an hour, boy. You ain't going to make no kind of a guide sleeping all day. Let's get the hell out of here," Sanders said.

Everyone in the shop crowded to the windows to watch as Matt loaded his clients and their gear into the truck. The men were in his face the entire time. Before climbing into the wreck, Grundy put his hands on his hips, shook his head, and kicked a front tire. Then they were off to the river in a cloud of dust, a bellow of smoke and a cacophony of banging and roaring with their terrified and unproven guide at the wheel.

That morning in the shop Grundy and Sanders and I had agreed to meet at the Bottoms Up Tavern on Hebgen Lake for dinner. I was having a scotch when the boisterous old men came bouncing in. They ordered drinks at the bar before joining me. Matt headed straight to the restroom.

"Damn, Henry, I believe that boy's going to take your job," Grundy said, after taking a seat across from me. He was smiling broadly.

"Did he do okay today?" I said, dreading what was to come.

"After we got to fishing, he did a great job. It was touch and go at first, though. He let the boat get away from him at the ramp and fell in over his waders running it down. Then he dropped and spilled the cooler getting it in the boat, and the ice and everything else was covered in dirt. Half mile down the river we almost sank because he forgot to put the plug in. Took him almost an hour to bail it out, but from then on after he got over the nerves, he did great. As good a day fishing as I've ever had," Grundy said.

"Guess everybody at the ramp had a good laugh then?"

"They did, but he didn't let it get to him. One of them asshole Ennis guides gave him some shit about it all when he floated by later, but Matt handled that fine. Where'd you find him, Henry?"

"Under a rock. Now tell the truth, what do you really think about him?"

"Seems like an all-right kid if he'd get a haircut and throw that ridiculous earring in the river. I'll say this for him, though, he sure put us on fish. And he knew which flies to use, too," Sanders said. "And by the way, I witnessed a miracle today. We floated what, ten or twelve miles down that rock and boulder strewn torrent in a strong wind and he never touched a single rock. He's a marvelous rower, too, Henry. He's going to make a great one if he keeps at it."

"He wants to guide so bad it's about to kill him. And if he can make it through a few days with you two riding his ass, I figure he's probably got a chance."

"He did a superb job with his limited experience. We sure gave him hell at first, but it didn't seem to daunt him any. He really seems to have a passion for it all right."

"That's good. I'm not wasting my time on him if he doesn't. You sure it wasn't that bad?"

"Hell no. Matter of fact we want him the rest of the week if we can get him. There's something about that boy that makes me enjoy his company, same as with you, Henry."

A few days after Matt's first guide trip, I was in the Yellowstone Fly Shop killing time before heading to Swan Creek when a young couple came in. None of the other clerks were around, so Ethan went to help them. "What can I do for you folks?" he said.

"Are you the owner?" the man asked with a stern tone.

"Yes, I'm Ethan Macstatts."

"There's a young man with a ponytail rowing a wooden boat with your shop's name on it. The past several days he's been guiding two older men."

Emma had been listening since she'd noticed Ethan gawking at the shapely woman, and she immediately came over. Ethan's mouth started moving, but nothing would come out, so Emma took over. "What's he done?"

"So far he's helped make our fishing trip out here miserable," the man said.

Ethan headed back to his desk looking at me like he wanted to kill. "Damn you, Henry Ball," he said, under his breath as he passed by.

"How?" said Emma.

"Seems every time we see him his clients are playing a fish, and we've hardly caught any. And the few we have caught are mostly whitefish. Our guide floats us down the middle of the river while your guide walks his boat along the bank so his clients can fish the best water. My wife needs instruction, but our guide has ignored her."

"So, I still don't understand what the problem is," Emma said.

"There's really not a problem. I guess we just feel slighted and jealous. It's just that he's so good we feel we deserve him to guide us."

Ethan got to his feet and started to say something, but Emma's glare put him back down. She pulled the schedule book and turned some pages. "He's booked the next two days, but he's available this weekend."

They both broke into smiles before they hugged. "Awesome. We'd like to schedule him both days."

Ethan had given a slide presentation at the Phoenix Trout Unlimited Banquet during the previous winter, and a pharmaceutical corporation had booked several of the shop's guides to fish groups of their clients over a two-week period beginning the first of August on the Big Horn River. Because of Vic's dislocated shoulder, Matt was called on to go in his place.

While Matt was away, I fished fruitlessly for the Swan Creek trout most every morning. I read and tied flies in the evenings, but mostly I was miserable without Matt's company. And to make it worse, I finally worked up enough backbone to call Doc Holmes and he confirmed that Hope had closed the house down and moved back to Massachusetts like she'd threatened. Then he gave me ten minutes of unmitigated hell for not coming back for the chemo treatments and out of frustration he finally hung up on me. I called Timmy Carter as well and he informed me his wife had taken over the responsibilities of caring for my clients. She'd found guides for most of them but had to cancel others.

I'd spoken to Sara just after Matt had left to go to the Bighorn and she seemed satisfied with his situation after I'd convinced her that he'd just run away again if he went home against his will. She eventually agreed, and I believe she realized he was better off with me for the time being. As soon as he was back from the Big Horn and I could get him out of Ethan's grasp, I intended taking him to meet James Mason. Maybe he could talk some sense into Matt and persuade him to forget his idiotic notion of guiding, and for my sake, to go home.

Fog had the mountains grappled in obscurity and daylight came grudgingly under the sooty, roily clouds. Despite the steady drizzle, the day was pleasingly cool and windless. Though the weather was dreary, I knew it would bring on an abundance of aquatic insect hatches that would possibly persuade the Swan Creek trout to leave its lair and feed. When I drove by Hebgen Lake, I figured the smart thing to do would be to fish there instead of wasting another day on one fish that most likely wouldn't show anyway. It'd been over twenty days since I'd hooked the fish, and I hadn't seen it again. If I fished the lake, mayflies would emerge for hours in the dismal weather, and with the surface like a windowpane, the trout would feed in the calm meniscus until well into the afternoon. But I was consumed with the Swan Creek trout, and the sight of the brightly and varied colored armada of belly boats scattered on the lake convinced me to go on.

By the time I'd slipped to my vantage below the log pile, mayflies were hatching in droves. I decided that if the fish wasn't enticed to come out to gorge on this feast, I was giving it up. Twenty days of driving to the river and walking over a mile through the muck and grass to get to the log jam without seeing the fish had diminished my determination and was wearing me out physically as well.

As I was sifting through fly boxes for a suitable fly pattern to try if the fish should appear, the unmistakable gulp of a surface feeding trout came from near the logjam. I was right. The gloominess of the day and the bounty of food had drawn the giant fish out to feed.

For ten minutes I marveled watching it feed before I made the first cast. But drifting amid the myriad of natural duns, my imitation was ignored. Another cast, and the fish again chose a natural instead. Something amiss with my next offer caused the fish to stop feeding, so I quit casting and began searching through my fly boxes for a different fly. Eventually I came across a pattern I hadn't tried in years – a Marinaro thorax pattern – and decided to tie it on.

After fifteen minutes the fish reappeared, and I didn't cast till it was sipping insects in confident rhythm again. And on my second offer, the fish ate my artificial in a leisurely rise. After setting the hook the trout raced for the logjam. I pressured the leader as hard as I dared to keep it in open water long enough for me to dash into the stream and block the path to its lair. Then the spooked fish had no alternative but to go upstream and lie in a deep run where it stayed and eventually tired a quarter hour later. After it floated to the surface exhausted – its gill plates flaring gulping oxygen – I waded out and hand-tailed it to drag it to shore.

But as I was wading backwards out of the stream, ill fate struck again. I stumbled and lost my grip on the fish, and before I could clear my cramped hand, the fish bolted, the reel handle whacked my fingers and the fragile leader broke. Then the great spotted fish swam leisurely downstream and dissolved back into the safety of the jumble of logs.

I was so engrossed in agonizing thought over losing the fish while slogging back to my truck that I didn't notice the bear till I was on top of it. He was apparently snoozing near the path hidden in the meadow grass and I was within yards of it when it rose on its hind legs. I started backing away explaining with my quaking voice that everything was going to be okay. The bear kept rolling its head and snuffling air. Then my feet tangled in the grass and I fell hard on my ass. A jolt of terror coursed through me and my voice left when he looked down and his beady little pig eyes locked with mine. They seemed void of any capacity of feeling, except for death. When he dropped back to all fours, I expected a charge, but instead he ambled into the nearby timber like our meeting was an everyday occurrence and never looked back. It was a great effort making my rubbery legs function going the short distance to my truck. Then it took both hands to steady the key into the ignition a half-hour later.

I stopped by the fly shop on my way through town in hope some conversation might lift my mood after the disastrous and gloomy day. Ethan looked up from his vise when I came in from the pouring rain. "Any luck today, old timer?"

"Nope. Aren't Matt and the guides due back today?"

"They left Hardin this morning and should be rolling in anytime now."

I went behind Ethan's tying desk and took a seat next to him. "I wonder if I did the right thing by getting him into this."

Ethan's meticulous hands stopped working and he swiveled his chair around to face me. "I'd say definitely yes and that you were his salvation."

"He could be doing better things you know, like getting an education."

"There's plenty of time for that. Let him live his dream for a while. He'll make the right decision when he grows up and is forced to be responsible. That day will come fast enough. After all the time and effort you've gone through getting him to where he is, you surely don't want to quit on him now, do you?"

"I just don't want him to get caught up in it like I did and wake up one day old and broke and to find his life was a fantastic waste that's passed him by."

"Thanks, Henry. I'm glad Emma didn't hear you say that."

"Now wait, Ethan, that doesn't mean I don't appreciate all you and Emma have done for me."

"You've reformed Matt from a worthless pothead to a responsible young man. You should have pride in that. Stop worrying. He's going to be fine. But how about you? How are you doing?"

"Do you mean with my health or losing Hope?"

"I mean your health. I know you're agonizing over her."

"Most days I feel okay, but some I feel weak and fatigued. Guess I should be grateful I'm doing as well as I am. For his sake, I hope I can make it a while longer."

"Hard to believe you'd gamble your life over this."

"You just don't understand it all, Ethan. If Matt comes in soon tell him I'm at the restaurant down the street."

I went back out into the miserable day and bought a pack of cigarettes at a liquor store walking to the cafe. I got a table up front and smoked while watching the endless parade of tourists cruising by. They were people who could afford vacations and had families to share their lives with. They had set routines with clear bearing. They had responsibilities to others. I'd always felt sorry for them because they were unencumbered for only a few weeks a year to go someplace like here, then they were slaves to routine and misery, living an existence and not a life. The path I wanted Matt to take suddenly became confusing. I didn't want him to end up like me, but neither did I want him to be miserable and unhappy suffering through what is considered a mundane, normal life, especially with having the addiction for what he was doing that he'd inherited from me.

Someone bundled against the weather jogging up the street brought me out of my twisted thoughts. His build or mannerisms or something looked familiar. But then a gust of wind blew his hood off and exposed a short haired, copper-faced kid I didn't recognize. He came on into the restaurant and paused to hang his parka by the door. When he spotted me, he waved and came to my table wearing a big grin. "What's the matter, old man? I've only been gone a few weeks and you act like you don't recognize me."

I struggled to hide my astonishment as I shook his hand. "Welcome back, Matt. How'd it go over on the Big Horn?"

"Great. That river is amazing. Hatches and rising fish all day."

"Did they scalp you at Fort Smith?"

He grinned and rubbed his close-cropped head. "It was getting to be too much trouble."

"I sure like it."

"I figured you would. You griped about it enough."

"You know, I've been thinking since you've been gone. You really need to consider going back home and to school. Then when this guiding thing wears off, you'll be able to get a good job in the real world."

His face clouded. "I don't want a real job. This is the life I want, Henry. This is the first time in my life I've really been happy. I don't have any desire to go back home or to school."

"At least think about it. You could guide out here in the summer till you finished college. The Marine Corps would pay for your education if you joined. You could do a hitch and see the World and all that bullshit."

"Stop wasting your breath. Nothing you can say will make me change my mind."

"Fishing shuts down here after October. What will you do the rest of the year?"

"Guide elk hunts or something. Vance said he could use me on the ranch he manages in the winter in Arizona."

"I told you to forget about guiding big game hunters. I told you before, bird hunters are the clientele you want. They're like fly fishermen, a more sporting and professional class of people."

"Since I don't know anything about bird hunting, would you be willing to teach me?"

"Suppose you want to have a family someday? Even if you guided year-round you wouldn't be able to support a family on guide's wages without a struggle."

With that, his insolence and defiance surfaced. "What I do with my personal life is no concern of yours, so keep out of it."

"I thought for a minute you might have grown up some, boy, but you've still got a long way to go. You think you know about life and what it takes to survive, but you don't."

At that, he got up, grabbed his coat and disappeared back out into the storm.

Later that week Ethan and I were in the basement of the fly shop. Neither Matt nor I had brought our argument up about his future again, and things seemed to be back to normal between us. Ethan was wearing yellow, elbow-length, rubber gloves leaning over a vat dipping a white hackle cape into ginger colored dye. I was searching through some old boxes of fly-tying hooks hoping to find a discontinued style I liked. It was nice down in the quiet and coolness of the basement, even though the dye and formaldehyde stench of the animal skins was atrocious.

"What's the matter, Henry, you get so old you quit fishing?"

"What do you mean?"

"You haven't been all week, have you?"

"That's right."

"Why not?"

"I'm not into it right now. I've got more important things on my mind. If you ever gave Matt a day off, I'd go with him."

"If he's not working, he's off with that girl, so forget ever fishing with him again."

"I can't blame him. She'll be going back home to school soon and then he'll be brokenhearted."

There were no treasured hooks hidden away in the box, so I started packing them away.

"I'll let you in on something if you'll give me your word you won't say anything," Ethan said.

"You got it."

"Cleatis said he gave her a ring. They're getting married some-time soon. She's supposed to stay here with him through the winter."

I slammed the box back in its place on the storage rack. "Bullshit, Ethan. Don't joke about such stuff."

"I'm not bullshitting you. I swear it's the truth."

"I wondered why he got so defensive when I mentioned how hard it would be keeping a family up on guide's wages. I'll have to figure out some way to talk him out of it. Ruining his own life is bad enough, but he shouldn't ruin Sandy's, too."

"Henry, you're so full of shit. When a man gets the notion to marry, nothing's going to change his mind. You know that."

"I didn't realize they were that serious. It'll be hopeless. I need a morning whiskey. Come with me, Ethan. Let's go to the Kozey Bar and have a drink."

"You go on. It's too early to be drinking, and anyway, some of us have to work for a living."

The Kozey Bar was empty except for a female bartender scribbling on a clip board replenishing the liquid inventory. I interrupted her and ordered a double scotch hoping it would relieve the shock of the news of the engagement. Shortly after Labor Day, Matt would be unemployed. He could possibly hire on to drive a snow buggy through the Park during the winter for minimum wage. Sandy could wait tables for tips and suffer the abuse of the snowmobile freaks. As I went to the bar for a refill a tour group of elderlies began filing by on their way to the dining area. In passing, most of them cast thirsty glances at the neatly lined bottles behind the bar. One man looked my way with an envious stare, and I held up my glass as an invitation to join me, but his wife jerked his arm and he followed her obediently on.

I was on my third drink when a woman came in appearing as dejected and despondent as I was. She took a seat at the bar and ordered a drink. After sampling it, she got up to study the game heads and artwork hanging on the walls around the room. Though she was plump, I imagined she'd once had nice legs and a world-class ass. The more I watched her the more her mannerisms seemed familiar. Eventually, she looked my way, and after a thoughtful stare, her spirits seemed to lift. I was bewildered when she came and collapsed in a chair across from me with an appeasing smile. "Do I know you?" I said.

"I know I've aged and gotten chubby, but I hope not so much so that you don't recognize me, babe."

I knew her voice but couldn't place it. Her eyes I knew I'd peered into before. "You look familiar, but I can't remember who you are."

"You haven't changed much, Henry Ball."

The whiskey on an empty stomach was hitting me hard. If I'd had a clearer head, I might have recalled who she was. An old client's wife from the past, I guessed.

"Don't you remember fucking me that night on the Missouri? The sunset and moonrise? Humping all night on the prairie like coyotes in heat? If you don't remember that, you're a hopeless son of a bitch."

"Laney!"

She got up and ambled around the table and hugged and then kissed me on the lips. I wanted to gargle with the scotch when she turned to go back to her seat. "Do you hate me, darlin', for running out on you like I did? I just had to get out of that dumpy town. Oh, Henry, it was so hard for me to leave as much as I loved you."

"I couldn't hold a grudge for forty years, now could I?"

"Where you been all this time, love?"

"Here and there. I live in the Keys now. How about you?"

She giggled and glanced around the empty room and lowered her voice. "I wouldn't tell just anybody this, Henry. I started an escort business in Vegas with my Aunt Charlene. I never told you about her, but she got paroled from prison for tax evasion and for running a prostitution ring back in Philadelphia just after I got to Helena. That's why I left when I did. She had a tidy sum stashed away before she was sent up and I left when I did to help her get the business going. She died some years back and left it all to me. I sold out two years ago. Made a killing, too. Damn, I wish you'd come to see me. We could have had such a grandiose time."

"I couldn't have afforded a high-class whorehouse like that."

"Please don't call it that. And you know I wouldn't have charged you, Henry."

"It's ironic, but when we first met, I figured you were a virgin. I was reluctant to even touch you for fear of offending you."

"I remember. I can still see the fear in your eyes – like a boy his first time."

"I'd never have figured you for a prostitute till James told me the truth about you. It was all over town, too. But even though you broke my heart and made a fool of me, I've got to admit, you're the best fuck I've ever had."

An angelic smile formed on her haggard old face. "Why, thanks, Henry. What a nice compliment. Why don't you come up to my room right now and we'll relive some old memories?"

"I'd love to, Laney, but I've got to meet somebody in a few minutes."

"If I remember right, it won't take but one."

I had to laugh. "How about a rain check?"

"I'll be here the next few nights. Leave a note at the desk. I'd love to spend some time with you, Henry." Then she lifted her brows and smiled. "If you know what I mean."

"I'll look you up. I promise."

We toasted, and I killed my drink and got out of there like the fuse on a bomb was burning under the table.

After the news of Matt and Sandy, and the encounter with Laney, I wanted to be alone. Nobody would bother me at Swan Creek, except maybe the bear, and at that moment I'd been happy if it ate me.

The sun was hot and heavy, my sweat-soaked shirt clung annoyingly to my back. I had to bend against the howling wind walking the mile to the logjam. Conditions were perfect for the giant trout to be out gorging on grasshoppers. Tussocks of grass overladen with seed had collapsed and curtained the undercut by its lair. If it hadn't deserted the log jam because of our last confrontation it should be waiting behind the tussocks to ambush any struggling hopper the wind delivered.

I'd left town in such a rush I hadn't thought of water, and it became an effort to swallow from the coagulated phlegm collected in my throat. My head pounded as if a derrick was inside. All were the results of the morning whiskey. After an hour, I started thinking about leaving when the sound of slashing and splashing of aggressively feeding fish in the bend below made me reconsider. But by mid-afternoon I couldn't take anymore, even though a lot of nice fish were in a frenzy feeding up and down the creek. I was so thirsty in fact I began thinking of chancing Giardia and drinking from the creek. As I stood to leave, a broad crease from the undercut went up and then back down the creek. At first, I thought I'd spooked the giant trout, but five minutes later the water furrowed again as it came from the undercut to take another hopper.

The fish then began feeding with abandon making a great commotion devouring every hopper that came down the creek. I became mesmerized by the display and for some time forgot I had a rod in my hand. When my presence of mind returned, I stripped some line out and then cast near the overhanging grass where it was holding, and on my first offer it boiled out and took. The great fish fought hard against the heavy leader, but after fifteen minutes of unrelenting pressure I lead it onto a gravel bar whipped and finished. I laid my rod beside it to show a perspective of its size before snapping a dozen quick photos. Then I slid it back into the creek and watched as it swam slowly back into the jumble of logs. I felt vindicated for my previous blunders, full of pride for the accomplishment, but I still felt disappointed the finale hadn't been more challenging and spectacular. It was as if it'd wanted to be caught it'd been so easy. Only my old age blunders had prevented it from being done sooner. I was elated, too, in knowing I'd made my last hike up the valley and that I could put the trout behind me and concentrate on the most important matter, which was Matt and his future and wellbeing.

I waited at a photo mat while the pictures were developed, then went to the shop. Ethan was scribbling on a clipboard checking the fly bin inventory and looked up when I went in. "You sure look happier than when you left here this morning," he said. "That's the first time I've seen you smile in a long time."

"Take a look at these, Ethan."

He took the package, then spilled the photos onto the counter and began flipping slowly through admiring them. "Holy shit, no wonder you've been spending so much time on Swan Creek. That's the biggest trout I've ever seen caught around here. Looks like something out of a horror movie with that hooked jaw."

"Just don't tell anybody where I caught it. I don't want to be the cause of Swan Creek being over-run."

"If it weren't for the bear stories, it would be anyway. Matter of fact, Cam told me he was in there the other day and saw an old boar that had no fear and acted like he owned the place."

"I know. He and I met, and close enough to shake hands. I was going to tell Cam he needed to close that area off. It really is dangerous in there. That old bear's starving and he's going to hurt somebody if they screw up and blunder into him. I don't know why he didn't eat me."

"That's what Cam's afraid of. He's going to take the bear patrol in there in a few days and dart him and haul him off somewhere to the backcountry."

I felt my blood begin to rise. "He's too old to go through that stress. Those idiots will end up killing him. That place belongs to him. There're signs on every tree warning people to stay out. If somebody gets eaten, it's their own damn fault. Cam could close the area off and let the poor bastard die a natural death this winter like he deserves."

"Calm down. You know people out of their environment get dumb. You've got to remove situations like that bear from them. Some fool would wind up wandering in there regardless if the Park closed it off or not."

"Just don't tell Matt where I caught it. It's too dangerous and he's hard-headed enough to go in there to try to catch it."

"Okay, Henry. Mind if I keep this photo to hang on the fish board?"

"Sure, Ethan, but tell everybody I caught it on Duck Creek. There aren't any big trout in that stream and there's not any bears there to hurt anyone either."

At breakfast the next morning, the conversation began with the big trout. Matt had seen the photo I'd left at the shop when he'd gone to check in after his guide trip the afternoon before. Now he was ecstatic and insisted he go try to catch it. But after a lot of arguing and lies I was satisfied I'd convinced him that I'd caught it on Duck Creek and then I changed the subject. "So, how long since you've checked in with your folks?"

"I call every week or so."

"Don't they want you to come home? You've been gone a long time. I'm sure they miss you."

"Mom always asks if I'm ready to come home. I keep telling her no. I might go back Christmas if Sandy does."

"She isn't worried about you?"

"I told her about you helping me and she seems okay with it. I sent her a picture of my haircut. She was blown away. Said it was a great improvement, that she didn't recognize me."

"Does she know you do dope?"

"I don't anymore, Henry. I didn't take any when I went to the Big Horn and threw it all away when I got back. And you're right about what you said about friends. I know now who they are, and you're the best one I have. I should have told you that a long time ago. And thank you for all you've done for me. I just wish I knew why you were doing it."

He reached across the table and I punched his fist. "I'm not sure myself, Matt. Maybe it's because I never had a son and you've become like one."

We sat in silence eating, then something came to mind I'd been holding back asking for some time. "I've got an odd question for you, Matt."

"What is it?"

"Do you ever dream about a man that hunts with a spear? He's small and has long blond hair and brilliant blue eyes. He may run with a big lion sometimes."

He choked on the bite of sausage he was chewing and took a long drink of water. "You must have been reading my mind. I was just thinking about him. How did you know?"

"Just a hunch," I said.

"I've had the dreams since I was a kid. But how did you know?"

"You talk in your sleep."

He studied me long and hard but didn't say anything. I could tell he'd surmised something, but hopefully not who I was. I was all but sure he had, though, because of the way he changed the subject so quickly as if he suddenly knew but didn't want me to know he did.

"I know where you really caught that big fish," he said.

"I know you do. Duck Creek."

"You lie, old man. It was Swan Creek. I got it out of Ethan."

"That son of a bitch."

"He didn't come out and tell me. I saw the photo on his desk and fooled him into it. He tried to tell me you caught it on Duck Creek, but I know you never fish there. You've spent most of the summer on Swan Creek. Cleatis told me about that place and how big the trout are there."

"Okay, but I want you to promise me you won't go in there. An old bear's using the area and he could be dangerous."

"I know, I know. I've heard enough about the damned bear from Ethan."

"I'm serious, Matt. Don't go in there or you'll really piss me off."

"Don't get mad. I was just kidding. You just don't want me catching your big fish and showing you up is all."

Next morning, I went to the fly shop to see when Matt had a break in his guiding schedule long enough to allow us to pay James Mason a quick visit. My state of mind about him and Sandy getting married had improved since we'd talked the morning before. I planned to talk to Sara about it and hoped if the two went home for

Christmas their folks would talk them out of it, or at least convince them to wait a few years.

"What's up, Ethan. Seen Matt this morning?" I said.

Ethan glanced up from a piece of mail he was reading. "He left with Sandy a few hours ago."

"Say where they were going?"

"Said Grayling Creek."

"By the way, I don't appreciate you telling him where I caught that fish. He was going in there this morning if I hadn't crawled his ass. Your word isn't worth shit anymore."

"I didn't tell him. He figured it out on his own. He's smart."

"No, you're just easy. Now I'll worry about him going in there. He seemed determined last night he was going to despite my warnings."

I was leaving the cabin for a walk the next morning when a truck came boiling up the drive. I saw the emotion on Vance's face as his rig slid to a stop. "Damn, Vance, what's up?"

"Seen Matt today, Henry?"

I knew what was coming. Matt had lied and disobeyed me. My heart started to race. "No. He didn't come in last night, but I figured he snuck in the dorm with Sandy and spent the night with her like he does most every night now."

"She didn't come back to the Laurel last night and the people at the Inn are worried."

I tried more excuses to ease the dread. "They probably just got to having fun and camped on Grayling Creek. They're probably hiking out now."

"I hate to tell you, Henry, but Cam went looking for them and found his old rig parked at Swan Creek this morning. He sent me to get you."

Cam and a young Park Ranger were waiting at the parking lot. I went over to the old Harvester and looked in. A photo of the big trout was on the cracked and faded dash.

"We waited on you, Henry. Figured you'd want to go with us," Cam said.

"Nobody else coming?"

"It's just going to be the three of us. I want to keep this quiet. I don't want to stir up a commotion and get a bunch of curious tourists in here."

I studied the Park Ranger. He looked too young to be shaving yet and I doubted he had any idea of the danger and tragedy that was likely waiting for us up Swan Creek. "That's good, Cam. Let's get going. If they're alive, they need our help."

Cam offered a chubby, bolt action rifle. "Better take this, Henry."

I put my hands up. "No thanks."

Cam then handed the rifle to the young Ranger. I could tell by the way he handled it he'd had little experience with long guns. "Why don't you leave those here?" I said. "That bear hasn't done anything he wasn't supposed to." Then I turned to the young Ranger. "You ever fired a rifle before, son?"

Cam broke in. "We've got to get them out, Henry, and I doubt he's going to give up a kill without a fight."

"If somebody panics with one of those cannons, it could be worse than the bear."

"Then why don't you take it?"

I shook my head. "Stop wasting time. Let's go."

"I should have removed that bear from here weeks ago," Cam said. "This wouldn't be happening if I had."

We stopped on the hill overlooking the valley and hung there peering out over the foreboding and lifeless landscape. "I got a feeling this ain't going to be good, Henry," Cam said.

"I knew that before I drove out here. Now let's go."

I led the way for a half mile, then I turned to Cam. "You ought to cross over. We could cover more ground if we spread out." He crossed the creek and left me with the young Ranger.

We went on for another half mile or so without incident, then the stench hit me. It was the foul smell of blood, brains, busted guts, and feces, the odors of brutal and violent death, the hellish-battlefield reek I'd never wanted to experience again. I motioned the young Ranger to get in front of me. "He's close so be ready," I said quietly.

Then the Ranger realized the foul smell and his face twisted in horror. He began to tremble, and I could hear his strained breathing. I glanced around looking for any sign of the bear. Across the creek was the rise where I'd cast from fishing for the mysterious giant trout. Guilt came crashing down on me with the realization that this nightmare wouldn't be happening if it hadn't been for my egotistical determination to catch the cursed thing. "Goddamn me," I said out loud.

The Ranger turned. "What'd you say?"

The sound of our voices brought the charge on. It lasted only seconds. The Ranger jerked around as flies exploded off the bear's cache as it came bounding out of the willows in great strides, low to the ground, padded feet thudding rhythmically. But most conspicuous was the rumble I felt more than heard when it growled and its teeth clicking like hailstones on rock. As the Ranger turned to run, I jerked the rifle from his grasp and flipped the safety. I shouldered the stock, touched the trigger and a gusher of red exploded from the bear's head as it closed to within yards.

There were body parts protruding from the mound of dirt where the bear had buried what was left of Sandy. A piece of leg with a ripped-off calf wearing a dainty hiking boot was most prominent. Globs of long glittering black hair were hanging in the willows. I heard a moan from the log pile where the misplaced trout lived and went over and pulled Matt out. He was in shock and his back had been clawed, but his ripped backpack had saved him from serious injury. Cam called on a satellite phone and an air ambulance came and took him to Bozeman. A group of high-ranking Park staff came to investigate. I hung around till they put what was left of Sandy in a body bag. I don't know what they did with the bear. Most likely left him there for nature to consume. Cam and I didn't see the young Ranger again till we were back at our rigs at the trailhead.

I didn't sleep that night, and next morning before daylight, feeling miserable and to blame for Sandy's death and languid and hungover from all the scotch I'd drank, I stowed mine and Matt's belongings in the camper and drove to town. I dropped the elk cabin key through the mail slot at the fly shop with a thank you and goodbye note to the Macstatts and then headed to Bozeman.

The hospital smelled of the antiseptic stench I despised. The nurses' white shoes squeaked like they were in a full court press bustling about on the shiny linoleum floor. Matt was in bed gazing transfixed out a window when I went into his room. "How do you feel?" I said.

After he emerged from his sedated stupor and realized it was me, he broke down and couldn't talk. He put his hand out and I took it. "Seeing someone you love get killed isn't pleasant, is it?" He sobbed and shook his head. "When I was your age, I saw a lot of my friends die and those memories have haunted me ever since. They'd faded some over the years but seeing and smelling what the bear had done brought them back as if they'd happened yesterday. You'll always see her, so get used to it."

His face twisted and I felt bad for being so blunt and squeezed his hand. Then I went to a window and started staring out. "It wasn't your fault, boy. I'm the guilty one because I had to catch that fish to prove a senseless point and satisfy my ego. But I do blame you for disobeying me. Take my advice and get over your crazy notion about guiding and go back home to your folks where you belong. Get an education and make something out of yourself." I waited for an answer, but it never came. I turned back to him. "How's your shoulder?"

He spit and drooled and sobbed and snot and tears streamed. "I'm going to be okay."

"I'm glad you weren't hurt badly, but I'm sorry for Sandy, I truly am. Did he eat your earring?"

He felt his ear where the pierce was. "I don't want the stupid thing anymore."

"Do your folks know?'

"Not yet."

"Call and tell them to come get you. I've had all I can take. I'm going home. I'll leave your gear downstairs."

He got out of bed and when I hugged him, I'd never felt so much pain, sorrow or sadness. I turned to leave and was almost out the door. "Henry, wait! I'll listen to you from now on. I love you, Henry. Oh, God, please don't leave me now."

I stopped and looked back and saw myself a long time ago hunched over propped against the bed, white robe undone and open, as much as naked, sobbing, crying and so pitiful. He needed me now more than ever and I knew then I wasn't going to abandon him then or ever.

"You ever heard of P.T.S.D., Mr. Ball?" Matt's psychiatric physician asked.

This was the third meeting I'd had with Dr. Glenn Hamilton. He was a fit and handsome man who appeared to be in his late thirties. He came across as being very professional. I had all the confidence in the world in his opinion and expertise in treating Matt's mental state. "Never heard of it, Doctor," I said.

"Post-traumatic stress disorder is a mental condition that's usually caused by severe fear and or trauma. Most cases are men from combat situations that have experienced imminent encounters with death. Matt experienced such fear during the bear attack when the bear tried getting him out of the log jam after he'd seen it kill his friend. Can you imagine an innocent kid like Matt having to listen through the night while she was ripped and torn to pieces and eaten? And then the bear trying to get to him again and again in that jumble of logs? It's unimaginable. It's going to take time for Matt to get over this. He needs to be in an environment of peace and serenity where he feels secure. The busier he stays and the more his mind is kept from the attack the better off he'll be and the sooner he'll recover. Since you're his closest friend I want you to know and understand that. You've likely never been in a situation of inevitable death like he was in, so it's hard for you to understand. He'll experience moments of uncontrollable anger and periods of deep depression so severe it may bring him to suicide. I hope you can help him recover."

"I'll see to it he makes it through."

"By the way, have you ever been in a terrifying situation like he was in?"

"I was at the Chosin Reservoir."

He cocked his head in thought for a long moment, then said, "Oh, I see. Then you do understand."

"I do now. And he's my grandson and not just a friend, just so you know. But he doesn't need to know that." And I explained why.

CHAPTER 17

We were over an hour behind schedule heading to Wolf Creek to visit James Mason after having been stopped at every other milepost as work crews repaired the winter's damage to Interstate 90 between Belgrade and Manhattan. The air conditioner was gushing for all it was worth as the Eagles blared out one of their rock and roll songs, which was more to Matt's liking than my preference to their country rock. Matt's patience came to an end when yet another manly-clad, weather beaten woman in an orange vest flipped her yellow sign that read 'Slow' to the red one saying 'Stop'. "Damn! Come on," he said, and stomped his foot before twisting the volume on the radio down. "We're never going to get there like this."

We were again in for another long wait for the 'follow me truck' to come lead us through the one lane construction zone. I couldn't help but laugh. "Why don't you get out and tell her we need to get through so you can go fishing?"

A sheepish look appeared. "Because she might kick my ass." We didn't have to wait as long this time and when we passed the 'End of Work Zone' sign his spirits lifted, and he got back in the mood to talk. "Seems like everybody likes Judge Mason, even Ethan."

I rolled a half-smoked cigar stub back and forth between my lips as I contemplated. "The yuppies would say he's charismatic, but in my opinion, he's just full of bullshit and knows how to dish it out accordingly to dazzle the weak minded, so you'd better be careful."

I glanced over at him and there was no humor in his stare. "You're not much of a comedian," he said. "You know that don't you?" I grinned but said nothing. "How long have you known him?"

"Over forty years."

"Does he still fish?"

"What difference does that make?"

"Whether a man fishes or not is foremost in judging his character, for a man that doesn't fish is a man without purpose."

"Where did you come up with that line of bullshit?"

"Just now. And it's the truth."

"That's pretty smooth. Yes, he still fishes, but he enjoys drinking and pontificating more now that he's old."

"What's pontificating?"

"Don't worry, weak minded, you'll find out soon enough."

"You're an asshole, old man." He was smiling this time.

It'd been over two weeks since the bear attack. Dr. Hamilton had counselled Matt through the early stages of his grief and trauma. Considering what he'd been through I thought he was recovering well. But there were times when he'd break down and cry uncontrollably, but those times seemed to be getting further apart. And there were days when he was quiet and sullen and lethargic – symptoms of depression Hamilton had lectured me about. I well-remembered those times. The more Matt's mind was occupied the better he seemed to be. I thought a visit with James Mason and some days of fishing on the Missouri and the Little Prickly Pear would do him good. Then I wanted to take him to the White River bottoms. The peace and serenity there seemed to have helped me more than anything getting over the post trauma of the Chosin now that I understood why and what I'd gone through during those dark years.

Sara went into hysterics when I called and told her about the bear. She demanded I bring her boy home immediately, but I asked her to consider whether he would be better off there with her having to spend all her time caring for Ginny or in Montana with me doing what he loved. She talked to Dr. Hamilton and he told her Matt would most likely be better off with me because that was what Matt had told him he wanted. Matt put an end to the dilemma when he told Sara he wasn't coming home. He was eighteen and an adult now and she couldn't make him. In the end she wasn't happy but knew she had to let it go and thanked me for what I was doing.

James Mason was waiting on his front porch when Matt and I pulled up. Last time I'd seen him was the past spring boarding a plane out of Key West. His thick raven hair was streaked with white now, but he looked fit as ever and his eyes still held their playful sparkle as he put his hand out. "So, you must be Matt I been hearing about?"

"That's him. He's the troll I found living under the bridge on the Madison," I said.

"I bet he didn't look half as bad as you did when I found you. You were a filthy, whiskey reeking pig beat all to hell. I should have left your sorry ass in jail with all those other reprobates."

Matt was enjoying hearing how I was during the worst time of my life, but being my grandson, I'd rather he didn't know.

"And I won't elaborate on his womanizing since you appear to be a refined gentleman and a most unlikely companion for the likes of this old miscreant," Mason said.

"I'm not a fighter anymore, and I don't have much interest in women now days, either," I said.

"You're still just like you were forty years ago when you got us into all that trouble in West Yellowstone with the chief of police. Neither a leopard nor a redneck ever changes their spots."

"Damn, how many times have I heard you say that?" I'd had enough and went into the cool of the house. Mason laughed, and he and Matt followed me in.

Matt hadn't fished in over two weeks, and with his boundless enthusiasm still intact despite the recent tragedy, he was waiting with his flyrod before James Mason and I could finish lunch. He then herded us off to the Little Prickly Pear and Mason and I watched from the shade of a cottonwood grove as he probed the glimmering runs and sparkling riffles of the pacing little stream under the depthless blue sky. A warm breeze stirred the lush smell of a nearby mowed alfalfa field and the scent took me back to my first days on the ranch. Overhead, two Swainson's hawks screamed their contempt at our intrusion into their rookery as their paths intertwined riding the wind thermals. Mason scrounged his faithful dinged flask out and took a long drink. He grinned wiping the seepage off his chin. "So, do I call you Papa now, or Grand Henry, or what?"

"Always the lame comic. I need serious advice, James, about him," I said, tilting my head towards Matt.

"You're asking the wrong person if it's about child rearing. You know I have no experience with that. All I know, and it's only my personal assumption, is that when a child comes into this crazy world it's innocent and pure. Unless it's born mentally unstable, how it turns out depends on its environment and how its parents raise it. I was lucky and had a wonderful mother and father. They provided me food and shelter and made sure I got an education. They were always there when I needed advice, or love and kindness, and they were always ready to discipline me when I stepped out of line and needed it. But most importantly, they taught me the significance of morals and ethics, not to mention responsibility – crucial things that apparently aren't being taught today."

"I get down when I think about what a failure I was at being a father."

"You didn't have a chance with Sara, but you're making up for it now with what you're doing for Matt. You've obviously helped him get his life straightened out and on the right track. And you're teaching him how to make a living from what he loves. With what you're sacrificing you're doing more than most people can claim they do for their own children. These days public schools have been stuck with doing most kid's parenting since usually the parents are too busy working to do it or are just apathetic because they have someone else to do it. It's a bad thing, too, for the child and society. Crime statistics are proving that. Unwed mothers are a big part of it, but mainly it's because fathers won't take on the responsibility of raising their sons to be responsible men – not teaching them the importance of ethics and morals and the responsibility to care for their own. It seems that nurturing children is a diminishing instinct in this day and age, but obviously you still have it. I'm afraid bad times are coming to our society because men are abandoning their duties as fathers."

"But am I doing the right thing getting him involved in what I did? He could do better by going back to school and getting a professional job in the corporate world. He's too bright and ambitious to be a fucking trout guide."

"Being smart doesn't have anything to do with it. Being happy is what's most important. And you were the consummate throwback, so you must understand his undeniable motivation for doing what he's doing."

"I know. It's the damned curse of my ancestry, and unfortunately, he inherited my chromosomes. He even has the dreams of the little man and the lion."

"So, if he's so compelled and can be happy like you were, what difference does it make?"

"I wouldn't say I was happy. I did it because I don't think I could have led what's considered a normal life. I would have been miserable working a regular, regimented job with that incredible urge constantly pressing on me. And money didn't mean anything to me while I was young, and I thought I'd live forever. But now that I'm old I'm not so cocksure. My confidence fades a little more every day as my anxiety builds thinking about when I won't be able to work anymore, especially since I don't have any retirement and hardly any savings."

"Remember what you told me about that Cleatis Jones kid that guided with you in Yellowstone? The one that rebelled and ran away when his parents tried making him go to law school. If Matt wants to go back to school, he'll decide on his own. If he's half as stubborn as you were you won't force him. Here, shut up and drink some of this and give me one of those cigars."

I swapped a cigar for a pull off his flask, and he went on. "What you're doing with that boy is the most important and right thing to do, Henry. My advice to you is to teach him all you can so he can be his best at whatever it is he decides to do."

"But there's more to it than just Matt, James. For one thing, Hope couldn't accept me choosing to help him over going back home to her and she's left me, and I can't blame her. Losing her and the guilt for what I've done to her is tearing me apart inside, even though Matt's more important than anything else to me now."

"Look, you need to get this thing with him right in your mind, Henry. And don't go on feeling guilty about the way you lived your life, accept it. We all second guess what we did, whether we lived it right or wrong. Help the boy get started with his life if it's that important to you, then go home and get things straightened out with Hope and your business."

The three of us fished the Missouri and the Little Pear for the next several weeks and then Matt seemed to become bored with fishing, or most likely, he'd had all he could take of me and James Mason constantly bantering at one another. The only thing the two of us agreed on was the excellent upland game bird hatch that spring. The cut alfalfa and wheat fields along the Missouri and on the ranch were loaded with pheasant and Hungarian Partridge. When bird season opened, Matt was more than happy to abandon the drift boat and his two old grumpy mates for birds and a gun – for a chance to experience something novel.

We started the season out on the ranch hunting in the cool of the mornings, and there were plenty of birds. Mason had a young, inexperienced Labrador bitch from wonderful bloodlines he wanted me to start training and to my extreme delight Bess took to flushing and retrieving like a veteran that'd done it all her life. She instinctively knew how to quarter into the wind to locate birds, and of course to retrieve. I explained to Matt that certain breeds of dogs were born with selected traits, and the exposure to game ignited those inborn qualities like throwing a match to gasoline. And I explained it was like the killing instinct bred into him that ignited the first time he swung on a partridge and it erupted in a cloud of feathers when he pulled the trigger.

One night after dinner just after bird season opened, the three of us were in Mason's game room. Matt had kindled a fire and Mason was in his big chair nursing a dark brown drink.

"Matt, what kind of gun do you have?" Mason said.

"I'm using one of Henry's. It's worn out and I call it the jam-o-matic."

Mason shot me a look of disappointment as he got out of his chair. "That figures. If it's Henry's, it'd have to be a cheap piece of junk. Come here, I want to show you something."

Mason went to his cabinet and took out a gun that had a gold quail inlaid in the receiver. "My old man bought me this when I got my law degree at Austin. It's a Winchester Model 21. It was a great quail gun and ought to handle Hungarian partridge just as well. I haven't shot it since I moved here. I'd like for you to have it."

Mason offered the gun, but Matt put his hands up. "I can't take that."

"I don't have anybody to leave my guns to, or anything else I have for that matter. I don't know what will happen to it all when I die. Go on and take it. It'll make me happy knowing you'll put it to good use."

"I don't know what to say."

"You don't need to say anything. Just use and enjoy it."

After Matt hugged and thanked him, he admired the gun and shouldered it. It was long in the stock, and Mason saw that it was. "It needs to be fitted to you. I'll send it to Marty Fajen and have it done over the winter," Mason said.

Matt was gulping down corned beef hash saturated with runny egg yolk when I came down to breakfast the next morning. A stream of yellow had drooled down his chin and coagulated there. Mason was Two Stepping to Hank Williams, but Junior now.

"Grab a chair and sit down and eat. The boy's dying to try out his new gun. Bart Hendrix won't wait on you long. He'll be off and gone working if you don't get moving."

My appetite was waning, and I ate part of an egg and a few bites of sausage. Mason had been scrutinizing me. "You need to eat more, Henry. You're starting to look like a gaunt old man."

"I'll take a biscuit with me. What time you want us back?"

"I'm putting a brisket on the smoker this morning. It'll be ready by four. You'll be back before then, I'm sure."

The drive east to the Hendrix Ranch took almost an hour. Bart and a barking blue healer came out onto his front porch to greet us when we pulled up. Bart was dressed in a worn flannel shirt and soiled and stained blue jeans. A pair of ragged leather work gloves were hanging from a back pocket of his jeans. His roper boots were as dilapidated as the gloves. His sun-weathered face looked as abused as his boots. "Darn good to see you, Henry. You've lost weight, but you look well."

"Thanks, Bart. Looks like they're working the hell out of you."

"As always." Bart turned towards Matt. "Who's this here?"

Matt offered his hand. "I'm Mathew Whitaker. Glad to meet you, Mr. Hendrix. Thanks for letting us hunt."

"You bet. Long as you're a friend of Henry's, you're welcome on my place anytime. Don't hardly let nobody else on. Ain't been much bird hunting on the place since Henry quit guiding. He kept 'em thinned out pretty good." Bart stomped his foot. "Get damn you, Gus!" The heeler stopped nipping at Matt's calves and dashed onto the porch.

When I stopped laughing, I said, "Got to where I couldn't walk that much, Bart."

"Ought to get this boy here guiding, Henry. There're more birds now than ever."

"He's thinking of doing just that, Bart. He might come calling on you next fall if you don't mind."

Hendrix turned to Matt. "Son, you plan on it. Show him around the place, Henry. I got to get to combining alfalfa seed. If you get more of them grey partridge than you need, I'd like a few."

"They'll be cleaned and waiting in your fridge, Bart," I said.

Hendrix went shuffling off towards his pickup kicking up clouds of dust but stopped abruptly. "Hey, Henry, how about killing all the damn deer you see. Them vermin are eating all my alfalfa. Want my rifle?"

In the old days, I would have jumped at the chance to poach some fresh venison, but not now with Matt. I winked so Bart would understand. "It isn't deer season, Bart."

"Who the hell cares? They're going to eat me into the poor house. Now get going. I got work to tend to."

The first covey of Huns flushed out of range from the edge of a cut wheat field, but Bess found them again in a nearby coulee where they held tight in the heavier cover. Further down the draw she flushed a bunch of sharptail grouse. There were birds all down the coulee and Matt shot well with his new gun even though the fit was off. By the time we reached the end of the draw our game bags were bulging, and the weight on the straps had our shoulders burning. We then skirted an alfalfa field and finished filling our limits. I snoozed under a willow by a creek while Matt skinned and cleaned the birds like I'd taught him. Ethan would gladly pay him, and handsomely, for the skins to resell to fly tiers.

Several days later we left the Little Prickly Pear Ranch and rambled over Montana to line up more property for Matt to guide on. The ranchers still alive from the old days remembered me, and most of them gave Matt permission to guide on their land. And while Matt and Bess hunted, I mostly stayed in the camper reading and pining over Hope.

We drifted northeast above Plentywood, then turned down at the Canadian border. From the Breaks we went south to Winnett, then to Grass Range and Roundup, and then to Lewistown, and to Utica and on and killed prairie birds wherever we hunted.

It seemed Matt became even more compelled to hunt than to fish, and he combed the fields and scoured the coulees from daylight till dark searching for birds. The rancher's wives were elated to have the ones he killed that we couldn't use. For future reference I made Matt log the locations of the areas that held the most game on Bureau of Land Management maps. Through my old acquaintances, Matt obtained permission to guide on more land than he could hunt in a lifetime. Grocery sacks of curing bird skins filled the camper. Bess dwindled to a bag of bones and became too footsore to walk. Matt became so short of temper from exhaustion from walking the hours and miles every day that I couldn't stand him anymore, and after two weeks on the road we headed back to Wolf Creek.

CHAPTER 18

"Somebody knows where she is. Call your friends in the Keys. I bet she'd come if you asked her," Mason said, from his big leather chair.

"Doc's already told me she's gone back home to her mother. When Matt and I get done in Arkansas I'll try to talk to her. I doubt it'll do any good at this point, though," I said.

"Matt doesn't need to get mixed up with those river people, Henry. They're mean. They'll corrupt him."

"You don't know those river people. They're good folks. They just have different ways than other people do. Some of them are mean, I'm not denying that, but there're mean people everywhere. Seeb and Lewis are good and like brothers to me."

"Henry, there's something wrong with all this you're not telling me. Why are you in such a rush to get all this done? Matt can do all the guiding he needs to right here in Wolf Creek. He doesn't need to go to Arkansas. He could live with me and guide on the Missouri. There's plenty of ducks to hunt here. If you didn't take him down there, he wouldn't know the difference."

I considered what he said. I really didn't want to go back to Arkansas and get involved in duck guiding again, but I'd promised Matt we'd go. And I did want to see Seeb and Lewis Stokes again.

It might be my last chance. But most of all I remembered how well the serenity and security of the bottoms had helped me through my problems after the war and I felt it would help Matt with his. "If it doesn't go well, or if he finds he doesn't like it then we'll leave and come back. I just feel I owe him the chance to experience it. No matter what you say, it isn't the same as hunting here. You just don't understand."

"Oh, but I do understand one thing. You're going to do what you want, just like you always have. Be damned anybody else's feeling. I've never been able to reason with you. Just keep in mind that we're old, and one day soon one of us isn't going to be around anymore. Why can't we spend as much time as we can together? For once I'm coming out and telling you, I don't want you to leave. Now you've got me attached to that boy, and you're going to drag him off and leave me here all alone again."

"I know how you feel, James. He left me for several weeks last summer and I got gloomy as hell, but some things are more important than feelings. You told me that yourself, remember? The most important thing for me is making sure he gets a fair start in life. And now that I've gone this far, I feel impelled to carry it through."

I saw defeat in his eyes for one of the few times I'd known him. "You're right, Henry. Guess I'm just feeling sorry for myself. It's just that I hate being lonely in my old age. Since Lula Mae died it's been mighty tough. Just come back as soon as you can and bring him with you. Life feels almost normal again with him and his youth around."

"If you ever need me, I'll be here. You know that."

"You'd been through a lot before you went down there. You knew how to take care of yourself and Matt doesn't. I don't want him getting hurt or corrupted on that miserable river."

"The river isn't miserable. It's a place filled with life and beauty. I wish you'd have come just once so you'd understand."

"I've never regretted staying clear of that place. There's something foreboding about it."

"Matt will be fine. Now stop worrying. I've got to get my rig into town to get it serviced and I won't be back till late. We'll see you in the morning before we leave."

I was up well before dawn the next morning. Matt and I were packed and ready to leave for Arkansas and I wanted to get an early start. When I went to the kitchen to make coffee the dreary sight of James Mason at the breakfast table with his head resting in his hands staring blankly into space took me aback. He looked as if he'd aged ten years overnight. "You don't look well, James. Something wrong?"

He shifted his blank and dreary eyes from the wall to me. "Yes, there is. It came to me last night in my sleep – the reason for your determination to help Matt, and all the urgency, not to mention your physical deterioration."

I couldn't look him in the eye. Of all people, I shouldn't have kept it from him. "I knew you'd figure it out, but I thought I'd be long gone when you did. I know I should have told you, but I didn't want you to worry."

He dropped his hands from his chin. "I understand your reasoning, and I'm not upset with your secrecy, but I am deeply troubled because of your condition. How much time do you have?"

"When I left the Keys, they gave me six months to a year unless I had treatment. It would be experimental and no guarantee it'd work. I swore I wouldn't go through that hell six months ago, but I'd reconsider now that he's come along."

"Then you need to stop this and go back home. When you get well, you can finish it."

"I can't take that chance. He's still got so much to learn, and I'm the only one that can teach him. If I stopped now, I might die and not get it done. Then where would he be? No, I'm not quitting. If you don't understand and if it offends you, I'm sorry."

"Damn, man, you're insane. You've lost Hope over him and your business is in ruin. You're even giving your life for him. No one owes a debt that great. Listen to reason, Henry, he wouldn't let you go on with it if he knew."

"And that's the reason I can't afford to let him find out. He'd leave if he knew I was dying because of him, and he'd likely run if he found out who I really was. I can't afford to lose him now. You've got to play along with me and keep this to yourself. Promise me you will."

An emotional spasm overtook him, and he broke down, but he promised.

CHAPTER 19

The White River Bottoms of Arkansas

Matt studied the brilliantly lit towering rice bins as we drove into Stuttgart. The wipers squeaked mist from the windshield as a gusting wind rocked the truck and skittered litter across the road. The late Sunday night streets were all but deserted as I pulled up to the gas pumps at an all-night convenience store.

"I forgot how dirty humidity makes you feel," Matt said.

"You'll get used to it again."

As Matt pumped gas, endless and disoriented formations of low flying snow geese circled the grain bins. The gloomy night was filled with their incessant and hideous squalling. Their white under parts illuminated by the powerful bin lights made them look ghostly floating in formation amongst the blowing-broken fog. Matt was excited and impressed by the spectacle and pointed towards the sky as I came out of the store carrying a brown sack splotched with oily stains. Having seen the raucous, nasty crop and habitat destroying vermin thousands of times before, I only gave them a casual glance. I pulled away from the pumps to an empty church parking lot across the street, and half starved, we devoured the last few pieces of chicken that had remained and turned to greasy leather after a day under the convenience store's heat lamp.

I reminisced about the White River bottoms and of Lewis and Seeb Stokes as I choked the disgusting meat down. Over two years had passed since I'd last seen them. Even though I'd as much as begged them to, they wouldn't visit me in the Keys. To my knowledge neither had ever been outside of Arkansas.

When we finally pulled into Lewis' mobile home driveway in Boone's Bluff it was well past midnight. The trailer was unoccupied except during duck season. Then it served as the gathering place for the Stokes' hunting clients and as Lewis' home. Lewis and I had bought the house on wheels at an auction from a repossession company in Pine Bluff back in the seventies. I'd lived in it through fifteen hunting seasons, and when I'd quit the bottoms, to avoid taxes and liability, I'd deeded my part ownership over to Lewis.

The large and very stale convenience store coffee had my bladder in agony, and I went to the edge of the river to pee and gazed down on the reflections of the White River. While listening to the sucking and swirling sounds of the heavy current, I breathed memories of forty years past from its damp-earthy smell. I thought of Howard Stokes and his family. Most of them were dead now, and the few still living despised me for starting my own guiding business in the bottoms and for taking Lewis and Seeb with me back in the mid-sixties.

I came near wetting myself when a blaring barge horn startled me out of my thoughts. As it passed, I watched through the eerie river haze as the ghostly looking deck hands went about their work under the blinding white deck lights. I could feel the throb of the powerful diesel engines through the ground as it bore out of sight. Collected litter along the bank bumped and clinked in the wash. The floating dock below rattled and squeaked with the roll of the waves.

I rustled through the collected debris in the gutter over the backdoor for the key that had been kept hidden there for the past twenty years. After prying open the swollen door, I gagged on the stench of rodent piss. Luckily a few lights worked as I went around opening what few windows that weren't seized with rust. The linen hadn't been stripped from the past season and rat and roach pellets dotted the sheets and pillows. I thought of Matt and smiled and wondered how much misery he was willing to invest to be an Arkansas duck guide. When I went back out, he was still in the cab snoring contentedly, so I left him and went to the camper to sleep.

At first light, a loud and incessant pounding brought me slowly awake. I opened the door to a stout man with thick, black graying hair grinning broadly with a fine set of teeth. "Well I'll be, if it ain't old Henry Ball. I couldn't believe it when I got your message sayin' you was a comin'."

"Yeah, and I'll explain why later, Lewis. Looks like you've put on some weight, old timer."

His big grin came again. "I have, but you look the same. Might even be skinnier."

"Appears nothing else has changed around here since I left."

Lewis Stokes gazed at the ground while rummaging his pockets and brain. "More people's huntin' and movin' in on us, that's about all. Since they opened the bottoms up to the public, it's gettin' crowded. Seeb has to go to the lake at four every mornin' now to try to keep other hunters from claimin' our blinds. We can't say nothin' about it if they do, though. Sometimes we even have to let 'em hunt with us."

"I saw that coming when talk started about that land swap between the Feds and Black Kettle. I had a feeling it was time to get out."

"Yeah, but business is still good even with all the other people huntin'. You know, Pappy wouldn't believe that anybody that wants to can hunt our lakes now."

I laughed. "Wonder what Howard would have done if he'd gotten to his blind and found somebody in it."

"Hell, they would have left or there would've been a shootin'."

"Times have changed, Lewis. Come on in. I'll fix some coffee. Where's Seeb?"

"He'll be here. I told him you was a comin'. He's sposed to start brushin' blinds today, but hell, dependin' on what kind of mood he's in, he might not get to it fer weeks."

I put the coffee on and started breakfast. "How's he doing?"

"Awe, hell, he got caught a stealin' persimmon trees again. At three hundert dollar a load, it's just too hard for him not to. Daddy could get him out of stuff like that when the timber company owned the land, but he might do some time over it now. The Feds don't put up with that kind of shit like Black Kettle done."

"He'll get off. They know better than to make an enemy out of Seeb Stokes."

"They already have. He just can't understand that things ain't like they used to be. The law ain't afraid to come down here like when we was a growin' up. Specially the Feds. You got to be kearful. But Seeb ain't changed. He never will. He's forty-eight-year-old now and as wild and bull headed as ever."

Matt appeared at the camper door rubbing sleep from his eyes. Lewis studied him curiously. "Somethin' I can do for you, boy?"

"I'm with Henry."

"Lewis, this is the friend I told you about in the message. Matt wants to be a duck guide."

"Awe, hell? You must of kilt a lot of ducks then if you're good enough to be a guide?"

"No, sir."

"Well, can you blow a duck caller? You ever won a contest?"

Matt lowered his head. "No, sir. I've never tried."

"Hell, boy, everybody around here wants to be a duck guide. Duck guides gets to frazzle all the purdy girls. You ever even been duck huntin' before?"

Matt dropped his gaze again. "No, sir."

Lewis scratched his graying stubble as he pondered. "You look like you ought to be a schoolteacher, or a politician, or maybe even a preacher. You don't look like no duck guide to me."

"I'm willing to learn if somebody would teach me."

"Seeb's a need'n a runnin' buddy to help him cut cane and strip Cyprus bark to brush blinds with the next few weeks till duck season opens. He might learn you if you helped him. But I warn you, he ain't easy to work with."

"I'll help him. I'd be glad to. I can get along with anybody."

"Think you better meet him first. Might change your mind."

Matt left to go pee and I went back to cooking. "Lewis, think Seeb will want breakfast?"

"Better have lots of whatever it is you're a cookin'. He ain't never turned no food down."

"I've got a dozen eggs, a pound of bacon and a can of biscuits. That should be enough."

Lewis grinned and shook his head. "I doubt it."

"I'm sure you're right. I wasn't thinking and should have bought more."

"How long you a plannin' on stayin', Henry?"

"Till you or Seeb run us off. We don't want to get in your way, but I'd like to see if Matt really wants to duck guide like he says. I'd appreciate all the help you and Seeb would give him. It'd mean a lot to me."

"You know you can stay long as you like. Seeb can find plenty for him to do."

"Thanks, but if we start to wear out our welcome, just be sure to let me know."

"Don't worry, Seeb'll let you know. Back your camper up by the back steps and hook up to the trailer house. Matt can sleep out here and you can stay inside and keep me company."

"Bullshit. Matt can move in with you and the rats. I'm staying out here in the peace and quiet."

I stopped what I was doing and gave Lewis a questioning stare as the sound of a vehicle came rumbling down the drive. Lewis smiled and nodded.

The engine sounded on the verge of blowing as the badly abused and ancient truck squalled to a stop. I slammed the camper door to keep the oily exhaust and dust out. Then shortly the camper door banged back open and a severely pocked-faced, red-haired gorilla filled the doorway. He was wearing a threadbare flannel shirt and faded jeans worn through at the knees. "Damn its lazy-ass-Henry-the-prick Ball. Thought we'ens was rid of yore sorry ass," he said.

"Good to see you again, too, Seeb," I said.

"That bacon smells good. Glad I got here fore you hogs et it all. Pour me some of that coffee."

Matt then reappeared and Seeb turned and began to eye him up and down. Matt's eyes widened and jaw dropped as he studied Seeb. "Who the fuck is you, boy?" Seeb said.

Matt offered his hand. "I'm Matt Whitaker, Henry's friend."

Seeb bent and jerked Matt's feet from under him and he fell hard on his ass. Then Seeb lifted him off the ground by his ankles and started shaking him. After a knife and a few coins fell out of his pockets, Seeb let him go. Matt fell in a heap crimson faced and cussing. "Damn, Henry, he's poor'n we are," Seeb said.

Matt got to his feet humiliated and livid and started throwing punches. Seeb started laughing and lowered his head to the rain of blows. "He's a fightin' little bastard, ain't he?" When Seeb had had enough, he gave Matt a slight shove and he went sprawling on his ass again.

The truck springs creaked, and the camper yawed and listed when Seeb climbed in. He scrunched in next to Lewis at the small dining table. I struggled to keep from gagging on his body odor.

"Hell, I thought fer a minute I had me a wreslin' buddy, but he ain't nothin' but a pussy." Then he turned back to Matt. "Get on in here, you little fucker, and let's eat. You're lettin' flies in."

Matt came in and slammed the door still puffed up and red faced. I thought for a minute he was going to start the fight again.

"What's your name, pardner?" Seeb said.

Matt blew a few times and his anger seemed to settle. "I already told you. My name is Matt."

"You a feisty little bastard. What you a doin' here?"

"I'm with Henry."

"I know that. You done already told me. I ain't no dumbass. What you here fer?"

"I want to learn how to duck guide."

Seeb's deep voice rose to falsetto as he giggled while he talked. "You don't look like no duck guide to me. What kind of duck caller you use?"

"I don't have one."

Lewis broke in. "All he's got is the wants, Seeb. But he said he'd help you brush blinds if you'd learn him how to be a duck guide."

It was an involuntary mannerism Seeb had developed in childhood when he had trouble articulating. His eyes fluttered, and he stuttered as he attempted to form words. "Ah, ah, damn, Henry, hurry up with them eggs. I'm hawngry. Me and Mark's got work to get done."

Seeb calling Matt by the name of Mark caused Lewis and I to exchange surprised glances, but we realized why he had.

Seeb grabbed the bowl of scrambled eggs as soon as I sat it on the table and then nearly emptied it on his plate. Then he layered most of the bacon on the eggs. He made a pile of biscuits on the table beside his plate and started eating. "Go on 'n eat, Mark, so we can get on up the river."

"There's not enough left for me, much less for Henry and Lewis. And my name is Matt not Mark."

Seeb kept spitting egg on Matt as he talked. "Well whatever your name is, hurry up. You ain't gonna learn nothin' bout duck guidin' a layin' up on your ass with Henry and Lewis. Them's the two laziest bastards in the world. They don't deserve no food no way."

Seeb scooped the last spoonsful of egg from the bowl and gulped it down. "Damn, Henry, cook more next time. Come on, Mark."

Matt grabbed the two biscuits that were left and the cup of coffee I'd poured for him and followed Seeb down the steps to the dock. After some rattling and banging from Seeb loading tools and equipment, an outboard cranked and then Lewis and I watched as they went speeding out of sight up the river in a small skiff.

"You think it's a good idea to let that boy go off with him alone?" Lewis said.

"All they're going to do is brush a few blinds. What could go wrong?"

"With Seeb, any and every thang."

"My god, Lewis. What have I done?"

That evening I was getting ready to cook dinner when I heard Seeb's outboard coming down the river. I hit every other step going down to the dock. All day I'd been dreading what disasters might have happened with Matt in Seeb's care and my fears were justified. Seeb was hauling Matt out of the boat by his collar and the seat of his pants when I made the last step. After Seeb dropped him, Matt tried to stand but couldn't. He then crawled to the edge of the dock and hung his head over the river and started heaving. I kneeled close by him and was overwhelmed by the reek of alcohol.

"What in the hell happened to him, Seeb? He's drunk and covered in mud and blood and fish slime."

"He ain't worth a shit, Henry. He got into my moonshine when we stopped to cut cane and before we was through he got to where he couldn't climb up and down the bank haulin' the cane to the boat without fallin' and rollin' down in the mud. Then he got into it again when we got to the lake and was shit-faced drunk when I got done brushin' the blinds. I stopped where I knowed some deer bed when we was a comin' back and when I run four of 'em out of the canebrake he only hit that one out of five shots," he said, pointing to a small doe on the deck of the skiff that was speckled with seeping chest wounds from a load of OO buckshot. The bottom of the skiff was filled with croaking and squirming catfish.

"Is deer season open already?"

"Hell, I don't know. What difference does it make?"

"It makes a big difference if you get him thrown in jail. He'd never get to duck guide in Arkansas for doing something like that."

"Henry, you worry too much."

"But what about the blood and puke and the slime?"

"We et some of the liver when I gutted the deer. He was so drunk I had to carry him out on one shoulder while I drug the deer. Guess the liver made him sick cause he started pukin' on me and his self and everything else. It weren't bad till it ran down and started squishin' in my shoes. The blood come from him droolin' eatin' the liver. He was passed out in the bottom of the boat when I emptied my catfish baskets on him. I thought it'd sober him up, but he just laid there a snorin' with them cold fish a floppin' all over him."

CHAPTER 20

Two weeks passed quickly and as far as I knew Seeb and Matt hadn't done any more poaching or other law breaking. But I knew Seeb acted out of impulse and not reason and when an opportunity to kill something he wanted arose, he'd take advantage of it, legal or not. And Matt informed me that Seeb had practically forced him to drink the moonshine that first day they worked together and he assured me that after puking his guts out plus the hangover it'd given him that he'd never take another drink of it unless he was bound, and it was forced down him. So far, the two seemed to be tolerating each other, maybe even to the extent of becoming friends, which in Seeb's case was extremely unusual.

A lot of winter nights I'd read to the Stokes brothers in the one room shack we'd slept in when they were kids. One story they all seemed to especially enjoy was of the Pilgrims at Plymouth Rock, of how they'd hunted game and had cooked the feast for the Indians. Something in that tale of how Thanksgiving had come to be must have struck a chord in Seeb's psyche. Whether it was the hunting or the feasting or the Indians, the story induced a mania that it was his duty and obligation from that time on to hunt ducks on Thanksgiving morning regardless of weather, his state of health or if the season was open or not. I had no reason to believe his rationale had changed in the few years I'd been away, and so I set my alarm for 4:00 a.m. that Thanksgiving morning to find out.

Just before 5:00 I wasn't surprised to hear the unmistakable rumbling of his truck before it shut off a short distance away. Then I made him out tiptoeing down the road in the ambiance of the three-quarter moon. Matt had already slipped out of the trailer and was waiting at the top of the dock steps. Then in the moonlight I watched the hulk and his minion paddle upriver. My inclination was to stop them, but I resisted. Matt could make the decision whether to let Seeb coerce him into breaking the law again or not. He'd been warned more than once to not let it happen again. Now he was in jeopardy of my unabridged wrath. When they were well upriver the outboard cranked and then they faded out of sight in twin trails of phosphorescent wake and blue smoke heading up the river.

Just before sunrise I woke Lewis and we sat on the dock listening to the booming echoing through the bottoms. There was no doubt who it was. Only Seeb would be dumb and brazen enough to shoot ducks on Federally controlled land out of season. I could only hope they wouldn't be caught. I didn't want to spend Thanksgiving Day getting two idiots out of jail and seeing Matt's opportunity to duck guide in the river bottoms squandered away.

Matt was sleeping like a corpse on the sofa when Lewis and I came back from visiting Lewis' invalid brother Willard later that afternoon. Thinking back on the bear, the more I thought about Matt disobeying me again, the more my temper rose. My entry into the trailer sounded like an artillery piece when I slammed the door. And as I went about the kitchen, I made a great commotion banging pots and pans and slamming drawers. Matt began to squirm as he slowly came awake. But when I went and stood over him, he was wide-eyed awake and trembling with anticipation of what he knew was about to come. "What were you and your big brother up to so early this morning slipping around in the dark like two burglars?" I said.

His expression was that of a condemned man peering down the barrels of a firing squad. "Were you awake when we left? We tried not to wake you up."

"Stop trying to avoid the issue. What were you doing?"

"We went to Coot Lake to see if any ducks were in yet."

"Who did all that shooting down there?"

His lip quivered. He had to clear his throat several times getting it out. "Me and Seeb."

"At what?"

"Ducks."

"I didn't know the season had opened. How many'd you kill?"

Again, he hesitated, but then he brightened seeming to think I'd be impressed. "Fifty-three," he said, smiling proudly.

I grabbed his collar and pulled his face close to mine. "You'd better listen and listen good. Seeb Stokes doesn't have the mental capacity to think beyond today. Your duck guiding career isn't going to get far if you're going to let him turn you into a poacher. I warned you about this. Now you've disobeyed me again. I sacrificed more than you'll ever know bringing you here, and this is the appreciation I get." I shook my fist in his face. "I'll turn your ass in the next time you violate a hunting law. That's something I won't tolerate. Understand?" He nodded, and I went on. "I want you to spend time with Seeb. He can teach you everything about the bottoms you need to know, but don't let him lead you astray. If you'd been caught with those ducks, not only would you be in jail facing a heavy fine, you'd never be allowed to guide in Arkansas. It's up to you to decide. You're supposed to be a grown man able to make the right decisions for yourself. You don't need me telling you what's right and wrong – you're old enough to know. If you ever do it again, I swear I'll turn your ass in just like I would any other common criminal, because that's just what you are. I won't tolerate it."

I let him go and he put his hands in the air as if hoping for help from above. "I'm sorry, Henry. I didn't think about it like that. I shouldn't have let him talk me into it."

"I bet he had a real hard time. It's going to start a war, but I'm going to deal with him, too. We all did it back in the old days, and I can say it was alright because times were different then, but that's no excuse. I'm ashamed I ever poached, but we lived off the land back then. We didn't always have money to buy food. There was a lot less hunting pressure in those days, and a lot more ducks, but there's not enough excuses I can use that makes it right. You have a choice."

"I swear I'll never do it again, Henry. I swear it."

"Did you even bother to clean them, or did they wind up in some backwater for the coons to eat?"

"We cleaned them all. They're in the refrigerator. We wanted you to grill some for us tonight."

I went back to the kitchen to let my anger cool thinking that maybe I'd been too harsh letting my emotions get away from me with Matt in the condition he was in, but if they'd been caught it would have been serious for Matt, especially with being an accomplice of Seeb Stokes. There'd likely have been some jail time tacked onto a hefty fine as well. I'm sure Seeb had easily convinced Matt by saying they'd only shoot a few ducks, and then how out of control they'd become when the opportunity for a slaughter presented itself. I'd been party to such many times when I was young and still bloodthirsty. When I left the kitchen, Matt was still on the sofa with his face buried in his hands.

"Hell, if I don't cook them, they'll just be thrown in the river and be nothing but wasted turtle food. Take my truck and go to DeWitt and see if there's a store open. Buy some Italian dressing, some limes and a pound of bacon. And some horseradish if they've got any. And if you've got even an ounce of brains, don't let anybody know what you did this morning, or the law will be down on us before nightfall." He fell twice getting out the door and down the steps to the truck.

Seeb was stumbling drunk when he came up the dock steps later that evening. He knew I'd be mad about getting Matt involved in the morning hunt and I had no doubt he'd been hiding in the bottoms drinking all afternoon to get his courage up to face me. Though he had to hold the railing to keep his balance, he wasn't so drunk that he didn't notice the glowing coals in the grill beside the back steps. And as usual, he threw the door open so hard it shook the trailer when it slammed against the wall. "Henry, I ain't had no grilled duck breasteses since you left."

"How do you know that's what I'm cooking?"

"Mark said he'd talk you into it."

"I'm cooking a dozen or so and Lewis took the rest to Willard. We don't have room for them all here. And by the way, it took me an hour to clean all the spilled blood and feathers out of the refrigerator."

"Think a dozen 'ill do?"

"Surely with all the squirrel and dumplings I've cooked it will."

"Hot damn! Squirrel and dumplin's. You make 'em good as Mama did. She learned you how, didn't she?"

"She did, but I've added some things."

"I ain't et all day. Can I have some now?"

I thought that if he ate it might sober him up some. "Want beans, too, I guess?"

"That's a dumbass thing to say, Henry."

As I expected, he heaped enough squirrel and dumplings in a serving bowl for three people. Then he staggered to the dining table and started gulping and smacking like a starving dog. "Where's them beans at, Henry?"

In short order, he devoured the dumplings and a can of cold pork and beans. "Guess that'll hold me till them duck breasteses gets done. Where's that Mark at? He off pokin' my niece Pearle again?"

"No, for once in a good while he's not. He went with Lewis."

Seeb had a pint jar of shine in his coat pocket and was quiet for several minutes after taking a long drink from it. He sounded on the verge of breaking down when he spoke again. "I'm shore glad you come back, Henry. I shore missed you. It ain't been much fun here since you left. You know you're like a brother to me, don't you?"

At first his tone and the compassion of the comment touched me, then I realized it was nothing more than a preamble to the apology he was about to give for the poaching episode. I wasn't going to give him the satisfaction, though, and went towards him wiping my hands on my apron. "You're like kin to me, too, Seeb, but I want you to promise me something."

"I'd do anything for you, Henry."

"Don't get Matt in trouble down here. He's a good boy and I don't want him getting mixed up with the law, especially with the Feds for poaching ducks. Promise you won't let him do it again."

I could hear his teeth grinding as his jaw muscles worked and his eyes began to flutter. It was a transformation like Jekyll to Hyde I'd witnessed many times before just as he was about to go out of control with rage. I prepared for the storm that was about to come. "You old bastard you, don't be a preachin' to me about breakin' the law. You was the biggest damn poacher in the bottoms at one time. I was just tryin' to teach the little shit about duck huntin' before the season come in." He shoved the table away and stood. His chair toppled over. "I'll stomp your skinny ass if you mess with me."

"I'm not preaching to you. I know what we did in the old days. I just don't want Matt doing it."

He was shaking with rage. The last thing I wanted was to be beaten to a pulp. Lewis knew how to handle Seeb better than I did and I should have let him deal with him. I grabbed a cast-iron frying pan off the counter.

"And if them wardens ever come back here again, I'll stomp their asses, too."

The rage died as fast as it'd come. His jaw dropped as a look of amazement washed over him. It took a long moment for the full implications of what he'd said to sink in. "You mean Federal Agents came here today?" I said.

"Yeah, but they didn't find nothin'. We outrun 'em and hid the ducks fore they got here."

"Who were they?"

"That prick Tommy and a new one I ain't never seen. Fore that bastard was a warden he used to poach with us. That's how he knows where I hunt at. Lazy bastard didn't try too hard to catch us."

"You'd better be glad it was Tommy. The reason he didn't try any harder was because he grew up with your family, but even Tommy's not going to keep letting you go. It's his job and he's only doing what he's supposed to do. This isn't a game, Seeb."

He giggled, picked up his chair and sat down. "Mark kicked their boat out in the river while they was a lookin' for us back in the woods. That's how we outrun 'em. That new warden had to swim it down. Tommy told me that when he come here. That young warden was shakin' and water was still drippin' off him."

"Where was Matt when they were here?"

"He'd done hid in his bedroom. Tommy never knowd he was with me."

"Where were the ducks?"

"In the tool closet on the dock. We had it locked and everything cleaned up so good he didn't even try to look in it. He must of thought we hid the ducks back in the timber."

"No, that's not the reason. He really didn't want to catch you is why he didn't look. Don't you realize they would've shut your guiding business down if he'd found those ducks? Six or eight would have been one thing, but fifty. You'd probably have done jail time."

"It was fifty-three, Henry."

I knew I was wasting my time and walked off in disgust and went back to cooking. My only hope was that I'd gotten through to Matt and he wouldn't do anything so stupid again.

After Seeb had several more pulls off the pint jar, he said, "I'm sorry, Henry. I won't do nothin' else bad around Mark. I give you my word."

I turned and faced him. "How long will it be before you forget and do it again?"

"I won't forget. Cross my heart."

He seemed sincere, but I knew in a matter of time he'd be poaching again. It was too embedded in him not to. "We'll see, Seeb. Just don't get Matt involved if you do. Now get some more beans out of my camper while I get the duck breasts ready to grill."

Just before he went out the door, he stopped. "Did Mark tell you we got a duck band?"

"Which one of you shot it?"

"Mark did. He's a lucky little shit, ain't he? It was his first duck hunt, too."

"I can't believe you didn't claim it, and falling in with you isn't lucky, but at least we've got something to celebrate tonight. Now go on and get the beans and a bottle of my whiskey while you're at it. I need a drink really bad."

CHAPTER 21

Duck season opened the following Saturday, and it was like Christmas morning down on the river. Seeb and Matt left for Coot Lake giggling like schoolgirls at 4:00 to go spread the decoys. Lewis was up and pacing the yard waiting on his clients an hour before they were scheduled to arrive. All their noise and turmoil woke me well before I intended to.

At five, a caravan of pickups rumbled into the drive. A great commotion ensued as the trucks emptied and the boisterous mob of twelve or so men went about digging out their equipment under the security yard light. They were attired in an array of garb from bibbed overalls to jeans in green and blue, bright orange bird hunting jackets from eras gone by, steel vamped brogans stained with mortar and grease. Their cap crests bore names of heavy equipment manufacturers that had been rendered illegible with sweat, grease and grime.

Disordered voices and laughter overwhelmed the whine of the outboard after we were underway going upriver. The repugnant stench of whiskey breaths filled the cabin as bottles were passed around in the dark. After five miles on the mist laden river we reached the loadout dock, then started a renewed chaos of transferring the drunkards and their gear to a cotton wagon that was attached to an ancient John Deere tractor – our final mode of travel on the journey to the blinds. With a can of starter fluid Lewis eventually managed to bring the archaic beast to life and we started chugging the final two miles to our destination through the woods on a winding, oozy logging road. A faint glow was showing in the east when we finally arrived at Coot Lake.

We eventually got the hunters settled in the three blinds scattered along the oxbow lake after another fiasco of unloading and sorting equipment. It took fifteen minutes alone to discern whose gun was who's after having to remove each one from their cases for identification, then another ten was spent deciding who would hunt with who. By then flights of squealing woodducks had begun moving in the faint dawn light going to their secret spots for the day.

The sun strained forever rising above the trees before exploding into a blazing-golden sphere. As the mist blanketing the lake slowly faded under the warming glow, the decoys took life on a freshening breeze, then the high flights of passing mallards started taking notice of our spread and in swarming bunches they came, and in bunches they died and in less than an hour the hunters were close to filling their limits. But then the flocks curiously began flaring off the lake. Seeb began paddling from blind to blind looking for someone that might have been wandering around looking for a place to squat. As he came to the last group of hunters they began pointing across the lake. Seeb paddled to the spit of ground beside the blind and got out of his paddle boat. Lewis and I were on a bench behind the blind, and neither of us had noticed the four men until then. We immediately knew by their uniforms it was a group of federal wardens and they were being led by Tommy McMahan, the agent Seeb had had the run-in with on Thanksgiving morning. Seeb raised his gun to fire over their heads, but I grabbed his arm. "Damn, Seeb, ease up."

He jerked his arm free. "I don't give a fuck. They're messin' our hunt up." He turned back to the approaching men. "Get your asses down from there. Can't you see we'uns is a huntin', you dumb bastards?"

"Don't you see that's Tommy," Lewis told him.

Seeb then realized who they were and emptied his gun and then his pockets and threw the illegal lead ammunition in the lake. In minutes they were upon us. "Y'all having a good hunt, Seeb?" Tommy said, the sarcasm distinct.

"Till you snoopin' bastards come we was."

"Better check that talk fore it gets you in trouble."

Lewis came between them and put out his hand. "Tommy, good to see you."

Tommy ignored Lewis' hand. "This ain't no social call, Lewis. Need to check y'all out."

Tommy turned to Seeb. "Empty your pockets and gun. I want to see your shells and check your gun for a plug."

Seeb handed his gun to Tommy, and Tommy passed it on to another warden to check. Then Seeb turned his pockets inside out. "I run out of shells an hour ago," he said, under Tommy's menacing glare.

The other two wardens were picking up spent hulls making sure they were stamped "Steel" in front of the nearest blind. Disappointedly, they shook their heads when Tommy gave them a questioning look. Then Tommy's attention went back to Seeb. "It'd be best you stay here and keep quiet while we check your hunters." Tommy motioned with his chin, and the other three agents started away to check the hunters, then he turned to Matt. "Guess you're the new guide I been a hearin' about. Let's see your guide license then."

Seeb broke in. "He ain't no guide. He's just a helper."

"I said for you to keep quiet and I meant it," Tommy said, before turning back to Matt. "If you're just helpin', then let's see your huntin' license."

Matt produced the license and Tommy studied it. "Were you the one doin' all that shootin' down Bear Bayou Thanksgivin' mornin'?"

Matt's hands were shaking refolding the license. He fumbled several times getting it back in his wallet and didn't answer. Tommy's lips were twisted in a smirk as he stared down on him. Seeb broke in again. "You know it was them Lefonts. You just want to fuck with me is all."

"I checked on the Lefonts and they had an alibi. They were in town with their mama havin' Thanksgivin' dinner. Don't try to put the blame on them. And I seen you throwin' them shells in the lake when we come up. Your time's a comin', Seeb."

Seeb started towards Tommy with his fists balled, but Lewis stopped him. After a long, daring stare, Tommy turned away from Seeb and went down the lake to join the other wardens. Lewis and I followed.

The three agents had the hunters lined up and standing outside the blinds. One was counting ducks and arranging them in limits while the other two were checking licenses and guns. Tommy went rummaging through the blinds and came out of each carrying empty whiskey bottles. Several of the hunters were ticketed for minor violations that could have been ignored. One an unplugged gun, two others for not signing their waterfowl stamps. Tommy gathered us all together when he was done writing tickets an hour later.

"I should take the whole bunch of you in for huntin' while under the influence of 'alkyhal'. Now, who killed which of them ducks?" Tommy said, pointing to the bunches of dead birds.

The hunters looked so ridiculous staring at the ground while fumbling in their pockets like a bunch of guilty kids that I almost laughed. It was obvious no one was going to answer, so Tommy turned to Lewis. "I want the ducks with the men that shoots 'em. You know better, Lewis. I could charge you with killin' 'em all and you wouldn't have a chance in court."

"I know who killed what but I ain't had time to separate 'em yet."

"Yeah, right. Me and you need to talk. You too, Henry. Come on with us."

When we were out of hearing of the others, Tommy turned to Lewis. "Me and you go back a long ways, Lewis. You and Seeb are like family. Now, I know you and Henry ain't goin' to do nothin' illegal, but Seeb killed a bunch of ducks Thanksgivin' mornin' on the refuge. I know he done it and you do, too. With all the spent shells and feathers we found in that baited hole it must of been a real slaughter. The empty hulls was lead, too. He got lucky and got away from us after he kicked our boat out in the river while we was in the timber lookin' for him. That young warden yonder had to swim it down. And then when we tried to check him on your dock, he threatened us. You'd be better off if you broke away from him. He's goin' to cause you and your hunters a lot of inconvenience if you don't." Then he turned to me. "And I know that boy was likely with him, Henry. Better keep him away from Seeb before he gets into real trouble. He wouldn't do well in the state pen with them real animals."

"Look a here, Tommy, he's my brother. I just can't far him. He owns half the business. Me and Henry had a talk with him about poachin'. I really do believe he's going to try to go straight. How 'bout cuttin' us some slack. You could have just give them men warnin's instead of fines for that minor bullshit. They probably won't never come back huntin' with us again now."

Tommy put his finger in Lewis' face. "You tell that crazy brother of yours if he ever threatens any of us again, I'll shut y'all down. And if I catch him breakin' the law again, I'll see to it he never steps foot on Federal land again. I could kick myself in the ass for not gettin' a warrant and searchin' your place for them ducks the other mornin', but I figured even that dimwit had better sense than to have hid them that close to home, but now I wonder. I started to come back with a warrant that night and look around, and the only reason I didn't was because of you and Hired. I could lose my job if it got round I was bein' slack on you cause we're friends."

"I appreciate it, Tommy. I'll talk to him some more."

"And I'll tell you another thing, anybody comes wantin' to hunt with y'all, out of the blinds or what not, you better let 'em. This ain't y'alls no more. It belongs to the gov'ment now."

Lewis' face was aglow with rage. He'd helped build the blinds years before when he was a kid. They'd belonged to his family, as did the sole right to hunt the lakes at one time. Now all of it had been taken away and turned over to anyone that wanted to use it.

"I'll make him understand," Lewis said.

As Tommy turned to leave, he said, "Yeah, good luck with that.

Days quickly turned into weeks as groups of hunters came and went, and over a month of duck season passed in a blur. Thankfully there'd been no more run-ins with the law. By then, Matt had learned most of the mundane tasks involving duck guiding. He'd become a fair caller under Seeb's harsh tutelage and had learned to operate the boats and other equipment and learned his way around in the bottoms. And over that time, he'd come to be good friends with Lewis and Seeb's niece Pearle who we'd hire to clean the trailer ever so often. She was cute but ill-mannered and almost as rough as Seeb with her profane talk, but I was glad to see Matt getting away and spending time with someone more his age. Their relationship seemed to be helping him deal with the bear incident as well, though Lewis was still waking him screaming on occasion during the night.

It was Saturday evening and I was alone in the camper. As usual, just before seven, Pearle Stokes' spot rusted, paint peeled red Firebird came roaring into the driveway. I watched from the camper as she sprinted up the steps in her skintight jeans and knee-high boots to the trailer door. Like her uncle Seeb, she didn't bother knocking and slammed the door open against the wall with a startling loud bang. "Come on, baby doll, and let's get goin'. Seeb's done bought us some beer," she yelled into the house."

I figured it best I intervene and stepped outside the camper. "You two aren't old enough to be drinking, and you sure shouldn't be drinking and driving that hot rod like you do."

Pearle exhibited Seeb's defiance glowering down on me from the porch. "You can't tell me what to do, Henry Ball. You ain't my diddy," came the hissing reply through her crimson, painted lips.

"No, but I'll tell your daddy, and I bet he takes the keys to your car and blisters that ass for you, too."

She considered a short moment. "We'll leave it here then," she said in resigned defeat, then went moping off to get the beer.

Matt came out shortly. "Remember you got hunters tomorrow," I said. "Don't let her keep you out all night." He nodded, and I watched as they sped off in a haze of flying gravel and swirling dust.

It was earlier than usual that evening when the Firebird came rumbling back in. A door squeaked open and then came a brief exchange of heated conversation charged with female profanity. Then the door slammed, the engine revved, tires spun, and rocks clanged off the side of the trailer. I opened the camper door as Matt was going up the trailer steps. "Need to talk?"

He nodded and came in and took a seat at the dining table. He obviously didn't know his face was streaked with eye liner and splotched with red lip prints as he explained his situation. I struggled to keep a serious expression, not so much because of Pearle's black tear stains and lipstick, but with her story of the missed period and the likelihood she was pregnant. I'd sensed this was coming.

I was familiar with girls committing such desperate deeds to snare a husband, even to the extent of lying about pregnancy. It happened to me after having an affair with a girl from Dewitt many years before. I thought I was going to have a breakdown waiting for the days to go by until she finally admitted her pregnancy was just a scam to get me to the altar. I kept away from small town girls looking for a ride out of their destitution after that. I stayed down on the river at night far out of harm's way. Pearl and Matt had only been seeing each other for a little over a month. I doubted that was enough time for her to get pregnant and it be confirmed, even by a qualified doctor, much less a nineteen-year-old girl with a drug-store pregnancy kit. I was surprised they were having a sexual affair in the first place because of Matt's loss of Sandy, but he was young, and Pearle was cute and had a very appealing body. I'm sure it was hard resisting her certain seductions in the backseat of her Firebird.

"That's wonderful news, Matt. I can't wait to see the expression on Seeb's face when he finds out he's going to be your uncle. Did you and Pearle set the wedding date yet?"

Matt seemed to slip into a state of shock as I smiled and held my glass up to salute his coming fatherhood.

"I can't believe you just said that. I don't want to marry her, Henry. I want you to tell me what I can do to get out of it."

"Oh, that's easy. Pack your things and run off tonight. Nobody would miss you, except maybe your big brother Seeb. You're getting to be just like him you know, except you don't fart and then giggle about it at the dinner table – or at least you don't yet."

"Henry, this is serious. Her dad will kill me. I'm not ready to have a kid. I want to go back to Montana and work for Ethan next spring."

"That's no problem. She and the kid could go with you. She could wait tables at Jean's with Alice, or work in the fly shop for Emma."

"Henry, that wouldn't work. She wouldn't fit in. You got to help me figure something out. What would you do?"

I took a sip of my drink and sat in silence for a spell pretending to be contemplating his dilemma. "You know, I doubt we'll kill many ducks tomorrow. As warm as it is, there won't be enough mallards left in the bottoms to make a bowl of gravy. I'd bet they've all gone north again."

Matt's countenance turned from desperate to angry. I watched his face redden and then his knuckles whiten as he squeezed the edge of the dinner table. "For god's sake, Henry, don't you care anymore than that?"

"I didn't get her pregnant, you did. What do you want me to do, marry her and raise your kid for you? Why don't you just slip off tonight and save us all a lot of grief? Let the State Welfare Department take care of your mistake for you."

"I can't leave. My grandfather ran away and left my mother when she was a baby. I couldn't do that, Henry."

His words cut deep and angered me as well. My little fun session had turned sour on me. "You know, since the first day we met it's always been Matt that had a problem and needed help. Your financial situation, your pot smoking and using other drugs, your sorry ass attitude, the bear attack because you disobeyed me, and then poaching the ducks after I forbade it. And you constantly demanding I bust my ass to help you learn the guiding profession. That's just to mention a few. But what have you ever done for anybody? Oh, don't get me wrong, you've been helping out and doing your share of the work around here, but it seems like everything you do is for Matt's sake."

"I don't know what you mean?"

"Do you feel you're something special? That you're better than everybody else?"

He thought a moment. "I don't know."

"Our mothers dote over us so much when we're little boys that we come to believe we're the center of the universe. That's kind of the way you feel, right? That the world revolves around you?"

He looked away. "I said I don't know."

"Most men are too arrogant and egotistical to judge themselves honestly, or just too chicken shit because they're afraid to admit to themselves and to accept who and what they really are. Stop being ashamed to admit it. All of us are brainwashed by our mothers into thinking we're special and better than everybody else. And they do it because they truly believe their little boy is special and better than anybody else." I reflected a minute, took a drink, and started again. "Ever think of Sandy anymore?"

"What difference does that make?"

"It didn't take long before you were over her and banging another woman. It doesn't seem you grieved over her very long."

He leaped to his feet with his fists balled. "I ought to beat your ass, Henry. I hate you for saying that."

"I don't care what you think."

He slowly relaxed and then his eyes began to water. He sat down and put his hands over his face. "Damn you, Henry. You're like a brother to me. Like a father. I don't know. I'm so confused. You've helped me through so much. But now that I need you the most, you act like you hate me."

"Well I'll be damned, you're man enough to cry." I gave him a few minutes to compose himself while I mixed another drink, then I went on. "My senior drill instructor made me realize something very important. It was that my life was of no real value except to myself. Oh, my folks and wife might cry a few days if I died, but in a few weeks their grief would pretty much be gone and any thought of me would barely raise a sad memory. He was right, too. He made me realize my insignificance, that I'm but one person in billions that have lived and died before me, and one in billions that will live and die after me. He taught me that I'm no different or better than anyone else. That's right, Matt, stop thinking you're special. And don't try to make me feel sorry for you anymore. Be a man and do what you think is right with Pearle. Stop crying on my shoulder, okay?"

He spent a long time in deep thought before he spoke again. "You're right, Henry. My selfish and conceited attitude is what killed Sandy, and I'm the only one to blame for the fix I'm in with Pearle."

"When you're humbled enough to realize just who and what you are, and truly believe it, you become a better person – a better man."

He thought some more before saying, "Guess I'll marry Pearle then. I want my child to know its father. I don't want it to think of me the way my mother thinks of her father."

"Have you ever asked him why he left?"

"I never met him, and they never talked about him around me. The few times they did, they didn't know I was listening. It was like they didn't want me to know he existed. I've never even seen a picture of him. I don't even know his name."

"There're two sides to every story, Matt. He might have had reason to leave when he did. Suppose overpowering consequences forced him away, actions too powerful for him to control?"

"But if that's so, what can I do? Where do I start?"

"If your mother was a baby when he left, she won't remember what really happened. Confront your grandmother. Make her explain the truth."

"From what Mom says as sick as she is, I may never see her again."

The reality of that had slipped my mind. "Well, you may as well forget about all that for now anyway. You and your mother can try to settle it when you get home. Now, let's talk more about Pearle. Do you love her?"

"She's fun and I like her, but I don't want to marry her. I want to be free like you and live my life like I want."

"That's being selfish and conceited again. Believe me I know."

"Living your life like you did didn't affect anybody but you. How was it selfish?"

"That's my business."

"I can't help it if I feel I have to do what I'm doing. If that's being selfish, so be it."

"Listen, I'm going to tell you how I feel about your situation with Pearle. It's not the first time this has happened. She may be telling you the truth, or she may just be testing you. How did she act tonight?"

"Edgy, emotional, she even got violent and hit me."

"Have you been using rubbers?"

He lowered his head and reddened. "Sometimes."

"Or maybe a few times is more like it. Look forget about Pearle and her accusations for a few days. I bet she calls within a week saying everything's alright and that's she's not pregnant."

"I'll try, but I won't be able to keep it off my mind. And I'm staying clear of her from now on if she's not pregnant."

"That's up to you. Now get to bed. You've kept me up way too late as it is. There's a hell of a storm heading our way and the fog's going to make going up the river especially dangerous in the morning and I need to be clear-headed."

Matt stood and squeezed my shoulder. "Thanks for the advice. I promise I won't be such a self-centered spoiled brat from now on. And I'm going to find my grandfather someday to get his side of the story."

During the night the heavy fog I'd anticipated formed over the river and crept up the bank and enveloped the camper like a cocoon. Instead of putting the bottle away and going to bed like I should have, I stayed up drinking for several more hours till I fell asleep sitting up at the dinner table – or I passed out sitting up is more like it. The whiskey had done little to ease my conscience of guilt of what Matt had said about Sara and Ginny's attitude toward me, though. It hurt to know they detested me so that they wouldn't legitimize my being to my grandson. Then it came to me through the haze of inebriation just before I passed out that maybe it wasn't for Ginny's despise of me that I was kept anonymous from Matt, but instead was because of the shame for what she'd done to me.

I was still near drunk when I woke several hours later. I knew I shouldn't be operating a boat in the blanket of fog in the condition I was in, but there was no one else to do it and the show must go on. So when the crew of sixteen hunters arrived at five, I was on the dock waiting to boat them to the blinds on Coot Lake. It was their third and last day to hunt. The previous two had been beautiful weather-wise, and the shooting had been superb.

When we set out for Coot Lake the boats were as usual over-loaded with eight hunters each and their gear. The fog was a seemingly impenetrable white wall that wouldn't allow me to see beyond the bow of the boat. Though the wipers were beating across the plexiglass windshield, they had no effect on visibility. We'd been running just over idle for ten minutes and no one had spoken. Even though I was still high from the night of drinking, I was considering the lunacy of what I was doing. Then a tentative voice came out of the dark cabin. "Thick ain't it, Henry?"

"If we take it easy, we'll be okay. We got plenty of time," I said, trying to hide my apprehension.

I cussed Lewis under my breath for leaving the dock before I had my crew loaded. It would've been easier following his running lights in the slop, but soon I put that notion to rest. I would have had to have stayed within feet of his boat to follow his running lights. I kept just near enough to the bank to pick out the ends of the sweepers with my spotlight. Otherwise I would've been overtaken with vertigo.

"Watch out, Henry!" I was running at a slow speed when the reflectors appeared suddenly out of the fog. I crashed into the load-out dock before I could shift into reverse to slow the heavily laden boat. Lewis' hunters had just unloaded, and the impact sent them all sprawling across the dock. One almost toppled over the side into the river, but Lewis grabbed his jacket sleeve just before he went in. The livid bunch fell to cussing me as they struggled to their feet.

The fog thinned into spotty patches as the tractor left the river and chugged through the woods. The wind was building and charging the air with moisture from the Gulf as a low and roily black sky formed. The grey-barren trees swayed and creaked mournfully under the strengthening wind.

The fervor of the previous two days had vanished long before a subdued sunrise wielded pitiful light over the austere morning. Futile volleys were fired at the few straggling flights of ducks that were cast from the clouds like windblown ghosts. The gunners mainly sat in the blinds crouched in misery out of the blowing mist wishing they were bound for home.

I was right about what I'd told Matt about the mallards. By nine it was evident they'd left the bottoms to go back north with the howling south wind. There were no objections when Lewis called the hunt two hours early. As we pulled away from Coot Lake, I watched as Seeb and Matt collected the decoys in a torrent of rain. Then after loading the hunters in the cabbed-over boats at the river, Lewis parked the John Deere on a ramp to keep it above the coming floodwaters and disconnected the battery. It wouldn't be used again until the next fall after the river had receded back into its banks.

In the dead of the night, I was jarred awake by a blaring horn. As Seeb was topping the steps to the trailer in the downpour, lights flicked on inside and then Matt opened the door rubbing his eyes.

"Wake up, pardner, and get dressed. We got to get to the lake and let the cables out on the blinds. The river's comin' out of its banks tonight."

"Can I at least get something to eat first?"

"You can eat and layup sleepin' on your lazy ass when duck season goes out. Now hurry up. I'll be on the dock a waitin' on you."

Matt and Seeb spent the next two days in the bottoms running chainsaws to keep the roads to the blinds clear of logs and drift and they slackened the cables on the floating blinds when needed as the water rose. They slept in the blinds and had charcoal buckets to dry their clothes and to stay warm. Seeb had soft drinks and food caches of sardines, potted meat, Vienna sausages and other such delicacies scattered over the bottoms and I knew they wouldn't go hungry.

During those two days the bottoms became what appeared to be a sea of chocolate milk. Late in the second afternoon, a meek south wind reversed and started gusting from the north. The last dark clouds went scudding south and snow showers came from the last few whipping by. The leaden sky turned turquoise, and in the clean washed air, flights of chattering waterfowl came pouring down from the north in droves. Matt fell in bed so tired that night he didn't bother to take his sodden clothes off.

A group of young investment executives from Nashville were first to hunt after the timber flooded. I listened to their conversations which were mainly of college and fraternities and the Market as they unloaded their gear from their shiny new SUV's under the brilliant yard light. Lewis complimented their fashionable attire and expensive scrolled guns while they studied the trailer house, the littered yard and Lewis' unusual dialect. "Jim, y'all foller Henry there on down to the dock and load up. We got about a five-mile run to make upriver."

"Do you think we'll kill any ducks today, Mr. Stokes?" Jim said.

"Name's Lewis. Ought to. Lots of new birds come down on this cold."

Volleys from all points echoed throughout the bottoms that morning as the newly arrived and tired and famished ducks poured into the decoys. By the time the sun had come over the trees limits on Coot Lake were close to being filled. But shooting suddenly waned as the birds lost interest in the lake and began scattering into the sunlit timber to feed on the abundant mast available to them now because of the flood waters. After watching what appeared to be a great tornado of mallards funneling into the timber for thirty minutes, Seeb paddled to the blind Lewis and I were in and then called Matt over.

"Matt, take some decoys down to the Choctaw blind and see if you can get anything to work in down there. Till the water falls out, they'll be eatin' akerns and the lake won't be no good. Looks like we got to move in the timber for a while."

Matt loaded some decoys from our spread into his boat and paddled away, but in less than an hour he was back. His face was bruised and his nose dribbled blood. He was shivering and I realized it was from the chill of his dripping clothes. "What in hell happened to you?" Seeb said.

"Two men were in the Choctaw blind when I got there. When I told them to leave one of them knocked me out of my boat."

"Who in hell was they?" Seeb said.

"I don't know. They didn't bother introducing themselves."

"What'd they look like?"

"Big, fat and ugly with long, dirty beards."

Seeb's face went blank as he thought, then rage replaced the confusion. "Them damned Lefonts. Them two bastards ain't sposed to be on my side of the river. They snuck in down Little Bayou. I heared their outboard down there at daylight. I'll be a waitin' down the road a piece on you, Henry," he said, and got in his boat and paddled away.

"He's liable to wind up killin' 'em if you don't get down there," Lewis said.

"You're probably right. Let me have your boat, Matt. I'd better get down there," I said.

I didn't run into Seeb on my way to the Choctaw blind, and I'm sure the Lefonts were expecting him, because after realizing it was me paddling into their decoy spread, one casually jettisoned a long string of dark brown spit my way, and said, "Well, if it ain't Henry Ball. Thought we was shed of your wormy ass. Made all that money out of our bottoms and moved on. We figured you was that idjit Seeb come to start trouble."

"What in hell do you mean roughing up that boy, Big? He's helping the Stokes. I thought you two hunted the other side of the river."

"Ain't none of your damned business where we hunt, Ball. Now that this is all public, you and the Stokeses ain't got the run of the good shootin' holes no more. We'll hunt anywheres we like, and that little shit don't need to be a tellin' us what to do. And neither do you."

Then he left the blind and came splashing towards me in the knee-deep water. The other one, his younger brother Dumas, followed. I stepped out of the paddleboat knowing there was going to be trouble. I'd been reluctant bringing Lewis' gun, but now I was glad I had.

Big took a swing at me, but I ducked, and butt stroked him in the groin. Then I lost my grip on the gun when Dumas grabbed and lifted me up from behind in a headlock. Big had recovered and hit me in the face and drew back again, but a hollow thud resounded, and his eyes whitened as he sank to the water. Dumas loosened his grip when he saw it was Seeb that had hit his brother, and I turned and knocked him down. Then I broke a piece of rotted oak limb on his head. When I turned, Seeb had his gun aimed at Big's face. "No need to kill him, Seeb," I said.

Seeb was incensed and seemed not to hear me, so I grabbed his arm and he flung me away like a piece of chaff. Dumas was out cold, so I figured I'd better get him out of the water before he drowned. Seeb was still standing over Big with his gun to his head after I'd gotten Dumas to a dry piece of ground. Big's face was twisted in fear. He had a trembling hand inches from the gun barrel as if he would stop the load if Seeb fired. After I got between them, Seeb slowly lowered the gun.

"If I ever catch you two motherfuckers on my side of the river again, I'll kill your asses, you hear me?" Seeb said.

Big struggled to his feet and stumbled and splashed over to his brother and looked at the gaping, bleeding gash in his head. "You 'bout kilt him, Ball. You done put a lump on his head the size of a turkey egg," he said, and started towing his limp brother's incredible mass to their boat. Blood was dribbling down Big's neck onto his coat where Seeb had bashed the back of his head.

"Don't you'ens never come back over here or I'll kill your worthless asses," Seeb said.

"You better watch it, Seeb Stokes. If we'ens ever catch you alone, your ass is had."

Seeb went into another tirade and I struggled to restrain him. "Get your ignorant asses out of here while you can and be thankful you're alive. Best thing for you to do is drop all this and stay away from here. You know what I mean," I said.

"Fuck you'ens. We ain't a droppin' nothin', Ball."

I kept my shoulder pushed against Seeb's chest holding him back till the Lefonts had motored out of sight up the bayou. "They better not come back here again. After what they done to Mark the turtles are goin' to have a hell of a meal off their worthless asses if they do," he said.

CHAPTER 22

With the coming and going of the groups of hunters, time passed quickly, and it was suddenly Christmas. Lewis went home to Pine Bluff to his family and I stayed in hunting camp trying to regain enough strength to help the Stokes through the last weeks of the season. Seeb and Matt didn't miss a beat, though, and hunted every morning, including Christmas.

The skim ice in the backwater never thawed under the brilliant sun that day, and on a perfect wind the mallards worked eagerly into the blocks on Round Lake. They were back at the dock by early afternoon with their limits and Seeb left soon after without saying a word. I figured Christmas had put him in one of his melancholy moods and he wanted to be alone. That was fine though. It would be good to spend some time alone with Matt. I started a brace of Cornish hens roasting and opened a bottle of cheap champagne so we could toast. Then we sat down to talk.

"You know it seems stupid to have duck season open today. Nobody hunts on Christmas," Matt said.

"You and Seeb did."

"No, I mean paying hunters. We didn't hear any shots except ours today."

"I can assure you that duck season dates aren't set so duck guides can make more money. It's done for the management of waterfowl and for the benefit of the public. You haven't even gotten through a season yet and you're already thinking like a self-centered, arrogant Arkansas duck guide."

Sara was upset because Matt hadn't come home for Thanksgiving, and I could feel her rage through the phone when I told her he wouldn't be home for Christmas. But after I explained how well he was doing and how happy he was, it seemed to mollify her. I didn't tell her that her little boy was as much as a man now and that she needed to get used to living without him, unless she was prepared to move around the country forever how long the compulsion had him under its power.

Matt interrupted my thoughts. "What's on your mind, old man. You were in another world. Did you hear a thing I said?"

"I'm sorry. Guess my mind wandered off."

"No more champagne for you if you can't hold it any better than that."

"Tell me again."

"I said, why didn't you tell me Seeb had a son?"

"I didn't really think it mattered. The Department of Family and Children's Services took him after his mother abandoned him and Seeb. It was heartbreaking, especially for Seeb, but you should realize the boy's better off. Seeb had no business trying to raise a baby. With his past criminal record of poaching and bootlegging and history of violence a judge deemed him an unfit parent. The boy, especially being that young would have suffered miserably living with a single father so unqualified as a parent. It was a tragedy for Seeb but best for the child."

"It doesn't seem right, the government taking babies from their parents."

"I agree, but sometimes it's better for the child."

"You knew the boy's name was Mark, didn't you?"

"Yes, and Lewis and I picked up on it the first time he called you by his name. Are you upset with me for not being more upfront?"

"Not really, but it gave me a shock when he told me all this today. He really seems upset I'm leaving in a few weeks. He can't understand I have other important things to do."

"Believe me he'll get over it in no time after you're gone. It was the same way when I left when he was a kid."

It was New Year's Eve and Matt, Seeb and I were on the dock getting the boats ready for the next day of hunting. I was thankful the last few weeks had shot by so fast and the end of the season had come down to a matter of days. Seeb had become despondent and had started prowling the afternoons in the bottoms alone almost every day since Matt had told him he was leaving after the season closed, so we weren't surprised when he headed upriver after we were done with the chores. "Come on, Matt. I'll make some coffee," I said, as we watched Seeb go out of sight up the river in his skiff.

"No thanks. I'm going to take a nap. I feel like a zombie I'm so tired and sleepy."

"Sleep deprivation – a duck guides worst enemy and most faithful companion. May as well accept it, because you'll never get used to it."

"I'm really worried about Seeb. He's been acting strange lately. He doesn't talk much anymore and acts like he doesn't want me around."

"That's depression, Matt. His main passion in life ends for almost a year the day duck season closes and it always puts him in a low mood. And of course, the fact that you're leaving is making it worse. In a few weeks, he'll get back to normal. I know because I witnessed it for a lot of years."

"You think the Lefonts will really make trouble if they catch him alone?"

"I doubt it. They're mainly hot air. I don't think they want to take Seeb on."

"Do they live around here? That day we had the fight is the only time I've seen them."

"They live in a floating house on Goose Lake across the river from where we hunt. They pretty much stay to themselves and make their living off the river just like Seeb."

"Seeb said you beat one with an oak limb and he cracked the other's head open with his shotgun barrel. I'd like to have seen that after what they did to me."

"I hated getting mixed up in it, but the Stokes have always considered me part of the family and everything is family down here. It's a code they live by. Be glad you got accepted. You'll always be welcome here, Matt. That rarely happens. Just keep in mind that with the acceptance comes the responsibility of taking up for the family."

"Lewis told me this morning he wanted me to come back next season, so I guess I'm in."

"You are, but you need to understand that the Feds aren't going to allow commercial hunting in the bottoms much longer. They're choking it off slowly but surely. It could end at any time. Then you'll have to start leasing land to guide on, and you'll lose most of your profit when you do."

"Then we'll raise our prices. Hunters will pay most anything for a chance to kill a duck. But my main concern is with Seeb right now having to leave him in the condition he's in."

"Then why don't you stay here and go ahead and marry Pearle like she wanted you to? Then you'd be Seeb's nephew and could partner with him in his commercial fishing and whiskey making business."

"That's not funny. You know I've stayed away from her since she told me she wasn't pregnant. I just hope you're right about Seeb. I'd hate for anything bad to happen to him."

"You don't need to worry about Seeb. He can take care of himself."

Though Seeb didn't come back from the bottoms that night, Lewis and I weren't too concerned. During his low moods over the years Seeb had stayed out late in the bottoms many times before, getting so drunk he'd pass out in a blind for hours. But when he didn't show the next morning when the hunters did, we began to worry. He rarely missed a hunt even when he was deathly ill, and with enough shine he could nurse himself through a severe morning hangover when necessary.

"If he don't show up by the time the hunters leave out at lunch, we'll go lookin' for him," Lewis said.

"Maybe I should call the sheriff?"

"If there's trouble we need to handle this ourselves, Henry. We don't want the law buttin' in if them Lefonts are to blame for anything."

Seeb didn't show during the hunt that morning, and after the hunters left, we went back to Coot Lake to look for him. "To cover more ground let's separate and meet back here at dark. Far three shots if you find anything," Lewis said. Then he headed off towards Stinking Bay, I to Millers Bayou, and Matt to the Choctaw Blind.

The river was falling back into its banks and the current in the timber had become listless. A rotten smell issued from the trapped backwaters. The mallards had departed, and the woods were lifeless. Warm somber breezes moaned and squeaked through the barren trees.

I checked several blinds paddling to Millers Bayou, but all I found were spent shell casings, sodden ammunition boxes, food wrappers and some drained whiskey bottles – the normal refuse left by duck hunters.

It was another two hours before dark when I was to meet Matt and Lewis back at the lake when I'd finished searching up Millers Bayou, so I headed on up to Little Bayou, an unlikely but possible place Seeb might be. I hadn't gone far when a murder of crows rose cawing from a dry ridge off the creek back in the timber. The indignant raucous black mob took me back to the Chosin and the carrion crows whenever they were disrupted by a low flight of Corsairs on a bombing run. Except for something that had drowned during the flood there would be nothing else to interest them back there. Then I saw Seeb's overturned paddle boat in the backwater and knew the search for him was over and I fired my gun.

The crows slipped back while I waited for Matt and Lewis but rose noisily again as we approached Seeb's body. They'd picked hard, but he hadn't rotted enough for them to have eaten much. Only his eyes and slivers of flesh from his face were gone.

The murderers had bound his hands with zip ties and tied him to a tree. His face had been bludgeoned. A deep incision emitting rivulets of blood ringed his throat. After we untied and laid him out on the ground Lewis covered him with his coat and we stood around wailing and grieving till well after dark.

"Well, let's get him in the skiff and take him home," Lewis said, after he could cry no more.

"The law won't like it if we move him," I said.

"I don't care. I'm takin' him home."

"Those worthless bastards are going to pay for this," Matt said. "And you told me they wouldn't hurt him, Henry."

Next morning, I called the sheriff's department in Dewitt and Sheriff Ralf Bates and an ambulance came out to the trailer. Tommy McMahan knew the place where the crime had been committed and took some deputies and an investigator to the scene. After they carried Seeb away, the sheriff sat us down at the kitchen table. "Look boys, I can see your pain and grief. I'll leave you alone with it as soon as you answer a few questions. First of all, any idea who done it, Lewis?" Lewis stared back and said nothing, defiance glaring in his eyes. "Lewis, better let the law handle this. You're about to get in an ass of trouble. Now tell me, who do you think done it?"

"I ain't got no idea."

"That's a damned lie. I'll tell you one thing, there'd better not be no more killin's over this. It ain't like the old days, Lewis. You can't settle this on your own."

The sheriff adjusted his gun belt, clenched his fists and stormed out. The sparse gathering drawn by the flashing blue lights milling about in the yard watched him drive away. Then they began to slowly drift off shaking their heads and mumbling accusations. They were river people and knew as the sheriff did that river justice would prevail as it always had.

"I'm goin' to Goose Lake to kill them bastards tomorrow night. You comin' with me?"

"I have no qualms about killing them, Lewis, but we need to think about the others that depend on us. And you're forgetting one thing – their dogs."

"I ain't forgot. I'll see to them."

Lewis mixed a concoction of antifreeze and hamburger before going upriver later that night. He left his boat and went the last half mile on foot to Goose Lake. When the Lefont's hounds heard rustling in the woods they went to barking and howling after the noise. The brothers kept their dogs near starvation believing hunger made them hunt better and they eagerly lapped up the poisoned meat as Lewis slipped away in the dark.

Next morning after breakfast Lewis and I made plans for our visit of retribution to the Lefont's floating house that coming night. I only wanted revenge. A good ass whipping and getting them to jail would have to do. Murder was out for me. Likely they'd spend the rest of their days behind bars anyway, or most likely get a lethal injection at some point since Seeb's murder was premeditated and first degree. But Lewis wanted quick self-imposed equal justice. "I'd still like to blow their ugly faces off with a load of buckshot and sink 'em in the river," he said.

"That's what they deserve, but we can't do that. Kicking the shit out of their sorry asses and turning them in to the law is going to have to be good enough. Killing the worthless bastards isn't worth spending the rest of our lives in prison for."

"For killing my brother, it is to me."

"But it isn't for your family's sake."

"That's the only reason."

"I want to make one thing clear. Matt's not to know anything about this. I don't want him involved in any way. We'll leave after he's asleep. And I still think we should give it a few more days. They'll be expecting us I'm sure after what we did to their dogs."

"The sheriff's liable to get 'em if we wait around. I at least want the satisfaction of stompin' their asses and makin' them shit their pants thinkin' we're goin' to kill 'em."

Another storm had begun to form in the Gulf and a warm, moist wind started building as we motored upriver. The sky was starless and inky with low, heavy clouds rolling in. When we pulled in to tie off well above the entrance to Goose Lake a skiff with no running lights came speeding past us going on upriver. We sat in the boat till it went out of hearing. "What do you think, Lewis?"

"Probably just some coon hunters. I ain't turnin' back now. Let's go."

Walking the distance through the dark woods to Goose Lake was an endeavor of torture and frustration from constantly tripping and falling and being ripped by saw briars while clouds of mosquitos converged on us.

The planked gangway leading to the back of the house squeaked under our weight. Lewis was ahead of me and stopped and cocked his head for a long while listening for any movement inside. I became inpatient and pressed my hand against his back and he moved on to the door. It was slightly cracked and with a slight push it creaked open. I covered my nose as the putrid scent of ripe body odor and rancid food greeted us.

We stepped inside and the only noise was the faint crackling of dying embers coming from a wood stove in the far corner. A faint-flickering-golden glow from its partially opened door eerily lit the room. I was thinking we'd wasted our time, and that no one was home when a blinding light flashed in my eyes. There was brief scuffling and then Lewis fell backwards knocking me down. I struggled against his weight to get on my feet, but a pain sent galaxies of shooting stars though my brain, and then all went black.

I came to on the front porch of the floating house with my hands and feet feeling on fire from being so tightly bound with heavy zip ties. The back of my head throbbed from where I'd been clubbed. Lewis was beside me, his eyes unfocused. Then I realized the blood oozing from a gash in his head and great dread rose inside me. "Oh my god, Lewis, can you hear me?" To my relief he nodded.

I listened to the rattling and banging and voices from within the house. "This ought to be enough rope. Damn, I can't believe them bastards was that dumb. Let's throw water on 'em and talk fer a spell."

The Lefonts them came out on the porch, and after rolling us over, saw that we were conscious. Big laughed and emptied the bucket of icy water on us anyway. "You boys have a good nap? You're about to have a real long un," he said.

"Why, Lewis Stokes, you as big an idjit as that retarded brother of your'n. Only a fool would of come back so quick after killin' a man's dogs. We knowed what you was up to. Now you goin' to pay just like Seeb done," Dumas said.

A kick to my ribs from Big lifted me off the floor and onto my side and left me breathless. "And you, Henry Ball, you uppity sombitch, you never belonged in our bottoms no how. You was with Hired that day he shot my pappy and crippled his foot. Then you hogged them good shootin' holes all them years and made all that money. I've always hated your ratty little ass. Now you fixin' to get what you deserve."

They dragged us to where a gate was open at the edge of the porch so our heads were hanging out over the water. I figured to keep our splattering brains from making such a mess. "You assholes aren't going to get away with this. Better let us go," I said.

Big kicked my ribs again and laughed. "Wish we had time to cut on you boys like we done Seeb, but we ain't got all night. After I blow your brains in the lake, we're gonna weight you down and drop you'ens in the river for the turtles to eat on."

"I'm gonna kill Ball after what he done to me. You ain't havin' all the fun," Dumas said.

"Better step back then if you don't want to get covered. I'm fixin' to splash old Lewis' brains all over creation."

After Dumas stepped back, Big put his gun to Lewis' face. He sounded like an old lady the way he cackled. Then a gun thundered nearby out on the lake and Big pointed his out into the darkness. "Who's that out thar, damn you?"

Matt's voice came clear and steady. "Put those guns down or I'll cut you two lowlife motherfuckers in half."

After a long silence, another shot exploded from out of the black and then the metallic clacking of another round being pumped into the chamber. The impact of the load cracked against the porch above our heads ripping some boards. Along with the splinters settling onto the floor, Dumas' gun banged down, too. "Oh god, don't shoot me!"

"Lay down then and don't move. How about you, asshole. I will shoot you."

Big had seen the muzzle flash from Matt's second shot and as he shouldered his gun and aimed, another shot boomed and Big went down like his legs had been chopped off. He fell beside me screaming and writhing. Little rivulets of blood were spouting in heartbeats from his thighs. "Thank goodness he didn't kill your sorry ass," I said.

Then Matt's voice came again. "I'm coming in. I've got my gun on you, so don't try anything dumb."

Matt came silently out of the dark sculling the small boat with one hand, pointing the shotgun with the other. Big was still squirming and moaning leaking blood as Dumas pled for his life. When Matt stepped onto the porch, Dumas started to raise up and Matt whacked him on the head with the gun butt and he didn't move again.

"What in hell are you doing here?" I said.

"I knew you were going to do something like this. You keep treating me like I'm a stupid child. You shouldn't have left me out of it. I loved Seeb as much as you do."

"You better be glad he come, Henry. We'd be dead now if he hadn't," Lewis said.

"Now you're involved. Your mother will kill me if she finds out. Are you okay?" I said.

"I think so, but I've got the shakes really bad. What do you mean if my mother finds out?"

"I don't know. I'm half out of my head and not thinking right. How are you holding up, Lewis?"

"I got a hell of a headache, but I'm okay I guess."

Matt cut me free and I lost my breath and yelled sitting up from the pain in my ribs. As I massaged my wrists Matt cut Lewis free. "Where did you find the paddleboat?" I said.

"It was tied off with their skiff in the cove over there."

"Better yet how did you find us?"

"I followed you until you pulled over and I went on by. I drifted back down and cut through the woods and came out where they tie off their boats. I saw the lights on here and that's how I found you."

"You could've got killed pulling a stunt like this. I should be mad as hell, but right now I'm mighty glad you came."

"Now that it's done you was right, Henry. It was a bad idea tryin' this so soon," Lewis said.

"He's right," Matt said. "So, how much trouble you think we're going to be in with the law?"

"I don't know. Right now, we need to get this lump of shit to the hospital. I don't want him to bleed to death on us," I said. "And I'm sure Lewis needs some stitches in his head."

Just before we left the house Matt pointed to a shotgun propped in a corner. "That's Seeb's," he said.

"Leave it," I said. "That's evidence."

Matt left the gun but picked up a knife he'd given Seeb for Christmas from the kitchen table as we left.

We managed to get Big and Dumas loaded into one of their skiffs and motored back upriver to the trailer. Big couldn't walk and it was a chore dragging him up the steep dock steps. We loaded the two into the back of my truck and went to the emergency room in Dewitt. Big had a palmful of number 2 steel shot removed from his legs. There was no real damage done though, just some lost blood. Lewis got some stitches in his head. They checked my ribs. Nothing was broken, just badly bruised and terribly painful. I had a headache straight from Hell, but after several Oxycodone I was pain free, on top of the world and as loquacious as a drunk parrot. Several deputies came to the hospital and stood around with their hands gripping their pistols while we were being treated. Two of them stayed with Big and Dumas at the hospital while the rest of us went to the sheriff's office.

It was nearing dawn when we pulled into the county jail parking lot. A deputy questioned us individually about the incident, and then we hung around the visitor's area of the jail drinking lukewarm stale coffee while waiting for Ralf Bates. When he came in, he gave us a brief, angry glance as he passed through the lobby heading to his office.

After a long wait Bates came back, but with a stern smirk on his face this time. "I figured you boys would show up here one way or ta other. Didn't think it would be this soon, though. I read the report, but I want to hear it in yawl's own words."

We each went alone into Bate's office and told him our version of the ordeal with the Lefonts. I gave my testimony last and Bates kept the same featureless expression the whole time. He walked around his office in thought for five minutes after I'd finished and then he gathered the three of us together again.

"So, it was the Lefonts. Should have known, but I didn't think they had the balls or the meanness to kill anybody. And what am I goin' to do with y'all? You broke into their house and for all I know was plannin' on killin' 'em. But they are the murderers of your brother and friend. Even though I feel you had the right, I doubt the District Attorney, or a grand jury will. And if they were about to kill you, I can't charge this boy with usin' force to stop 'em, especially since no real harm was done. But I can't just let you off scot-free."

The painkiller still had me in a talkative mood, and I started pleading our case. "If you check you'll see we didn't break in. The door was open when we got there. We only wanted to talk to them about Seeb to see if they would admit to killing him, but they jumped us first. If Matt hadn't come along, they would have murdered two more innocent people, Sheriff. All we did was pay them a visit and their guilt overtook them, and then they decided to kill us, too. No Arkansas jury is going to convict us for what we did. Who are they going to believe, us or those two cold-blooded murderers?"

"You got a point, Henry. Guess you could call it a citizen's arrest. Guess y'all can leave, but don't go anywhere far till I hash this out with the D.A. If you do it'll only make things bad for you."

"We'll be at the trailer house, Sheriff," Lewis said.

We had one other group of clients that had been hunting with us for years. The impact of Seeb's death dampened the hunt, but we made it through. We spent the next few days after the season ended gathering up and storing decoys and other equipment, and free-floating the blinds. Matt and I packed for the trip home to the Keys and were waiting on the D.A.'s decision on whether we were going to be allowed to leave Arkansas before a trial. We were eating breakfast when Ralf Bates came a few days later. Lewis answered his knock. "Come on in, Ralf, and have some breakfast. We just set down."

"Believe I will."

The Sheriff filled his plate from the stove and sat down. As he blackened his eggs and grits with pepper, he started the conversation. "Have a good season, Lewis?"

"It was, cept for losin' Seeb. Matt here says he's comin' back next season to help in his place."

"How about you, Henry? You a comin' back?"

"I doubt it, Ralf. I've had all the duck hunting I want."

"You goin' to be around for a while, Lewis?" Bates said.

"After we get Seeb in the ground tomorrow I got to get on back to work, Ralf. I 'bout stretched my string far as it'll go at the far station."

"I'm sorry about Seeb. We had our run ins, but I reckon he was a good enough feller. If it weren't for makin' half my constituents mad, I'd found that still of his'n, and blowed it."

"There's goin' to be a lot of thirsty people round here now, that's for sure," Lewis said.

And then we ate in silence waiting for Bates to break the news. He held us in suspense until we'd finished eating. "Guess y'all want to know what the D.A. had to say?"

We nodded, and I prepared for the worst.

"Well the main thing that went good for you is that Dumas confessed to everything when we got him away from Big and put a little pressure on him. It's his story that Big did all the dirty work and he just went along with it. He told us they left the door cracked on purpose figrin' you'd pay a visit, so they'd laid a trap for you with intention of murderin' you. D.A. promised to get Dumas a life sentence if he'd testify against his brother, and he jumped on it. Henry, you and the boy need to come by in the mornin' to give depositions, then y'all can leave. Just let me know where you'll be if I need you. And by the way, that citizen's arrest bullshit didn't fly."

CHAPTER 23

Home
20 January 1991

I was so eager and determined to get home to Sugar Loaf Key that, except to buy gas and coffee, I drove straight through. But after pulling into the drive and studying the house my joy and enthusiasm began to wane. After being gone for so long the house looked old and alien all shuttered and dulled with mildew. The grass and shrubs had gone wild, and the yard was littered with dead palm fronds and other dead herbage. All that could be fixed with a few hours of hard work, though. It was the thought that it was just a charitable and temporary abode that I was being allowed to dwell in that really killed my spirit. I didn't really own it and as soon as I passed, it would become the property of the Florida Keys Nature Conservancy. The property was a valuable piece of real estate I'd loved to have passed on to Matt, except it wasn't mine to pass on. And making it all the worse was the reality that Hope was truly gone. To compound it even more was the state of my health and the ruination of my guide business I'd worked so long and hard to build. With all those miserable thoughts racing around in my head, if there had been another place to go, I would have backed out of the drive and gone there to try to escape the misery and despair I was feeling.

The south Florida heat soon ran Matt out of the camper, and his tapping on my window brought me out of my self-pitying trance. I slid out of the truck and reluctantly went to open the house I'd loved and had missed so much that now seemed so desolate and strange.

Hot, stagnant, and mildewed air engulfed me like clinging wrap when I opened the front door. The shades were drawn, and it felt as gloomy as a funeral parlor once I was inside. When I drew back the living room curtains the months of accumulated dust threw me into a sneezing fit. Opening some windows helped clear the air, but not the dismal feeling of Hope not being there. Then I showed Matt to his bedroom.

"You can sleep in here, Matt. Hope it suits you okay."

He looked it over and smiled. "It's great, Henry. It's a big change from the trailer house. Glass windows instead of duct taped plastic bags. Carpet and not sticky linoleum. No stench of rat piss. No box springs on cement blocks." The paintings of various species of flats gamefish hanging on the walls took his imagination over. When I opened a window the ocean air blew him back to reality. "You really got a neat place. I love it," he said.

"I love it too, but I've been gone from it way too damn long thanks to you." I realized after I'd said it that I was trying to put the blame on him for all my problems when I was the one that had made the decisions that had caused them. My uncalled-for comment killed his exuberance and made me feel ashamed and sorry. We stood in silence a long moment as he again studied the various fish portraits, then a clatter from across the canal caught our attention. It was a girl in a yellow thong bikini unfolding a lounge chair. Being my closest neighbors, I knew Lea Sanchez and her parents well. Lea was of Spanish descent, dark complexioned with coal black hair. As I watched her, Sandy came to mind. After coating her immaculate body with tanning oil, she spread out a towel, and after dropping her top and sprawling out on the chair, Matt turned to me with eyes wide as saucers. "Damn," was all he could manage.

"Haven't you seen boobs before?"

"Not like those I haven't."

He turned back to gawking at her like a wild-eyed randy goat. "Oh hell, here we go again," I said, and left.

I went to my bedroom to unpack and when I opened the closet, the sight and scent of some unwanted clothes Hope had left behind sent a jolting ache through my chest. The emotion brought on an overwhelming urge to call Doc Holmes. Of all people he would know best of her sentiment towards me and wouldn't sugar coat the truth to protect my feelings.

When his receptionist answered, she told me that Doc was busy and couldn't talk. "I know as always, but please tell him Henry Ball needs a few urgent words with him."

After several minutes of depressing chamber music, the receptionist returned. "He'll call you back. He's with a patient."

The wait wasn't long, and before the second ring I jerked the receiver up. "Are you back, Henry?" Doc said.

"We just now pulled in."

"How do you feel?"

"Like shit. I just finished a thirteen-hundred-mile drive. How else do you think I'd feel?"

"I'm just concerned, Henry. You don't have to be short."

"I'm sorry, Doc. I'm out of my mind over Hope not being here. The true reality didn't set in till just now."

"Hope? You mean that wonderful woman you deserted? The one you drove bat shit crazy with all your lies. The one you promised and swore to that you'd only be gone for two weeks to go chase down some runaway brat you'd never seen before. And now you drag your worthless ass back eight months later and say you're upset because she isn't spread-legged in your bed waiting on you. Fuck you, Henry. Hope is a friend of mine and you shit on her. My only concern for you now is from a professional standpoint. If you want to talk about your health, fine, but don't bother me anymore with your personal life, especially concerning Hope after the way you treated her."

"Look, Doc, I know I screwed up, but if you'll let me explain all this, I think you'll understand, and so will Hope. I really need to talk to you."

"Like I said, Henry, I don't owe you any of my personal time. If you want to make an appointment to talk about your health that's fine. I'm obligated to do that. Otherwise I'd just as soon we break ties. I thought you were a better person."

"Okay, Doc, but if you were half the man I thought you were, you'd at least give me the chance to clear the air. Guess I can't blame you, though."

I waited anxiously expecting Holmes to hang up, but mercifully he didn't. "I'll come by around five-thirty. I'm busy now and can't talk anymore."

As Doc eased his Jag through the crowded streets of Key West, I studied the ambling masses herding down the sidewalks like asylum trustees on furlough. Key West seemed strange after Arkansas, but I figured if it were a place for the deranged then I was truly at home. They were two different worlds. "If only Seeb could have seen this," I said, under my breath.

Holmes glanced over. "Beg your pardon."

"Just talking to myself, Doc."

"Miss these freaks, Henry?"

"Surprisingly yes. Damn it's good to be home, Doc. I just wish Hope were here. It's torturing me she's gone."

"You're the one that fucked that up and I don't feel any sympathy for you. Now where do you want to go?"

"Somewhere quiet where I can sit in the sun and feel warm and at peace, if that's possible."

We went to a restaurant that had an outside bar on the water. The afternoon sun felt wonderful out on the deck after the cold of

Arkansas. Two quick double scotches put me in a better frame of mind.

"When did you start drinking again, Henry?"

"After you gave me the news that I had cancer last June. I figured it didn't matter anymore. I started smoking again, too. What of it?"

"I know I don't like your asshole attitude after you've had a few. So, stop the obnoxious bullshit and tell me what's happened over the past eight months."

I spent the next hour conveying the events that had transpired during the time I'd been gone. I related everything of importance concerning Matt I could think of hoping it would get me back in Doc's good graces. And I guess I was trying to convince myself I'd done the right thing, as well. Doc's admonishing glare had softened considerably by the time I'd finished.

"I'm still disgusted with you, Henry, but now I partially understand your idiotic reasoning. But you need to understand just how crushed Hope was from all your lies and deceit. Did you even try to call her after she left here and went home?"

I turned my gaze to the Gulf to avoid his eyes. The ocean had calmed and looked afire from the golden hue of the setting sun and the reflection gave everything a buttery tint. "After we left Yellowstone, I figured it best to leave things as they were till I got back here. I got sick of making excuses to her. My calling was only making things worse and making me feel more like a liar, which I was. I had to stop giving her false encouragement. It made me sick listening to her pleadings for me to come home."

"I guess you were screwed either way you went, but I'm still on Hope's side. If you could explain it all to her just as you told it to me, you might convince her to come back. But I'd have to say it's doubtful. Loathing you would be an understatement of her feelings when she left here. She loved you and the Keys and the house so much, and you abused her so bad."

"You aren't giving me much encouragement, Doc, or making me feel any better."

"She's been gone for months, Henry. For God's sake, a lot can happen in that amount of time. Hope's a beautiful woman and she could have found somebody else by now, or more precisely, somebody could have found her. Could you really blame her for not coming back? And don't act as if any of this is my fault, you bastard. It was you who deserted her, not me."

"Sorry, Doc, my emotions are running away with me right now. And no, I couldn't blame her for not coming back."

I emptied my glass and summonsed our waitress to bring another. "If only I could talk to her, Doc, and make her understand."

Holmes slid a slip of paper across the table towards me. "Here's her number, Henry. I called and told her you were back before I left the office. She didn't seem to be very concerned."

I'd gone over the line with the whiskey and was on my feet screaming out of control before I realized it. "Don't fuck with me, Doc! This isn't the time."

The deck hushed, and everyone turned their eyes on me. I sat down and dropped my head. Doc seemed to enjoy seeing me make a fool of myself. He was grinning when I regained enough composure to show my face again. "Feel better now? Why don't you have another one," he said.

"I'm sorry. I've had enough."

"Just call her, you jerk. That's all you can do. And now that we've discussed Matt and Hope, let's talk about you. How do you feel? And don't lie."

"I have very little appetite. It doesn't take much to exhaust me. But it comes and goes. Some days aren't as bad as others. I can feel it more every day, though."

"You're a sack of bones and I can see signs of jaundice in your eyes. You should have started treatment as soon as you were diagnosed. You'd probably have it in remission now."

"I didn't have time. I had to do this for Sara and Matt – and for myself. Why can't any of you understand it was something I had to do?"

The Maverick had mildewed in dry storage during the past eight months, and the Yamaha needed carburetor maintenance. Since I hadn't figured on being gone so long, I didn't take the time to winterize it before I left. After backing it in the driveway, I started working on the outboard while Matt scrubbed on the boat. When he'd worked himself to the polling platform, he climbed onto it. "Ever fallen off this before?" he said.

"Plenty of times. You're going to fall. Just try to land in the water. It doesn't hurt as much. Last time I fell, I hit the gunnel and broke Doc's favorite rod and my ass was bruised black for a month."

"Isn't it hard to pole a heavy boat like this?"

"At first it is, but it'll get easy after a while and become as automatic as rowing did after you get used to it. Finding and spotting fish is going to be your biggest challenge."

"I doubt it'll take me long to figure it out."

"We'll see, smart ass. We'll see."

He was quiet for several minutes and I began to feel his stare on the back of my neck. When I looked up, he was glaring at me intensely. "What's that look for?" I said.

"Henry, are you alright? Just since we left Arkansas you look thinner and your eyes don't look so good."

I wasn't ready for him to know I was dying just yet. He needed to learn all he could about the flats while I could still help him, and he didn't need to be distracted by that. "Yeah, I got a bug from the water in Arkansas. It's working on my bowels. I'm taking an antibiotic and it'll be gone soon." The look he gave me was one of doubt.

Next morning as we were launching the Maverick at the Sugar Loaf Marina for Matt's first day on the flats, Tim Carter came out of the office when he saw my truck. His ravaged sun splotched face lit up as he offered his hand. "It's good to have you back, Henry. You've lost weight since you've been gone."

"It's good to see you, Tim. I got a bug in Arkansas, but it's about gone. Meet Matt Whitaker. Matt wants to be a flats guide. I hoped you might help me out getting him started."

Timmy's happy expression turned sour as he looked Matt up and down. "There's too many wannabe guides in the Keys as it is."

"You don't care about fly fishing clientele, Tim. Matt could make you money from all the fly fishermen you turn down if you'd work with him."

Tim went back to giving Matt a hard looking over. "You're right. I could use another guide. Harry just went out on his own, the bastard. But I'm tired of training assholes that leave and go on their own when they've learned enough and then take my clients and fishing spots over when they do. How do I know I could trust you not to do the same?"

Timmy's brazenness surprised Matt and he turned to me for intervention. I decided to let Matt handle Tim on his own and I smiled and shrugged.

"But I wouldn't do anything like that," Matt said, after a long pause.

"You say that now, but when you didn't need me anymore, you'd leave just like the rest of them have."

I interrupted. "I'll show him my places and I've got enough clientele to keep him busy, but I'd feel good knowing you'd help him, as well. You don't have anything to lose and everything to gain."

As Tim thought he scrutinized Matt even more. Matt took his sunglasses off and began fidgeting with the head strap. "Okay, I'll give him a try, but it's mainly for you, Henry. He looks halfway honest at least. Yeah, I might be able to work with him."

"That's good, Tim, and I want to thank you and your wife for taking care of my clients while I was gone. I'll never be able to repay you."

"It all worked out pretty well except for that old Marine General. He was pissed you didn't let him know you weren't going to be here."

"He'll get over it, Timmy. How was he?"

"He's a scrappy old codger. Ever see him smile?"

"Once a long time ago."

"When you get back from fishing come by my office. I've got a commission check for your share of the trips we did for you."

The skiff skimmed smoothly over the light chop as we headed out into the Gulf to Simms Flat. Simms was a haven for feeding schools of bonefish and permit on the right tides, and by far my favorite place to fish. There were few other guides willing to make the long run to Simms with so many flats almost as good nearby, but the long run was worth it to me just for the solitude.

Near the mainland, skiffs and cruisers were running rampant, but as the distance from Sugar Loaf grew, the presence of other craft diminished. After running thirty minutes I pointed ahead, and Matt watched the emerald fleck floating on the horizon grow and connect to the sea and eventually become the small cay that marked Simms Flat.

I killed the engine and coasted onto the flat, then unclamped the push pole and climbed onto the poling platform. "Get the nine-weight rod out, Matt."

Matt took the rod from the holder and stepped onto the casting deck and began scanning the flat for bonefish as if he'd done it a thousand times before. The water was clear as air, and with so many sandy spots, I'm sure he believed he could see any bonefish that came near the boat. It wasn't long before he pointed his rod, and said, "There's one, Henry."

"Just a baby shark," I said, trying to constrain my laughter.

Matt dropped his head. "Oh."

I poled on and saw movement coming our way fifty yards out. "Ray at two o'clock."

The ray was easy to distinguish, and Matt pointed at it with the rod when he spotted it. Its wing tips were making twin spouts of mud as it casually winged along. "Get your fly out, Matt. Bonefish are feeding behind the ray."

He was on his toes straining to see. "Where?"

"Just get your thumb out of your ass and get some line out. Cast behind the ray and hurry it up. They're moving our way fast." He stripped line off the reel and made several pathetic false casts. It was as if he'd never had a flyrod in his hands the way the line struggled going back and forth in huge, wide loops. When he cast, the fly went ten feet and snapped to a stop. "You're standing on the line. Pick your foot up and shoot please and make it fast. They're going to see the boat."

"Where?"

"Just cast damn it!"

Matt heaved the fly and it went less than twenty feet in a miserable heap of fly line and leader. He shook his head as he stripped in line and started to pick up to cast again, but the pod of fish was coming towards his fly.

"No. Leave it. Now strip, strip, strip. Drop it. Now set." He was so tense he overreacted and broke the fish off on the strike. "We're not tarpon fishing. Put on some new tippet and a fly," I said.

His hands were shaking so much it took him three tries to tie the tippet on. While he was repairing the leader, I explained how to strip-set instead of raising the rod tip like setting the hook on a trout. After climbing back onto the casting deck, he turned to me with a sheepish look. "Guess I was a little overconfident. It's not as easy as I thought it'd be. I never even saw the fish."

"Forget it. You didn't do so bad for your first try. At least now you understand a little of what you're up against. Remember what I told you about being humbled and realizing who and what you are?"

"Yes, sir."

"These bonefish will do that for you."

I thought back to the first time I fished for bonefish. In the mid-seventies on the Madison River, Horace Simington convinced me to visit him in the Keys. I was reluctant to go at first surmising ocean fishing would be boring. I tried begging out, but Simington was relentless.

The first day on the water I became infatuated with bonefish, of how they would explode off the flats at even the mere passing of a tern's shadow. I remembered the muscle locking tension created by the first school I saw moving across the flat leaving trails of mud plumes, tails sparkling waving in the sun nosing along searching for food. If the cast was short, the fish wouldn't see the fly. Too close, it was worse than the tern's shadow. There was always the capricious wind to spoil even the perfect cast. It was the challenge of a sport that captivated me, and stalking bonefish on the flats with a fly did so entirely.

Then I thought of how the so-called experts try to make it all seem so easy. They make you think with their cheap and erroneous instructional videos you can learn to catch trout and bonefish consistently on a fly with little effort in little time. They leave out the part about the real casting skill it takes years to acquire, and they omit the wind, too, and how much havoc it wreaks on you both physically and mentally. And they never touch on the immeasurable desire it takes to become truly accomplished. As James Mason had told me in the beginning, "No matter how much you learn and how good you get they'll still kick your ass." And now after forty years and thousands of days of it I'd add that the more you learn the more you realize how little you know.

I put the pointless thoughts out of mind and began poling toward the channel that cut the flat. We were still a distance away when I detected a slight bulge just where the incoming tidewater broke out on the flat. "Matt, look to one o'clock. Keep your eyes on the water about sixty yards out." I detected another minor disturbance. "There's fish there, Matt. See the ripple?"

"I can't see anything."

"Just keep looking." A glinting forked tail then broke and waved above the water. "See that don't you?"

"What is it?"

"A bonefish tail. There's a whole school. You must be blind if you can't see them."

"I see 'em now! I see 'em."

Spouts of mud plumed as the feeding fish nosed the marl for buried crabs and other crustaceans as they worked quickly and methodically towards the boat. "Get your back cast higher this time, Matt. The wind is over your right shoulder. It should be easy." But it wasn't. He could only manage a thirty-foot cast instead of the needed sixty. "Try to relax and put your fly out further at two o'clock."

He paused to gather his wits and this time he wasn't frantic when he started to cast. The line dragging against the water helped load the rod and he hauled the line back high and shot a fifty-foot cast precisely where it needed to be. "Great job. Now leave it there. Leave it. Be ready. They're coming up on it." A tail broke near the fly. "Now strip. Strip. Stop. Stop. Strip. Strip." A fish tailed up on the fly. "Set! Set!" He kept the rod tip pointed at the fish and stripped hard.

The water erupted as the startled school headed for deep water. Line began dissolving off the spool and then backing began pouring out as the hooked fish sped off across the flat. A dozen wakes furrowed the water as it tried staying with the school, but after a hundred yards it slowed and eventually stopped and turned on its side.

"Shake the grass off your line before the weight breaks you off," I said.

He cleared the line and began reeling. The fish gave little resistance. It seemed to be finished when he finally brought it near the boat five minutes later. "Get the net, old man."

"Let me worry about the net. You keep your mind on the fish."

"He's done. Get the net."

When the fish sensed the boat, it exploded out across the flat again and caught Matt off guard. It was a miracle the leader held when the spinning reel handle banged his knuckles. The fish was spent after the second run and Matt soon brought it alongside the boat. As I went for the net, two flashes streaked out of nowhere. The rod bowed deeply and then straightened, and the bonefish's head popped out of the water and into the boat.

Matt was dumbfounded at first, and then he became angry realizing what had happened. "Those bastards! It didn't have a chance."

"That happens, Matt. I know they're part of the scheme of things, but damn if I don't hate them sometimes. Want some payback?"

"What do you mean?"

I rummaged in the rod compartment and brought out a spinning rod rigged with a gaff sized hook and a steel leader. I punched the hook through the bonefish's head and handed the rod to Matt. "Cast in the channel. I bet you a double sawbuck the nasty bastards are laying out there on the edge. And hopefully one's about to become our special guest for dinner tonight."

The bonefish head shimmered as it rolled and twisted sinking into the dark shadows of the cut. Matt started to reel but I stopped him. "No wait. Give them time to smell it." In moments the rod bowed as the hooked shark started down the channel. The drag purred as the taught mono hummed in the breeze. Matt had a grand time fighting the shark and in ten minutes it was whipped. After he led it to the side of the boat, I hit it with a gaff and hauled it in chomping and thrashing. Several blows to its head with a lead-weighted priest ended its struggles. "Small blacktips and bonnetheads off the flats are good eating, Matt. Maybe the best fish there is. We'll steak him out and broil him over charcoal tonight."

I got a filet board and knife out and started steaking the shark. Matt came back to watch. "I wish Seeb were here. He'd love this," he said.

I began packing the meat into a zip lock bag. "Knowing Seeb, he'd love supper tonight more than the fishing, especially if we had some moonshine. And anyway, what makes you so sure he's not here?"

"What do you mean by that?"

I leaned over the gunwale to wash the blood and slime off my hands and then the knife and board. "Maybe he is here. Don't you believe in reincarnation?"

He let out a loud laugh. "Coming back from the dead as an animal? Come on, Henry, you don't believe in that nonsense."

"As much as anything I've heard in a church sermon. It's nice to think Seeb's spirit came back in some animal and that he's watching us now. What animal would you think he'd come back as?"

"I don't know. A bobcat or maybe a hawk. Some kind of predator, I'm sure."

"I'd agree with that. If you had the chance what would you like to come back as?"

"I don't know. I've never given it any thought it's so stupid. What would you like to come back as?"

"A dolphin."

"A fish? Come on, Henry, anything but a fish. That's stupid, too."

"Dolphins aren't fish. They're mammals just like we are, and they're very intelligent. Think about it. They can travel all over the world picking the climate and places they want to live. They have an endless menu of all sorts of fish. The only real enemy they have is man and the orca. But you know what the best thing about being a dolphin would be?"

"What?"

"They can make love anytime they want to just for fun just like humans."

"If you're telling the truth you just made my mind up for me."

"Thought so. Now look behind you."

The discussion of reincarnation ended with the sight of forked tails waving in the sunlight as another school of bonefish came feeding our way.

The phone rang forever before she answered. I'm sure it was because she saw it was my number on her caller ID and she was trying to decide whether she wanted to answer or not. "Hello, Henry," came the dour greeting.

"Hope, it's wonderful to hear your voice. How are you?"

"I'm fine. A bit lonely, but I'm okay. And you?"

"I'm sick with despair that you're not here. The house feels strange without you."

"I know the feeling. I got it a few weeks after you left and realized you were lying to me and that you weren't coming back. When I realized you'd traded our relationship for someone you didn't even know."

"That's not exactly the way it happened. If you'd just let me explain. Just listen a few minutes."

A long pause. "Okay, but it's just to clear my conscious knowing I did what was right by giving you the chance. But whatever you say it won't change my mind because I won't believe it."

As I related the story of the past eight months, soft moans and sighs came from her end. At first, I thought they were because of emotion for what I was telling her, but then it came to me they were from the hurt of her believing that what I was saying were just more lies.

"And that's about it, Hope. I couldn't just leave him to the wolves. I had to help him."

"But you promised me and broke it. You lied to me again and again and I lost all faith in you. I could never pick up where we left off. I could never trust, much less ever love you again. Just too much anguish and heartache has happened." She began to sob. "You never loved me anyway. Never truly loved me. The nights in your sleep when you called her name. You never got over her. You think you love me, but you don't. You love her and her only. I know that now. Call her and see if she'll take you back. But leave me alone."

The click was painful. She was gone forever and just as well for her sake. Now she wouldn't have to see me waste away, and she was right about everything she said.

Chapter 24

Instead of having to endure the antiseptic stench of Doc Holmes's office amid a waiting room full of infectiously ill, groaning and coughing patients to discuss my recent test results, I convinced him to a meet me at a sour smelling, smoke filled dive up on Big Pine Key that was full of hoodlums, alkies, drug abusers and convicts. Expecting the worst, I ordered a gin and tonic and lit a cigar to ease my nerves while I waited for his arrival.

As usual he was fifteen minutes late. After he took a seat across from me, a waitress with bad teeth and even worse blown-out tattoos on the back of her hands came to take his order. Her cheeks were hanging out of her cut-off jeans and there were homemade tattoos gone wrong on them, too. I grinned and pointed at her jiggling ass as she walked off. Doc's morose expression didn't change. "Well, Doc, I can see by your lost sense of humor the test results weren't good."

He began kneading his fists and dropped his gaze. "You're right, it's not good, Henry. But you've still got a small chance if you'll start treatment immediately. I can't understand why you didn't start them last June like I insisted."

"There were more important things last June, Doc."

He gave me an incredulous stare. "I've never known such an obstinate bastard. Nothing's more important than your life. Matt could have waited."

"No, he couldn't."

Okay, Henry, I'm not arguing about that anymore. It's a waste of time. Have you talked to Hope yet?"

"Very briefly last night."

"How did it go?"

"It didn't. We're through and it's just as well."

"I was afraid of that, but why do you say it's just as well?"

"You and I both know I'm going to die soon, so what does it matter? You didn't tell her anything about my state of health, did you?"

"Damn it I told you I wouldn't!" He slammed his glass down and the sticky contents splashed out onto his hand. As he wiped his fingers with a paper napkin, the crimson melted from his face. "If she isn't coming back then I guess she'll never know then until, until –"

"Have some balls, Doc, say it, till I'm dead. Death doesn't scare me. It's just that I'd like some more time, that's all. I'd like to enjoy some of what normal people experience, like a family, a home, some real happiness." I waved to our waitress and pointed to my empty glass.

"So how is Sara taking him being with you? She must resent it?"

"I don't think so. I've made her understand how strong his desire is to do what he's doing. She almost ended it, though, when she found out about the girl being killed by the bear. I haven't told her about Seeb's murder yet. It would be the end of it if she knew how Matt had gotten involved – that her little boy had shot a man. I asked her to come and be here when I tell Matt I'm his grandfather. After that they can do whatever they want. But if he does leave after I tell him it'll break my heart after all we've been through."

The afternoon breeze felt good sitting in the shade out on my deck. I raised my face to catch more of it as I watched the Maverick idling up the canal. Matt stopped on the far side to let Lea out. They'd become near inseparable since meeting at a dinner her parents had given for us shortly after we'd returned home. I couldn't blame him. She could have been the star in that sports magazine with all the bikini models. She was every bit as beautiful as Sandy.

From the hours on the flats under the subtropical sun Matt now looked like a white-haired aborigine. He idled up, tied off and stepped up onto the pier wall. "How was fishing?" I said.

"They were where you told me they'd be, and lots of them. Lea caught three on her spinning rod. I caught two on a fly and lost another one. I got a shot at a permit, too, but as usual, he ignored my fly."

"Typical of those snobs. Get used to it. Did you by chance catch anything for supper?"

He gave a 'thumbs up' before jumping back down into the boat. When he opened the livewell a startled tail kicked a spout of water in his face. Then he brought out a nice grouper gripped by its bottom jaw. "I caught it by the big-coral mushroom."

Our dinner then gave a flip and went flying. Matt pinned it to the gunwale for a second, but it squirted from his grip and went into the canal.

"So, what do you do for an encore?" I said. "Now don't start sulking. Just rinse the rods and clean the boat so we can go get something to eat." I watched as he unloaded and rinsed the tackle and then began hosing the boat. "You and Lea seem to be getting mighty tight. Do I need to get fitted for a wedding tux?"

He gave me a squirt with the hose. "Not hardly. She's too busy with medical school, and I'm too busy with bonefish right now. But who knows what the future holds?"

"Ask her to have dinner with us tonight. I want to forewarn her to what disappointment and misery she's getting into if she hooks up with you."

"You keep out of it, old man. I don't need you putting stupid notions in her head." He stared at me a long moment and a quizzical look came on his face. "You don't look like the same person I met a few months ago. You look years older and terribly gaunt now. Are you sure you're telling me everything about your health?"

"Thanks for the compliment. I told you I'm fine. I just picked up a stomach bug. Now let it go."

The chemo treatments were even more vicious than I'd expected and for several days after enduring one, I was weak and bedridden. I looked more depleted each morning, and the struggle to get out of bed became increasingly harder. After several weeks Doc revealed – with tears streaming – that the treatments were having no effect. He said it was time to get my business concerns in order while I had the chance. Matt had become more inquisitive by the day and commented more and more about my health and appearance. He was even more disturbed seeing me after a treatment. With my time running out fast, I decided it was time to put his mind at rest and tell him all.

Matt had been living on the ocean since he'd come to Sugar Loaf. He'd taken the Maverick over as soon as he'd felt confident enough to maneuver the channels and flats alone, and he spent almost as many hours a day on the water as there was daylight. He used my charts to navigate to my favorite flats, and my logs for the optimum tides to fish them. He became adept at spotting fish, and poling became second nature to him. Timmy had gotten over his bitterness over Harry shafting and leaving him and he and Matt had become good friends and fished together whenever possible. After their last trip out, Timmy felt that with a little more experience and a captain's license Matt would be ready to guide on the flats.

In the peace of the pre-dawn few boats had left the docks, only the cruisers going out to the deep blue. The ride to Simms Flat wasn't as bad as I'd expected. I glowed with pride as Matt steered the channels handling the Maverick with the confidence of a seasoned captain. We had to raise our voices to be heard above the whining engine. "You know fishing won't be good this morning, old man. Tide's not right," Matt said.

"I know. I just want to be on the water for an hour or so before it gets too hot. Sure you don't mind taking me out?"

"You know I don't."

"Sometimes it's good just to go out and enjoy the beauty of nature rather than with the intent of killing or catching."

"I wouldn't know about that. I only see it one way, like you did when you were young."

"I know, Matt, I know."

I never visited Simms Flat on a neap tide because there were never any bonefish feeding there without a strong tidal flow, and without it being covered with rushing water Simms looked like a different place. The calm and flat water appeared lifeless except for the apathetic winging of a small ray and the doodling of a baby shark. On the slack wind the cooing of the nesting Crown pigeons in the mangroves seemed more mournful than usual. Out on the Gulf a dolphin rolled and whistled when she blew. I pointed towards her. "There's good luck, boy."

Matt watched her roll and blow again. "Why don't they come on the flats, Henry, like the other fish do?"

"I told you, they're not fish, and they don't have to come in here to feed. They catch all the food they want in the open water."

"They never come on the flats?"

"No, because of barracudas and sharks and their fear of getting trapped. I told you how smart they are. Only something very powerful and unusual would make them come into water this shallow."

"That one seems lost."

"I don't think she's lost, I think she's lost somebody, like her mate. He must have met tragedy somehow, possibly a net, maybe old age. They may have just got separated somehow. Maybe she'll find him and they'll be together again."

"She sure acts like she wants to come on the flat with us."

"Oh no, she won't do that. A dolphin will never come on a shallow flat like this one. It would have to be something more important than its own life. She is acting very curious, though."

"Want me to rig a rod so you can fish?"

"No, Matt, I just want to talk."

I slid up onto the casting deck and started what I'd been dreading for months. It was now or maybe never with the way my health was going. "You've been asking about my health and physical condition a lot lately, and when I look in the mirror I understand why. I've been lying to you, Matt. The reason I'm like this is because I'm dying from a form of leukemia. I waited too long to start treating it and now it's too late. My organs have started wasting away and soon will start shutting down. I didn't want you to know because I didn't want you to worry or be distracted from all you needed to learn before I die."

Matt moved his mouth, but nothing came out. He slid off the poling platform with tears in his eyes and came and took my hand. "I knew something was bad wrong, but not this. How long have you known?"

"Just before I left here to go find you last spring. It may sound strange but dying didn't matter so much to me then. Finding and taking you home to your mother was the most important thing at that time."

"Taking me back to my mother?"

"She called and asked, or more exactly, demanded that I go find you and bring you home. Do you believe our meeting was simply a coincidence?"

He broke down sobbing. "I love you too much to pretend anymore after what you just told me. I figured you were my grandfather the day you found me fishing that day in the rain, but I wasn't completely sure. It didn't take long to figure it out though."

"And how was that?"

"I knew somebody would come after me sooner or later, and I knew it wouldn't be my dad. He's so helpless he couldn't find his way out of Georgia. And Mom wouldn't have come because she was taking care of her dying mother. It just started adding up, especially since I look just like a young you. And I overheard them talking about you more than once when they were well into the red wine. I heard my grandmother say your name more than once. She never said anything bad, though. Sometimes it even sounded as though she missed you. It had to be you. It just made sense."

"So why didn't you tell me you knew in the beginning?"

"That first night you found me, after I realized who you were, I left when you started snoring. I was going to hitchhike as far as I could to get away from you so you wouldn't make me go home. But I was so broke and desperate and starved I decided if you were playing a game with me, I'd play along and milk it for as long as I could. Free food, shelter and transportation for as long as I could get it. I didn't go to Beaver Creek fishing like I said that first morning. I hid in the camp restroom until daylight and watched you unload the camper and then leave. While I was hiding, that's when I decided I'd use you for as long as I could. I slipped back in the camper when you left, and I made up the story about going to fish on Beaver Creek. Then after we went to the Big Hole, I figured that through you I could get and do what I wanted for as long as I went along with your charade. I knew I had you in the palm of my hand. But as time went by and I began to care about you, I started feeling guilty and when you brought up the dreams of the Nomad at lunch that day, I started to call you on it, but I was afraid to. And again, I wanted to tell you I knew when we were having the talk about Pearle being pregnant and I hurt your feelings so bad. I knew I did. I could see it in your face. So why didn't you tell me in the beginning you were my grandfather?"

"Because you'd know I came to bring you home and I knew you'd run away, especially after I realized how determined you were to stay in Montana. And I figured you hated me so much from what you'd heard that if you found out I was your terrible grandfather you'd surely leave. Then as time went on, I became attached to you and never wanted to lose you. I became possessed with teaching you all the things I have so you could make it through life with me not being around. I did it, too, though I was almost too late. We lied to each other to keep from losing each other. They weren't bad lies. In fact, they were good lies because look how it all turned out. And now I'm glad the truth is finally out so we don't have to go on pretending anymore. I just hope someday you're lucky enough to have a son or grandson that you love as much as I do you to bring out the good and best in you like you did for me."

"But nothing will matter without you. Everything we've done won't mean a thing."

"It will mean everything because now you'll be fine after I'm gone, and I can rest in peace knowing that. You've got Lea and everything you ever hoped for. Now let's talk about your mother. I want her to come down here before it's too late. I want to see her one more time. I don't want to die with her feeling like she does about me."

After all you've done for me, I think she's trying hard to forgive you. Maybe now that's she's free she can come here."

"What do you mean by that?"

"I don't know how you're going to take this, but her mother passed the other day."

I turned away so he wouldn't see the anguish. After the initial shock subsided, I was amazed I felt so much grief and sorrow for someone I hadn't seen or talked to in almost forty years. I struggled to regain my composure. "I'm sorry to hear that. I'm sure your mother is devastated. Now be done with those tears and let's head back. I'm getting hungry and can hear your stomach growling as well. And the pain pills are starting to lose effect and I'm not looking forward to the rough ride home."

Once in open water I became engrossed watching the dolphin. It was sad and strange how for several miles she tried keeping up with us before eventually tiring and turning back towards the Gulf.

"I called to give my condolences. Matt told me this morning. I'm sorry she went that way. You know I never stopped loving her."

"And she still loved you, Dad. She called your name a lot there at the end. She even asked if you were coming to see her. And she told me what really happened – the reasons you left when you did. I don't blame you anymore. Forgive me for not listening to your side."

"There's nothing to forgive. You believed what you were told."

"And thank you for all you've done for Matt. I miss him, but know he's safe in your care, and happy as well. You're better than any father he could ever have had."

"Thank you for that. It means a lot. Now I need to tell you something you need to know. I've got leukemia and not long for this world. I wanted to see you again, but not now, because I don't want you to see me like I am. You've been through enough of that misery already. Your understanding and forgiveness are enough and mean more than you'll ever know. It'll make it easier for me when my time comes." She started to cry. "Don't be sad. I've had the best life anyone could have had. Did she suffer?"

"At times. Hospice did miracles though. After she accepted the fact she was going and I told her it was okay to go, she became happy and started babbling about dolphins and calling your name even more. Maybe it was the medications making her delirious. It didn't make sense."

"It does to me. She's happy where she is now, Sara. Believe me."

"You mean in Heaven?"

"No, not yet. Matt will explain it to you someday."

CHAPTER 25

Instead of taking the air shuttle from Miami to Key West and then making the short drive north to Sugar Loaf Key, Major General Robert Johansson, USMC, Ret., always rented a car in Miami and then drove the 150 miles to Sugar Loaf. Once I asked him why he went through the misery of the long drive when he could fly from Miami to Key West, and he told me it was because he enjoyed the sights of the Keys along the way. But I knew he drove the monotonous and frustrating four hours amid the pokey sightseeing tourists and speed traps because his military ingrained frugality prevented him from wasting the money on the short flight. And out of politeness and respect I never told him that taking the air shuttle was much cheaper than renting a car and paying the exorbitant price of south Florida gas to drive the 300 roundtrip miles.

Johansson seemed to enjoy his visits with me in the Keys. I supposed it was because I was the closest person he had to family. And though he wasn't worth a damn at it, he loved fishing the flats. If he had any interests outside of the Corps other than that, I never knew of them. I was aware of several serious love affairs he'd had over the years, but I figured he never married because he was afraid matrimony might have interfered with his military obligation.

Johansson was shocked by the appearance of the emaciated cadaver that opened the door to his knock. I thought it was hilarious that a hardened combat veteran of three wars would be so emotionally struck. He stood stunned and speechless with a mortified look on his face till I finally said, "Come on in, Bob, you're wasting my air conditioning. And get that morbid expression off your face before I pass out laughing."

He came in and hugged me and then went to the liquor cabinet and poured a big whiskey. He gulped it down and poured another. He'd never been much of a drinker in all the years I'd known him. Always too disciplined. The alcohol eventually settled him, and then he was able to talk. "I called Tim to make sure you were home. He said you were sick and to be prepared, but I wasn't ready for this."

"Sit down and stop being so dramatic. If you're going to ruin this beautiful day with despair, get your old ass out. I don't have time for it. When it's time to go, it's time to go and my time has arrived, and I've accepted it."

I took a seat in my recliner, and he sat down on the sofa across from me. "I'm sorry, Henry. This really dampens the good news I've brought for you."

"It's been a long time. I could use some good news for a change. Let's have it."

He set his briefcase across his knees and opened it. Then he took out a small box and an envelope. He opened the box and there was a Medal of Honor medal in it. The gold star with the blue ribbon embellished with the seme of stars was overwhelming and I broke down. "How can I ever thank you?" I managed after I was able to stop sobbing.

"You bastard, you wanted that medal as bad as I wanted you to have it, but you'd never admit it. I knew once you got it, you'd be proud."

After I'd composed myself and was able to talk coherently again, I said, "If you'd messed around a few more weeks I'd never have gotten to see it. But then you could have had a big posthumous ceremony with the Marine Corps Band and all. A battalion of young Marines could have wasted a day standing in the hot sun in dress uniform on a parade deck listening to you bullshit about some insignificant bastard they'd never heard of. And you could have worn that gaudy blue uniform with all your medals and shown your ass like you like to do so much. I'm glad I lived long enough to cheat you out of all that."

He broke into unrestrained laugher. "You're right. I'd have had a ceremony with a band, a pass in review, and all, but you've got to ruin everything. I should have flown away that day from that hill and let those dinks have your worthless ass. Now tell me, where have you been for so long? I tried to find you, but no one knew where you were. By the way, where's Hope? I must have called fifty times and never got her."

"She left me over this. She's been gone for months."

"Sorry to hear that, Henry. She was a good woman."

"No, she was wonderful and way too good for me." I pointed to his drink. "If you're going to get shit-faced right here in the middle of the day, pour me one too, then I'll tell you where I've been."

After he filled our glasses, I started the story of mine and Matt's travels. When I related the part about Matt shooting Big Lefont, he stood and applauded. When the final chapter ended, we were wasted.

"You know, Henry, sounds like that boy would make a fine Marine."

The whiskey had me tongue heavy and slurring. "I've been telling him that, but he wants to travel around the country and guide like I did. I've begged and pleaded for him to forget it, but he won't listen."

"Why you pompous ass. Why hasn't he the right to do what he wants? What are you, a communist or something?"

At first the comment made my temper flare, but after I gave it some thought I realized he was right. "It's only that I care so much for his wellbeing. I just don't want him ending up like me."

"From what you've told me, thanks to you he's well prepared for life. Sounds like he's far from being helpless. He may change his mind someday and want to do something different, but you won't change it. Oh, by the way, you sure don't deserve this, but it comes with the Medal. With it, you'll end up pretty well off."

I removed the Kansas City government check from the envelope that he handed me and was stunned when I read the amount typed on it.

"That's for over forty years of retroactive backpay for the Medal that you're owed, tax free and with interest. It dates back to when you were on that hill all alone machine-gunning gooks off the road so the battalion could get away, and for coming out on that frozen lake to save me. It's a pretty astounding amount. You'll never know how much satisfaction it would give me to shove it up that arrogant, doggy colonel's ass, whatever his name was, that stopped it from going to Congress when it should have."

My concern wasn't about a hearing forty years ago. My thoughts were on buying the Simington estate for Matt now that I had some money. But something else came to mind Johansson might possibly do that would be even more important and possibly more beneficial to Matt's future than buying the estate. "I need one more favor, General?"

"Ask away, Henry. If it's in my power, I'll do anything I can."

"Doesn't an appointment to Annapolis for my kids come with this?"

"It does, if they qualify scholastically. But I think your daughter's a little old now, don't you?"

"I'm not talking about Sara. I'm talking about Matt if he ever wanted to go back to school. He claims he has the grades to get in. If you're so high and mighty in the political and bureaucratic end of the military, couldn't you pull a few strings for me?"

After he reasoned a moment, a big conniving smile appeared. "There are several Congressmen that owe me favors. I could probably get that done."

"Good. Now thanks to you I can die in peace."

We were so drunk by then he called the Naval base at Key West and requested two Marines be sent to drive him back to Miami to catch his evening flight home. The Marine Lt. Colonel commander of the base gladly obliged so as not to jeopardize his career.

The next day I called the director of the Florida Keys Nature Conservancy, and he told me he couldn't give an answer as to whether I could make an offer on the Simington estate before I died or not. He'd have to consult their attorney and the conservancy board. He said the request that I wanted to buy the house sounded strange and was unusual, since it was mine till I died anyway. I was too tired and hungover to explain the reason was because I figured the money from the Medal would go farther in helping Matt if it were invested in something that would appreciate like the Simington estate. I asked the director of the Conservancy to call me back when he had an answer.

I hadn't considered using the Colt 1911 I'd smuggled home from Korea to blow my brains out since I'd left Oldale in 1951. But now that I'd depleted to a near helpless invalid, I was considering using it again, and soon. It hadn't come to Matt putting adult diapers on me yet, but that wasn't far off. And the thought of it more than repulsed me. I didn't want to linger around until my condition got that bad. The look on Johansson's face seeing me so helpless and depleted had been humiliating. My vanity insisted I be remembered as Henry Ball, not the shriveled, helpless corpse I was now. I figured if I slipped out on the beach one night and did it, there would be no mess to clean up. The tide would take my splattered brains and wasted body away and Matt wouldn't be troubled with the time and expense of my cremation. And the crabs and fish could eat well for a while, too.

"You stubborn son of a bitch, let me have some morphine. You won't lose your license over it." My pleadings were just as well to a deaf man. Doc Holmes wouldn't relent and put his professional integrity at risk, not even to help his best friend. I remembered how good morphine had been when I was wounded during the war, and that's how I wanted to feel now. The pain killer I was taking was doing a decent job, though it made me sick at times. What I wanted was the euphoria morphine produced. The way I was back then, I would have likely been a drug addict as well as a drunk if I'd known how to get it after Korea. Being on the threshold of death now, I couldn't understand what difference it made.

"Can't do it, Henry. It's against my ethics as a doctor. When you're under hospice care they'll administer morphine."

"Why do you smart people have to be so simple minded? I'll be dead in a few more weeks, and who's ever going to know? They didn't spare any of it when I was blown up in the war."

"I'll give you some pain pills that are more potent than what you're on now, and that's all. Keep your insults up and you won't get any damn thing from me."

I backed off knowing Doc would be true to his word and decided it best to change the subject. "Doc, I need your opinion. What's your thoughts on the Conservancy selling me my house before I die?"

He was scribbling on my chart and stopped. He thought a minute and grinned. "Maybe they will. Kipling O'Brien is the head of the Conservancy Board. Would you like for me to see if he can get the issue resolved? He owes me a few favors. His son's drug problems, my getting him into rehab and keeping it quiet. You know what I mean."

"Your professional ethics won't allow you to give me a little morphine, but you'd turn around and bribe a rare honest man because you kept his son's drug problem swept under a rug? Jesus, what's the world coming to? Of course I want to get the house issue resolved before I die, but are you in the process going to bleed money out of O'Brien like you do your helpless patients like me?"

That got Doc laughing, and he promised to get things moving on my purchasing the Simington estate. Then he gave me a lecture on the new prescription of pain pills.

"Look, Henry, this pain medication is different than what you're on now. You've got to be careful and not take more than prescribed. Not only will it impede your physical abilities, it'll cause mental impairment and irresolution as well. In other words, your ability to reason and make logical decisions will be impaired dramatically if you take too much. And the worst thing you can do is to drink alcohol with it."

CHAPTER 26

Two weeks had passed since Doc put me on the new pain medication. I was taking the prescribed dosage and couldn't tell much difference from the previous one, even with a few slugs of scotch. I still wanted morphine, but the pills and whiskey would have to do. No matter how I persisted, Doc wouldn't relent and prescribe morphine.

But Doc had done me one great favor. He'd talked to Kipling O'Brien who'd in turn consulted with the nature conservancy board and its lawyer and they'd determined that since it was to be sold immediately upon my death for funds to preserve the Keys flats and coral reefs there was no reason I couldn't buy the estate now at its appraised market value. O'Brian had the appraisal and contracts expedited and I'd bought the house and immediately made a Last Will and Testament making Matt the executor and sole heir of my estate. I wanted to go to Simms Flat one more time and use the opportunity to reveal our great fortune to Matt. And at the speed my health was going I knew we should go soon and that it would be the last trip I'd make anywhere because I knew the little man with the horrible lion were coming soon.

The NOAA computerized voice was forecasting severe storms just before dark with 25 knot and gusting winds. I was determined to chance beating the weather to finish my business with Matt. He was in his bedroom studying a chart when I tapped on the door. "Let's take a boat ride," I said. "We need to talk."

He nodded, rolled up the chart and put it away and then helped me down the steps into the boat. Lea came out when she heard the outboard crank and threw her hands up in disbelief when she saw us about to leave. "We'll be back in a few hours," Matt shouted to be heard above the wind as we motored past.

People along the canal securing boat lines and storing deck furniture stopped and gave us incredulous stares. When the roiling-open sea came into sight at the end of the canal, Matt shifted the Yamaha into neutral and gave me a questioning stare. I smiled and motioned him on.

The spray off the waves was like quirt lashes on my face. The jolting of the boat was torture and I prayed the extra pills I'd taken just before leaving would kick in.

It took forty-five minutes of teeth rattling pounding, but the skiff and I endured the sea's abuse, and we pulled into the lee of Simms Flat drenched but unscathed. Matt noticed the dolphin rolling nearby and pointed her out.

The concern was distinct in Matt's voice. "I'm not sure it was smart coming out here in this weather, Henry."

Seeing the dolphin and the effects of the pills and scotch made me laugh. "Awe, everything's going to be alright now, boy. Just you wait and see."

In the time it took Matt to stake the boat, the wind went from a howl to a roar and the rain had turned the distant ocean white. As I watched the deluge easing our way, I began to explain to Matt about Johansson's visit and the house that was soon to be his. He seemed unable to concentrate on what I was saying, either because of the noise of the storm, or his fear of it, or both. He kept glancing over his shoulder in the direction it was coming. I was going in and out of my head from the overdose of pain medication I'd taken. The big drink of whiskey I'd washed it down with hadn't helped my reasoning capacity, either. I stopped my senseless rambling as a waterspout dropped out of the black storm cloud and began drifting our way. I pointed to it, and said, "Is that what you've been looking for, boy?"

Matt turned and watched for a moment as the funnel danced back and forth like a vertical snake, then he went fumbling in the storage compartments for life jackets. He strapped one on and handed another to me. I tossed it into the air and the wind whipped it away. "Can't you leave me alone and let me die like a man instead of a shriveled invalid!" I screamed.

Matt tore his attention from me and climbed onto the poling platform. He pulled on the push pole to dislodge it, but the wind pressing against the boat had it wedged so tight he couldn't pull it free, so he unclipped the stern line and the wind sent us surging sideways across the flat. He jumped down to the console and got the engine cranked, and we went tearing down the channel to open sea. Once out of the protection of the key, the full force of the wind slammed us. Our hats went first, and then the seat cushions, and finally the cooler with cans and bottles spraying out as it went whipping away skipping over the waves like a piece of confetti. Because of the medication everything had become dreamlike and comical to me. "Ain't this great, Matt! We're right in the heart of it."

Matt wasn't paying any attention to me now. He couldn't hear me anyway with the noise of the wind and the whine of the maxed engine. He was trying to outrun the storm and to stay in deep water so the following swells wouldn't swamp the boat. And he did a good job for a mile or so, but eventually the outboard grounded, the boat slowed, and then we were buried by a wave.

Just after I was swept out of the boat something hit my chest with a tremendous force. Then the power of the swell rolled and scraped me across the ocean floor. I succumbed to the comforting realization I'd end my life then, but something began pushing and nudging me along. I thought it was Matt at first, but it possessed too great a power. It pushed me to the surface and then to the boat and nosed me over the gunnel. I began coughing and gagging helplessly out of strength.

In the clutter of bobbing cushions, coolers and floating equipment strewn downwind across the sea, I spotted Matt riding the swells swimming toward the boat. He climbed over the side and gave me a look of disbelief. "How did you get here? I was looking all over for you out there."

I pointed to the dolphin circling the boat and he turned back and stared at me in dumbfounded amazement. Then he realized the gash in my chest. "On my god, you're bleeding, Henry."

"I don't think it's as bad as it looks. See if the engine will start. If not, get on the radio. I don't want you to have to spend the night out here."

Matt ground on the engine until the starter began making staticky clicks. Then he found the submerged radio handset and drained it. After he flipped on the power, he beat the console and banged the handset, but there was nothing but silence.

The sea settled in stages. In an hour, it went from windswept and frothing, to gentle and swelling. Blood was seeping freely from my chest. The cooler with the water was gone, and the first aid kit, too. Even the flare gun had been swept away. As night fell, we were drifting at the mercy of the wind and the tide.

The stern was the only place on the boat above water and Matt pulled me to it and held me in his arms. Then exhaustion and the overdose of pills put me to sleep.

When I woke the sea had calmed and the storm had passed. Stars were flickering, and I could see either the glare of the rising moon or the glow from the lights on the mainland and then I was out again.

I figured it was past midnight when I woke the second time as the Maverick started dragging bottom. When we finally ground to a stop, I was still in Matt's arms, and the moon was straight overhead. We were on a flat a short distance from a mangrove key.

Matt slung my arm over his shoulder and struggled dragging me to shore. He tripped several times on the mangrove roots and gashed his shins. Even with the full moon, it was dark in the heavy growth, but he forced his way through the wet limbs until he found an opening to lay me in. He used his shirt to soak the oozy blood off my chest. "The prop must have hit you, Henry."

"Must have been."

"Why were you acting so crazy when the storm hit?"

"Just before we left, I took twice the pain medication I should have with a big drink of whiskey I shouldn't have, and it put me out of my head. I almost got you killed because of my stupidity. I'm sorry. We should never have come out in this weather."

He glanced at my chest. "Does it hurt?"

"Not yet, but the pills haven't worn off. I'm sure I'll have hell to pay before long, though."

"What do you want me to do?"

"I'd drink some water if you could get some."

He went back to the skiff with both of us knowing his search would be fruitless. Everything that hadn't been strapped down had been lost. He went through the storage compartments and found nothing but a couple of life jackets. He used one to cover me and put the other under my head. Then he left to look for something that would hold water.

By the glare from the moonlight, in the mangrove roots he saw the glint of a sunken can and worked it back and forth till it broke apart. Then he collected what raindrops he could from shaking the mangrove limbs. I'd barely swallowed the few sips when it came back up. Matt took his shirt off and soaked it in the saltwater and cleaned my wound again. "I'm sure Lea has every boat in the Keys out looking for us. Somebody'll be here soon," he said.

"You never were a good bullshitter, Matt."

"Just don't die here like this. I'd never forgive myself."

"Listen, Matt, I'd rather go like this than waste away like a poisoned rat in a hospital. This is the way it was meant for me to go – by the hands of nature."

The droning of the no-see-ums and the mosquitoes converging on us, and the soft lapping of the slight surf were the only sounds. If there were boats searching for us, they were still a long way off. The pain medication was about gone, and Matt must have sensed it because he took my hand. "Are you hurting?"

"I'm starting to. Can you feel them, Matt?"

In the moonlight I could see him glancing around. "Yes. I can even smell the cat. I've never felt fear like this before. Not even the bear."

"Don't be afraid. They aren't here for you. Oh, they'll come for you someday, but right now it's me they want."

The effect of the medication was gone, and the pain from the chest wound began to surge and eventually became so unbearable I passed out. When I woke it was coming daylight and I could hear Matt wading nearby on the flat. Then I heard the faint whine of an outboard heading our way. I felt the presence weighing heavy on my chest and knew I was about to die when Matt came hurrying back. "Old man, I hear a boat! You're going to be okay."

"Better go wave them down then."

"I'll just wait here with you."

"Go wave the boat down, Matt."

"I know they're here. I can feel them stronger than ever. If I leave –"

"You don't need to worry about that. It'll be better for me, you'll see. Just go on now."

"But I know if I leave, I'll never see you alive again."

I smiled. "Oh yes you will. Just look for the dolphins. Now go on so I can get this over with."

Matt forced himself away, staring hard at me as he pushed from my sight through the thick foliage. Then I could hear him splashing through the water shouting to the boat.

Epilogue

15 May 2038

I was off in my mind thinking about the dolphins. I always thought of them when I was on the water. And when the boy and I were together, I thought about them even more. Now that I was old and understood the true value of what he'd done, if I could see him just once more, I could properly thank him. And I'd like to tell him again how much I loved him for doing all he'd done.

Had it been a coincidence that the dolphin had come onto the flat and circled the boat that morning while I was tossing his ashes? It'd been well over forty years, but the memory remains as lucid as if it'd been yesterday when I watched him jumping and spinning and frolicking away with his mate into the boundless sea. I realized later that being with her and having her love again was all he ever really wanted. Every time I'd gone out on the ocean since that day, I'd expected to see them, but I never had.

He was right about most things, but he'd been wrong about one – that I'd forget about him and my love for him would diminish over time. He'd been right about the man and the lion, though. I'd felt their horrible presence and then saw their tracks on the edge of the shallow water fading in the sand that morning they took him away out into the Gulf. And I'd felt them again even stronger when I was wounded and dying on a snow-covered mountain in Afghanistan with my command under siege. Maybe after our final meeting he'd arrange it so I could tell him all those things I wanted to. I'd been told he could, and I truly believed it.

The boy with me had just reached his teens, and though he was small, when his weight shifted, the skiff rocked and brought me back to the present. I watched the line come low behind him, and then the fly kiss off the water. He pushed the unloaded rod forward and the line fell in a miserable heap at his feet. I started to shout but held my anger. "How many times do I have to tell you, don't drop your wrist on the back cast? If that's the best you're going to do, let's just quit and go home."

I'd taken an unusual liking to the boy several years back. There was something that caused a passion deep within me to stir and I couldn't get enough of the scrawny brat now. I hadn't been so close to my son who'd been very much like his mother. Both had an affinity for wealth, and I never understood why she'd married me in the first place. My son had cared nothing about nature, instead he'd played computer games and such growing up. And now his job entailed watching a screen all day with numbers speeding by showing how the Market was doing. And he didn't resemble me either but was instead a close replica of his mother – dark skinned and raven haired of Spanish descent. I was like my grandfather in respect that I loved women of dark complexion and raven hair. It must have been that it was in our blood.

I also had a daughter, and she resembled me in more ways than just appearance. Unlike her brother, she loved nature and had fished and hunted with me a great deal growing up. The boy with me now was her son.

The kid turned with an indomitable glare that startled me, and I shuddered in the mucky heat. I opened my mouth and took a deep breath to keep my emotion from coming up. I'd seen that determined stare, and it shook me to the core. "I ain't never quitin', you old fart." Then he gave me the finger.

I stared hard at him trying to hide my amusement. "Damn you're hardheaded, boy. You remind me a great deal of your great grandpa at times."

The boy turned his back on me and seemed to focus for a moment. Then he rolled the slack out of the line and stripped it off the water. He made a nice high back cast and then hauled. This time he stopped the tip high and the rod loaded nicely when he cast, and the line rolled out in a wonderful tight loop and settled soft and straight on the calm water. Though there were no bonefish or permit to test it, it was a good cast. When he concentrated and used his resolve he could cast reasonably well. After he stripped the line onto the casting deck, he turned back to me. "Say, Colonel Matt, will you finish the story of the Nomad tonight? We could build a fire outside in the pit like we do at the Pear."

When he wanted a favor, he called me by my retired rank to placate me, I guess. "If you'll stop being so vulgar and disrespectful towards me, I might."

"I promise if you'll tell me the rest of the story, I won't call you an old fart or other bad names anymore. Or give you the finger."

"And for how long?"

He shrugged. "Forever I guess."

I knew him too well to believe the promise would last for long. "Do you remember where I was when you fell asleep last night?"

He acted as if he were in deep thought for a moment. "It was where the man and the dark girl met on the river."

"You're fibbing again. I told the story well beyond that and know you were awake."

He looked down at his feet. "Oh alright. I really fell asleep after the dark people let the Nomad come live with them, but I liked the part about the Nomad doing the dark woman so much I wanted you to tell it again."